Send Off Sir

MARK BASFORD

Originally published 2014 under the pen-name Marc de Caen

This edition published by Mark Basford, 2017

ISBN: 978-0-9934345-4-9

CHAPTER TITLES

Author's Foreword

"WARNING: This product may contain nuts." That was the notice I once saw displayed prominently in a supermarket relating to jars of ... you've guessed it... NUTS. In a similar vein I feel I should include a warning here: "This work of fiction contains characters whose views may offend you." Let me say it is not my intention to offend; it is simply to allow characters to express original opinions appropriate to their characterisations. Of course, offence – uniquely – is something that is taken more often than it is given. So, if you are considering being offended by any of the contrary views expressed herein, do reflect on the words of Evelyn Beatrice Hall in The Friends of Voltaire (1906), "*I disapprove of what you say, but I will defend to the death your right to say it.*"

Dramatis Personae

POLICE

Chief Superintendent Barbara "Babs" Watt
Superintendent Richard "Richie" Yelland
Detective Chief Inspector Bryn Castleton
Detective Inspector Marcus Priestley
Sergeant Robert Oldham
Detective Constable Neil "Witty" Whittington
Detective Constable Lily Martello
Detective Constable Anthony "Berry" Beresford
Constable Linda Plummer
Constable Elias Dunn
Gloria Naylor, Receptionist

MEDICS & FORENSICS

James Kinder, Paediatric Surgeon
Gordon Mallory, Forensic Pathologist
Nina Buxton, Senior Anatomical Pathology Technician
Joanne Carpenter, Paramedic
Philip Obaku, Paramedic
Jenny Merton, Lead CSI
Nick Evans, CSI

SCHOOL STAFF

Gilbert Verbane, Headmaster
Glenda Oaken, Headmistress
Victoria Clifton, Head of Sixth Form, Geography
Sophie Cleese, Classics
Anthony Ashbourne, Maths
Julie Goode, Maths
Jeremy Benn, Maths
Nathalie Dupont, Modern Foreign Languages
Étienne Platini, Modern Foreign Languages
Jane Leveret, Performing Arts
David Pratt, ICT (Computing)
Christine Nunn, Religious Studies
Barbara Saxon, History
Joanna Jackson, Head of Administration
Margaret Webster, Administration Assistant

FOOTBALL TEAM – STAFF
Hugh Cassidy, English Literature and Greek Classics
Thomas Collins, Chemistry
Graham Rendel, English
William Hart, Biology
Dafydd Davies, History
Brian Hunter, Physics, Deputy Head
Francis Offial, Modern Foreign Languages
Cameron Finlay, Psychology
Edward John Newhouse, Physical Education
Arthur Decker, Art
Terry Cullen, Politics

FOOTBALL TEAM – SCHOOL
Robert Henderson
William "Billy" Huntsman
Vincent Hardwick
Jack Stanage
Quentin "Tommy" Thompson
Gary "Gazza" Talbot
Daniel Harris
Mark Hope
Alexander Peveril
Dean Bonsall
Robert Bolsover
Kenneth Derwent
James Woodhead
Nathan "Nosher" Smith

OTHER STUDENTS
David Williamson, Ball-boy
Simon Green, Ball-boy
Zachariah Peck, Ball-boy
Mickey Blackstone, Smoker
Becky Worthington, Special Needs
Rosie, Girl with Dog

ANIMALS
Brownie, a dog

FAMILY MEMBERS

Helen Priestley, Wife of Marcus
Edwin Priestley, six-year-old Son of Marcus
Alice Priestley, four-year-old Daughter of Marcus
Theresa Whittington, Wife of Neil
Samuel Dunn, Father of Elias
Cynthia Newhouse, Mother of John
Susan Newhouse, Sister of John
Janet Henshaw, Sister of John
Mrs Blackstone, Mother of Mickey
Gwendoline Cassidy, Mother of Hugh
Gareth Cassidy, Father of Hugh
Sylvia Worthington, Mother of Becky

VARIOUS OTHERS

George Westmorland, Bank Manager
Boy Black, Pub Landlord
Ginny Bakewell, Shopper
Michael Gough, Chef
Charles, National Trust Volunteer
Shelley, National Trust Volunteer
Keith, National Trust Volunteer
Steve Nugent, Birdwatcher
Clive Oxley, Father of a Student
Andrew Logan, Biology Teacher (retired)
Rowland Ryland, Newspaper Reporter
Manny Gilder, Divorce Lawyer
Sol Schaeffer, Criminal Lawyer
Edward Tomkins, CPS Lawyer

PART 1

CHAPTER 1

A Body in the Changing Room

November, Wednesday Afternoon

John Newhouse lay motionless on the pale green tiled floor of the girls' changing room, the crimson rivulet of blood seeping from the wound to the back of his head turning brown and cloudy as it precipitated in the shallow pool of soapy water that had formed near the girls' showers; in contrast, the blood that had begun to congeal on his raven hair remained shining bright as it darkened and set against the black background.

The ten men looked down at the sports master lying prone, his sightless eyes staring at the damp ceiling; the shock made shivers pass through several of them, exacerbated by the evaporation of sweat chilling their shoulders and backs.

Dr Brian Hunter, Head of Physics, at thirty-five was the oldest of the assembled teachers by a couple of years; as Deputy Head he was also the most senior. He found he had unconsciously moved to the front of the group, propelled by some invisible osmotic force. At his right-hand was Terry Cullen, a newly qualified politics teacher and one of the youngest at twenty-two, impelled by character and short stature always to strive to be at the front. The other eight teachers had fallen into two ranks behind them, those at the back craning their necks to catch a glimpse of their fallen colleague.

Hunter turned to William Hart, a biology teacher at the school for the past six years: 'Bill, are you able to check if John is, um ...' His voice trailed off, unable to bring himself to choose between the words "dead" and "alive".

Bill accepted the invitation, not so much in the confidence that he knew what to do, as in the belief that those around him probably knew less. He knelt to the left of the motionless shoulders and placed the ends of the first two fingers of his right hand in the area to the far side of Newhouse's neck where school text books indicated blood should be pumping through the carotid artery. He put the index finger of his left hand vertically across his own mouth to request silence, as though he might also be listening for the sound of the pulse. After a full fifteen seconds of hoping to detect some sign of life, and without rising from his almost religious posture, he declared 'I can't feel a pulse in his ... neck'. He had considered using the term "carotid artery", but instinctively felt this was not a time for asserting his biology credentials. 'I'll try his heart and his wrist as well.'

Thomas Collins, thirty-year-old escapee from industrial chemical production in Teesside and now enjoying his fifth year in the chemistry department, had retrieved his mobile phone from the pocket of his hanging jacket and was now speaking from two metres ahead of the others, in their line of sight and on the other side of the body. 'Ambulance!' There was a short pause. 'I'm speaking from Midshaw School, the girls' changing room. Someone has been badly injured and may be dead – we need an ambulance right away.' ... 'I'm a teacher here. Mr Collins. Tom.' He wondered if "Tom" was too informal for such an occasion. Perhaps Thomas, or... He responded to the next question. 'Mr E. J. Newhouse is injured and may be dead. There's blood coming from a head wound.'

Hart looked in Collins' direction and enunciated in a raised voice for Tom's benefit, in case the information needed relaying to the emergency services, 'No sign of a pulse at the neck or wrist, and his heart doesn't appear to be beating.'

As Collins continued his phone call, Hunter addressed the remainder of the group. 'Everyone stay in here for now. I'll let the Headmaster know what's happening.'

Hunter left the changing room, ran up the steep steps to the playing field and loped the thirty metres to where Mr Gilbert Verbane was standing; Cullen, uninvited, followed in his wake. To the right of Verbane stood Miss Glenda Oaken, Headmistress, a large and heavy forty-something, having been a determined old maid for almost thirty of those years. To his left was Ms Victoria Clifton, Head of Sixth Form; in her mid-thirties, she was the Amazon Hippolyta waiting in vain to be asked for her girdle. These three were standing together near the half-way line of the pitch where just minutes earlier they had applauded the teams as they left the field at the end of the School versus Staff football match.

Hunter arrived slightly behind Cullen, the latter having put on a spurt just as Hunter had slowed. Cullen blurted out his unnecessary message. 'Dr Hunter has …' – he snatched a quick breath – '…something important to tell you'.

Verbane looked at Hunter, who delivered the heralded message in short bursts. He had intended to whisper, but the volume varied in intensity like the breeze, as his chest heaved in syncopation with his words. 'Mr Newhouse has been injured and may be dead. He's on the floor of the girls' changing room. Mr Hart has checked for a pulse but couldn't find one. Mr Collins has called for an ambulance.'

Verbane acknowledged the concise report with a curt nod of the head. 'I'd better take a look myself.'

Clifton grasped Verbane gently on his left shoulder to make sure she had his attention, instinctively recognising this as one of those rare occasions when physical contact would be acceptable in a school. 'I'll go down to the gates and make sure the ambulance knows exactly where to go.'

Verbane looked in her direction for a moment, but his eyes had a far-away, glazed look, and he turned away without acknowledging her. He marched quickly, avoiding running, like a major on a military parade ground, lacking only a swagger stick to complete the impression. Oaken remained transfixed, her face revealing her shock at the news; then she trailed after him like a somnambulist, dropping further behind with every step. He entered the changing room and walked up to where the games master was lying, the group of teachers backing away to maintain a respectful distance, with Hunter and Cullen joining them at one edge. He gave an instruction to his staff in a tone more familiar to them as his Headmaster-to-children voice. 'Everyone, collect up your clothes and leave as quickly and as quietly as possible.' The stock phrase had come to him unbidden. 'Go to the staffroom; I shall see you there shortly.' He turned to Hunter and Cullen. 'You two please stay here until the ambulance arrives.'

No one had yet moved when Oaken entered the changing room seconds later and immediately fell to her knees as though in supplication. As she knelt parallel to Newhouse's head, she leaned forward and put her right ear against his chest, then began pressing on it rhythmically with both hands in an awkward manner from her sideways position. Hunter was thinking that a more efficient position could be sitting astride Newhouse, but the momentary image this conjured up ensured he kept the suggestion to himself. He believed he saw a more substantial flaw in Oaken's action. 'Isn't CPR for restarting breathing? Don't we need a defibrillator to start his heart first?'

Oaken stopped for a moment before declaring, 'I have to try.' She then began to pound Newhouse's chest with her fists. After half a minute she looked up at Verbane. 'It's hopeless.' Her voice cracked with emotion as her "hope" was strangled and choked in her throat.

Verbane bent down to place the four fingers of his left hand on the right side of Newhouse's neck. On discovering no pulse there, he steadied himself by resting his left hand on the floor, getting some blood on his shirt cuff in the process. With his right, middle finger he pulled down each eyelid on the still-handsome face of Newhouse, in the manner he had seen in countless films.

The eight teachers recognised the end of Verbane's performance as their cue to collect their clothes and leave the changing room. They filed out in silence, not speaking until they had passed through the portal, as though they were leaving a church after a funeral service.

CHAPTER 2

Paramedics and Police Arrive

The sound of a distant siren was heard in the girls' changing room by Verbane, Hunter, Cullen and Oaken as they stood looking down at Newhouse; the volume indicated the emergency vehicle had passed a near point at a tangent as it headed for the school's main entrance. Clifton intercepted the ambulance at the gate and gave a concise explanation of where they should go. The dull grey tarmacked route to the girls' changing room was not wide enough for the broad wheelbase ambulance, which therefore had to straddle the path before veering to one side and stopping in front of the changing room main entrance with the near-side tyres on the grass.

Philip Obaku emerged from the front passenger door, his green cotton suit looking slightly oversized as it billowed around his voluminous body. Joanne Carpenter jumped down from the driver's side, her matching green jacket having been discarded to reveal a blue polo shirt that neatly fitted her lithe body but looked barely adequate for the cold weather. The prominent logos on their clothing matched the design on the large black bag that Obaku retrieved as Carpenter rushed into the changing room. Verbane raised his head and looked directly at her to indicate his seniority. Carpenter asked him, 'We were expecting to find a girl – is she somewhere else?'

Verbane responded, 'There is no girl. Mr Newhouse is the only casualty.'

Obaku was already kneeling at the left side of the body and checking for signs of life. He turned to Carpenter, giving a slight shake of the head. Carpenter knelt at the right side and quickly confirmed his assessment. Clifton had chased after the ambulance, her initial trotting having graduated to running as she felt an increasingly urgent need to discover for herself what was happening. She entered the changing room as Carpenter spoke into her radio to say that a Mr Newhouse was dead on arrival, and that there is no Teri Newhouse.

Outside the changing room a liveried Volvo adorned with blue flashing lights arrived unguided, drawn to the correct place by the presence of the ambulance. Uniformed police officers PC Elias Jobs-Dunn and WPC Linda Plummer had been attending a domestic incident in Nethershaw when the call came in for them to go to Midshaw School. Though they had delayed their short journey just moments to close off the Nethershaw incident while discouraging the couple from going into the next round of the bout, they nevertheless arrived after the ambulance which had been close enough to Midshaw School to negate any need for a First Responder car to be summoned.

The first to emerge from the Volvo was Plummer; her stab-proof vest masked the slenderness of her frame, making her appear short and round. Dunn exited the driver's door, his emaciated frame emphasising his considerable height advantage. Plummer physically blocked Dunn from barging into the building. 'I'll go in first, Elias; it's a girls' changing room. Wait until I tell you you can go in.' She went into the room and addressed the four teachers. 'Please don't touch anything – I'll be right back.' Hunter reflected on the physical impossibility of satisfying the request; even under these circumstances the pedantic physicist in him remained fully functioning. Plummer stepped outside through the inner swing doors and the outer lockable doors, and beckoned Dunn to come inside. Mutual nods of recognition were exchanged between Obaku and Dunn; they spoke together quietly, away from the body and the assembled people, while Carpenter and Plummer also held a brief, muted exchange. Dunn and Plummer conferred, following which Plummer turned to Verbane. 'Is there anything you can tell us about the injury?'

Verbane offered what for him was the briefest of explanations. 'John Newhouse was playing in an eleven-a-side football match for the staff team against the school. He left the match a few minutes before the others and will have come back here into the girls' changing room – it had been reserved for the staff team. When the rest of the team came in here they found him in this state, but no one knows what happened.'

Plummer responded. 'The cause of the head injury will have to be investigated, which means we need to secure the room to avoid any further contamination of the scene of the incident. First of all we need to clear the area of all non-essential personnel. Could you and your colleagues please go outside without touching anything.'

Hunter caught himself almost smiling at this request, which he masked by turning it into a grimace as he filed out of the room behind Verbane and Oaken and ahead of Clifton and Cullen. They retraced their steps to their earlier place by the football field as though winding back time. Plummer followed after them to record their details and to confirm the identity of the deceased, while Dunn stayed inside with the two paramedics.

Moments later two more vehicles arrived at speed: an unliveried white Ford Focus with a blue light on the roof, closely followed by a black Range Rover with a green light on top. Detective Constable Neil Whittington – widely known as "Witty" – parked the Ford on the grass to the left of the ambulance so as not to block its exit. At five feet nine and average build he appeared unexceptional; his crumpled dark blue suit and wrinkled white shirt, together with his untidy, dark brown hair, suggested a lack of care over his appearance.

Witty heaved himself out from the driver's seat and stepped quickly away from the car, watching Detective Constable Lily Martello unfurl herself from the other side, an imago emerging from the chrysalis. He looked at her surreptitiously: five feet ten, straight blonde hair, piercing blue eyes, aquiline nose and cupid's-bow mouth with full lips; she had a face that would have launched a thousand ships. Together with her slender body and quite large, apparently firm breasts, she was his ideal of exquisite beauty. He sighed inwardly, knowing how unprofessional it would be to treat her as anything other than just another colleague.

Witty and Martello began to stride toward the front door of the building that prominently displayed the restriction "Only Girls Allowed". They were overtaken by the small, light figure of Paediatric surgeon Mr James Kinder; though a kindly man, his name was pronounced kin-der by association with Kinder Scout, the highest plateau in Derbyshire. Kinder had no thought of how undignified he may have looked as he sprinted past them and into the girls' changing room. He had parked his Range Rover further back on the grass so as to leave the way clear for the ambulance to make a rapid dash to the Children's Hospital near Weston Park,

Sheffield, where he himself was employed. Immediately on entering the changing room Kinder looked down at the body, then turned to Dunn and demanded, 'Where's the girl?'

Dunn replied, 'There is no girl, only this man. And you are?'

'I'm the doctor who was called out by the police. I'm James Kinder, a paediatric surgeon – a children's doctor. DC Whittington telephoned me and provided me with an escort to get me here ASAP.' Unusually for him he had used the acronym "ASAP", pronouncing it A-sap; it was his attempt to sound less like yet another condescending doctor and more like someone familiar with what he imagined was the world of practical policing. He had added the description "children's doctor", not deliberately to talk down to Dunn, but because he had been frowning and looked a little confused; Kinder had come into contact with enough people who did not understand the meanings of such words as paediatrician, paedophile, paederast, podiatrist, et cetera, that he sometimes felt safer saying "children's doctor". He reflected on the difficulty doctors often experienced when meeting someone for the first time, needing to pitch their conversation at a low level until they proved themselves capable of deeper comprehension; he found addressing groups of people even more problematic, with the need generally to aim for the lowest common denominator.

Witty and Martello entered the room as the exchange was taking place between Kinder and Dunn. Kinder turned to Witty. 'You called me and said a girl was either badly injured or dead; but there is no girl.'

'I'm sorry, Mr Kinder, I passed on the information I received.'

Hearing Witty address him as "Mr Kinder" rather than as Jim, he knew Witty was embarrassed about the mistake. Witty and Kinder had known each other for several years, from a time when Witty had been driving a patrol car in the early hours of a morning and had stopped Kinder who had been travelling at over ninety miles an hour. Instead of waiting in his car for the officer to come and talk to him, Kinder had jumped out and run up to the driver's side of the police car where he had bellowed, 'I'm a surgeon. Get me to the Children's Hospital in Sheffield. Blue lights. Do it NOW.' Kinder had not waited for any reply. Witty had accepted the order and had given him the required escort. Witty had later paid Kinder a call at his home to see if a procedure could be put in place that would enable the police to help in the future with high-speed escorts. Consequently, Witty had on several occasions led the way for Kinder to speed to the hospital. The meeting had also sparked a personal friendship between the two; they now regularly, though infrequently, went out for a drink together, where the conversation would eventually, yet inevitably, turn to the subject of Ollie, Witty's disabled son.

Martello, who was unaware of the personal connection between Witty and Kinder, decided to intervene in the awkwardness she perceived. 'As you are here now, would you mind confirming that the man's life has been extinguished?'

Kinder repeated to himself the word "extinguished", triggering other thoughts. 'His life guttered and was extinguished like a candle in the wind.' His mind flitted to an old painting with unlighted candles around a corpse, then to a black-and-white Swedish film with a similar tableau.

Accompanied by an unintended sudden intake of breath, he bent down to perform the usual tests. He checked the carotid artery but found no pulse. He shone his pencil torch into the dilated pupils, but they remained unresponsive. He even checked the heart and the wrist for signs of a pulse for the benefit of the assembled audience, though he knew he was just going through the motions as the conclusion was obvious. He declared, 'No sign of life.' After a moment he added, 'There isn't anything I can do for him, so I'll leave it with you to take things from here. I'm on call from the Children's Hospital, so I'd like to go back home to be ready in case they need me. The paramedics may as well leave too – they may be required elsewhere.'

Martello responded, 'Yes, I'll give the paramedics the word, but could you hold on here for a couple of minutes? I need to check on procedure.'

He angled his straight hand away at the wrist so that his fingers pointed toward the paramedics. 'They were here first, so ask them to complete a Validation of Death form; then there's no need for me to do a Certification of Death.'

'I'll just ring my boss first, if that's alright.'

She instructed Dunn to seal off the changing room. Before going outside to put up the blue-and-white police tape, he relayed to her and Witty the brief explanation Verbane had given them earlier. When he had stepped outside to stand guard at the door,

Witty and Martello held a brief discussion before making phone calls.

Kinder stayed as requested; to refuse the request of a gorgeous woman was somehow to insult her, and yet he had often rationalised how unfair it was of society to favour those with conventional beauty, as its counterpart was to act against all those not deemed to be so endowed. Practically, he was more concerned with prejudice shown against visibly damaged children. He reflected on other prejudices. Those against race, creed, disability and sexual orientation were diminishing, at least overtly; but others were being recognised – obesity, heightism, even gingerism. He often found many ordinary people were now unsure what they were allowed to say to him within the latest rules of Political Correctness – in effect, they acted as a form of censorship which curtailed their freedom of speech. He recalled several who had clearly been uncertain how to tiptoe safely through the PC minefield in responding to his explanations of why Caucasian children are more likely than other races to suffer from cystic fibrosis, or how sickle-cell anaemia indicated they had ancestors who had originated from sub-Saharan regions where malaria was rife.

Kinder looked around the changing room, observing the notices specifying "entrance" and "exit" to the shower area. Six chrome spray-heads were arrayed along the external wall, equally spaced, visible above the white-tiled, one metre eighty interior partition. He felt a twinge of guilt as he remembered how, in his mid-teens, he had ached to see inside the girls' changing room at his old school when they had come in from games lessons, heaving and sweating and needing showers. His thoughts were interrupted by Witty who had completed his phone call.

'I've been checking on the confusion about the incident report.'

Before he could explain further, Martello completed her call and immediately proceeded to speak, cutting across Witty's conversation. 'As the paramedics arrived first, it makes sense for them to be the ones to record the time they found him dead. That means there isn't really any need for you to stay, Mr Kinder. Thank you for coming at a moment's notice.'

Witty added his own appreciation. 'Yes, thank you Mr Kinder, you're a good scout.'

Kinder attempted to give different responses to each: smiling at

Witty at his attempted humour; looking suitably appreciative at Martello for her seriously-delivered expression of gratitude. The attempt to smile with only half a mouth resulted in it twisting awkwardly, causing him to fail on both fronts. Kinder and Witty proceeded to leave the changing room as Martello spoke to Carpenter to check that the Validation of Death form had been completed. Kinder turned to Witty, 'Kinder Scout; got it.'

The inner, swing doors moved quietly, whereas the outer doors shrieked, suggesting two pieces of metal grating together in unoiled hinges. Kinder shuddered slightly, perhaps not so much due to the noise itself as to the fact that no one had taken the trouble to address it. Of course, his NHS hospital had someone permanently employed to fix little things such as that, whereas school budgets were, according to the media, stretched to breaking point in all directions. Even so, he thought he might have taken it upon himself to fix the problem if he had been a teacher at the school.

Dunn had put up the police tape to seal off the locus, and Witty now held this up for them to pass under. 'Duck under the tape, Jim. By the way, I've been listening to the original recording of the emergency call. As it related to a girls' changing room, it isn't too surprising that the words "Mr E J Newhouse" were transposed to "Miss Teri J Newhouse". So the mystery is solved. The Miss Ter-ee is solved.'

Kinder restricted his appreciation of the underlying humour to a brief smile, in view of the circumstances. 'It's not a mistake that's likely to be repeated, then.'

While Witty and Kinder were having their conversation, Martello exited the changing room with the paramedics, instructing Dunn to go back inside and stay with the body. As Kinder departed, Martello turned to Witty with a look of self-satisfaction. 'I've just been speaking to our DCI – Castleton said he'll be the SIO until he hands over to DI Priestley when he's back from his latest jolly. I described the scene and he says two CSIs will be enough – he'll be arranging for them to come over straight away. He reminded me that an unexplained death should be investigated as a homicide until it proves otherwise, and that there's five principles for the initial response phase: preservation of life – too late for that; preserve scenes – keeping everyone out of the room until the CSIs have processed it; secure evidence – we need to talk about that; identify victim – the headmaster can do that formally; and identify suspects – anyone nearby. And then he said that for now I'm in charge.'

Witty was irked by Detective Chief Inspector Bryn Castleton making Martello the officer in charge of the incident. He assumed Castleton had favoured her with increased responsibility because of their personal relationship, as her experience and past performance did not justify her preferment. He wondered if Castleton had used the term "jolly" or if she had invoked it herself; he knew what Priestley was working on with the National Crime Agency and it was definitely not a "jolly". He tried to keep any hint of the annoyance he felt from creeping into his voice as he responded, 'Well, what do you propose we do?'

'Castleton agreed it was a suspicious death, so he'll arrange for a Forensic Pathologist to attend, even though he reckons it could cost about three and a half grand depending on exactly what tests are needed, instead of just a hundred for a Routine Pathologist. We should stay here for when the pathologist and the CSIs arrive.'

Witty was concerned their inaction would result in the loss of valuable material – information, intelligence and evidence. He suggested, with a relaxed-sounding voice that masked his frustration, 'While we're waiting, perhaps we could get a clear idea of what happened, find out who was where, check for CCTV, and then start talking to the key witnesses. Plus any other fast-track actions you can think of.'

Martello realised Witty was quite right. To assert her leading rôle she responded, 'I'm going to ask the Headmaster some questions. After that I'll talk to the senior staff while you interview the teachers who were in the football match.'

The automatic bell that signalled the end of the school day generated a rush of escapees from the buildings, but then the news of the death of Newhouse spread among the children like wildfire as they prepared to leave the grounds. Many of the younger children chose to leave school as usual – those who were not returning to empty homes would be bursting to be the first to deliver the shocking news to their parents or carers. In contrast, many of the older children chose to remain at school to see what further developments might occur; this was not so much from a ghoulish desire to see or be near to a dead body as simply the wish to experience something new.

Carpenter and Obaku alternated responsibilities for incidents. Whoever drove to an incident would also drive back, thereby avoiding losing time adjusting seat and mirror positions. Obaku was relieved not to need to be in the back with a patient, where they would be bounced around by the hard suspension. The slow, quiet departure of the ambulance was in marked contrast to its arrival, as Carpenter navigated past the many children who were now standing in groups or wandering around the grounds. For some of them the departure of the ambulance signalled the end of a phase of that experience which thereby left them free to depart; others, especially those for whom no one was waiting to welcome them home, chose to remain to see what else would happen for their edification.

Plummer met Martello and Witty near to the changing room and directed them to where Verbane, Oaken, Clifton, Hunter and Cullen were gathered together on the touchline of the football pitch. Plummer took up sentry duty outside the front door of the changing room.

Witty and Martello rushed up the steep steps to the games field where the five teachers were shaking their heads as they asked themselves brief, unanswerable questions. Martello and Witty introduced themselves as "Detective Constable Lily Martello" and "DC Whittington". Martello began, 'Headmaster, I have some questions I need to ask you, to find out what may have happened, and who will need to be interviewed. Would you like to begin by telling me how many people there were playing in the football match?'

Witty felt embarrassed for Martello – she may not have registered Dunn saying it was an eleven-a-side game, and may not realise what questions were vital to be asked at this stage. He enhanced her question. 'She means how many substitutes, as well as the two teams of eleven. Just to make sure we don't miss anyone.'

Verbane responded, with a nod in Cullen's direction, 'Mr Cullen will be able to provide you with full lists of the teams.'

Martello looked at Witty to give him a direct instruction. 'You can pick that up after this briefing.'

Witty nodded before turning to Verbane. 'Actually, until we know what has happened we may find it difficult to ask the right questions. Does the school have CCTV?'

'I'm sure there isn't a school in the country that has CCTV in their changing rooms.'

'What about other parts of the school?'

'The governors are currently considering a proposal for CCTV safety cameras to be installed in classrooms, but there's resistance from the unions. For now we don't have any at all.'

'Then could you perhaps tell us what you know of Mr Newhouse's movements from the point that you last saw him alive, and where he went afterwards so that we can, um, pick up the trail from there, so to speak.'

Verbane swelled visibly as he felt himself to be centre-stage. 'Everybody watching the match saw Mr Newhouse sent off the field with about five minutes left to play; a very unfair decision I believe. I saw him heading for the changing room, that is to say the girls' main changing room, which the staff team were using. The school team were using the boys' changing room. I suppose it's possible he stayed long enough to see the free kick that the school team took, and from which they scored what proved to be the winning goal. Most people would have had their eyes on the match in those last few minutes, so it may be difficult to find anyone who saw exactly where he went, and when. I'm fairly certain he had gone down the steps to the changing room by the time the final whistle blew. The school team then formed two rows which the staff walked through to suitably generous applause. Then the staff team formed two rows and applauded the school team. It's something I reintroduced here, showing appreciation for the opposition. I noticed my staff team putting on brave faces despite having come second in the match.'

Witty queried this explanation. 'Come second? Was it a league? You said the school team won.'

'Yes. For the past year we haven't had losers in my school, we prefer the term "came second" as this avoids any suggestion of outright failure.'

'Right; that's very, um, fair-minded.'

'Indeed. It was just a few minutes after the match had ended that Dr Hunter...'

Verbane indicated Hunter with a slow, sweeping gesture of his right hand, reminiscent of a cricket umpire signalling a four, '...came with the terrible news.'

Witty enquired as to Verbane's own alibi – it was always a difficult matter so he thought it best to get it over with as soon as possible. 'Where were you during the time between Mr Newhouse leaving the field and Dr Hunter coming to see you?'

'I was here with my colleagues, Miss Glenda Oaken, our Headmistress, and Ms Vicky Clifton, our Head of Sixth Form.'

Clifton interjected. 'Actually, Headmaster, the three of us came together right at the end of the match. Just before then I was over on the far side reprimanding a few boys who had been rather unsporting about Mr Newhouse – after he'd been shown a yellow card one of them had shouted "Send Him Off", and then they started chanting "Send Off Sir" over and over again.'

'Yes, indeed, that's correct. Anyway, I'm sure I can find lots of witnesses to confirm my whereabouts. As Headmaster I find I'm never alone on social occasions such as these. Frequently, members of staff like to take the opportunity to bend my ear about any little gripes they have, where I'm something of a captive audience and have little choice but to listen. However, there were very few staff about, so I was standing with some of the students, mostly girls who wished to quiz me on things to do with university applications. Not many of the boys were with me – I think they were more interested in what was happening on the field. I do remember Miss Leveret coming to talk with me, and then Miss Nunn came over and joined the conversation. After that, Miss Oaken and Ms Clifton also joined me.'

Witty nodded slightly, Martello more vigorously. Witty asked, 'And what happened after Dr Hunter had spoken to you?'

Verbane explained the events to the best of his recollection. 'I went to the changing room, where I checked to see if Mr Newhouse was alive. Sadly, he was not, so I closed his eyes.'

Oaken interjected. 'Don't forget I tried to revive him.'

Verbane confirmed this had happened, continuing, 'I asked Dr Hunter and Mr Cullen to stay, and I asked the other eight members of the team to go to the staffroom and wait for me. Do you wish to see them straight away?'

Witty nodded. 'Yes. Could you keep them together for now?'

Verbane turned to Hunter. 'Will you let them know the situation – I'll be over there myself soon.' Verbane turned back to

Witty. 'Mr Cullen here ...' Verbane used the same sweeping hand gesture as before, '... will help you with anything else you may need.'

Martello confirmed the briefing was over. 'Thank you, Headmaster; that was all very clear. I'll keep you informed of developments.'

Martello returned to the girls' changing room, putting Dunn on sentry duty outside at the front, and posting Plummer to the back entrance, while she waited inside with the body for the arrival of the CSIs and the pathologist.

CHAPTER 3

Witty Obtains Football Team Lists

Witty left the playing field at a brisk walk, accompanied by Cullen. As they headed toward the main school building Witty wondered why Cullen was walking quite so close to him. Was it the sense of protection some people felt with policemen? Was it a way of expressing a wish to be helpful? Or perhaps inviting him to be accepted as a friend? Did Cullen have something to hide? Or maybe it was associated with the idea of "Keep your friends close and your enemies closer"? Witty tested the water by inviting Cullen to chat. 'So, what position were you playing?'

Cullen gave his automatic smile, the one that he used dozens of times every day in his lessons. 'There's a full team sheet in the staffroom. I was put on the left wing – someone suggested it as a joke – they said that's where I belonged because of my politics. It wasn't my ideal position – I'd have been better as an attacking midfielder in the thick of things. We could have won if I'd had my chance to drive the team forward.' Conspiratorially he added, 'There's a team list in the boys' changing room where they've added extra comments – what you might call "schoolboy humour".' Then, remembering dead Mr Newhouse, he changed his expression to a frown that overshot the mark and looked like he had just suffered an intense migraine attack. 'Or you could get a clean list from the office.'

Witty responded lightly. 'I'd like to see what passes for schoolboy humour nowadays – which way is it?'

They changed direction and headed for the boys' changing room, outside which several teenagers were looking shiftily as though they might be infringing some school rules. The boys quickly moved away as Cullen and Witty approached. Witty decided he would make no assumptions about this little group, as some innocent boys look naturally guilty and some guilty boys look like absolute angels.

17

Cullen led the way through the two sets of doors, taking a right turn and pointing to the notice board. At top centre the word "Teams" was in thick black writing on a piece of yellow card attached with two drawing pins. Underneath were half-a-dozen team sheets. As Cullen pointed out the staff team sheet Witty also noticed the school team sheet for the same match. Both had been printed double-spaced; extra comments had been hand-written on them between parentheses, arrows indicating they should be read immediately before surnames. Witty read the staff team sheet first.

School vs. Staff Football Match
Wednesday OK 1:30 p.m. *dyslexic?*

STAFF TEAM

1   Mr (*Butch*) Cassidy
2   Mr (*Cool*) Collins
3   Mr (*Really Good Work*) Rendel
4   Mr (*Hand It Over*) Hart
5   Mr (*Do NOT*) Davies
6   Dr (*Head*) Hunter
7   Mr (*OUT!*) Offial
8   Mr (*Freud*) Finlay
9   Mr (*Nobby*) Newhouse, Captain
10   Mr (*Daisy*) Decker
11   Mr (*Caring*) Cullen

'What do you think's meant by the added comments? I see you're described as "Caring".'

'I expect they're just showing their appreciation for my attitude to them.'

'And what about: "Mr Cool Collins"? Is he cool?'

'Not really. He tries to be, but he's more the opposite because it isn't cool to try to be cool.'

'I suppose "Mr Butch Cassidy" is fairly obvious.'

'Yes, another opposite – he's not at all butch.'

'Oh. I assumed it was from the cowboy film, Butch Cassidy and the Sundance Kid.'

'I didn't get that till now. I'm sure I've heard of the film, but I've never seen it.'

SEND OFF SIR

Witty read through the school team.

School vs. Staff Football Match
Wednesday OK 1:30 p.m. *dylsexia rules KO*

SCHOOL TEAM

1	Robbie (*diver*) Henderson
2	Billy (*bites yer legs*) Huntsman
3	Vinnie (*that's my ball*) Hardwick
4	Jacko (*psycho*) Stanage
5	Tommy (*bone-crusher*) Thompson
6	Gazza (*dribbler*) Talbot
7	Danno (*bomber*) Harris
8	Marco (*dodger*) Hope
9	Alex (*up n at 'em*) Peveril, Captain
10	Deano (*nutter*) Bonsall
11	Bobby (*killer*) Bolsover
12	Kenny (*belter*) Derwent
13	[number not in use]
14	Jimmy (*jammy*) Woodhead
15	Nosher (*smasher*) Smith

'Some of the boys sound a bit dangerous – psycho, bone-crusher, nutter, killer. Are these reflections of their character, or maybe opposites?'

'I don't think they mean anything.'

'They make interesting reading, anyway – I'll take both sheets with me.'

He pulled out the drawing pins that held the team lists to the green baize board, taking the two sheets and folding them gently to avoid creasing, then placing them in an inside pocket. 'Could you show me to the office? I'd like originals as well – ones without comments.'

Cullen led the way to the nearest entrance to the main school building. 'The office is at the other side. It's quicker to go through than around.'

Cullen began a string of questions.

'Do you think it was an accident?'

'That's not for me to say'

'Who'll be in charge of the investigation?'

'That hasn't been settled yet.'

'Do you expect the investigation to take long?'

'Investigations vary enormously. It all depends.'

'Depends on what?'

'What the forensics team discover.'

'When will they arrive?'

'It could be any time soon, depending on what other work they have right now.'

'Will we all be fingerprinted?'

'That's a decision for the future.'

Cullen recognised he would be unlikely to get any inside information from Witty; he also saw him as unimportant as he was clearly not in charge of the investigation – otherwise he would have said so. He therefore looked for a way of off-loading him. He saw a young woman heading toward them; the thick, black rims to her glasses did little to cover the prettiness of her face, and the contrast only accentuated the effect of her long blonde hair. The small, slightly upturned nose gave her a childlike quality that supported an overall untroubled look which suggested she had not been in teaching long enough to have developed the care-worn gaze that so many adopted. Cullen seized his opportunity, speaking to Witty loudly and timing his words so as to be heard by the approaching woman. 'I believe I should go to the staffroom. It's where the Headmaster is going and I'm sure he'd want all the team there. Perhaps I could pass you on to Miss Goode.'

Cullen moved to his right to block Goode's path. 'Julie, this is … '

He looked to Witty to introduce himself. 'Detective Constable Neil Whittington.'

'… and he's needing to go to the office. I have to see the Headmaster, so could you take him?'

Goode looked at Witty rather than Cullen, as she smiled without affectation. 'Yes, of course. I'll take you through here – it's a bit of a maze.'

Cullen departed with a self-aggrandising 'Thanks for doing this for me, Julie.'

Goode ducked through an uninviting door and depressed a rocker switch to turn on a single, low-power bulb that made the room appear more like a dingy corridor. She commented brightly, 'Something of a rabbit-warren, isn't it?'

They exited through the door at the far end and turned left into a bright corridor illuminated with strip lighting and with rooms off to both sides. Witty enquired: 'Does everyone know this route?'

Goode gave the official line. 'It's not for use by the children; they probably know it though. The staff use it all the time. You may have noticed signs around the place that show there's a one-way system in operation. In theory the staff are exempt, but have you ever tried walking against the flow of dozens of children? This passage avoids that problem.'

Witty commented, as much to consolidate the thought as to respond. 'So, people can get around quickly if they know the way.' He added to himself, 'without being noticed'.

After passing two doors on either side they turned right to where a solid mahogany door displayed a large sign identifying the Administration Office; a second sign indicated the incumbent as "Mrs J Jackson, Head of Admin". Witty noted how this door was in marked contrast to the flimsy, plywood doors seen elsewhere throughout the school. Goode turned the handle quietly, as though not to disturb any sleeping occupants. Witty followed Goode into a brightly illuminated room that was dominated by three large desks. Two of them bore large triangular nameplates indicating the names and titles of the occupants: Mrs Joanna Jackson, Head of Administration, and Mrs Margaret Webster, Administration Assistant. Jackson was seated at an impressively large computer screen that was placed in the centre of her desk, and was scrutinising the keyboard below it. Webster had a smaller computer screen on the left side of her desk; she appeared to be inspecting the carpet tiles from the comfort of her seat. On the third desk were three printers, one small, one medium and one tower, and several piles of A4 paper of various colours. Down one side of the room was a large, free-standing printer with multiple positions for feeding in paper of different sizes. In a corner of the room was a large photocopier, also with multiple paper-feeding options. Next to it was another machine, capable of both printing and photocopying. The rest of the room was filled with wooden cupboards the colour of beech.

Goode's erstwhile bright demeanour seemed to dim on entry to the office. Witty speculated on whether this was due to the death of

Newhouse, or more to do with entering this room. He decided to check whether she knew what had happened. 'Are you aware of the incident involving Mr Newhouse?'

She jutted her chin forward and gave a slight frown. 'No, I'm not. Has there been a complaint? If so: you should really be talking to the Headmaster.'

'Mr Newhouse has died. It happened suddenly, after the football match.'

Her immediate response was to put forward an argument against this preposterous idea. 'But he was very fit.' She shook her head repeatedly from side to side as she added, 'He couldn't just die from playing football.'

She fell silent, blinking slowly, looking directly at Witty as though inviting him to justify his unreasonable statement. He responded in an apologetic tone. 'It happened after he had left the field; I'm sorry I can't be more specific.'

Goode turned to Jackson who had been listening to the conversation without apparent interest. 'Were you aware of this, Jo?'

Jackson responded without the least hint of emotion. 'Yes, Dr Hunter called in to let us know, on his way to the staffroom. He said to get a message out to all the staff.'

'And have you relayed the message?'

'Not yet. I was just thinking up the appropriate wording, so I could type a note for the Headmaster to approve. Then he'll need to sign it and I'll photocopy it. That way everyone gets the same message.'

Goode spoke in carefully restrained tones, knowing how Jackson tended to stand on her dignity whenever there was any suggestion of her authority being undermined. 'You're too late to get the message around the school properly today. I suggest you and Mrs Webster go round the classrooms – separately – and if you find any staff then let them know straight away. If there are any children still in the classrooms with the teachers, speak only to the teachers and ask them to relay the message.'

From the top of a large pile she took two copies of the buildings' layout leaflet – the type given to all children on their first day at the school. Taking up a red pen, she circled one group of classrooms on one copy and the remaining classrooms on the other. Clifton entered the office as Goode was handing one leaflet each to Jackson and Webster. Goode turned to Clifton. 'Did you know Mr Newhouse has died?'

Clifton nodded slightly. 'Yes, I was at the match standing with the Headmaster when I heard. I came over here to make sure people are being informed.'

Goode nodded vigorously. 'I've divided up the school classrooms into two groups for Mrs Jackson and Peggy to spread the message.'

Clifton addressed Jackson. 'We need to get the message around the school right away. Just say he has died after the football match and more information will follow when we have it.' Seeing Jackson hesitate, she added, 'You need to do this now, on my authority.'

Jackson noisily opened a drawer, huffing a little as she removed a set of keys. 'I'll have to ask you all to leave this room, then, as I have to lock it behind me: Headmaster's orders.'

There was just a hint of triumphalism in Jackson's voice as she cited the Headmaster, saying it a little too loudly than was necessary for the close audience. She ushered the other three from the office and walked out with Webster, locking the door, and then checking it twice to ensure it hadn't miraculously unlocked itself in the meantime. Jackson and Webster hurried away, showing a turn of speed not previously observed in them.

Goode turned to Witty, apologising, 'I'm sorry, was this why you were needing the office? I should have asked.'

Witty nodded yes while saying, 'No. I agree, though, it was right of you to organise letting the staff know first. Actually, I need the team sheets for the Staff v. School football match.'

'I can do you a copy. The lists are held on the common database under Physical Education. I know, because there was a long debate in the staffroom about whether they should be under Social, Staff, Physical Education, or several other possible sub-directories. It would seem one person's idea of logic is another's idea of wrong-thinking, so in the end Mr Newhouse just told the others they would go where he said, under Physical Education.'

Goode took Witty to the Maths staffroom, a title that belied its main rôle as a storeroom for various teaching aids that were deemed useful in enabling children to grasp key mathematical concepts. She entered a four-digit code number into a keypad, and when the brass and black metal box clicked she immediately pushed open the painted plywood door and stepped into the room. She held the door by its edge for Witty to enter.

'The door unlocks for five seconds. The maths department trialled the system before it was installed on the main school entrance. Apparently, the thinking was that it needs numbers to be entered, so it should be the maths department to test it out.' Goode giggled for a moment in an almost childlike way as she recalled the heated debate that had been generated by the whole saga, appearing already to have put aside any thoughts of Newhouse. She turned to Witty to explain the origin of the door locking mechanism. 'Mrs Jackson hasn't forgotten or forgiven us yet – she was determined to be the first to have a keypad system; she claimed it should be installed on her office door as that was the most important part of the school and so it should also be the most secure. It's what lost her the argument – the Headmaster didn't like the suggestion that his own room wasn't the most important, but had the nouse to know not to claim the first keypad for himself. Since then, it was decided not to install any more because of the cost. So Mrs Jackson has to carry keys with her whenever she leaves the office; apparently the keys are very heavy and get heavier the longer she carries them … it's an interesting physical concept.'

The room they had entered was more like a long corridor, made narrower by the four battleship grey, thin metal cupboards running the length of the left side, each one peppered with dents and scratches that perhaps gave testament to teachers returning over the decades from lessons that had not gone according to plan. Goode sat at the light oak bench that ran the full length of the opposite wall, pulling a laptop toward her and releasing the lid using its broken, plastic slide. It was already plugged into one of the many sockets that stood proud of the wall in groups of four. The laptop had been left on stand-by, so it took just a few seconds to warm-boot the machine and bring up the security logon screen.

Witty made a show of turning away from the screen, moving his feet as well as his head so as to emphasise he was not observing her logon or password details. He looked at the lists of contents attached to the cupboards, wondering just what these things looked like, and how he had succeeded without them when he was at school. He read some familiar words – cards, dice, hexagons; others he could guess at – KS3, KS4, Celtic Knot; and some that meant very little to him – tesserae, MATs, hypercube. He wondered if anyone ever performed stock-checks, counting the listed fifty regular dodecagons, hundred hexagons, two hundred pentagons, three hundred equilateral triangles…

In little more than a minute Goode had the two documents open on screen and had printed them on the small, slow, rattling printer at the end of the room, just a couple of metres away. 'I've charged them to my own cost code rather than the maths department. You'd be amazed how tight the budgets are for some things.' Her emphasis on "some" made it clear there were other things where she regarded spending as not tight enough. Collecting the two sheets, Goode handed them to Witty, asking, 'Would you like to go to the Headmaster now, or is there somewhere else I can take you?'

Witty nodded in the affirmative, though it was unclear what he was assenting to. 'Could you take me to the main staffroom? The headmaster asked the staff football team to wait there – I've some questions to ask them.'

Goode closed the laptop lid, the green light embedded in the front edge quickly being replaced with the amber. She stood up and pressed the door lock release button, awkwardly pulling open the door a little way with the small, round handle, before grasping the outer edge of the door and forcing it open. After Witty had stepped outside, she released her grip on the door, which proceeded to close slowly; they were fully ten metres away by the time the self-locking mechanism had finally clicked to indicate the room had been secured.

CHAPTER 4

Initial Statements Taken from Staff Team

Witty accompanied Goode to the staffroom where he found the ten surviving members of the football team sitting drinking tea or coffee. The Headmaster had paid them a brief visit before heading for the sanctuary of his office, having given them a pep talk on how everyone needed to be strong to cope with the unhappy loss of a much-loved and much-respected colleague. The term "much-loved" had caused a few of them to frown. None of them looked especially pepped up. Eight had changed into their usual clothes, having first taken quick showers in the single cubicle across the corridor from the staffroom, a place normally used only by the few members of staff who regularly jogged in when the weather was fine. Hunter and Cullen however were still wearing football kit, and both of them looked uncomfortable about being under-dressed.

Goode opened the staffroom door and asked Witty, politely, 'May I leave you here, Constable?'

Witty gave the expected, appreciative response. 'Yes. Thank you for your help.'

'Should I put up a "Do Not Disturb" sign?'

'That would be marvellous. Please do.'

She entered the staffroom silently, avoiding eye contact with any of her colleagues. Going to a set of pigeon-holes, she picked up a ready-printed sheet and some green blobs of tacky, rubbery material with which she then attached the sheet to the door. As Witty stepped into the room she closed the door behind him as quietly as she could, making sure the handle was first turned sufficiently to avoid its usual clicking sound.

Witty noted how everyone had looked up as he followed Goode into the room, but no one had spoken. He had the impression they had been silent long before the door had been opened. As he looked around the room he realised why none of them had been talking despite having an obvious topic of conversation. Most of them were reading through exercise books, marking scripts. Others were trying to look interested in various textbooks, perhaps so as not to disturb their colleagues. He wondered whether the main factor for this unexpected behaviour was due to the time pressure they felt to mark children's work during the school term, or if there were some other consideration such as silently marking their respect for a dead colleague. He hoped this indicated they had not been comparing their recollections of the time between Newhouse leaving the field of play and their discovery of his dead body.

Having decided to adopt an unusual method for obtaining their initial testimonies, he gave an artificial cough as a prelude to speaking. His usual style was to add a little of his trademark humour, so as to lighten the mood and perhaps relax everyone into doing as he asked without too much resistance. However, under the present circumstances he felt he ought to reflect the gravity of the situation. Well, perhaps just a little humour would be alright, he thought, as he launched into his opening speech.

'Gentlemen, I am sorry to be meeting you under these unhappy circumstances. Whereas in the police force we have an expectation that colleagues may be lost from time to time, in a school it is not something that is ever expected. Consequently, you may be feeling a much greater level of shock than I can appreciate. If anyone feels especially distressed at this difficult time, please let me know.'

Witty interpreted their silence as his cue to continue. 'As you might expect, I need to collect some information from you all. I would like you each to get a sheet of paper and something to write with – ink rather than pencil, as the sheets will be taken into evidence – and to find somewhere to sit where you're not overlooking anyone else's paper. Please remain silent. Just like exam conditions, if I remember correctly.'

Francis Offial stood up and opened a drawer marked Modern Languages, from which he extracted a dozen or so sheets of lined paper. He handed a few each to three colleagues who took one and passed on the others as though they had trained for this eventuality; within seconds everyone had one sheet and the few remainders were back in Offial's hands. Each of them conjured up a pen of some sort. Following three changes of seat, within half a minute they had all found somewhere suitable to sit. Six of them occupied a large, oak desk that dominated the room; four were sitting in well-worn, comfy chairs with wooden armrests.

'Now, first of all write down your name at the top of the sheet, and today's date and time.' Witty could have given them this latter information, but chose not to do so as he saw an opportunity to keep the mood light; he was correct in assuming there would be murmuring as they agreed on the current time. Witty beamed his biggest smile as he pretended to reprimand them. 'Exam conditions, gentlemen – no talking!'

Witty noticed a few smiles being exchanged around the room, though none were directed at him. He also noticed a couple of good-natured grimaces and the odd sigh of apparent despair. 'Now, without referring to anyone else, I would like you to write down the words "WITH ME" in capital letters, followed by the names of the people with whom you entered the girls' changing room at the end of the match. I know you may think at first that you all entered together, but try to refine your thoughts. Think who was right there with you, up close and personal as the expression goes. Then, write down "BEFORE ME" in capitals, and enter the names of those who were in the changing room before you. And thirdly – and I'm sure you've probably all guessed what's coming next – write down "AFTER ME" in capitals, followed by the names of those who entered after you. Finally, the fourth heading, for completeness: write down "NOT SURE ABOUT", and write down the names of those you don't know were with you, before you or after you. When you've finished, please check your answers to ensure you have exactly nine names listed in these four sections, with no duplicates and every team member entered just once. Finally, sign your name directly below the last thing you wrote. Does anyone have any questions?' They remained silent. 'If there's anything you'd like to ask me while everyone is completing their papers, please put up your hand.' Witty beamed around the room as he added, 'Just like I had to, when I sat my school exams.'

Witty observed that all the teachers focused steadfastly on their papers, no one looking around. It was as though they were all concentrating on doing well in a written examination paper, no doubt as they had done all their lives. Witty wondered if anyone would play the part of the naughty boy, or ask a question just so as to make contact with him. Such action could have been revealing, either about the person, or about whether they had something to hide. However, no one asked anything while the exam conditions prevailed.

SEND OFF SIR

After a little less than a minute, Cameron Finlay, a recently appointed psychology teacher, turned to look at Witty for recognition that he was the first to complete the task. Several others followed, and Witty made sure he acknowledged each one individually with a smile and a nod of the head. Eight of them completed the task in just a couple of minutes, most of them sitting back and looking contentedly at their finished work. Witty looked closely at the two teachers who remained stubbornly staring at their sheets of paper, like self-deceiving students who cannot believe the exam would contain only those questions for which they were unprepared when there were so many other questions they had revised for and could have answered brilliantly. The two laggards were Graham Rendel who had taught English at the school for six years, and Arthur Decker, a Newly Qualified Teacher (NQT) who had joined the Art department after giving up his dream of becoming a commercially successful post-modern artist. Witty looked over their shoulders and saw they had not progressed beyond writing the headings. He recalled his own senior school first year geography exam, where he did not know how to answer one of the earlier questions and felt unable to go to the next question, thereby ending up bottom of the class for that subject. It was amazing, he thought, how such embarrassing memories could spring back at a moment's notice.

After another minute, Witty decided to move things forward. 'Those of you who have finished, will you hold up your papers and I'll collect them, and then you can leave. Those of you who are still working, thank you for your diligence and please keep going – there's no time limit.' The teachers did as instructed. He collected completed papers from eight of the teachers, checking each one against the names on the team sheet and recording their team position number in the top right corner to make cross-checking easier.

The two who were still in football kit remained behind as the other six left the room. Hunter spoke to Witty. 'It was interesting that you compared the different expectations of death in the police force and in schools. When you talked of colleagues being lost I think you were referring to sudden, violent death. Does that mean you believe Mr Newhouse died after being attacked?'

'I'm sorry if I gave that impression. Mr Newhouse may have died by accident. We just don't know yet.'

'Well, you see, if it's deaths that are not to do with violence, then teachers, sadly, do have such an expectation, though more often to do with students than with colleagues. Sometimes we have children who are very ill, and we just try to make their lives as normal as possible until the inevitable happens. Other times, death happens from predictable behaviour such as teenage boys taking risks – there's an age when so many of them seem to imagine no harm can come to them. The worst is when death occurs suddenly and unexpectedly. There was one such loss at my former school; it was four years ago. A sixth form girl went down with meningitis in the morning and was dead by tea-time. She wasn't especially brilliant, or beautiful, or athletic. No, she was a girl who was doing her best with what talents she had been given, and …'

Hunter seemed to be losing the thread of his argument, suddenly looking very emotional. It was as though the memory of the loss of a child from a previous school four years ago was more painful to him than the loss of a colleague that afternoon. Hunter restarted with a question that was clearly intended as a third-party accusation. 'Why do the media almost invariably find someone to describe every child that dies under such circumstances as having been exceptional in some way? Why do people mourn the loss of a beautiful child more than the loss of a plain one?' His physicist's logic attempted to assert some sort of scientific angle to his monologue. 'But then why do people get upset about the death of an actor, an actress, or some other celebrity they never knew personally. Every day there are thousands of deaths around the world of people we don't know. We should just focus on the ones we do know.'

Witty probed gently, 'And did you know the girl very well?'

Hunter considered whether this question, being from a policeman, may have been loaded with a suspicion of impropriety – the fear of an unjustified accusation was always just below the surface for male teachers. He responded defensively, 'I knew her as well as I knew other students in my care, no more and no less.'

The painful memory drove Hunter to reveal rather more than his conscious mind might have intended, as he was gripped by the overwhelming feeling of grief that had struck him four years earlier. 'I know I was not the only teacher who shed tears at home in the evening, where no one could see us being weak. In the end the little reminders around the place were just too much to bear, so

I moved to another school.'

Hunter appeared still to have something to say, so Witty remained silent. 'Of course, as a humanitarian, I believe all loss of life is equal. But I'm not perfect – which of us is – so I know I do see differences in loss. When an adult has been in an awful accident and now can't do anything, and they want to die, I believe that society should help them to fulfil their wish.' Hunter was suddenly uncomfortable with the extent to which he was revealing his personal views to someone he had only recently met for the first time. Remembering why Witty was there, he brought the subject back to that reason. 'I know I should mourn the loss of John Newhouse just as much as I mourned the loss of that schoolgirl, but it's still sinking in.' Hunter knew this may have sounded like admittance of some sort of guiltiness about the death of Newhouse; he hoped Witty would not confuse guilt of feelings with culpability for actions. He decided to move the conversation in another direction. 'I really could do with collecting my clothes from the changing room. Mr Cullen is in the same situation. What's the procedure?'

Cullen stood up and walked over to them to show he also wished to know. Witty explained, 'The changing rooms are out-of-bounds, so that everything can remain undisturbed until the forensics people have done their job. It may be possible to have your clothes checked by them inside, and then passed to you outside.'

Apparently satisfied that this was appropriate under the circumstances, Hunter nodded agreement and left the staffroom. Cullen, however, remained behind and returned to his chair.

Witty spoke with the two remaining examination candidates who were still staring blankly at their sheets of paper. 'Is there anything I can help you with? Is there some particular problem you're having?'

Rendel responded first. 'I think I was probably the last to enter the changing room; I know there were colleagues in there before me, but I can't remember if there was anyone behind me – I don't think there was.'

Witty offered a way forward. 'In that case, write that no one entered with you, list everyone as there before you, no one after you, and put on an additional comment of "I think I was the last one in, but I'm not certain." Then sign it and we'll leave it at that for now. There'll be an opportunity later to revise what you've written if you need to.'

Witty looked over Rendel's shoulder until he had completed the task. Rendel handed him the paper and made his departure.

Arthur Decker waited until Rendel had left before venturing, 'My problem is that I don't really know everybody, so I'm not sure who was with me, who was there before me, or who was there after me. I'd probably recognise them, but I can't put all the names to the faces. I'm in the art department, and we're not exactly in the swim of things up there in the garret. I don't come into the main staffroom very often, as my breaks and free periods are usually spent with students working on their paintings or other art-work. Some of them have to be prised out of the place at the end of the day. It isn't really my fault I can't answer the questions.'

Witty thought Decker may be on the point of bursting into tears, though the timing suggested he may be more upset about his inability to complete the question paper than about the death of Newhouse. He knew many members of the police force made the mistake of having an unjustified confidence in their ability to read people's true emotions and the underlying causes, and consequently he had always sought to keep his own confidence level in check; he therefore consciously decided to keep an open mind on how to interpret Decker's apparent emotional state. Whatever was behind it, Witty decided it would nevertheless be best to smooth things over as quickly and as gently as possible. He nodded sympathetically. 'Yes, that's completely understandable. Are there any definites that you can place?'

'Just Dr Hunter and Mr Davies.'

'OK. Put them down and then list everybody else as uncertain.' Decker did as instructed. Witty showed him the original team sheet that Goode had printed for him. 'Now copy the names of the others from the list.' Decker worked quickly, looking relieved at being able to make progress on a task that the others had long ago completed. Witty concluded, 'Now write: "I do not recognise all my colleagues, which has made it difficult to answer the questions." Then sign it.'

Decker gushed his gratitude. 'Thank you ever so much. It was really helpful of you to let me do it that way. Thanks again.' Decker leaned his body forward as he left the staffroom, appearing to be about to break into a sprint.

SEND OFF SIR

Witty had been wondering why Cullen had remained in the staffroom. He was hoping he might be waiting in order to make a confession after all the others had left, but he was quickly disabused of this notion when Cullen broke into a strident harangue. 'We all went into the girls' changing room after the match. When we found Mr Newsome, eight of them took their clothes out. Why can't I just take my clothes out as well? I mean, without having them searched? If they could do it, why can't I? You don't have any right to search my clothes. This is not a police state. I know my rights. You need a warrant for that sort of thing.'

Witty thought Cullen may be hiding something, but that it may not be relevant to what happened to Newhouse. Perhaps he was just another of the "I know my rights" brigade, who almost invariably did not. He ventured, 'Is there something in your clothes that you don't wish the police to discover?'

Cullen snapped back. 'If I answer that question I might as well let the clothes be searched.'

'Well, most people wouldn't have any problem with having their clothes checked, under the circumstances, unless they had something to hide.'

'Do you know, when I used to demonstrate, when I was at the LSE, the police were always pushing us back and holding up batons and threatening us. We were all treated like criminals. But we weren't. I mean we weren't criminals, we were just protestors.'

'You were something of a radical were you, then?'

'I supported workers' rights. If that makes me a radical, then, yes, I was a radical. Communism is the only moral system, and workers have every right to be paid as much as the bosses. The police had no right to harass protestors. And you have no right to search my clothes.'

'So, the idea that your clothes will be searched is like a red rag to a bull. Or should I say a red flag.' Cullen remained looking grim, so Witty laughed out loud to make sure Cullen recognised it was an attempt at humour; he would not normally laugh at his own jokes, but he thought it might just help to ease the tension. Cullen for once in his life felt lost for words; he had never before met a neo-fascist running-dog of the establishment authoritarian state who liked to make jokes. Witty decided to quit while he was ahead; he left Cullen in the staffroom and headed back to the girls' changing room to meet up with Martello.

CHAPTER 5

CSIs Examine the Scene

The children who were still on school premises observed the arrival of a van bearing the words "Scientific Services Unit", the police authority having not yet followed their neighbouring forces whose vans now displayed the more familiar term "Crime Scene Investigation". In the past the purpose behind a scientific support vehicle would have been comprehended only by the *cognoscenti*; nowadays the general public recognised the function due to the popularity of various US TV programmes. Even those in the business had largely given in to the unstoppable tide, and now referred to the occupants as CSIs, despite official documentation still using the identifier SOCOs – Scenes of Crime Officers.

Jenny Merton, lead CSI, allowed her junior partner, Nick Evans, to do the driving. Nick was a slow, careful and deliberate driver who did not so much enjoy being at the wheel as disliked having to suffer anyone else's driving; even the most careful of drivers would rack up a whole series of misdemeanours under Nick's close scrutiny, and Jenny did not generally appreciate having them enumerated to her if she were the driver. As she had once explained to him in a quarterly performance review, 'The very close attention to detail that you display at crime scenes is really excellent, but when you apply the same approach to explain what you perceive to be the shortcomings of my driving, well, it's just bloody annoying. Pardon my French.'

She saw it as part of her drive for personal professionalism to avoid swearing, and certainly never to aim an epithet at a junior colleague. She had covered her embarrassing slip by immediately proposing Evans should do more of the driving, which quickly became established as doing all the driving.

Evans waited for Merton to close her door before he closed his. He had once explained to her that she tended to use more force than was necessary when she closed the van door, especially if a

34

window or another door were open as that would enable the air under compression to escape thereby avoiding a back-pressure from the action of her closing the door and so requiring less force. She had explained to him in a voice cracking like ice, separating each word with clinical precision, 'Don't lecture me on how to close the bloody door because it pisses me off. Pardon my French.' Adding a moment later with normal elision, 'But I'll bear it in mind in the future.' She now always took great care when closing the van door, except when she wanted to annoy him.

Merton stood five feet seven tall with Amazonian musculature. Though her fit forty-four-year-old figure might have passed close scrutiny for ten years younger, the bags under her eyes told a different story: sleepless nights from three children followed by sleepless nights from crime scenes, both needing her attendance and attention in the wee hours. Last Christmas she had been fully prepared to be scrutinised, but in the New Year she had changed her mousy-brown flowing locks in favour of a severely short hairstyle, to give the impression she was ready to repel all boarders of the male variety.

Evans, at twenty-five, had the unblemished face of a new-born, having always avoided late nights on the basis that it would impair his ability to think clearly in the morning. He also severely limited his consumption of alcohol for a similar reason, and at a concern for the number of cells that he calculated would be shed by his brain. At five feet five and under eight stone, with short-back-and-sides mid-brown hair that could be mistaken for basin-cut, and a voice that maintained a monotone irrespective of circumstances, he had had no opportunity to resist that other common cause of being up in the night.

Evans quietly opened the back of the van to access their equipment. Merton and Evans stepped into their Tyvek white scene-suits, zipping them up to their necks. They pulled the elasticated matching boot covers over their shoes, before donning clear plastic shower-caps – bankrupt stock bought at a rock-bottom price – then pulling over the suits' integral hoods; the precise coordination suggested a well-rehearsed choreographed dance-routine. Evans covered his mouth with a face mask, whereas Merton allowed hers to remain for now hanging loosely at her neck. First Merton then Evans added a dash of colour with a pair of purple latex gloves, stretching their fingers deep into them and then releasing the open ends to tighten on their arms above the wrists with satisfying thwacking sounds. They walked to the front of the changing room where Dunn was stationed at the blue-and-white cordon.

Dunn lifted the police tape, speaking to Merton as she led the way. 'Hello Jenny. DC Martello is in there.' He lowered the tape before Evans could follow. 'Hi Nick. Don't let the ice maiden make you get all steamed up inside your bunny suit.'

Evans attempted a smile as though it were payment of an entry fee for Dunn to raise the tape. He hated that sort of humour, especially when he felt he was the butt of it.

Inside the changing room Martello was standing quite still, emphasising she was not contaminating the crime scene. Being currently in charge of the investigation, at least at the site of the incident, she felt a need to be giving orders. She proceeded unnecessarily to tell the CSIs how to do their job. 'Hello Jenny, Nick. There's a head wound, so you'll need to check the room for any weapon that might have been used.'

Evans immediately responded, 'Such as a coat hook?'

Merton turned to look at Evans; he was not known for making light of incident scenes, so she assumed he was making a serious comment. Evans was pointing with his right hand, the thumb upright and the index finger extended, repeatedly moving his hand forward and backward like an animated cartoon character. His hand finally came to a halt a few inches from one of the long row of hooks that had not previously been considered a health risk under the school's Health & Safety policy. 'This one has blood on it. Most of the other hooks have a knobbly end to them, but this one hasn't, and there's a couple more over there that are the same. I can't see any broken bits, so they may have been damaged before today.'

Merton looked at the sharp end of the broken hook, commenting to Evans, 'That's damn bloody dangerous.' Knowing not to jump to conclusions – a mistake she had made herself on occasions – she knew they should still process the entire room; she explained her plan of action to Martello. 'The pathologist will be processing the body – we'll do an outward spiral search starting next to it. The room's virtually empty so it doesn't look like there's much to be checked through apart from the three sets of clothes.

SEND OFF SIR

As far as fingerprints go, a place like this is bound to be covered in them, so unless we see some bloody ones we'll just focus on the area near the hook. The chances of finding forensics on a wet, tiled floor are really low, but we'll give it a shot. We'll check for glove prints as well – have to try to make use of our Glove Mark database if we can. Nick's already spotted what's probably the most useful thing we'll turn up, so don't be too optimistic there'll be anything else. If you wish to take a closer look you'll need a scene-suit – there are some spares in the van.'

Martello was thinking this could prove to be a very quick case, and that perhaps she could solve it before Priestley came back to the station at Midshaw and took over the investigation. She asked Merton, 'How long do you think it'll take you to complete your forensic examination?'

Evans offered the standard reply on Merton's behalf. 'It'll take as long as it takes.'

Merton suggested, 'Perhaps a couple of hours. We need to stay until the pathologist has dealt with the body – in case there's anything he wants us to do. Any idea who it'll be?'

Martello responded, 'It's Dr Mallory.'

Merton blanched. 'Not that bugger. Pardon my French.'

'I've met him before; he's very good.'

'He's one of the best forensic pathologists around, but we just don't get on very well together.'

Martello decided the fault must lay with Merton, so chose to leave her alone. 'I'll go outside and wait for him.'

Martello left the room and spoke briefly to Dunn who was guarding the front entrance. 'Nick spotted some blood on a broken coat hook. Just make sure no one comes in here without authority. If anyone comes too close, tell them to go further back.'

Dunn felt offended by Martello's detailed instruction. He responded, 'Thank you. I wouldn't have thought of that.'

Martello replied, 'You're welcome.'

He realised her response was intended genuinely so made no further comment. He mused to himself something he knew he would be censured for if he said it aloud in the wrong company. 'Don't worry about not knowing what sarcasm is, Lily. Just think of what you've got – gorgeous face, great body, fantastic tits – I know I think about them all the time.'

37

Martello went around the block to where Plummer was guarding the back entrance. Plummer spoke first. 'There's been a few children trying to take a closer look; I told them they had to keep away while ever the place is being examined.'

Martello nodded in approval. 'I had to tell Elias what to do; he never seems to have much common sense. Anyway, we have to treat this place as a potential crime scene – Nick spotted some blood on a coat hook, though we don't yet know if it's related.'

Martello circled the changing room block from the back to the front entrance, staying just outside the police tape-defined exclusion zone.

Hunter approached the changing room's back entrance and spoke to Plummer. 'Hello. I'm Dr Hunter. My clothes are still inside. DC Whittington said I should just ask for them to be checked and then I could have them.'

Hunter had spoken confidently and calmly, so Plummer saw little reason to doubt his word. If Witty had indeed advised him to ask for his clothes to be released, then she had no basis for refusing Hunter's request, though the CSIs could do so if they deemed it essential for maintaining the integrity of the incident scene. 'I'll check whether your clothes can be released yet. Please stay behind the tape.' She entered the changing room, stopping just inside the doorway. Merton looked up to see who was entering the CSI's domain. 'Jenny, there's a Dr Hunter here.'

'I was told the pathologist would be Dr Mallory.'

'He's not a pathologist; he's one of the staff here. Witty said to ask for his clothes to be checked so he can have them. Would that be OK?'

'Bring him to the door but no further. I'll talk to him.'

Plummer invited Hunter to come to the outer door while she held open the inner door. After brief introductions, Hunter explained, 'My clothes are hung up in the corner: dark suit; blue tie with some red on it. I understand you need to check them first.'

Merton interrupted any further explanation as she was in a hurry to complete her work; the sooner they could finish the forensic processing, the sooner she could go home to her teenage children. She dived back into the room and went to a set of clothes in the nearest corner: dark suit, blue tie with a red design. In the course of examining the jacket she discovered a small clear plastic bag containing a minute amount of an organic substance. She called over to Evans. 'Nick, have a smell of this.'

They sniffed the contents of the bag and nodded in agreement that they had identified marijuana. Merton took the bag to the door and beckoned Plummer to come closer and take a look for herself. Then she spoke to Hunter. 'Do you recognise this? Is it yours?'

Hunter leaned forward and looked closely. His first reaction was to answer the questions literally, "Yes, I recognise the substance; and no, it is not mine", but then a more sinister interpretation came to him and he drew back, his eyes widening to reveal more of the whites. 'I don't believe this. Have you just planted that in my clothes? It's like something from a bad American film. Are you expecting me to say something like "That is not my stash"? Let me say quite clearly, I have never seen that stuff before.'

Plummer and Merton both knew that the vehemence Hunter was displaying did not necessarily indicate innocence. However, Merton had an uncomfortable feeling about his response and was inclined to believe him. 'Just wait there a moment please, Dr Hunter.'

Merton returned with a tie. 'Is this your tie?'

Hunter's response was emphatic. 'No. My blue tie has a red motif of an atom with two orbiting electrons on it, not a repeating red pattern like that has. I believe you're holding Mr Cullen's tie.'

Merton asked Hunter to wait again, as she dashed back inside muttering under her breath, 'Bugger, bugger, bugger, bugger, bugger, bugger, bugger, bugger.' She returned clutching a tie that matched the more detailed description Hunter had given. 'Is this you tie, sir?'

Hunter looked more annoyed than pleased as he confirmed, 'Yes; it is.'

'Just wait a moment.' She rushed back into the room and checked through this second set of clothes. In the inside pocket of the jacket she found Hunter's photo-id driving license. She quickly put everything into a large plastic bag, tearing off the adhesive strip cover and sealing the top, thinking she could do with a big red ribbon to tie in a bow as gift wrapping to deflect Hunter from raising a complaint. She went to the door and handed Hunter the bag, adding by way of apology, 'I'm sorry about the balls-up with the clothes. I mean the mix-up. Sorry.'

Hunter now looked more relieved than annoyed as he took the

39

bag of clothes. 'Thank you. I'll be on my way, then.'

Merton went back inside, hoping there would be no repercussions.

As Witty left the main school building he saw Hunter returning, carrying a plastic bag. He enquired, 'You got your clothes all right then?'

Hunter scowled. 'I'm not impressed, you know. Is it a regular trick to see how people react?'

Witty had no difficulty in looking puzzled. 'What exactly do you mean, Dr Hunter?'

'I was shown a little bag of marijuana and asked if it was mine. Were you in on the set-up?'

Witty remained silent, not so much as an application of a technique that may lead suspects to incriminate themselves, as the fact that he could not think what to say. Hunter was clearly intending not to speak further until he had a response. Eventually Witty offered, 'I think it must have been an honest mistake.'

Hunter remained unconvinced. 'You're saying the police don't plant marijuana on people?'

Witty looked for a way of relieving the tension, risking a joke. 'No sir, we find it grows much better in soil.'

Hunter was taken by surprise and released a laugh that he quickly cut short. 'Well, why do your people carry such things around with them?' Before Witty could reply, the dawn of realisation broke over Hunter's brow. 'It was someone else's!'

Witty decided he needed to investigate before engaging further with Hunter on this subject. 'I think I'd better find out what happened. Please excuse me Dr Hunter.' He scuttled off without giving Hunter time to respond.

Martello was standing with Dunn at the front entrance to the girls' changing room as Witty approached. He called out, 'All quiet on the Western front?'

Martello responded, 'Yes, there's nothing happening here.'

Witty could not decide whether Martello was in the dark about the little packet of marijuana or whether she was intending to keep him uninformed. He decided to see if Plummer had anything to say about it; he walked casually around the block. 'Hiya, Lin. Anything been happening?'

Plummer's radar was on red alert. It was one thing not to broadcast the mix-up with the clothes; it was quite another to deny it had happened if asked directly. The look she perceived in Witty's eye suggested he already knew, but, in case he didn't, she saw no reason to drop Merton in the mire. She therefore decided to fence a little, parrying his first enquiry. 'What sort of anything?'

Witty almost invariably found Plummer to be straightforward in her dealings with colleagues, so her defensive response suggested to him she knew what he meant but did not wish to reveal it. He decided to play the game, knowing he held the winning cards. 'Oh, just anything.'

The smile that played on Witty's lips told her not only that he knew, but also that he knew she knew. The smile that had been threatening to break out on Plummer's mouth now emerged fully, revealing she knew he knew she knew. Witty reciprocated with a full smile of his own, indicating he knew she knew he knew she knew. Plummer offered, 'I didn't see what happened inside, only what happened at the door. Jenny told me about it afterwards. It's probably best if she explains it all.'

Witty nodded and combined a few metaphors. 'Get it from the horse's mouth, before the horse has bolted, while you keep the stable door locked.'

Witty performed a limbo to pass under the tape. He went through the outer door and pushed open the inner door, extending his neck so his head was visible in the inner sanctum. 'Anyone at home? Can I come in?'

Evans picked up on his error. 'You can, but you may not.'

'What?'

'You are clearly capable of entering, but you do not have permission. I'm just checking this area near where you're standing, so you may not come in. You'll have to wait until I'm finished.'

Merton offered an alternative route by picking up a stack of square aluminium stools with tiny legs and placing four of them carefully onto the floor in a line with gaps of about thirty centimetres between each. She explained, 'Stepping stones. Walk on them over to here.'

Witty walked carefully to the point Merton had indicated, close to where she was standing. 'I was wondering what happened when Dr Hunter came to collect his clothes.'

'Oh. So the shit's already hit the fan.'

Witty picked up the theme. 'No. I'm just the sewage operative seeing if there's anything to be cleaned up.'

Merton gave a detailed explanation of what had happened, pointing to the corner where Hunter's clothes had been, and the corner that now contained a plastic bag holding the clothes that had previously included the marijuana. Near the centre of a side there was one further set of clothes still hanging, which she suggested probably belonged to the deceased. Merton concluded, 'I hope there's no repercussions from letting Dr Hunter know about the marijuana – I'm sorry I let the cat out the bag.'

'You mean, let the skunk out the bag.'

Merton grimaced. 'Ha-ha bloody ha.'

Witty dropped his grin before continuing. 'There's a Mr Cullen, a young guy, who was very upset at the idea of having his clothes examined, and now we know why. At some point he'll be coming here asking for them. I think it's best if he's confronted sooner rather than later. I'll track him down.'

Witty was about to leave when Evans called out to him. 'Has anyone mentioned I discovered a quantity of blood on a coat hook? It's fresh, and there's enough of it to suggest that it may be directly relevant to the investigation. Jenny's taken swabs of it and of some other matter on the hook – we'll need to run tests back at the lab but we know what we're expecting.'

Witty generally found Evans had a long-winded and overly-formal style of delivery that grated on him a little, but right now he just felt grateful for letting him know. 'That's very interesting, Nick. Is Lily aware of it?'

'She was here when I spotted the blood about five seconds after I came in.'

Witty resisted giving Evans the congratulations he appeared to be inviting. He exited the changing room via the back entrance and confirmed to Plummer that Merton had explained about the clothes and the marijuana. He walked around to the front where Martello was standing and looking into the far distance like someone waiting for their sweetheart's ship to appear from over the horizon. Witty put Martello in the picture straight away about the discovery of the marijuana in Cullen's jacket without mentioning the circumstances under which it had come to light. Martello did not ask him how he came to know this before she did, but responded peremptorily, 'You go and find Cullen and confront him about it.'

SEND OFF SIR

Witty reflected on why Martello had not checked that he had been informed about the blood on the coat hook, even though it could be a key determinant of the direction the investigation would take – and who should be leading it. He wondered if it was a deliberate act on her part to withhold this from him – she did sometimes appear to be very keen to be running the show, and one way of keeping the upper hand was to restrict the flow of information. On the other hand, perhaps she was simply unable to marshal her thoughts and ensure adequate communication, in which case, why was she leading the investigation?

Witty walked over to the main school building and headed for the staffroom. The "Do Not Disturb" sign was still on display, which had no doubt dissuaded members of staff from entering. He went inside and found Cullen seated, back in his original comfy chair; he wondered if he was perhaps the type of person who claims some sort of proprietorial ownership of a thing by repeatedly using it.

Witty had not seen Hunter and so could not ask him whether he had mentioned the marijuana to Cullen. He looked for an angle that would play equally well in either circumstance, but accepted any such compromise approach would inevitably be second-best to one based on knowing what Cullen knew. He decided the best strategy was to take it one small step at a time and to see what developed. "Softly, softly, catchee monkey", he thought. 'Mr Cullen, would you not be more comfortable getting changed into your normal clothes?'

Cullen responded in a dogmatic, sulky tone. 'Like I said before, I'm not going to allow them to be searched.'

Witty interpreted this as indicating Cullen was unaware the marijuana had been discovered, so decided to delay revealing the fact. 'Your clothes have been sealed into a plastic bag and are waiting for you in the changing room. You can't go in there, but someone will pass them out to you if you go and ask.'

Cullen jumped to his feet as though a spring had been released under him. 'Right, I'll go, then.'

'I'm going that way myself. I'll walk with you.'

Witty observed Cullen clearly looked relieved, no doubt thinking the marijuana had not been discovered; he hoped Cullen's defences would be down as a consequence, and focused on when to perform the *coup de grâce.*

As they walked along a metalled path, Witty encouraged Cullen to chat. 'Do the staff and the students often play football against each other, or was this a special – a one-off?'

'It's special, really. It happens once every year, I'm told, though it's my first time.'

'So, if it's only once a year, does the school provide the kit, or do you have to bring your own?'

'We use school kit. The school team used the first team's kit and we used the second team's.'

'Do you often play football?'

'No. Not really. I mean, I used to play, every week. It isn't that I can't play. It's just that I don't have the time anymore.'

'I keep hearing teachers are really overworked, with no time for anything but school stuff.'

'Yeah. That's right. We're all martyrs to the cause.'

'So you never find the time to go partying?'

'Well, sometimes I go to the Fever Pitch with mates.'

'That place has a bit of a reputation for being a drugs scene. Is that something you're into?'

'Are you fishing, Constable Witty?'

'Not really, Mr Cullen. But I was wondering why you had marijuana in your coat pocket.'

'Fffuuuckk!'

Witty smiled to himself, thinking, 'What a cruel bastard I am, leading him on, letting him think he'd got away with it. This is one of the few remaining perks of the job, though if I were a Catholic I'd probably go straight to hell for enjoying it so much.'

Cullen waited for Witty to speak, being unsure how to play this situation. 'It isn't very much, so let's not overreact to it. Best thing is if you sign a statement about it, and we'll do our best to make sure it's kept in perspective. Are you OK with that?'

The fire-brand protestor of Cullen's slightly younger days appeared to have been fully extinguished, as he meekly responded 'OK.'

Witty was relieved he would not have to be wasting time on someone going through the usual set of denials. They reached the changing room and Witty spoke to Martello. 'Mr Cullen will be admitting possession of a small amount of an illegal substance, so let's just get his clothes for him and he can be on his way.' Though

Cullen had not formally agreed to anything and had not yet been cautioned, he was convinced the best way to proceed was for the offence to be treated in a matter-of-fact manner; also, by Cullen not denying possession when Witty spoke to Martello in his presence, he was in effect admitting it under the legal maxim *qui tacet consentit*, "silence implies consent". The last thing Witty wanted was for a minor issue to interfere with the investigation into the death of John Newhouse. He was therefore relieved when Martello responded, 'Yes. OK. You go and get them.'

Witty went into the changing room and asked Merton for the clothes, which she provided minus the marijuana. He returned and gave the clothes bag to Cullen, who nodded curtly. Cullen departed slowly, dragging the bag along the floor, looking as burdened down as Sisyphus pushing his rock.

Witty went back inside to check on progress. He asked Merton, 'Has the remaining set of clothes been processed yet? Not found anything else that shouldn't be there, have you?'

Merton walked over to him and showed him a brown envelope inside a clear plastic evidence bag. 'This was in the inside pocket of the jacket. There's five ten-pound notes in it. We'll check it all for fingerprints.'

Witty considered whether to let Martello know straight away about the money, or whether it was his turn to withhold information – even if only for a short while. Before he had decided, he heard the sound of Dr Mallory's black BMW, its throaty roar proclaiming its unnecessarily powerful engine for the UK's speed limits.

CHAPTER 6

Pathologist Examines the Body

Dr Mallory drove to the same patch of ground where the ambulance had been, but left it too late to brake and consequently skidded on the grass which was becoming increasingly slippery due to the frost that was forming with the falling temperature. He stopped just a metre or so short of the small wall that defined the outer boundary of the path that partially skirted the girls' changing room block. Without the least hint of embarrassment he emerged cool and unflustered, his sculpted, finely muscled body adorned with a tanned face topped off with slicked-back black hair – possibly bottle-enhanced – that approached to within an inch of the collar of the immaculately shaped jacket of his stylish suit, the overall effect suggesting a Mediterranean gigolo.

Witty noticed the full strength beam of rapture Martello was directing at Mallory, as he glided toward the welcoming committee with the grace of an ice skater. He wondered whether she was looking to trade up from DCI Castleton. Comparing the two, forty-eight-year-old Castleton was a decade and a half older, and lacked his intelligence, charm and sophistication. But of course his saving grace from Martello's perspective was that he could enable her to rise through the ranks. Witty reflected she was already at the maximum level of her current ability, and sometimes failed to make it even to competent detective constable standard. Realistically though, her figure and her looks could overcome most obstacles to her achieving whatever she desired, and Witty reckoned she desired Mallory. The question for Witty was: would he reciprocate that desire?

Witty saw the fleeting smile that Mallory threw at Martello as comparable to that of a film star who might briefly acknowledge a fan who has stood for hours in the teeming rain to catch a glimpse of him as he walks the red carpet before sweeping past and into the carefully rehearsed embraces of the people who really matter most to his career. It was as though Martello's obvious adoration of him was no more than his due. He thought Mallory was probably far too much in love with himself to consider giving away that precious commodity to others. As Mallory passed by Martello without further acknowledgement he felt strangely insulted on her behalf.

Mallory slowed as he reached Witty and asked him the brief question, 'Body?'

Witty's response was briefer: silence, accompanied by a jerk of his right thumb in the direction of the changing room. Mallory floated through the two pairs of doors and looked around without lowering his gaze, notwithstanding the fact that most bodies gravitate toward ground level. Martello rushed in after Mallory, leaving Witty to follow in her wake. The three of them stood just inside the inner, swing doors, none of them wearing scene-suits.

Merton became monosyllabic on Mallory's arrival. She issued him the instruction, 'Suit!'

Mallory retaliated with verbosity and deliberate misunderstanding. 'Yes, it's one of my favourites. It keeps me warm in winter yet allows the air to breathe through it so that I don't overheat if the temperature rises.'

Merton felt her own temperature rising. 'You're got to wear a scene-suit.'

'How much more do you have to do? You could help me with the body once you've finished with the room.'

Evans called out, 'I'm just finishing.'

Merton scowled at Evans for not assisting her in keeping Mallory waiting. She addressed Mallory disingenuously, 'I've still some things to do.'

Mallory chose not to press her for a more accurate response, simply requesting, 'Will you fill me in on the background?' Merton proceeded to give a comprehensive explanation, drawing attention to the head wound and to the coat hook in turn. Mallory responded, 'So there is little point in testing liver temperature to establish time of death; though it gives a more accurate estimate than the old rectal temperature test, the associated standard calculation would still give a window that is much wider than is already known. Not that I use the standard calculation. I have developed my own computer-based mathematical formula that is far more accurate than the standard one. Though it begins with the

47

simple premise that the fall in temperature of any organ within the body is linked to the ambient temperature by Newton's good old Law of Cooling and the heat retention capacity of the organ in question, it then extends much further, taking into account the amount of fat and muscle that insulates the organ, the changes in the ambient temperature over time, the mass of the organ for which the temperature has been taken, the mass and nature of the organs nearest to it, and various other special factors if they are relevant. The accuracy of the result is highly dependent on knowing the exact temperature of the body at the time of death. This may be known if someone has kept adequate records, though factors such as illness can affect anyone's normal body temperature. Otherwise, average body temperature for that type of person has to be used, which may be misleadingly inaccurate if they have an unusually high or low normal body temperature. If the normal body temperature for someone has to be estimated, then many other factors have to be considered in calculating the expected value; the parameter values are linked to anything and everything from body shape, fat content, even ethnicity. I could go on at length about it, but I'm ever so busy today. The point is, even my sophisticated technique could not provide a more accurate estimate of time of death than has already been established.

'Then there's the question of the wound to the head. I shall only be able to match the coat hook to the skull when I have them both back at the mortuary. As to the coat hook itself, when you've checked it for prints and taken samples will you please be so good as to detach it and bag it up, Nick.'

Mallory had addressed the entire speech to Merton, but turned to Evans on the very last word, his name. This had taken Evans by surprise and left him looking shocked and startled. Mallory continued, again addressing Merton. 'I'm considering just bagging up the head and hands and putting the corpse into a body bag fully clothed. On the other hand I could take the samples here – it isn't as though this is a hostile environment.'

Merton thought to herself 'I'll give you hostility if you want it.'

Mallory continued after a moment's reflection. 'I'll take samples here and remove the clothes; that'll enable me to make an early start back at the lab. At first sight it appears the cause of death is due to the head wound, but only the post-mortem will reveal whether it was directly due to damage to an essential part of the brain or whether it derived from some secondary effect, such as loss of blood, or pressure on the top of the spinal column closing down the breathing.'

Merton scowled at Mallory, convinced his verbosity was designed to delay her. 'I'll be finished in five minutes and then you can examine the body and give a proper prelim without contaminating my crime scene. It'll probably take you that long to get suited up.'

Mallory corrected her. 'Is this a crime scene? I don't believe that has yet been established.'

Witty wondered what sort of history these two had. Merton seemed to be on the edge of exploding. He did not like the idea of open warfare breaking out at the crime scene; for one thing, it could interfere with the investigation. He sought to pour oil on the apparently troubled waters. 'Your explanation about calculating time of death was very interesting, Dr Mallory. Have you had your method published anywhere? It sounds like it should be given the widest possible circulation. You're the only person I've ever heard express so deep an understanding of the subject. Other pathologists tend to give estimates that are so broad as to be, well, sometimes virtually useless.'

Mallory turned an appreciative smile on Witty. 'Yes, I've spent many an evening developing and enhancing the predictive equation, and I'm hoping to bring it to publication very soon.'

Mallory paused a moment for reflection before continuing to address Witty. 'I've had a very brief conversation with DCI Castleton as the Senior Investigating Officer, who for some reason doesn't intend to put in a personal appearance. I assume you're deputizing for now.'

Martello interjected. 'Actually, I'm the one who's deputizing. Perhaps we could go through your preliminary findings together somewhere when you're finished here?'

Mallory raised an eye-brow to Witty and flicked his eyes to the left to demonstrate a slow side-ways glance, before moving his head to face Martello. 'I don't expect there's a need for much discussion at this stage.' He turned to Merton. 'I do need to get on, though, so I'll put in a call for the meat wagon and get togged up.'

Evans called out to Mallory, 'You're not supposed to use that term, Dr Mallory.'

Mallory mocked him with enhanced inflexions, accentuating

the contrast with Evans' monotone. 'What, "togged up"? Why on earth not?'

Evans spluttered, 'I meant ...'

Mallory was already rushing outside, so Evans guillotined his unnecessary correction.

Witty decided to probe Merton a little, though carefully so as not to re-stoke her fire.

'You seem to know Dr Mallory very well.'

'Worked some scenes with him; wouldn't say I really know him.'

'I've heard it said he's all work and no play.'

'Yes, he has that reputation.'

'He doesn't socialise much, then.'

'Oh, he does. He likes formal dinners where they all get dressed up; that sort of thing.'

'Not one for an old knees-up then.'

'I doubt it.'

'So we shouldn't expect to see him at any Christmas parties this year.'

'I believe he does usually make an exception for Christmas parties, so you might.'

There was something undefined, something he could not quite put his finger on, about the way Merton had responded to this last question. He decided to try that theme again. 'Are you much of a party-goer, Jenny? Do you go to all the Christmas parties around?'

Merton looked suspiciously at Witty. 'Been gathering evidence, have you?' Witty raised his eyebrows and fixed a small half-smile, inviting Merton to say more. 'I did go to a Christmas party with him last year. Very swanky affair it was. I hadn't been to a "do" for years, not since Jim and me ... And anyway, it was the first time I felt the kids were old enough to look after themselves. So I did a full dress rehearsal for them the day before. They told me I scrubbed up nicely.' She changed her tone to a not entirely successful attempt at gracious. 'It was the occasion of the Annual Pathologists Ball. I was resplendent in a shimmering gold lamé gown bought especially for the occasion. Dr Mallory was even more resplendent ...'

Martello, who had been standing silently, now jumped into the conversation. 'Where was it?'

Merton was a little taken aback by the abruptness of the interruption. She responded in her normal voice: suppressed northern working class, through which much stronger overtones of her roots emerged when she was feeling stressed or tired or inebriated. 'London.'

Martello continued the questioning. 'Will you be going again this year?'

'No, it was a one-off for me. Never before; never again.'

Any further dialogue on this subject was terminated by Mallory's return, fully suited up to examine the body. Witty instinctively checked Mallory's white scene-suit to see if it came with cufflinks; he looked the same as the CSIs, except that he was sporting blue nitrile gloves. Provokingly, Mallory spoke deliberately loudly for Evan's benefit, who was currently tidying up in the furthest corner. 'I'm togged up, now. Sorry Nick, I mean I'm fully suited up. And the meat wagon is on its way.'

Witty observed Evans glowering silently, his cheeks reddening outwards from a central spot at either side, suggesting his body temperature was rising. He wondered if Mallory had taken into account raised temperatures of colleagues in the vicinity of a body when coming up with his all-singing, all-dancing, time-of-death calculation formula. He had to admit though, various people had commented on Mallory's dedication, brilliance and originality, someone even likening him to Da Vinci.

Mallory walked toward the body, choosing each step carefully, the loose-fitting scene-suit not entirely masking the bullfighter-like graceful movements of his hips. With a studied, prepared movement he bent down close to the head and turned it to one side, making the damage to the back of the skull easier to inspect. 'This is a deep, narrow wound.' Even though he knew the outcome before he began, he went through the ritual of testing for a pulse, and shining a narrow beam of light into the fully dilated pupils. Witty wondered whether that was just an ordinary torch he used, or whether it was some sort of laser beam. Mallory turned to Witty, while Martello looked at him in the hope that he would redirect his gaze in her direction. 'You'll need to know whether the wound was inflicted accidentally or deliberately. I won't be able to express a scientific opinion until I've checked a number of things back at the lab. If the wound dovetails with the shape of the coat hook, then I'll assess the bone density, establish the depth of penetration, and calculate the force required to inflict the injury against a fixed object. I may also be able to calculate the speed with which the deceased was moving. From thereon you can draw your own conclusions about the events that preceded the contact.'

'That's exactly what we need. How long will you take, do you think?'

'A forensic autopsy may last about three hours. A full report could take one to three months or more, depending on exactly what additional tests are requested; we should include blood tests for solvents, volatiles and chloroform. I'm wondering whether we can cut down on what else to test for, as it's fairly obvious where we should be focusing our interest. A routine autopsy would only take an hour, but then you wouldn't be offering to pay me my massively inflated fees for one of those, would you?'

'I'll arrange an iGene scan straight away – the key to the injury is the shape of the wound, so it makes sense to record it as precisely as possible. It's easier if the body isn't in rigor – the football kit suggests he had physical activity just before he died, which can cause the body to go into rigor a little faster than normal. Did you know the Sheffield mortuary has the UK's first digital autopsy machine? It's brand spanking new – well almost – and ideal for this case. Of course its purpose was to get around the tricky religious problem – people not wishing to allow their newly departed to be cut open. I'm assuming there are no religious concerns here?'

Martello responded, 'I'll check, but I'm sure there won't be.'

'In that case, I'll organise the first incision for seven o'clock this evening. You won't be wishing to wait weeks for the full report, so I'll put together an interim report of principal findings by morning. DCI Castleton is the SIO – will he be putting in an appearance at the post-mortem?'

Martello saw an opportunity and seized it. 'I'll be attending instead.'

Mallory's response was as knowledgeable as it was unexpected. He teased, 'Yes, please do, in case I have any questions.'

Martello looked startled at the idea that she would be welcome for answering his questions rather than *vice versa*. Mallory correctly interpreted her look and favoured her with a smile that was intended to be that of a teacher to a pupil, but, like pupils so often do, she misinterpreted it. 'Originally in some countries such as the good old U S of A the police would be required to have someone present at autopsies to assist the pathologist, or medical examiner as they call them over the other side of the pond. I, on the other hand, will be there for your benefit, so I'll be delighted to answer any questions you may have for me.'

Martello's misinterpretation ratcheted up a notch. 'I look forward to being there.'

Witty slowly and repeatedly shook his head a few degrees, observed only by Merton. Knowing how squeamish Martello could be, he wondered what was driving her to claim she was looking forward to watching the body of this dead man at their feet being cut open. He wondered whether Dr Mallory would take the route from the neck to the pubic area with just a slight detour for the belly button, or would he prefer, on the grounds of style or fashion, the large Y-shaped incision favoured by American medical examiners.

Martello exited the changing room and took out her phone. Witty left shortly afterwards and stood close by to listen in to her side of the conversation. 'A head wound. There's blood on a coat hook. Dr Mallory said seven o'clock start – I'm happy to attend. It could be very late. What about his family's agreement? Good, that's one less thing for me to have to do – I'm obviously going to be very busy all evening so we'll have to put it off for another time. Interim report could be tomorrow, maybe the day after. Right. Just until then. No, of course, that's more than I could ask. I'll get things moving right away. And you.'

Martello turned to Witty and gave him the news he was expecting. 'DCI Castleton has told me I'm to remain in charge here until he says otherwise.'

'And when might that be?'

'After he's had time to read the interim post-mortem report and decide what should be done next.'

'Tomorrow morning?'

'It could be much later than that.'

Martello allowed a frown to cross her brow for a moment. 'You didn't spend very long with those ten teachers. You need to be thorough.'

Witty responded without letting his irritation show. 'I've

collected some information that needs cross-referencing before we interview them separately.'

'You mustn't just assume it was one of the other players. It could have been someone else entirely.'

Witty remained tight-lipped and stone-faced at the suggestion he had made that assumption, so as to avoid his further irritation from leaking out.

Having received no contradiction, she continued, 'If we get a tracker dog and it leads us to one of them, then that'll prove you're right.'

Witty remained determined not to argue with her, so moved the discussion forward. 'I think they'll all have gone home by now.'

'Well, let's get a dog anyway; it may lead us to some sort of a clue. If we don't do it straight away it'll be too late.'

She made another phone call, asking to be redirected to a dog handler. The conversation was punctuated with pauses. 'This is DC Martello – Lily – we met once.' … 'It's nice of you to have remembered me.' … 'You had an Alsatian called Kaiser.' She nodded down the phone. 'Oh, really? Anyway, there's been a death at Midshaw School and it's probably not accidental. We need a dog to pick up any scent from around a school building.' … 'Why do you want to know the temperature?' … 'Oh, I didn't know that.' She put her hand over one end of the phone, mistakenly believing it would block out the sound of her question to Witty. 'How cold do you think it is?'

Witty observed the hoar frost that had started to thicken on the grass, enough to begin to obscure its colour. 'It must be around zero; maybe below.'

Martello relayed this information down the phone, adding, 'Well, maybe it's not quite that cold, yet.' She allowed a small frown to appear for a moment, suggesting concern at what she was hearing. 'You might make it here in half an hour.' The frown reappeared and lingered. 'Oh well, thanks anyway.' … 'No, I'm busy right now.' … 'I'm not free; not at all free.' … 'I've got to go.' Witty looked to Martello for an explanation. 'He said that his German Shepherd Dog can't detect a scent at sub-zero temperatures, and even if it isn't that cold now, it would be by the time he got here. He also said dogs smell better when it's damp.'

Witty could not resist the obvious misinterpretation. 'Well, I'm not going to go around sniffing dogs to see if that's right.'

Martello frowned at him. 'You do know what I mean, don't you?'

He nodded, trying to look contrite. 'And what else did he say? Something at the end?'

'Nothing, really.' Witty continued to hold her gaze. 'Well, it was just the usual.'

'He was sniffing around, was he? Like dog, like handler.'

'That isn't polite. But yes, you're right. Anyway, it's damp now, so it could work if we can get hold of a local dog straight away. There's usually lots of people walking around with dogs, so we could look for another German Shepherd Dog and see if it can detect a scent before it's too cold.'

Witty admired her determination, so decided not to register his misgivings. He felt he had to support her initiative while protecting her from looking foolish. 'All dogs have some ability to follow a trail, so it doesn't have to be a German Shepherd Dog. It could be a Border Collie, a Bloodhound, or any kind of scent hound, but it's probably best not to ask someone with a little poodle that's wearing a tartan coat.'

Martello nodded her agreement, the lack of a smile suggesting she was taking his recommendation very seriously. They set off in the direction of the school's main entrance. Despite the falling darkness there were still many small groups of older schoolchildren wandering around, reluctant to leave until they knew they had seen it through to the end. Witty observed there were three young girls standing together with a dog on a leash. 'Those girls over there have a dog. They look the right age to be at school, but I wouldn't have thought dogs would normally be allowed on the premises.'

Martello jumped at the opportunity. 'Perhaps it's a guide dog. We could just borrow it for a while; I'm sure the owner wouldn't mind being without it for a bit.'

Witty winced at the suggestion she might commandeer someone's guide dog. He slowed his pace to ensure Martello was leading. When still ten metres away she called out to them. 'Hello. I'm a detective. Have you heard about Mr Newhouse?' The three girls all confirmed they had. 'Is this your dog?'

One of them answered. 'Yes. She's my pet – she's a Chocolate Labrador. Her name's Brownie and I'm Rosie.' The girl added a little defensively, 'I'm allowed to have her at school, because of my diabetes – she lets me know when my blood-sugar level isn't right.' She gave a little giggle. 'My dad says she's the only chocolate brownie I can have.'

Witty noticed the words "Medical Support" on Brownie's red coat.

Martello continued. 'Is she any good at smelling things?'

'Yes, she's totally brilliant.'

'If I take her somewhere, might she be able to pick up a scent?'

'I'd have to take her. She's trained to stay with me all the time. She wouldn't like it if you tried to take her away from me.'

'Well, that's OK if you don't mind walking around with me a bit.' Martello turned to Rosie's companions, who she assumed would wish to stay with their friend. 'I need to keep to a minimum the number of different scents, so would you mind not following too close?'

The two girls nodded in agreement. Martello set off with Rosie and Brownie, Witty hanging back five metres and the other girls staying a further five metres behind him. They reached the front of the girls' changing room. Martello asked Rosie if she could get Brownie to look for a scent. Rosie looked doubtful, but bent down with Brownie and sniffed the air in encouragement. Brownie walked around, enjoying the game, setting off first in one direction and then in another.

Witty called over to them. 'With all the comings and goings there's been at the front entrance, I really don't think Brownie can be expected to find anything there. You could have more luck at the back door.'

Martello, Rosie and Brownie went around to the back while the other three stayed at the front. Rosie gave Brownie more encouragement with repeated sniffing. Brownie again played the game, setting off and coming back to the door. Then Brownie changed her routine and set off back around the block, eventually going to Witty and looking up at him. He bent down and stroked her. Rosie looked at him and asked, 'Do you have diabetes?'

Witty had recently passed a police medical assessment and knew he was in good health, so was able to respond with confidence. 'No, I'm sure I don't. I think Brownie picked up my scent from earlier when I was outside the back door. Would you expect her to look up at someone she thinks might have diabetes?'

'I wouldn't know what to expect – she's only been trained to respond to me. I know she always makes a big fuss of me when my sugar level needs fixing. For dogs that aren't pets, the training centre gets them to sit down when they find something that's not right; some of them can even detect types of cancer from breath or wee.'

Rosie went slightly pink, being unsure whether she should have said "wee" to a policeman, despite normally using coarser words with her mates.

Martello was encouraged by the first attempt. 'Let's give her another chance – she's a very clever dog.' This time Brownie set off in a different direction. She followed a path that led to a side gate and out onto a small road, turning right to go down a cul-de-sac. Near the end of this road she stopped and looked up at Rosie, as though asking what she should do next. Martello interpreted this as a dead end but had no wish to give up yet. 'Let's just get Brownie to walk around here and see if she comes up with anything else.'

They retraced their steps from the cul-de-sac before walking a short distance along a narrow road and exiting onto the main road. A bus pulled up fifteen metres ahead. Five women alighted, chattering together, all of them loaded down with shopping; they passed the dog and continued on their way. Brownie tugged at her lead to change direction and follow the women. Martello called out to them. 'Would you mind waiting? I'm a detective.'

The women came to a halt, continuing to talk. Martello beckoned Witty over for support. 'I'm Detective Constable Martello and this is Detective Constable Whittington. We're investigating an incident at the school. Would you mind telling us where you were this afternoon between three o'clock and three thirty?'

One of the women offered an explanation. 'We've been shopping. I can't say exactly what shop we were in, but it was over the other side of Sheffield at Meadowhall. We were all together. Have been all afternoon.' Brownie nuzzled up to one of the other women, who bent down and stroked her.

Martello continued addressing the spokeswoman. 'So you're saying you weren't anywhere near the school between those times?'

'That's right love. I'm saying it 'cos we weren't.'

Witty detected a prickly edge to the woman's voice and

decided to intervene. 'That's alright then. While my colleague takes the dog and its handler back to the school, could you just give me a few details? It'd be ever so helpful.' Witty smiled, and received smiles in acknowledgement, with maybe a hint or two of the type of grin that some women give when talking to a younger man. When Witty was alone with them he asked the woman who had been stroking the dog if he could have a word with her separately from the others. As the two of them walked away, the others began calling out.

'You've pulled there, Ginny.'

'When's it my turn?'

'What's she got that I haven't?'

'We'll not tell your husband.'

Witty spoke quietly to Ginny, despite the raucous banter. 'Just for the record, could I have your name and address?'

Ginny supplied the information, adding, 'I haven't done nowt, yer know.'

Witty nodded. 'I'm sure you haven't, but did you notice what the dog had on its coat?'

'Something to do with "Medical", weren't it?'

'Yes, it was. Now, it may be nothing at all, but that particular dog has been specially trained to look for people with diabetes. Do you know if you have diabetes?'

'No, love. I don't know, but I don't think I have.'

'Well, I know that I don't have diabetes, and the dog came up to me in the same way as it came up to you. So it doesn't mean that you do have diabetes. But, all the same, it would probably make sense for you to get yourself checked out by your GP, just to be on the safe side.' Witty returned with Ginny to her companions, thanked them for their help, and told them there was no need for anything further. They walked off, talking in more subdued tones, and with Ginny, looking paler, now the centre of attention.

Back inside the school grounds Witty met up with Martello who had taken her leave of Brownie and the girls. Martello asked about the women he had just interviewed. 'You reckoned their alibis were solid, didn't you?'

'Yes. It was too much to hope we'd get that lucky.'

'Well, it was a waste of time, then. You probably thought it would be, all along.'

SEND OFF SIR

She looked sufficiently downcast that Witty felt she needed some words of support. 'Actually, Lil, the idea of using a dog was good in theory. It was a bit impulsive just to grab the nearest one, but you showed the right attitude, refusing to accept defeat and finding an alternative solution to the problem. So, well done, and chin up, old girl.'

Martello looked at Witty through new eyes. He had called her "Lil", and "old girl", both firsts from colleagues. She appreciated Witty's words of support and gave him a spontaneous smile. She thought how Witty was one of the few people who seemed able to treat her like a normal person, speculating it was because for some reason he did not find her sexually attractive. Witty's heart skipped a beat when she smiled at him. Martello saw how pleased he was to receive her smile, and reflected to herself how he obviously appreciated her as a colleague.

Plummer walked over to Witty and Martello and told them the mortuary van had collected the body, and that the pathologist and the CSIs had left. Martello instructed her to let Dunn know they could both leave. As Martello walked with Witty she gave him a similar message. 'We may as well head off too. I need to go back home and make myself look presentable for the autopsy. I mean look professional.'

Witty could not stop himself from discouraging her from dressing up for Mallory. 'I'd have thought you're already suitably dressed; anything more would be gilding the lily.'

She laughed, seeing nothing beyond the witticism.

Witty recognised she was in danger of making a *faux pas*. 'We need to speak to the Headmaster before we go, of course. It's just etiquette. There's nothing we should report to him at this stage, but we want to keep him on our side. We can make it very brief.'

Martello blushed at this novice error. Witty closely observed a soft pink starting at her ears and spreading across her unblemished cream-coloured face and down her neck; he thought it made her look even more beautiful than ever, and found it stoking his sexual desire for her. He had to remind himself – as he did at least a dozen times every working day – that Lily was the most beautiful of flowers but not one for plucking. He reflected on how his family life was in enough turmoil without adding to it, and how there was also that brake called professionalism.

They went to the school's main entrance and rang the visitors' bell; Clifton arrived at the other side of the glass door, peering through it before letting them in. The three went together to the Headmaster's office. Martello began the awkward process of not divulging information to people who believed they had every right to know what was happening, and of extending expectations of timelines so as to give the police breathing space. 'In view of the circumstances surrounding Mr Newhouse's death, we have arranged for an autopsy to be performed as soon as possible. The results will then be assessed thoroughly and you will be informed of the outcome. The full report may take months to prepare as it involves specialists with various areas of expertise, but we may be able to give you some key findings within a week. I'm sorry there isn't more I can say at this stage, but we'll let you know anything as soon as we know.'

Witty pondered on whether it was really necessary to come out with such distortions of the truth, recognising that Martello was not alone in her attitude; so many of the police regarded it as their prerogative – even a perquisite – to lie to people. Nevertheless, he was not about to say that the report was due in the morning.

To Witty's surprise, Verbane accepted Martello's version of the plan, being more interested in the state of his shirt. 'As I explained to you earlier, I checked Mr Newhouse for signs of life. What I did not realise was that my shirt cuff had dipped into the blood that was present. Am I supposed to give you my shirt for forensic testing?'

Oaken weighed in with, 'And if so, would you need my blouse? It has blood on it from when I attempted to resuscitate Mr Newhouse.'

Witty thought Oaken sounded far too eager, and mischievously wondered if she was just wanting to strip off here and now. Martello hesitated, so Witty took the initiative. 'No thank you, Headmaster. The presence of blood on your shirt sleeve is entirely consistent with the events as you described them.'

Martello picked up the theme. 'And the same goes for you too, Miss Oaken.' After a moment she added, as though she were the domesticated type, 'Cold water is best for soaking blood out of clothes, and then use a biological powder.'

As the detectives were taking their leave, Witty made a request. 'We may need to keep visiting the school during the course of this investigation, and I can't say what times those visits will be. Would it be permissible for us to enter the main school building without needing to be let in, by giving us the access code for the main door?'

Verbane turned to Oaken as though asking for an opinion, though the nod of his head told her the answer to give was in the affirmative. She therefore replied, 'I'm sure that would be alright, Headmaster.' After Verbane had confirmed his approval she revealed the four digit number.

When Martello and Witty returned to Midshaw police station, he expected she would go inside to make a report of progress; instead she went directly to her car, leaving Witty wondering if she was avoiding DCI Castleton. Witty entered the cubist, white concrete building and spoke to Mrs Gloria Naylor, a civilian, who was on reception.

'All right, Gloria?'

She asked, as always, 'How's the family?'

He lied, as always, 'Everyone's fine.'

'I heard what happened at the school. Everything going OK?'

'Everything except the CSI's van; it broke down at the start of the week. A case of Sick Transit Gloria Monday.'

Naylor had heard Witty make this joke several times before and responded in her preferred manner, pretending to work out the exact number of times. She counted off the four fingers of her left hand using the index finger of her right hand, followed by counting off the index and second finger of her right hand using the index finger from her left. Having prepared said fingers, she slowly lifted the left hand to show the four, followed by a much quicker and repeated movement of her right to show the two, the fingers being splayed in that style favoured by Englishmen since the time of Agincourt.

The pleasantries over, Witty went into the shared office space and checked his e-mail account: nothing urgent. He checked his work queue: someone had removed items, no doubt in recognition that he would be otherwise engaged for the foreseeable future. He saw it as inappropriate to report events to Castleton as that should be left to the lead officer, Martello. He could not report to Priestley who was out on another case and was not due back until Monday. He decided not to stay any longer as there was little he could do at this stage.

As he passed Gloria she asked, 'Leaving already? Don't you have enough work to do?'

He responded, 'I always like to leave something to look forward to coming back to.' With an accent that hinted of some unspecific Southern State of America he added, 'After all, tomorrow is another day.'

CHAPTER 7

Martello at the Autopsy

Martello lived in Hope, the village rather than the state of mind. Her single-woman's flat was on the upper floor of a converted early Victorian two-storey house that had previously been occupied by generations of the Wright family for a century and a half. The house had been "tastefully converted into four modern flats with all amenities". It was "in an up-and-coming area" and "would suit an aspirational young professional". It also came "with access to the open countryside". Of course it would have needed a substantial journey away from that part of Derbyshire to find somewhere that did not have access to the open countryside – on a sunny day the whole region for many miles around was as idyllic as a pastoral picture postcard, being entirely unspoilt except for the cement works visible from her bedroom window that the estate agent had avoided mentioning in literature and on its website.

The flat had sounded, rather than looked, to be exactly what she was after. She had agreed to the asking price even though it was substantially higher than her intended maximum and really more than she could afford. She had then applied to Midshaw Bank for a mortgage. The young man at the bank had appeared uncomfortable with her, grinning rather than smiling, and sweating a little too much as he pulled at his shirt collar to try to give his windpipe access to more air. It was almost as though he were having an internal dialogue rather than speaking to her as he explained that her deposit and salary were outside the normal range to qualify for a standard mortgage. She had simply smiled in response, not the full-blown smile that could stop traffic at fifty metres, but the everyday, multi-purpose variety. The young man went on to explain that the credit-scoring system dictated what could be allowed, and that the only way around it was to have an application pre-approved based on the manager's personal recommendation. He had asked if she would like him to enquire about this option, and when she had responded with a "That would be very kind of you" he had scuttled away like a rabbit heading for an underground bunker. He had returned almost immediately with an invitation for her to enter the manager's office.

George Westmorland was perhaps the last of the old breed of bank manager in a farming community, knowledgeable about everything from animal husbandry through to livestock and feed prices. His half-moon glasses suggested a kindly Pickwickian character, though this belied his sharp accounting mind. In his earlier banking days he was known for being able to break down a balance sheet to understand the official strengths and weaknesses of a company, and to break down the characters driving the business to discover the reality of its health or otherwise. Nowadays he had less opportunity to read between the lines, as farming accounts were generally stark and simple; he knew many farmers who were struggling to make a living but refusing to forsake their heritage.

The impression he gave to his staff was of someone who played fair by everyone, rewarding the deserving and reprimanding only those who had earned his opprobrium. Customers generally saw him as quietly efficient, quickly responding to any issues they encountered with the running of their accounts. Customers of the Black Bull on a Saturday night after he had had an extra pint would find him rather more garrulous, as he dipped into his seemingly inexhaustible supply of anonymised anecdotes about farming and farmers for the amusement of anyone of a mind to listen.

Two local farmers had gained a different impression of George Westmorland when he caught them using a little ruse to inflate their balance sheets. On a Monday he had counted the cows at one farm which were floating assets in support of the farmer's ongoing borrowing facility, and on the Friday he had counted the cows at an adjacent farm for a similar reason. But he had noticed one cow with unusual features appeared to have been on both farms. He checked for transactional activity on their accounts and found no evidence of a sale having taken place. So the following week he made an unannounced return to the first farm to count the stock again, followed by an immediate return to the second farm for a recount there. The farmers were rewarded with an increase in the loan interest rates at their annual renewal, on the basis that their inaccuracy meant they represented a higher risk. He did not directly accuse them of having previously walked their cows over the fields while he was absent, but they tacitly accepted he knew the situation and took their punishment, which was made more palatable by the hint that accuracy of future stock accounting would result in a return to a lower interest margin over base rate at their next annual facility renewal. Following this, Westmorland had a clause inserted in the bank's Terms & Conditions that all farmers requesting loans would in future have to accept unannounced stock checks. As the background story leaked out – not from him, who remained at all times discreet on business matters – his reputation grew within the farming community of a shrewd operative who should not be crossed.

When Martello had entered the manager's office, Westmorland had risen and shaken her hand before closing the door behind her – an action that gave her a feeling of trepidation. However, her concerns had dissipated when he proceeded to open an inner door, calling out clearly across the open plan office, 'Will you work in here for a while, Miss Nettleton, in case I need your assistance with anything during this interview.'

Westmorland had begun by explaining the lending restrictions now imposed on him by Head Office, before going through the bank's application form with her. There was one question on the form that Martello was unable to answer, so he phoned the estate agent and asked about a "flying freehold", before terminating the call and carrying on with the next question. When all the questions had been answered, he explained that the bank's standard system would not approve the mortgage based on normal lending criteria. He then went on to ask about her work in the police force, her plans and intentions and even hopes for her future career, and whether she expected to remain based at Midshaw station for the foreseeable future. He appeared satisfied with all the responses, and informed her that he was pleased to say her mortgage would be authorised on his personal authority, subject to a satisfactory survey. Miss Nettleton had then been invited to leave and to take with her the loan application form so as to prepare another document for signing later. When Westmorland and Martello were alone he had then added it would be necessary for him to obtain an independent estimate of the value of the property, something which he would undertake personally by making an inspection of it. Martello had feared this was the sting in the tail, and that he might be looking to inspect rather more than just the property. Westmorland had recognised that look, having seen it so many times before in the course of his career. He had smiled at her as he opened the door to invite her to leave, adding, 'I shall make the appointment to inspect the property with the estate agent, rather than yourself, and then let you know my assessment.'

Two days later she had received a phone call from Westmorland to say he had inspected the flat with the estate agent's senior partner, and had informed him that, in his opinion, the property was considerably overpriced for the area, that the vendor would be unlikely ever to achieve their asking price, that no one who banked with Midshires would obtain a mortgage based on that valuation, and that they should inform the vendor of this and recommend a considerable reduction in the asking price, say twenty thousand pounds.

The estate agent, no doubt wishing to maintain good relations with the bank for the sake of future business, had spoken to the vendor who had agreed to accept the lower price. Westmorland had then gone on to describe to Martello the limitations of the flat, and how the cement works carbuncle would remain a blot on the landscape for many years to come, but that the reduced asking price now reflected these factors and incidentally brought her mortgage application to within the credit-scored application parameters. When he asked if she would like to proceed with the application she was delighted to give him the go-ahead. And, she had thought to herself, he never once made an improper suggestion. She had gained the impression that Westmorland was a kind, thoughtful, considerate, helpful, generous man to whom she would be forever grateful. The estate agent thought Westmorland as hard as nails.

* * *

Martello returned to her flat, parking her small, red Peugeot on the road, as the garage and hard-standing belonged to the two ground floor flats. She looked through the picture window from her open plan room and out over the Hope Valley, barely noticing the cement works that was determinedly refusing to blend into the landscape. She looked down at the rear garden to which she had no access, as it belonged in two narrow strips to the ground floor flats.

She was nevertheless very happy to have her flat, though felt it was lacking something as yet unidentified.

She checked her landline phone for messages; landlines were preferable in this area as mobile phone reception was weak and unreliable. There was a silent message – someone had phoned and not known what to say. Then there was a message from Castleton, trying to sound like it was work-related – asking for a status update on the latest case; she knew it was just another attempt to see her again outside working hours. She had bowed to pressure from him to go out for a drink at a distant pub, for a meal at a distant restaurant, to another distant pub, all the way to Derby to go to another pub, then another distant meal, and all the time she felt he was like a vulture circling, waiting for her to drop and be devoured. It had been difficult to refuse the allegedly innocent first meeting as he claimed it was something work-related that he wanted to discuss; in reality it was a thinly veiled offer to support her for promotion to sergeant if she in return showed her appreciation in the time-dishonoured way. She had tried to laugh it off, essentially telling him that she would be considering all proposals if ever she were made up to sergeant. And, she had thought to herself at the time, you are going to be disappointed.

There was a brief message from her sister Violet, a woman of twenty-five; with her short stature, unremarkable figure, unkempt brown hair, ears that stuck out just a bit too far, and a nose that had a slightly bulbous region half way down, she would have been difficult to recognise as a sister to Lily. Violet had grown up in her sister's shadow until, just after her twenty-first birthday, she had gone away unexpectedly one Thursday morning and returned on the Monday afternoon with a husband, Stuart. Since then she had blossomed into a happy mother of two delightful children, Harry and Beatrix, who were doted on by their loving parents. Martello phoned straight away and was rewarded with an immediate pick-up by Violet; they talked about anything and nothing for ten minutes while Harry called out randomly and Beatrix laughed and cried depending on how much attention Violet was giving her.

Martello went into her inner sanctum, her bedroom. This too had a view over the Hope Valley, unlike the second bedroom which overlooked the road and was a bedroom in name only, being used for storing Martello's accumulated clothes that were mementos of passing fads and fashions. From the extensive range in her current clothing wardrobe she chose something which she estimated projected the right balance between professionalism for an autopsy and allure for Mallory. She thought the deep red silk blouse with underwear of the same colour that left the observer unsure whether she was wearing a bra would be set off well by the grey pinstripe jacket with silver thread and matching straight skirt with rear slit. Black, buckled shoes reminiscent of a lawyer in court would complete the set, almost. She decided ribbed, red stockings would be an inspired finishing touch to vamp Dr Mallory. The medium-sized black leather handbag with gold-plated fasteners would be acceptable with this ensemble, though she feared her collection of handbags was the weakest part of her wardrobe as good ones were so ridiculously expensive. She collated the items neatly on the bench seat in front of her dressing table.

She decided to have some food so that she would not feel too hungry waiting for the meal at the expensive restaurant to which she expected to be invited by Mallory. Her small indulgence had to be chosen with care to avoid leaving anything on the breath. No meat, no cheese, no strong coffee. She settled for a boiled egg, a slice of bread and a cup of tea. She watched the kitchen clock intently – she knew she was an expert at boiling eggs. The egg was needing another twenty seconds when her mobile phone rang – it was picking up a signal, for once; she left it ringing until the boiling was complete. The sound level had increased close to maximum by the time she had turned off the heat and lifted the egg from the pan with a serving spoon. She grabbed the phone and answered it deliberately hurriedly, snapping out one word, 'Hello.'

Witty responded, 'Hi. You sound busy; am I interrupting something?'

'Boiled egg; it's just done. Can I call you back?'

'Yes; sure. Talk to you later.'

Martello placed the egg in the eggcup she had had since childhood, its picture of animals sitting at a table almost worn away. With a deft flick of a knife she took the top off the egg and was pleased to find the yolk was still runny. Eating so little food, she found she appreciated every quarter mouthful.

Following her meal she brushed her teeth with care, holding the minty flavoured freshness for a few extra seconds before rinsing her mouth; everything had to be just right, so no mouthwash as that would seem too obvious and would suggest evidence as to motive, m'lud.

As she dressed she considered phoning Witty back but decided against it. He didn't phone her very often and it was always genuinely work-related. She would be seeing him in the morning so she assumed he had something to say about the only thing happening before then: the autopsy. Well, that hadn't happened yet, so it must make more sense to talk to him afterwards, or even just leave it to the morning.

She switched her attention to lipsticks. 'The bright red would be wrong for this occasion – far too obvious. The purple's almost always wrong – it's more for old women; I only bought it for Fright Night. Baby Pink looks good on me, but not with these clothes. I'll use this light, dull red that makes it look almost like I'm not wearing any.'

She dressed with care, examining herself in the full-length mirror after each separate item of clothing was put on. She gave herself one final check, twisting her neck around to see her back in the mirror, before setting off for the Sheffield Medico-Legal Centre.

Though she found the route between Hope and Sheffield to be very pleasant in summer, her feelings were quite different when darkness had fallen and the frost with it, when the roads could be quite treacherous. She slowed almost to a halt at Longshaw, where Hathersage Road turns sharply left and continues uphill past the Fox House pub and restaurant. This was the corner where she had had her first and last professional, physically sickening experience of the aftermath of a car crash. She had been called out to a Road Traffic Collision and had found a car that had bounced up off the curb and embedded itself high in the stone wall that marks the boundary of the Longshaw Estate. One of her colleagues had drawn her attention to the painting of a fox on the pub sign, explaining how the name really came from a Mr Fox and not from the animal; the unspoken subtext was 'look at the pub sign, Lily; don't look inside the car.' Another colleague tried to make light of the RTC – a common protection mechanism – highlighting that the skid had started in Sheffield and ended in Derbyshire. She had thought how the young man whose mangled body remained within the concertinaed metal shell would never see any humour in it, being forever dead to all things of this world. She had felt unwilling to witness any more such horrors and the next day had written a letter of resignation. A senior male colleague had intercepted her letter and promised a quick transfer to CID rather than allowing her talents to be lost to the police force. He was as good as his word but showed far too personal an interest in her afterwards, and she was relieved when he was moved onward and upward and away from Midshaw station.

Martello drove carefully and sedately, nowhere near the limits that trigger the speed cameras, though enough to light up a "Slow Down" sign – except she knew it illuminated whatever her velocity. She passed by the end of DI Priestley's road, but he was away so she knew there was no point in calling in for guidance on the case. She arrived at the Medico-Legal Centre which houses both the coroner's court and the public mortuary and has a side-building for the iGene Digital Scanning Facility. She parked on Watery Street and went to the door; reception was now closed so she rang the bell and identified herself over the intercom – there was always someone available to let in visitors, twenty-four hours a day.

Senior Anatomical Pathology Technician Nina Buxton greeted her in reception. Buxton was an attractive thirty-something with strong hands and a pleasant smile; Martello wondered how she coped with seeing dead bodies every day and whether she was able to keep smiling through it all. Buxton noted how Martello was dressed; as she took her to a room just off the autopsy suite, she commented, 'You look like you're going out, after.'

Martello smiled and nodded, 'That's the plan.'

'The gear's in here; zip it right up – you don't want anything splashed on your glad rags.'

Martello followed Buxton's instruction to put on the protective clothing. She was disappointed that Mallory had not seen her before she had to cover up her carefully selected ensemble, thereby losing that initial impact. Buxton retrieved black wellingtons for both of them from the viewing room and took her into the autopsy suite where Mallory was already well-dressed for performing the post-mortem, right down to his green scrubs and matching Royal Green wellies.

Mallory looked up from a computer screen that was positioned near the door and well away from the large, stainless steel flatbed where corpses were dismantled. Without a smile, and with a business-like air that bordered on the brusque, he addressed Martello while Buxton walked over to the body lockers ranged across the back wall. 'DC Martello, come and take a look at this.'

'Do call me Lily, please.'

He repeated his earlier instruction a little less abruptly. 'Lily, come and take a look at this.'

She peered at the screen where two shapes were displayed separately, one in yellow and the other in blue. Mallory touched the keypad to make the images rotate, indicating their three-dimensional quality. He manoeuvred one image until it fitted into the other image, then made the combined image rotate. He explained, 'Do you see how most of the object on screen is either yellow or blue; the interesting parts are the white and the green. The white indicates a gap between the two images; the green shows where they overlap. You see how there's virtually no white or green – just a few little touches here and there. Do you know what this means?'

Martello was fairly sure but decided not to risk appearing foolish. Besides, she thought, Dr Mallory likes to show off his achievements so I should let him do all the talking. 'I'd like to hear it from you, if you don't mind, um, ...' She hoped he would invite her to call him by his first name which she had looked up and knew was "Gordon". She wondered if he had a diminutive form for close friends: Gord perhaps; surely not Gore; maybe Don, like the local river.

'The yellow is a three-dimensional image of part of the skull, and the blue is the image of the coat hook. The green and the white show where small distortions have occurred, but they're so small that I can say beyond all reasonable doubt that the damage to the skull resulted from the impact with the hook.

'Now for a little prestidigitation ...' With a flourish he lifted a shiny black plastic sheet that lay further along the side bench, revealing two plastic shapes, one yellow and one blue, sitting in trays of white powder. 'Here we have three-dimensional representations of the skull and the hook, hot off the fabricator machine. Though I prefer computer imaging, I know some people are more comfortable with the jigsaw puzzle approach.'

'That's marvellous, um, ...'

Mallory looked at Martello, puzzled by her hesitation –

normally she seemed so fluent and articulate. He put it down to concerns about witnessing the impending dissection. 'Well, we'd better get on with the post-mortem. I suggest you stand just where you are now – there's no need to see it from close up unless I have something to show you.'

Martello stayed firmly rooted to the spot, looking away from the body that Buxton had positioned on the autopsy table; she was determined not to witness the incisions being made. Mallory glanced over to her and saw how she was focused on the viewing window; interpreting this as a wish to be somewhere else, he walked over to her and offered her an escape option. 'Lily, I don't believe there's any real need for you to be here. I'm not convinced there's that much need for me to be here either, in a way, doing a full forensic autopsy – there's no doubt about what caused the wound. If you feel you have to remain as the official police presence I'm thinking I could cut this post-mortem down to a minimum.'

'I'm sure you're completely right. From a police point of view my only question is: are you able to say if it was deliberate?'

'Any bruising that indicates there was a blow or a push to propel Mr Newhouse into the hook may not show up for a day or two depending on exactly where contact occurred and what was used; we'll make sure the body isn't released to the family until we've checked that aspect. I'll be performing some calculations later to see how much force was needed to achieve the degree of penetration, based on the thickness of the skull and the tough mother ...' He stopped as he saw the shock cross Martello's face. 'I'm not using a crude Americanism, though perhaps I should be more careful about how I express things. Inside the skull cap is what is known in Latin as the *dura mater* which translates as "tough mother".'

'I'm sorry; you must think me very ignorant.'

'Not at all, Lily; there's no reason why you should know such terms.' Seeing Martello still looking dejected he offered some Latin that he believed she would know and that might help to restore her self-respect. '*Mea culpa; mea maxima culpa.*'

Martello smiled in acknowledgement. 'It isn't really your fault, but thank you for saying so.'

Mallory offered her another way out from what he believed she saw as a place of horrors. 'As I had to have the skull scanned for the wound shape, I took the opportunity to have the rest of the body scanned as well. So I believe it would be perfectly justified for you to take your leave, having done your duty. You could give me your phone number if you wish, so that I can contact you if there's anything I need to refer to you. How does that sound?'

'Or even better, I could stay in the waiting room. Then when you're finished we could go somewhere and have a chat about your post-mortem findings.'

'Once I've finished here I'll be doing my homework, so to speak; calculations to establish the force used ... that sort of thing.'

'I don't mind waiting. I'm sure you must need to go somewhere to relax after a long day. Perhaps we could go for a bite to eat and you can tell me anything else you think would be useful about the case.'

'I still have a lot to do here, but don't worry; I'll make sure my report is clear and detailed and easy enough to understand so that you'll know everything you need to know.'

'I really don't mind waiting for you. I mean, you must eat sometime, and I'd like to get to know you better, so a bit of socialising could be just the thing for you.'

The dawn of realisation finally broke through. He pondered on how to express his disinterest in Martello's repeated proposal.

'I'm flattered by your offer, Lily, but you're, um, how should I put it, um, attempting to shin up the wrong flagpole.'

'Ah. Sorry.'

'I'd appreciate it if you didn't broadcast it, though.'

'No, of course not.'

Martello turned away to hide her reddening face. She hurried out of the room and away from what she felt was the scene of her humiliation.

Mallory watched her depart, wondering if it was his earlier display of lack of interest in her that had made her become interested in him. Women can be perverse creatures, he mused.

Buxton interrupted his thoughts. 'In what universe did you scan the entire body?'

'This one – it just hasn't happened yet. We could do it now so I can cover my tracks, and then come back and do a proper forensic post-mortem – you never know what we'll find.'

'So you don't really need to do the scan. In that case it'll cost you six hundred smackers.'

'Is that the going rate for blackmail nowadays?'

'It's the going rate for using the scanner.'

'Only if they find out – I'm sure I can trust you to keep a secret.'

'You already have.'

'Ah, that secret.'

'What secret? The only way to keep a secret is to tell yourself you don't know it.'

'I thought the only way two people can keep a secret is if one of them is dead.'

'I'd prefer my method if you don't mind.'

As Martello drove home she had an internal dialogue that attempted to make some sort of sense of her confused thoughts. 'I must have been stupid for not guessing why Mallory had shown no interest in me at the school; virtually every red-blooded male this side of Leeds reveals their primal desire for me in some way, even though some make a bit of an effort to mask it. Witty doesn't fancy me though. Maybe he's Gay. No, I'm sure he's not Gay – he's married with a kid, though I suppose that could just be a cover. Anyway, he always treats me like a proper person, so I don't care if he is Gay. I could do with talking to somebody. And he did call me earlier. Perhaps he'd been intending to let me know about Mallory, or maybe it was about something else entirely.' She parked up and gave him a call.

'Hello?'

'Hello. I'm just on my way back from the city morgue. Dr Mallory showed me something interesting and I could do with letting you know about it. Could you see me at the Black Bull?'

'Sure.'

'I'll be there in ten minutes – can you get there before that? I don't like going in unless I'm meeting somebody and they're already in there.'

'Yep. I'll be there in five.'

'Right. See you.'

Witty drove the half mile to the Black Bull to make sure he was there first; and besides, he was expecting a work-related conversation and not a drinking session. Before today he had always walked there and always alone. His wife Theresa could not bring herself to leave the house in the evenings. Initially they had shared the duty of watching their son Ollie, but that quickly changed to her taking sole responsibility. He had accused her of wishing to play the martyr, and after that there was no going back to sharing the task, or anything else for that matter.

The Black Bull was technically "Black's Bull", a prolific creature that had covered many of the heifers of the region during the mid-nineteenth century, the charges for such servicing having funded the purchase of the pub. Though the old wooden sign hanging outside still proclaimed the original name, the wording was so faded as to be illegible, and the painting of said bull so obscured by decades of grime that it could be mistaken for virtually anything from a Black Pig to a Fell Pony. The pub was popular at the weekends with people from the nearby towns and cities, as it had that feeling of authentic Olde Worlde charm, which in this case was genuine as the décor had not been altered for decades. In midweek it was largely locals who frequented the place.

Witty was a weekday regular and a weekend stranger. The landlord, Boy Black, was an ex-boxer; he had won some regional bouts but gave up the game and took over the pub when his father had died from Alcohol-related Liver Disease. Recent customers speculated he had adopted "Boy" as his professional fighting name, like former British welterweight champion Dave "Boy" Green. Others with longer memories thought his real name was Tommy, like his father and his father before him, and as had been announced in the pub when the child was born. A month after becoming the new landlord, Boy Black had been worn down by the same question being asked with monotonous regularity, and had explained that "Boy" was his genuine name as shown on his birth certificate. According to his mother, his father had been so drunk when he had gone to the Register Office to record the birth that he had had difficulty keeping up with the questions, so he was still telling the registrar that the child was a boy when the "Name" question was being asked.

As a rule, Witty turned left into the Public Bar, where permutations of the same crowd of men would be found from Monday to Thursday. He wanted to avoid being drawn into conversation with anyone right now, so he ignored this evening's dozen or so regulars, and entered the Snug on the right. He went to the far corner, sitting with his back pressed into the centre of the red velvet-on-wood, curved, built-in seating, being the position that gave him the clearest view of the main entrance. He sat waiting without a drink. Knowing he was there for a work-related meeting, he could not have explained to himself why he felt as anxious as a schoolboy, with a fluttering sensation in his stomach like butterflies.

Boy Black saw him and came over, grinning. 'Sorry sir, there's no waiter service on today, but you can order your drink at the bar.'

Uncharacteristically, he was incapable of responding with suitable banter, and instead blurted out a factual response. 'I'm expecting a work colleague very soon. We needed somewhere to discuss something. She's a lady.'

Boy Black, at five feet eleven and packed with solid muscle, displayed some of his trademark fancy footwork and slapped four "Reserved" signs on Witty's table and on the three nearest to it – there was just a handful of strangers in the Snug so the tables would not be needed by other customers, at least not before nine o'clock. 'You can come back and reclaim your spot when the lady arrives. Now come through and have a drink with the others.'

Witty did as he was bid, collecting the pint of Pedigree that had been drawn without his asking. He remained at the edge of the usual crowd, not engaging with them, and peering over toward the main door with eyes that hardly blinked. The chatter died suddenly when a woman's voice was heard, clearly and distinctly like a public speaker. 'Stop bothering me. Leave. Me. Alone.'

Witty had recognised Martello's crowd control voice and was off like a shot, but Boy Black had the quicker access route to the Snug from behind the bar and arrived ahead of him. The landlord exercised his right to take the lead in his own house. 'You all right Lily?'

'He won't take no for an answer.'

He turned to the skinny lad who looked to be in his early twenties, if not less. 'Stop bothering the lady. And didn't you see the "Reserved" signs?'

'I was just talking to her. I wasn't doing any harm.'

Boy Black rested a heavy hand on his shoulder. 'Come away now.'

'Get your hand off me – that's assault – I'll call the police.'

Boy Black, knowing both Lily and Witty were on the force, thought this was too good an opportunity to miss. With the artificially high voice of a man imitating a woman, he turned to the watching audience that now included the regulars who had crowded into the Snug from the Public Bar. 'Oh, help me, help me. Somebody call the police.'

Witty took his cue, though delivering his lines like an actor who was performing a well-rehearsed part unconsciously and without engagement. 'Police here, madam. Now, what seems to be the problem?'

The lad was now red-faced, being shamed in front of his two mates who were still sitting at the far side of the Snug. 'You're not police – you're just his mate.'

Martello stood up with her warrant card in her hand. 'Yes he is, and so am I. And you're the one that'll be arrested if you don't move away now.'

Boy Black took hold of the lad's arm and escorted him to the door. 'I don't want any trouble-makers in here, so you're banned.'

'What about m' mates?'

'They're not misbehaving.'

The lad's voice was now whining – what the locals called "pewling". 'But I'm with them.'

'You were with them.'

The lad walked to the edge of the car park and stood, looking back, like a little boy lost. His two mates drained the last drops from their pint glasses and walked out without a word, looking down as they went.

The incident having put Martello into her assertive mode, she decided they should leave. 'This is too public for a work meeting.' She could have added, 'And I should know better by now than to sit in a pub on my own.'

Witty was feeling flummoxed and flustered. He was concerned to clear his name of any suggestion that he had not been diligent. 'It only took me a few minutes to get here, and I've been watching out for you ever since; I don't understand how I missed you.'

'I came in through the side door. I always do – I'm a regular.'

'I've never seen you here before.'

'I sometimes arrange to meet a friend here for a chat. He comes most Saturday nights.'

Witty felt this revelation strike like a blow to the solar plexus, leaving him breathless. He dismissed the idea that the friend was Castleton as everybody knew where he had been with Martello, and anyway this pub was far too close to home. He finally managed a few hoarse words. 'You kept quiet about that.'

Martello observed Witty's reaction that showed itself all over his face: the smile that was trying to break out but could find no way past the downturned mouth and extended lower lip, leaving his cheeks moving up and down like a nervous twitch in slow-motion; the nostrils that widened a few times every second, like a baby seal at an aquarium; and the eyes that blinked too frequently and each time stayed determinedly closed for too long. She decided he was disappointed that she had kept something secret from him, so gave a quick explanation that would enable them to get back to business. 'It's an old man that I like to talk to.' She knew George Westmorland at fifty-something did not really deserve the description "old man", but this was no time for accuracy. She wanted to get away from the audience, so ducked out of the back entrance, Witty following without another word. Outside, she stated rather than asked, 'You came in your own car.'

'Yes.'

'We'll go to my flat. Follow me. This is where I live in case you get lost.' She rattled off her address, then walked straight to her car, started the engine, and waited for Witty to do the same, before leading the convoy.

Back in the pub the regulars looked at each other, smirking like schoolboys. One of them offered, 'That's a turn up for the book.'

Another agreed, 'Yes, a real red letter day.'

Boy Black added his own observation. 'Amazing, it's the first time that's ever happened – somebody leaving a pint of Pedigree.' As he poured it away he reflected on how his father would never have let good beer go to waste.

CHAPTER 8

Witty on World Population

Witty trailed Martello's car, pulling up a metre behind her on the road outside her flat. She put her car keys into a side pocket of the black leather handbag and took out a separate key ring from which she selected the Yale key, opened the outer door and walked into the shared entrance hallway, then waited at the foot of the stairs. As Witty entered she walked up the stairs without a backward glance. At the top of the stairs she selected a second key, opened her door and walked in, again without looking back. Witty followed and closed the door behind him. Martello turned and faced him from close up. 'Neil, are you Gay?'

Witty had been through various scenarios on his way to Hope, but knew most of them were in the realms of fantasy rather than credible hopes and dreams. Not for one moment had this question featured, so he had no prepared answer. 'What?' he barked.

'Are you a homosexual?'

'No, I'm not.'

'It's all right if you are. I've nothing against Gays.'

'Well, I'm not.'

'Are you in denial, then? Perhaps you're Gay but can't admit it to yourself.'

'I'm not in denial. I'm just not Gay.'

'Well, why don't you fancy me then? Every other man does, unless they're Gay.'

Neil wondered if she had only allowed him into her home because she thought he was not a threat to her in any way. 'Look, if you're worried about me being in your flat, I promise to be on my best behaviour. But I'm just not Gay.'

'So answer the question then. Why don't you fancy me?'

Neil wanted to blurt out how he felt about her. 'Lily.' He stopped himself, knowing if he crossed the Rubicon there would be no going back, but the hormonal imperative overrode any conscious thoughts of consequences. He began again. 'Lily. To say I do not fancy you is so wrong. You could not be more wrong.' Like a snowball going downhill he launched into a reckless acceleration of the expression of his feelings. 'You are the most beautiful woman ever to grace God's earth. I desire you more than any man has ever desired any woman. There is nothing I would not do, nothing I would not give up, if I could be close to you all the time.'

Lily was taken aback by the strength of Neil's delivery – she was only familiar with his placid persona. She focused on his last words. 'Well, we're together every day.'

'Yes, and it's agony for me. I always have to put on a professional front and treat you like just another colleague, but all the time I'm wanting to tell you how I feel about you: the way you walk, the way your hair moves when you turn your head, the way you touch your eyebrows when you're thinking, even the way your voice goes all sharp when you're demanding to be listened to.'

'Is that why you're always so nice to me when we're working together?'

Neil felt a self-inflicted arrow in his chest, the barb making him wince physically. 'I'm not. I'm not always nice to you. Sometimes I should be nicer to you. I'm going to be better in the future.'

Lily thought for a while before responding. 'You're the only male colleague who treats me like a normal person. You're my best friend at work, and all this time you've been sitting on your feelings. When I phoned you, you came out straight away. I never understood how you felt.'

She stopped to think. Her need to be in control of situations had caused her to reject a long line of men who had asked her to go to bed with them. She had just begun to contemplate the reverse situation when her words came out spontaneously and overtook her uncompleted thoughts, taking her by surprise almost as much they did Neil. 'Don't say anything else. Let's go to bed.'

Neil remained motionless, his chest tightening; he felt barely able to breathe. Lily turned and walked to her bedroom; Neil waited a moment so as not to appear too eager, before following at a polite distance.

Despite the urgency he felt, Neil attempted to delay being ready to get into the bed until after her, but found himself undressed far too early despite taking his time over placing his clothes together in a neat pile so as not to make an untidy mess in her room. He sat on the bench seat wearing just his boxer shorts until she had completed her routine of carefully placing her clothes in their correct positions in the wardrobe. The first kiss was postponed until they were naked in bed together. Lily asked, 'Do you have a condom?'

Neil had the impression of something trickling within his abdomen, as though he had been penetrated by a bullet that was going to cut short his enjoyment of life. His throat became dry and constricted as he struggled to get out his words. 'No, I haven't.'

Lily rescued him from his anguish. 'According to the magazines, I'm near my least fertile right now, and there's a morning-after pill I could take anyway.'

Neil added his own birth-control contribution. 'I'll be really careful.'

The physical intimacy scored *nul point*, as Neil was so concerned about premature ejaculation that he withdrew a little too early for his needs and a lot too early for hers. He was embarrassed by his poor performance and immediately began to apologise. Despite his huge frustration, Lily's response overwhelmed him with relief: 'We'll get better with practice.'

After a decent interval, Lily observed, 'You seemed to be in a big hurry, there, Neil. I read in a magazine that married men are usually more capable than single men because they practise regularly with their wives.'

Neil turned to humour to rescue him from his embarrassment. 'I think married and single men both practise but in different ways. Practising is all I've been doing for a long time now.'

Lily did not appear to have understood the allusion, so he decided he should explain the reality of his home life. 'My wife and I don't have sex anymore. We haven't since the child was born.' He was conscious of the fact that he had said "the child", not "our boy", not "my son".

A silence hung in the air that neither of them felt able to break for a full minute, as they lay on their backs, his arm under the nape of her neck in the space at the front edge of her pillow. Lily eventually decided she needed to speak plainly with Neil, and that it would be best to have the conversation fully dressed so as to avoid distractions.

'Let's get up now and have a coffee.'

Neil thought she was so matter-of-fact about this that he was convinced she regarded the physical act of love-making as less significant than he did. He hoped it was not because it was commonplace to her, but recognised this was definitely not the time to ask. Lily went to the bathroom and took a shower, her need for cleanliness overriding her keenness to start the interrogation. Neil followed her example, and by the time he had re-dressed she had put on that day's third set of clothes.

'I'm having decaffeinated coffee; proper coffee stops me from sleeping.'

'I'm happy with the same. I've tended to rely on beer to send me to sleep.'

Lily decided that was enough small-talk so she launched straight into the first question. 'Why do you not have sex with your wife anymore?'

Neil was hoping for a permanent relationship with Lily, so decided absolute honesty without deceit or half-truths was essential from the start to give it firm foundations – though he sincerely doubted whether someone as ordinary as himself had any real chance of keeping her. He looked directly into her eyes as he gave his answer, refusing to use his wife's name for fear of giving substance to the spectre at the feast. 'My wife is a Catholic. She refuses to allow contraceptives. I don't want another child.'

'Did you know she was a Catholic when you married her?'

Neil remembered various religious issues surrounding their marriage, from the church to be used for the ceremony, to the faith in which they would bring up their children. Well, the Catholic Church was welcome to have the child brought up in their faith, for all the good it would do them or him. 'Yes, but I wasn't thinking with my head at the time. I remember imagining it would be alright to have as many as four children, and by then she'd probably have felt she'd had enough and would want to stop.'

'But you only have one child.'

'I don't have a child; not really. For me, a child is something wonderful that has certain characteristics: it laughs, it cries, it grows, it develops, it responds to people. What we have is a blob of human matter that does none of those things – and it never will.'

'Don't go saying that to anyone else, Neil, what with the Disability Hate Crime legislation and all.'

'Why are crimes against the disabled singled out like that? Loads of other crimes come out of hate, but they aren't given that extra dimension. And I'm sure there have been plenty of mercy killings that came out of love, and yet they could count as Hate Crimes. Anyway, I've nothing against disabled people. I wouldn't have minded having a child with a physical disability, but not a child who lacks the capacity to comprehend anything. With extreme mental incapacity the spark that makes us human just isn't there. And the worst of it is that we knew what to expect long before he was born. After she got pregnant she told me she had a heritable genetic condition; she'd known about it from before I even met her, so by keeping silent about it she had really lied to me. It was completely obvious from the ultrasound scan that it was a boy, though the nurse said she wasn't allowed to comment on our interpretation of the gender of the foetus; I believe the NHS doesn't hold with that particular piece of nonsense anymore.

'Shortly after we found out it was a boy, my wife told me it would be extremely mentally disabled. I wanted it aborted, but she wouldn't allow it – that's another Catholic thing. It's utterly stupid. It's like the celibacy thing for their priests, and they always feign surprise when someone who's prepared to have a life without sex with women is found out about having sex with boys. What do they expect?'

'You really don't like Catholics then.'

'I've nothing against Catholics – my friend Stephen is a Catholic, and he's a good person. I get the impression he runs his dentistry practice on a highly moral basis – no ripping off patients – because he believes it's the Catholic thing to do, though my guess is he'd still be moral even if he was an atheist.'

'Perhaps dentists tend to be good people?'

'I don't think it's that simple. I've heard patients in his waiting room complaining about other dentists. There was a woman who'd been going to one in Sheffield. He'd told her she needed private treatment rather than NHS, so she'd paid him thousands of pounds over the years. Then she had a crown done that was giving her some pain. He said the nerve had already been removed, so she should just leave it to settle down; she reckoned he thought it was all in her mind, but the pain was real enough. The crown was under guarantee, so he eventually re-did it, though he had such a surly look on his face she thought he blamed her for the problem. The new crown hurt as much as the old one, so she went to Stephen for a second opinion. He did an X-ray and discovered there was a different nerve nearby that was being put under pressure, so he re-did the crown somehow so it didn't hurt anymore. Not only did he fix the problem, but he also said she didn't need to have private treatment – the NHS was fine for her needs. She reckoned the other dentist had been ripping her off for years.

'Then there was an old bloke who'd been on holiday in Norfolk – I think he said he was staying in Cromer. He'd had a raging toothache and discovered the nearest dentist was in Sheringham, so he went there to ask them to extract the tooth. He never got past the receptionist. She went to speak to the dentist and came back to say he'd have to pay a load of money up front for a private examination, and even then the dentist wouldn't necessarily do anything. So, rather than potentially throwing money away for an examination but no treatment, his wife phoned NHS Direct and they located a dentist who agreed to whip it out. They had to drive for half an hour to get to this little place, and the guy wanted a wad of cash in hand straight away. He took out the tooth but left some root behind, which drifted in his gum until it stuck out the side. Stephen said leaving a bit of root behind could have happened with any dentist, and often it didn't matter, but the bloke thought maybe he was just being supportive of a fellow professional. Anyway, Stephen had to fish out the bit of root and then fit a bridge, which he did on the NHS. The bloke reckoned the dentist in Sheringham was trying to take advantage of him while he was in pain, and that the other dentist was more interested in the money than doing a good job.

'Clearly, some people don't see all dentists as paragons, whereas I haven't heard a bad word against Stephen about anything. So, I think he's a good guy, and it makes no difference to me whether or not he's Catholic; it's Catholicism I don't like.'

Lily looked thoughtful for a moment. 'Perhaps I should register with him – or does he have a waiting list?'

'I wouldn't be surprised if there is, though I think you have to register with the practice anyway, rather than just him. There's a second dentist, a really lovely woman.'

'You said that with a bit too much feeling, Neil; are you trying to make me jealous?'

He cast his eyes down and shook his head slightly. 'Ah,

jealousy, the green-eyed monster.' He looked up at her and put on a wistful smile. 'I should have mentioned she has the most beautiful green eyes.' He put on a far-away look, tilting his head and focusing with half-closed eyes at a point just above her. He was pleased when he heard her laugh, knowing she was certain he really only had eyes for her. After a few moments he shook his head as though breaking from a reverie. 'I've rather wandered off the point, haven't I? What I meant about being against Catholicism is that those at the top must know the world's population can't keep increasing forever. There's the obvious problem of feeding everyone, and a related one of climate change from increased meat consumption; then there's illegal immigration into Europe – the police as a whole see consequences of that every working day, and even rural Derbyshire isn't immune. So it's selfish of the Catholic Church to try to increase their share of the world's population by disallowing contraception.'

'Does that mean you think everyone should only be having their fair share – limiting the number of children they have?'

'There's a lot of ways of looking at that question. If everyone in the world had no more than two children then the total population would reduce slightly over time, but that's too simplistic a way of seeing things. If a country can't afford to support its current population and is forever dependent on international aid, then that country as a whole should be reducing its population. But on an individual basis if someone within a country can afford to support half-a-dozen children then why shouldn't they have that many? In the UK there are people who can't afford to have any children without relying on the state to pay for them, but it doesn't stop them from having lots. China has had a policy of restricting some couples to having just one child, and people in the so-called developed nations have complained it's an infringement of the Chinese people's inalienable human rights, but maybe China was being moral and it was the West that was wrong.

'Maybe a fair system for the UK would be that everyone has the right to one child irrespective of wealth, and the state would support them with their one child, whereas those who can afford more than one are allowed to have more without losing all their state benefits; but those who couldn't afford to pay the cost of looking after more than one would not be allowed to keep them and live off the state, which could mean forced adoption for any more children they have.

'There are other factors that affect population size in the UK, such as race or ethnicity. I wouldn't wish you to see me as racist, so I'll explain how I see myself first. Being prejudiced against someone due to their ethnic group is assumed to indicate someone's a racist, but strictly prejudice means having a negative attitude to someone that is not based on actual experience. As everyone's an individual, then the politically correct attitude is that it's racist to be against someone you've never met before, but if I meet ninety-nine people who are the only ones I've ever met from a particular group, and all of them are, say, drug dealers, then if I meet a hundredth I might well think they also may be a drug dealer, and it would be naïve to meet that hundredth and not have some negative expectations about them. If it's ninety-nine people of one race, then why shouldn't I expect the hundredth to be similar? You hear complaints about "racial profiling", but why should profiling be seen as best practice for some things and worst practice if it's based on race? I base expectations on experience, which is why I believe I can honestly say I'm not a racist, even though there are people I meet for the first time where I think there's more than an average chance of them being criminals. My guess is that many people who filled in a British Social Attitudes Survey and stated they're a bit racist may really not be racist at all, as they're actually basing their views on wider experience rather than individual prejudice. I saw a BBC news report where they lumped together people who say they're a bit racist with people who say they're a lot racist, but I think it's very misleading to bundle the two types of response into one. I know it's a nice distinction I've made, but I believe it's valid.'

'Nice distinction? I don't see what's nice about it.'

'Sorry, it means "fine distinction". I wasn't trying to be clever; I've obviously been reading too much, sitting up in my bedroom on my own.'

'Well, you have to remember I'm not much of a reader, so you'll need to make allowances for me.'

'Sorry, Lily, it's my fault – I really didn't think how best to express myself.'

'You're the second person this evening to apologise to me for my ignorance; I think it's making me feel stupider, so I don't want to hear any more apologies from you. Anyway, you were talking about population and then you started talking about racism. What are you trying to say?'

'I was thinking about the UK's ethnic mix and trying to get an insight into projected population growth. Experts have predicted that the total number of people in this country will grow considerably, and that the proportion that's white will fall from nineteen out of twenty now, to just two out of three by 2050. Looking at race or ethnicity or even skin colour could give us insights into different attitudes to preferred family size, except it probably wouldn't be PC to ask such questions officially. Obviously immigration is one factor that'll change the total numbers and so the proportion of people who are Caucasian compared to those who are from other ethnic groups, but another is that people from various ethnic backgrounds clearly have different attitudes to how big a family they should have; you see, it isn't just Catholics who are driving population growth.'

'How many children should people like us be allowed, then?'

'I think it's a question of morality, though different people have different perceptions; for me, morally, I would say it depends on income. I'd give the state powers to sterilise any woman who keeps having children and can't afford to look after any of them. Did you know there are women who've had fifteen children taken into care, one after the other? Sometimes they've even been pregnant with another when a Family Court is dealing with the previous one.'

'State sterilisation is not a popular opinion, Neil. Do you know of anyone else who thinks like you do?'

'It isn't something I've ever discussed with anyone. I certainly couldn't talk to HER about such things.'

'Maybe you've been left on your own too long.'

'Maybe I have, but it still seems a reasonable opinion to me. Anyway, thankfully, it doesn't apply to people like us.' He risked making the subject specific to them as a couple. 'I certainly don't see any issue with us having more than one.'

She missed the underlying suggestion, remaining focused on his attitude to genetic abnormality. 'Would you have wanted another child with her if it had been normal?'

'That's not something I've ever had to consider, as there's no way I was having another one with her, normal or otherwise.

There's a fifty-fifty chance another child would have been a boy and so would have had the same problem. If it was a girl it wouldn't show any symptoms so it would appear normal but it would still have been a carrier. In a way, it would never have been possible to have an entirely normal one.'

'So you wouldn't have wanted a girl either?'

'It would just be passing on a problem to the next generation. Most people want children of their own, and once a child is born they make the best of it they can, but for anyone who has a major genetic fault I think it would be better not to have a child in the first place. People can be so selfish, thinking only about what they want and not thinking about the child.'

Lily was still taking all this in when Neil started again on the subject that had dominated his recent life. 'My wife didn't tell me about her condition because she said she had the right to have children like anyone else. The idea that unborn children have a right to life is valid up to a point, though the people who debate it tend to have such strong views they go beyond the point of being reasonable. But the idea that all eggs and sperm have a right to life is just ridiculous – unless you're a Catholic. If only she'd agreed to have any male foetus aborted, we might have lived with that – but of course Catholics don't do abortion.'

Neil was finding being allowed to express his views to someone who would listen, though cathartic, was leaving him emotionally drained. After half a minute's silence that both of them felt was much longer, Lily offered up her own feelings on the subject of motherhood. 'My sister has two children. They're perfect. She's younger than me. I think I'd like to have children sometime, but it really messes with the figure.'

Neil had heard of women suddenly becoming broody and wondered if that was happening to Lily. He felt he should make his own attitude clear. 'I'd like to have children. I'm not saying they have to be perfect, but they do have to be something better than my wife made us have.'

Both of them felt comfortable in the longer silence that followed. Neil was reflecting on how his adult life had been up to now, and how much better it could be in the future. He realised this was the moment for him to change it; he took a deep breath and plunged head-first into the water, hoping not to hit a rock. 'Lily, I'm going to leave my wife. I'd like to live with you. I know I'm just ordinary and you're very special, but some marriages can be one-sided like that.'

'Jesus, Neil. We go to bed once, and then you want us to live together. And did you mean to let the word "marriage" slip out there as well?'

They both had enough experience of questioning suspects to recognise a slip of the tongue that revealed the truth. Lily's face maintained a serious look as she confirmed her agreement by asking about action predicated on acceptance. 'When do we tell them at the station? We shan't be able to work together once they know.'

'I suppose it depends on when we're actually living together. What do you suggest?'

'Move in tonight. Clear everything out at the weekend.'

Neil felt amazed by her directness; he had witnessed it often enough before, but never for something of this magnitude. Not wishing to dampen things, he nevertheless felt honour bound to add a practical consideration to the proposal. 'My wife won't agree to a divorce, so it will take longer before I'm free of her; that's another Catholic thing.' Neil found he started smiling at her and was unable to stop himself. She accepted his gaze for a while and gave intermittent smiles in return as they mulled things over.

Eventually she remembered Neil had phoned her when she was boiling her egg. 'You called me earlier on my mobile; the landline's more reliable – you've got the number, haven't you?'

'Yes, I've always kept it just in case.'

'Well, what did you call about?'

Neil cast his mind back to something that now seemed an eternity ago. Eventually he remembered, 'Did you...' His voice trailed off. He rephrased his question so as to avoid any suggestion of failure on her part as lead detective. 'Something about the case we're working on. The SIO should make sure next-of-kin are informed and that they agree to an invasive autopsy; that's often best done through a Family Liaison Officer. Did Castleton say anything about getting permission from the family, and what he was doing about a FLO?'

'He said he'd contact next-of-kin, but he didn't mention a FLO.'

'We should have checked whether the school had already informed next-of-kin. We should also have checked that Castleton did what he said he'd do – I don't find him reliable, and he might try to drop you in it if he's forgotten. We need to check if there's already a designated FLO; if not, and we get the preliminary results of the autopsy in the morning, we'll probably have to contact the next-of-kin ourselves.'

'You make it sound like being a lead detective is all about checking what other people are doing.'

'Well, it is to some extent. There's often a big difference between what people say they'll do and what they actually do. Leading a case is about making things happen, not just putting together a plan for what they'd like to happen.'

'You should be leading it, Neil – you're far more capable than me.'

Witty was torn between two mutually incompatible replies. Martello put him out of his misery, 'It's all right – you don't need to say it. We both know you're the competent one and I'm the good-looking one.'

Witty laughed with relief that Martello understood the reality of their abilities and attributes. After a pause he asked, 'Did Dr Mallory have anything interesting to say?'

Lily was torn between revealing Mallory's secret and detailing how his computer demonstration confirmed the injury resulted from impact with the coat hook. She decided the secret could wait a little longer. 'He scanned the coat hook and the damaged part of the skull and proved they were an almost perfect fit, so there's no doubt it's what caused the injury. He's going to work out how much force was used, to know whether it was deliberate.'

'And we'll know either way tomorrow morning?'

'That's what he said.' After a pause Lily decided the other secret really could not wait. 'Did you notice I'd dressed up a bit for the autopsy?'

'Don't undersell yourself, Lil, you weren't "dressed up a bit", you were Drop Dead Gorgeous, looking like a million dollars.'

She decided she should share more than just Mallory's secret. 'I had boyfriends when I was very young; the usual teenage explorations, but no serious relationships. Since then I've been out with a lot of fellas, but they've all been far too keen and pushy, and the harder they tried to grab me, the harder I pushed them away. I like to be more in control than they would let me be. So, I've kept them all at arm's length, except that now I'm thinking

I'm not getting any younger and I ought to consider settling down. Well, Dr Mallory is single, and I thought I'd take a run at him and see what happens; I might as well not have bothered getting dressed up, though – he never saw what I was wearing because I had to get covered up so I didn't get any blood on my clothes. Anyway, he turned me down, and he explained why by letting me in on his secret, though he doesn't want it spreading: he's just not interested in women. I suppose that means he's Gay, though he didn't actually say so, not in so many words. I thought your phone call earlier might have been to warn me – letting me know so I didn't make a fool of myself.'

'Well, I didn't know, though I suppose there were plenty of signals.'

'Maybe he's celibate.'

'Been there, done that. It's not easy.'

'You're not the only one, Neil. Anyway, he did us a big favour. I felt completely stupid when he told me he wasn't interested in me, so I wanted to talk to someone I could trust to try and make me feel better. You were my best hope and that's why I gave you a call.'

Neil decided he should show some of the decisiveness that Lily had been displaying. 'I'm going to drive back to my wife, pick up some things, tell her I'm leaving for good, and I'll be back here within the hour. I won't be staying to have an argument with her; that can wait.'

He headed for his old home via the all-night pharmacy.

CHAPTER 9

Interim Post-mortem Report

Thursday

Witty and Martello decided they should not rush into officially declaring their relationship, though they knew this was against Human Resources' rules; they agreed they needed more time to let the idea settle within themselves. Witty argued they should keep it secret to avoid being assigned separate duties which would disrupt the current case, not admitting it was more that he wished to be with her as much as possible. To maintain the deception they decided they should drive to work separately to arrive at their usual times, about seven fifty for Witty and eight o'clock for Martello. As Witty entered the office, Dunn greeted him enviously. 'You lucky dog.'

Witty muttered, 'Morning,' and went straight to a vacant interview room to phone Lily. 'Dunn knows about us, though I've no idea how, and I don't know how many more know.'

He went to his desk, logged onto the computer system and began checking e-mails. Martello's phone rang with the tone that indicated an internal caller. He punched in the group pick-up code to divert the call on his own phone; Reception informed him that someone from the mortuary had just delivered a package addressed to DC Martello. He collected it on her behalf. He was about to place it on her desk when, after a moment's hesitation, he decided it should be acceptable for him to open it as he knew it must relate to the Newhouse case. He found it was an interim report on the post-mortem of Edward John Newhouse. It specified Dr G. Mallory as the sole author, in contrast to full reports that always had a long list of signatories.

Witty began reading the report, trying to look fully engrossed in its contents while thinking of other matters. His tired eyes discovered the key statement regarding the force required to cause the injury. Mallory appeared to have made precise calculations that Witty could never claim to understand, and especially not this morning. He yawned as he attempted to condense the main conclusion, which appeared to be that the force had been close to the centre of the range of values that might be expected if someone had deliberately pushed Newhouse onto the coat hook. He closed the folder, intending to read it more thoroughly when he had the energy. He set off for the canteen in search of strong coffee with added caffeine; he vaguely recognised the woman who served him as she laughed pleasantly and commented, 'You look worn out, luv, like you've been up all night.'

Unsure whether the *double entendre* was intended, he replied with a weary nod of the head and trudged back to his desk.

When Martello arrived she slipped quietly into the office and prepared to check her e-mails. There was a yellow sticky label on her computer screen – her VDU as the techies called it – an instruction from Castleton to see her first thing this morning. Witty stood up and walked over to her, trying to look like he had always looked before today. He showed her the front of the interim autopsy report. 'I think Dr Mallory says it looks like he may have been pushed, though it's all long-winded and full of *caveats*.'

Martello showed him the sticky label. 'I'd better see him straight away.'

As she knocked on Castleton's door, she wondered if he knew.

'Enter.'

'Sir, you asked me to report to you straight away.'

'Yes. How's it going with the unexplained death at the school?'

'I went to the autopsy yesterday evening. Dr Mallory's established that the head injury definitely resulted from contact with a coat hook. He's calculated the force that was needed and says he was probably pushed.'

'You're obviously getting things moving quickly. What will you be doing next?'

'Going back to the school to interview people who were in the vicinity around the time of death.'

'I'll keep out of your way so that you can claim the credit for the investigation. Is there any help you need?'

'There's a lot of witnesses and it would be best if they're interviewed as soon as possible, so progress will depend on how many officers can be assigned to the case.'

'You and Witty should deal with the main players. Dunn and Plummer can take witness statements from the others. Keeping the numbers down avoids spreading the kudos when it's closed off successfully. This is a great opportunity for you, you know; if you can prove yourself on this case you can put in an application for the vacancy and I'll be able to present evidence for supporting it.'

'Thank you, sir, but there's a lot to be done before anyone can assess the case as a success or not.'

'I'm sure whatever happens I can find a positive way of looking at your contribution.'

'May I go now, sir – I have a lot to deal with.'

'Yes, off you go.'

Martello tried not to look too hurried as she walked quickly toward the door. Castleton called out to her just as her fingers were stretching for the door handle with its promise of sanctuary in the open office that lay beyond. 'Lily, you put me off yesterday evening and you didn't get in touch later. Are you avoiding me?'

Martello tried for innocence with a simple, 'Sir?'

'Look, we know exactly what this is about, though we've both been playing the game like we don't. When will you let me have your body?'

Martello strained a laugh. 'I need it for myself, sir – it's the only one I've got.'

Castleton refused to be fobbed off. 'You know what I mean, so don't mess me about.'

Martello tried for a full smile. 'I'm working too hard to think of other things.'

Castleton's voice rose in volume and pitch. 'Let's get it out in the open: when am I going to have sex with you?'

Martello had hoped to put off the moment of his rejection until after the case was solved, but could not avoid responding to his direct question. 'I believe it would be inappropriate, sir.'

'Are you saying "No"?'

'That's correct, sir. I believe HR rules disallow it.'

She turned and hurried from the office, relieved not to be called back a second time.

Martello beckoned Witty to follow her into an interview room. He doubted whether she had in her mind what he had in his, but nevertheless thought he should suggest it. 'Surely you don't want some more, Lily?'

She looked at him like thunder. 'Don't you ever know when to shut up with your quips?'

He decided he needed to learn, and fast. 'Sorry, Lily.'

'I've just been in with DCI Castleton.' Witty remained silent as he felt a wave of panic spread through him. 'He asked me for sex and I turned him down flat. He'll be causing trouble for me, you can be sure of that. Just get back to your desk and pretend like nothing's happened, but be on the lookout.'

Witty scuttled from the room without another word.

Ten minutes later Martello's phone rang and she was again summoned to Castleton's office.

'Enter.'

'Sir.'

'I've had another think about this case. It needs someone with more experience to lead it. Now send in Witty. Dismissed.'

Martello gave Witty a hurried explanation of her latest conversation with Castleton. Witty headed for Castleton's office, feeling he lacked the weaponry to face the monster.

'Enter.'

'Sir.'

'I gave DC Martello the chance to lead this case, but she hasn't performed well enough. I'm putting you in charge for now. Make sure you keep me informed of progress. Good luck.'

'Thank you, sir.'

Witty returned to their office and gave Martello a quick explanation of his conversation with Castleton, adding the obvious, 'I don't think he knows about us.'

Witty phoned the school and was put through to Verbane; he explained the need to interview all the members of the staff football team, and that four officers including himself would be setting off shortly. He held back the information from the autopsy for delivery when they were face-to-face.

The Headmaster at the beginning of his tenure had replaced the way that pupils were grouped into Forms within the school. Previously, Forms consisted of thirty or so children of the same Year, and were based largely on the science subjects they were studying. The new, vertical structure consisted of a few children of each Year and gender in each Form. He believed this grouping arrangement would help to break down the barriers that often developed between children of different Years, thereby minimising conflicts. For pupils, every day started with Form Time, where the roll-call would be taken and recorded on the school's computer system, and where messages would be delivered and announcements made; the new Form structure had the disadvantage that many announcements would have relevance only to a small minority of the Form members, but he deemed this inefficiency was outweighed by the benefits of the social cohesion that it engendered.

At the school every morning before Form Time, teachers, teaching assistants and lab technicians who were not on duty elsewhere would squeeze into the common room for a brief staff meeting. Today there were fewer absentees than usual; with so many having to stand, those who were normally guaranteed to have claimed particular seats chose not to use them but to stand up like the others. Verbane was struggling to see over the heads of the taller colleagues, so stepped onto the centre of a long, low, almost black, solid oak table that had been in the room since time immemorial.

Against tradition, he did not begin with the names of the children who were currently excluded, but went straight into staff absences. 'You are no doubt all aware that yesterday we lost John Newhouse, a colleague and a friend. There will be a time for mourning, and Miss Oaken will be liaising with John's mother to ensure her wishes and ours come together. There will also be a time for remembering John with silent reflection. Though most, if not all, students will be aware of our loss, every Form Teacher should begin today's Form Time with an official announcement. A minute's silence will be held ten minutes after the start of Form Time so the students can show their respect for Mr Newhouse. The school bell will ring to mark the start of the minute and will ring again at the end of the minute.'

Verbane paused for a moment before changing his sombre tone for a lighter one and using greater inflection. 'But for now we must be practical and make sure the school continues to run normally. Consequently, the Physical Education department must ensure suitable cover is provided for the lessons that John would have been giving today. Other departments will also need to provide cover for their own absent colleagues; there are now four on the list.'

He read out the four names, three of them being long term absentees, and the other, the French mistress Madame Nathalie Dupont, being a new addition. He continued, scanning the room and attempting to catch the eye of ten particular teachers. 'All members of staff who played in yesterday's match will be interviewed by the police who will be arriving this morning to take statements from you. This will also require a degree of cover, which Miss Oaken and Mr Collins have arranged; will you ten please stay for a minute or two after this meeting for details of how that will operate. In order for Miss Oaken to deal with the fall-out from the awful event she will be allocating her own duties to various members as staff as she thinks fit; please ensure you give her all the support she needs.

'Now to exclusions.' He reeled off the names of the three boys who had earned two days' exclusion, their reward or punishment, depending on attitude, for a joint enterprise; the "joint" in question was being passed around in the boys' lavatories when discovered by Collins' keen sense of smell.

Oaken took her turn to deal with pastoral matters. 'Jordan and Louis Cowley-Wesson are now living only with their mother, who has asked that we drop the name Wesson in all matters relating to her and her children, so she is now Ms Catherine Cowley. We can expect the children to be upset about the absence of their father, Mr Harry Wesson, who, she tells us, is living with Ms Penelope Smith, who is the mother of the Danny Smith in Year Nine. We also need to be on the lookout for any friction between Louis and Danny.

'Robin Loxley fractured his leg and it has been put in plaster. He is expected to be on crutches for at least a month. Allow him out of every lesson a few minutes early so that he isn't knocked down in the rush. Let a reliable student accompany him for protection; one only, please.

'Jessica Stanage and Karen Ringinglow had a physical disagreement at lunchtime yesterday. Their parents were given twenty-four hours' notice in the afternoon, and the pair of them will be serving detention together after school today. Be on the lookout for more, ah, empirical arguments.

'I think that's everything.'

Miss Nunn corrected her. 'I mentioned to you Becky Worthington's mum phoned me yesterday after school.'

Oaken looked to the ceiling to recall the conversation. 'Yes, thank you for reminding me. Mrs Worthington telephoned about Becky having gone home with wet hair. I'm sure you all know Becky is one of our Special children.' She emphasised the word "special", using it as a label rather than a descriptor. Oaken no longer used the term "special needs" after a member of staff with a highly developed sense of political correctness had asserted all children have special needs and the only difference between one child and another is what those special needs were. She continued, 'You all remember how we celebrated Autism Awareness Day last April to make sure our Special children are not in the forty per cent who suffer bullying in schools. We all have a responsibility to understand her. We need to be alert to reminding her about matters such as drying her hair, tying her shoe laces, fastening her coat when it's cold, all little things like that. So, just be sensitive to her needs.'

Verbane moved the meeting toward a close with a call for, 'Any other business?'

Miss Leveret raised her hand so as to be noticed above her taller colleagues. The red rims of her eyes were indicative of prolonged crying; the dark regions below them were more ambiguous – either a lack of sleep or mascara that had smeared.

'Should the school be closed today, as a mark of respect for John? I'm sure some members of staff will be very upset by John's death.'

Verbane adopted a look of great sympathy for Leveret. 'If you – or indeed any member of staff – feel the need to take a little time off, then please see me or Miss Oaken, and your requests will be dealt with sympathetically.'

No one else expressed a wish to raise any other matters, which was a little unusual as there were generally at least half a dozen items each morning under "Any Other Business", some of them genuine, others from members of staff just satisfying their wish to be noticed. Rather than using his usual expression to close the meeting – 'To the classrooms, troops!' – Verbane ended with 'Do your best, everyone.'

CHAPTER 10

Further Statements Taken from Staff Team

Witty and Martello followed closely behind Dunn and Plummer, knowing the latter's liveried vehicle tended to encourage other road users to give them precedence. On arrival at the school Witty despatched Plummer to check that the girls' changing room had been fully processed and cleaned before clearing the police tape from around the outside with Dunn. He wondered why on television programmes crime scenes were often kept cordoned off long after they had been compromised by lack of a twenty-four-hours-a-day patrol and were thus unable to provide any further forensic evidence.

Witty and Martello set off for Verbane's office. He suggested she should lead the discussion as she had attended the autopsy. Verbane opened his office door and she began the conversation.

'Good morning, Headmaster.'

'Good morning. Would you care for a coffee or tea?'

'Nothing for us, thank you. I'd like to give you an update on progress. We've made considerable headway overnight. I attended the post-mortem yesterday evening. The pathologist has established that the wound to the back of the head was the cause of death, and that it resulted from heavy contact with a coat hook that was attached to the wall. The evidence indicates it resulted from his being pushed, so we need to interview everyone who had access to the changing room, which essentially means the staff football team and any other people in the vicinity.'

'I see.'

'Also, I assume you will have made contact with Mr Newhouse's next-of-kin.'

'Yes, I telephoned his mother personally.'

'I'll need to make contact with her myself. Could I have the details, please?'

'You could get them from Detective Castleton – he telephoned yesterday.'

'He's often unavailable; would you mind repeating the information for my benefit?' She smiled, guaranteeing his compliance.

'When I spoke to John's mother she said she would inform his two sisters. I don't have their details, only hers. She lives in Chesterfield.' He gave Martello the address and telephone number.

'I called you earlier about the need to talk to the ten teachers who were in the staff football team.'

'It's all arranged. Miss Oaken is making her office available to you for conducting the interviews, and she'll also be liaising with you to bring people when you ask.'

'That's excellent, sir.'

Witty gave a parting thought to Verbane as they were about to leave. 'The injury involved a broken coat-hook and I noticed there were several more like it. You should really make sure all the broken ones are removed before anyone else is injured; maybe all the hooks need replacing.'

'Thank you for pointing that out – it's something that could easily have been overlooked with everything else that's going on. I'll get someone onto it straight away.'

Witty knocked on Oaken's door; she opened it and invited them in. Martello again led with a brief explanation of the pathologist's findings. Oaken enquired, 'How certain is it that Mr Newhouse was pushed?'

Martello saw no need to provide details, so responded simply, 'Enough to satisfy a court of law.'

Oaken moved onto the question of interviewing staff. 'Is there any particular order you require to see them in? It would be much better if you could fit into the school timetable and interview them as they become free, but it isn't essential as we have a system in place to cope with interruptions. Does the order matter? If not, could you leave it to me to bring them to you when it's least inconvenient for the school?'

Witty took over from Martello with a look in her direction. He confirmed that any sequence would be acceptable. He then asked, 'Did anyone consider whether the school should be closed, as a mark of respect?'

'The Headmaster asked my opinion, and I said it would be too disruptive to the students.'

'You have students here?'

Oaken looked puzzled. 'Yes, of course.'

It was Witty's turn to look puzzled. 'How many students?'

'I can provide a year-by-year breakdown if you wish. There are more than a hundred in each year.'

Witty realised his misunderstanding of the terminology. 'Ah, the children, the pupils, you call them students.'

'Oh, yes, all schools call their pupils students.'

'Right. Well, could we start with the first of the teachers who are currently available.'

'Yes, Mr Davies is available nearly all the time. He's a student.'

'So he isn't a teacher?'

'Yes, that is, he's training to become a teacher. He's on a PGCE course.'

Witty wondered why schools had dropped the specific term "pupil" and replaced it with the dual-meaning term "student". He hoped the rest of the day would be less confusing for his tired brain. 'Well, we'll start with him. Could you bring him here in, say, ten minutes?'

Oaken left for the staffroom to extract the first interviewee.

As lead detective, Witty felt he should be the one to phone Newhouse's mother to make an appointment for them to see her at home. He felt a little awkward as he asked Martello to round up Plummer and Dunn and bring them to the Headmistress's office while he made the call. The quantum shift in their relationship made him wonder if it might be better for them not to work together quite so closely in the future.

When the four officers were together he explained he would conduct the interview with the first teacher, after which they would discuss whether any other questions should have been asked so that a way of proceeding could be agreed by all of them.

Oaken delivered Davies to the door. He introduced himself, explaining he was a twenty-two-year-old History graduate on his first school placement as part of a Postgraduate Certificate in Education, and was based at Sheffield Hallam University. He looked more amused than worried as he entered the office to find four members of the constabulary all waiting to interview him, the two in uniforms standing either side of the desk where the two in mufti were seated. He accepted the chair that was offered, and opened brightly. 'I can't do lessons on my own until I'm qualified, so I have to go around with a proper teacher. Is it the same with you? Or are there four of you so three can hold me down while the other gets out the rubber truncheon?'

Witty brushed off the jibe without taking offence. 'Very droll, Mr Davies. Your colleagues will only have the benefit of two of us. This joint interview is to ensure consistency in the questions we ask.'

'Well, fire away.'

'I have the staff football team list and your statement concerning who entered the girls' changing room with you; also those who entered before you and after you, plus the ones you're unsure about. Your shirt number was five?'

'Yep. I was playing Centre Back.'

Martello began typing onto a laptop computer she had brought for the purpose of recording the interviews, a top-of-the-range model that a past senior officer at Midshaw had purchased for her use in the forlorn hope of some sort of reciprocation. The rest of the force still had to rely on the slow and laborious process of writing by hand, so Martello with her rapid touch-typing was often in demand for interviews.

Witty continued, 'I understand you have only been at this school for a very short time. Did you have any problem identifying everyone?'

'Well, yes and no.'

'What does that mean?'

'I wasn't sure who everyone was, so when we all came back to the staffroom after the match I compared faces with the photos that are on the wall in the corridor.'

'So, you weren't sure who they were when you entered the changing room, but you were sure later, after you had compared faces with the photos.'

'That's correct.'

'And so for the two you were not sure about, it isn't that you are not sure who they were, but that you weren't sure when they entered the changing room after the match in relation to the other players.'

'Do you go on courses to learn how to phrase things so that the average interviewee can't follow what you're saying?'

'I'm sorry – I didn't intend that to be quite so convoluted. I'll ask it in a different way.'

'There's no need. I did manage to follow what you were saying, and you are correct.'

'Thank you. So only Thomas Collins was before you? You were unsure about Hugh Cassidy and Terry Cullen, and the rest you were sure were after you?'

'Yep. Actually, I think Hugh was well before me. I think he was well before everyone because he was at one end of the pitch when everyone else was at the other. We were on all-out attack, trying to get an equaliser; even defenders were past the half-way line. I mean, if you're going to lose, you might as well risk losing by two as by one, if it gives you a chance to snatch a draw. When the whistle went for the end of the match he was on his own and nearest the changing room, so he went off first. I don't know if he realised about the Guard of Honour thing, where the two teams applaud each other. If he didn't he might have gone straight to the changing room. Otherwise, he'd have gone in with the rest of us.'

'And what about number eleven, Terry Cullen? You weren't sure about where he was.'

'Well, to be honest, I never noticed him. But my guess is he'd either be at the front or trying to get to the front, unless he was trying to get up close and personal with Dr Hunter. It's his nature.'

'Well, thank you for your frankness. Now, could you please consider whether anyone else – anyone who was not a member of the team – was near the changing room from the time you last saw Mr Newhouse.'

'After his sending-off I had my eye on the game all the time. I don't think I even glanced in that direction. Sorry.'

'If you do recall having seen anyone else in the vicinity, please let us know straight away. Now, would you read through your statement, and if you're happy with it then use the stylus to sign it directly onto the touch-screen.' Witty knew West Yorkshire Police regarded themselves as being at the cutting edge for using technology – they had recently spent five and a half million pounds on a project to replace paper notebooks with smartphones for four thousand frontline officers to record incidents. He wondered whether they would eventually be the first to claim the introduction of electronic signing of statements. Though he was aware of certain unresolved legal issues surrounding the method, he found its convenience overrode his concerns when it came to taking simple witness statements.

Davies read and signed, and was thanked for his assistance.

Witty waited for Davies to leave the room before asking for the views of all those present. Dunn responded first. 'Cocky young bloke, wasn't he? Totally unphased by having four police officers interviewing him. Ideal mentality for a criminal mastermind. Also he said "to be honest"; I read somewhere that means he was lying.'

Witty invited Plummer for her assessment; she took a more positive view. 'What you call "cocky" is just the way lots of young people are nowadays. He probably went straight from school to university and back to school. He may still have a childlike attitude to life, having never been exposed to the hard, real world. And though some children lie, and others say what they think adults want to hear, I believe he was just telling the truth. Also, I don't think you should try to read too much into the expression "to be honest"; the idea that it always indicates a lie is just, um, …'

Witty offered, "Bollocks?"

Plummer tittered. 'I was going to say "silly".'

Martello offered an observation that followed on from Plummer's perception. 'If he was telling the truth, it looks like Cassidy was the first into the changing room and could be the only member of the team to have the opportunity.'

Witty consolidated her view. 'We should leave Cassidy to the last. Then, if anything else useful comes out of the other interviews, we'll know all we're going to know before we talk to him.'

Turning to Plummer, Witty explained the need for another of the interviews to be postponed. 'The lab has confirmed the little plastic bag that was found in Cullen's clothes contained marijuana, so I think we need to deal with him in more depth. I'll let Miss Oaken know you're wishing to interview everybody except Cassidy and Cullen.'

Witty spoke to Martello, trying to keep that special softness out of his voice. 'We have an appointment to see Mr Newhouse's mother in half an hour.'

As Witty was about to follow Martello out of the office, Dunn directed at him a broad grin and a long wink coordinated with a slow nod of the head. Witty stopped dead in his tracks, and as Martello passed out of earshot he asked, 'Have you something to say?'

Dunn detected a hard edge to Witty's voice, but continued grinning as he explained, 'Our Lily of the Valley and the Twin Peaks was seen dressed up to the nines for you yesterday at the Black Bull. So it's too late to pretend nothing's happening. But good luck to you, I say.'

Witty felt his chivalric blood boiling. 'You will refer to DC Martello with respect from now on, formally. And if I hear any other derogatory remarks I'll be putting in a complaint about you, formally.'

Witty decided he should limit Dunn's involvement in the interviewing, as he had just displayed a lack of capacity for reading not only Davies but also himself. He turned to Plummer who had been observing the exchange closely. 'I expect at least six out of the seven teachers you'll be interviewing will be no more than witnesses, so if they're all treated like suspects we can expect six or seven complaints. You're the ideal officer for this sort of interview so I'd like you to lead them all; let me know straight away if any of them turn up something critical to the inquiry.'

As Witty turned to leave he offered an olive branch to Dunn, putting a hand on his shoulder and smiling while continuing to address Plummer. 'And just make sure Mr Dunn keeps his humorous observations to a minimum.'

As Witty disappeared from view, Dunn vented his spleen to Plummer. 'Who's he think he is? He's only a constable, the same as us. And he's one to talk when it comes to making jokes – he's always trying to be funny. How come it's funny when he says something, but when I say something it's out of order. It wasn't anything I hadn't said before about...' He decided to bite his tongue, metaphorically, '...DC Martello.' He began to run out of words, if not steam. Plummer took the opportunity to make an observation. 'But I think it may be a bit different, now.'

'What do you mean? Have you heard something – is he making Sergeant?'

'Not that reason; the other thing.'

'What other thing?'

'That thing called... love.'

Dunn and Plummer had nothing more to say to each other, so Dunn looked out of the window as Plummer checked the list of interviewees and their initial statements relating to the order the players had returned to the changing room. The statements appeared to be largely consistent, and Plummer was still looking for any anomalies when there was a knock at the door; she asked Dunn to open it. Oaken stayed at the entrance to her office as she introduced the second interviewee. 'This is Mr Rendel from the English department.'

Oaken left at once as Rendel entered the office. Plummer introduced herself and Dunn. Rendel accepted the invitation to sit, with Dunn sitting opposite him and next to Plummer. She riffled through the initial statements and fished out his sheet. 'I see you were probably the last to enter the changing room, but you were not certain. Have you had any further thoughts on whether anyone was behind you?'

'No. I'm fairly certain I was the last.'

Dunn interjected. 'Only "fairly certain"? How certain is "fairly certain"?'

'Well, I don't believe there was anyone behind me.'

Plummer spoke again. 'And you have listed all the other members of the team as having entered the changing room before you. That's nine people – quite a lot to be certain you could see each one of them. How certain are you about having seen them all in front of you?'

'I'm not "certain", but I am convinced they must have been, because they were all there when we discovered Mr Newhouse's body.'

Dunn jumped in again. 'It sounds like you're not at all certain about them having entered just in front of you. All you know is they were there at some point. Could any of them have already been there ahead of all the others?'

'It's possible. I was last in, so they were all already there. They could have gone in at different times. All I know is they were there when I went in.'

Dunn continued to pick holes in Rendel's testimony. 'You say you know they were there when you went in, but before you said you only knew they were there when the body was discovered.'

Dunn stood up and leaned over the desk, jabbing his right index finger in Rendel's direction. 'So why did you list them all as having entered before you when you don't know when they entered?'

Rendel jerked his head away from Dunn, pushing hard at the unyielding chair back. 'I did what Detective Whittington said to do. I told him I wasn't sure and he said to list them all and put down about not being certain.'

Plummer turned to Dunn, putting a restraining hand on his arm, looking him in the eyes and offering a smile. She turned back to Rendel. 'I see in your statement you wrote, "I think I was the last one in, but I'm not certain." So that's really as much as you can reasonably say about the order of entry into the changing room. Thank you. We'll move onto the next question. What happened between Mr Newhouse leaving the field and you entering the changing room? Start with what happened while the match was still being played.'

'I saw Mr Newhouse walk toward the changing room. He stopped to watch the match from the top of the steps at the edge of the playing fields. When he disappeared I assumed he'd gone down the steps. Then the match ended and the rest of us left the field. The school team formed into two lines and we walked between them while they applauded. After that we did the same for them, leading to the top of the steps. Then they walked down the steps and headed off for their changing room. The teachers' team including me followed them down the steps and then went into the girls' changing room.'

Dunn shook off Plummer's hand and walked around the desk to stand close to Rendel. 'You saw Mr Newhouse walk off the field and stop to watch the match. You were supposed to be playing in the match, and we've been told your team was on an all-out attack. How did you find the time to look at Mr Newhouse?'

'Well, I was playing Left Back, so I only ventured as far as the halfway line or maybe a bit further.'

'It sounds to me like you weren't part of the attack at all. You were too busy looking at Mr Newhouse walking and stopping and watching and walking again. It seems like you're claiming to be more interested in Mr Newhouse than the match that everyone else was interested in and that was coming to its climax. Did the rest of your team just ignore you, leaving you to stand around and look in the wrong direction? What if the other team got the ball and attacked your goal?'

'Mr Cassidy stayed back on his goal-line, so it wasn't as though our net was entirely undefended. No, I tell a lie, he eventually came to the edge of the penalty area.'

'So you were watching Mr Newhouse and Mr Cassidy walking about, and ignoring the match itself?'

'No, it wasn't like that. I kept looking around, so I saw Mr Newhouse walking, then I saw him standing still, and then I couldn't see him anymore. And I saw Mr Cassidy standing in his goalmouth, and then I saw him at the edge of the penalty area.'

Dunn leaned over until his face was threateningly close to Rendel's, as he delivered his damning assessment. 'It seems to me, Mr Rendel, that you're not much cop as a football player; you're forever looking around in the wrong direction. If the rest of the team were ignoring you, they wouldn't have seen what you were up to. How do we know you didn't leave the field after Mr Newhouse, and then come back?'

Rendel, trapped in his seat, snapped back. 'Well, I didn't.' He moved his head to one side from where he could see Plummer, pleading with his eyes for her to rescue him.

She responded with a single shake of the head at Dunn followed by a further jerk to her right. When Dunn had followed her instruction and moved away a little, she attempted to calm Rendel, who now had the darting eyes of a cornered, wild animal. 'I'm sure someone would have noticed if you had left the field. And of course it's perfectly understandable for you to have been looking around a bit, so don't worry about what you've just been saying. We were pressing you to check how certain you were of what you saw. Could I just clarify one thing you said? Mr Newhouse stopped to watch the end of the match. So, does that mean when the match ended he was still watching?'

Rendel's eyes settled down and he gazed directly at her so as not to catch a glimpse of Dunn. 'No, I only meant that he stopped for a bit; I saw him watching the match, but I don't know if he saw it to the end. In fact he wasn't there when the two teams did the mutual appreciation thing when the match finished, so he couldn't have stayed watching right until the end.'

'That's much clearer, thank you. And did you see anyone with Mr Newhouse? Or anyone else in the vicinity?'

'No, I'm sure he was on his own.'

'Right, well, that concludes this interview. Thank you Mr

Rendel. We'll write up your statement and you can check it and sign it if you're happy that it's all correct. I think we'll do that later, if it's alright with you.'

'Yes, of course. May I go now?'

'Yes. Thank you again, Mr Rendel, you've been most helpful.'

She stood up and walked around the left side of the desk before accompanying him to the door, as he appeared unwilling to move without an escort.

When Rendel had gone, Plummer closed the door and turned to Dunn. 'Now, that wasn't really the way DC Whittington asked us to do the interviews, was it?'

Dunn frowned. He looked down, tracing his right foot in a circle on the floor, giving a good impression of a naughty schoolboy brought before the Headmaster. 'Well, it's a football match and he's looking all over the place.'

'That may be true, but we're more interested in what happened to Mr Newhouse, aren't we?'

He grudgingly acknowledged this with a curt nod of the head, adding, 'At least he saw Mr Newhouse standing watching the match, so that squeezes down the window of opportunity even further.'

'Yes. There are several minutes before the match ended and a few minutes after the match finished when the incident could have happened, perhaps less than ten minutes in total.'

Plummer hesitated for a moment before addressing Dunn in a more formal tone. 'Your style of interviewing is better suited to a different situation than we have here. I think it would be better if I conducted the other interviews on my own. Is there something you could usefully do at the school? Perhaps sit in the staffroom and listen in on conversations? You might hear something that has a bearing on the case.'

Dunn was unwilling to accept the brush-off. He offered, 'I'll sit quietly and not say a word. If I think of something, I'll get your attention and talk to you about it. Promise.'

'Well, if you're sure you can do that. You can write up the interview notes for them as well; I'll do this one.'

Plummer had written up the notes from Rendel's interview by the time Oaken delivered the next interviewee. 'Mr Finlay is here from the Psychology department.'

Dunn stood silently as Plummer welcomed Finlay into the office. 'Mr Finlay, thank you for coming. I'm Constable Plummer and this is Constable Dunn.'

'You can call me Cameron. Mr Rendel has told everyone in the staffroom how you two operate – the good cop, bad cop routine. Well, it won't work with me. If I don't like what's happening, I'm just standing up and walking straight out of here.'

'I'm sure there'll be no need for that, Cameron; I'm just trying to get the clearest picture I can of exactly what happened yesterday afternoon.'

'While your colleague hovers nearby, threatening me with his silence.'

'Constable Dunn is just about to sit down.' She waited until he complied. 'I'll be conducting this interview on my own, and my colleague will write down your testimony for you to sign. Now, could we begin with the order in which you entered the changing room after the match? You came in with Dr Hunter I believe, followed by Mr Offial and Mr Decker.'

Finlay corrected her pronunciation by example. 'Dr Hunter and Mr Offial…' which he pronounced O'Fial as though an Irish name, '…were together until we reached the door; then I waited for Dr Hunter to enter ahead of me, and Mr Offial entered behind with Mr Decker.'

'Right, good, that's clear. And you saw Mr Collins, Mr Hart and Mr Davies ahead of you.'

'Yes. Mr Hart was directly ahead of Dr Hunter. I think Mr Collins was ahead of Mr Davies, before Mr Hart.'

'And you don't recall where Mr Cassidy, Mr Rendel and Mr Cullen were?'

'Mr Cullen seemed to be talking to someone as we were filing in, and then he disappeared – he'd probably just gone to talk to someone else. Mr Cassidy seemed to be already in the changing room, and I just didn't notice Mr Rendel.'

'Right. And did you notice Mr Newhouse once he had been, um, dismissed from the field of play?'

'I saw him heading for the changing room. He'd gone by the next time I looked in that direction.'

'And how many minutes before the end of the match was that?'

'Maybe five minutes, perhaps a bit less.'

'And did you see anyone else in his vicinity?'

'No.'

'What about after that, just before the match ended: did you notice Mr Verbane, for example?'

'Yes, it's always best to know where the Headmaster is. He was talking with Miss Leveret and Miss Nunn. I saw Ms ...' – he pronounced it "Mzzz" – '... Clifton rushing around the edge of the pitch from the far side, and Miss Oaken rushing from one corner on the same side as Mr Verbane; it looked like they were in a race to be the first to get to him – they were both not quite running, but nearly.'

'Right. And is there anything else you'd like to add, that you think might be relevant to the investigation?'

Finlay hesitated before responding, 'No, not really?'

'But there is something, isn't there, Cameron?'

'Well, Mr Rendel really didn't like your good cop, bad cop routine. Some of my colleagues are saying they want a union rep to be present, or even a solicitor, so you might find there's a bit of a delay while the others organise themselves.'

'I see. You know, we never intended to make Mr Rendel feel uncomfortable. Would you mind asking him to come back in, so that I can apologise to him?'

Finlay confirmed with a repeated nod of the head.

She turned to Dunn. 'Constable Dunn, is there anything you would like to ask Mr Finlay?'

Dunn was determined to maintain his vow of silence, so he shook his head with just the briefest of looks at Plummer before resuming his writing.

Plummer asked Finlay to wait until the statement had been completed. After a couple of minutes Dunn handed the script to Plummer who checked it and passed it to Finlay. 'Please read through this carefully, and if you agree with it, then please sign it at the bottom.' Finlay had reservations about some of the punctuation, but having no objection to the actual wording he signed it and left the office.

After a few minutes Finlay returned with Rendel and then took his leave of Plummer, studiously ignoring Dunn. Plummer invited Rendel into the office. 'I understand you were unhappy with the interview earlier. May I apologise for any discomfort or distress we may have caused you. Our keenness to get to the truth sometimes spills over and may create the impression of undue pressure. May I assure you, that was never our intention.'

Rendel's 'Apology accepted' sounded flat, as though this were a mere formality that had to be completed without sincerity. He was invited to read through his statement from earlier, which he signed before departing without further comment.

As soon as Finlay had left, Miss Oaken arrived with Offial. After introductions, he began, 'I'm not saying anything without a solicitor present.'

Plummer looked concerned and sympathetic. 'Of course you have that right if you're accused of something, though I was just intending to check the details of your brief statement from yesterday. Do you believe you need a solicitor? Is there something you wish to tell us?'

Offial's arms remained folded across his chest. 'I've heard all about your good cop, bad cop routine. There's two of you and only one of me.'

'Would you prefer to be interviewed by just one of us?'

'Just the "good cop"; that would be acceptable.'

Plummer was preparing to ask Offial which of them he would like to conduct the interview, but Dunn had already made the correct interpretation and was heading for the door. 'I'll leave you to it.'

She tried to suppress the relief from resonating in her voice or being displayed on her face. 'Thank you for all your help, Constable Dunn.'

In contrast to the awkward start, the remainder of the interview with Offial proved straightforward and unrevealing; he had observed nothing beyond the order in which the team had filed into the changing room, and was not entirely sure about that.

When Oaken arrived with Collins, Plummer asked them both into the office. 'We're really making great progress this morning, Miss Oaken. I had expected there to be delays as staff were needed for lessons. Your organisation has been truly excellent.'

As Collins was present she was unable to accept the praise personally. 'You can thank Mr Collins for that. We often have teachers who are absent at short notice, so we're very familiar with the idea of having cover teachers take over without much advance warning. This is similar, but not quite the same. I asked Mr Collins if he would organise getting individuals here quickly.' Oaken turned to Collins for further explanation.

'I just set up a system of roving replacements. It's a bit disruptive to lessons, no doubt, but all the teachers from the team were told what would be happening, so they just have to make sure they can do a handover to the cover teacher at short notice. Miss Oaken delivers the cover teacher and borrows the one you can interview next. Your interviews are proving short enough to minimise the disruption, so it's working well all round. I suppose the only extra complication is that it isn't a *bona fide* cover teacher, it's simply whoever's available according to the timetable.'

After Oaken had left, Plummer remarked, 'I'd never thought of teachers as great organisers.'

Collins gave a broad smile. 'And you still shouldn't think of them that way, either. Your average teacher couldn't organise...' he eschewed one of his more colourful analogies, settling for '...a drinking session in a pub. I have a good example from a few months back. I was asked to help with organising and costing out a school trip. For the costs, I put together a spreadsheet. Usual stuff: enter the projected variable costs, add in the fixed expenses, add in a contingency percentage, divide by the number of kids going on the trip, then tell them that's the estimated cost and they'll be refunded afterwards if the contingency fund isn't fully used up. But no, not here; it went to the Headmaster for approval and came back fifty quid higher per child, and no refunds to be considered because that might suggest we're not capable of working things out in advance. I raised it at the next departmental meeting and it was passed forward to the heads of department meeting. Response: they reckoned my calculation was incorrect – something to do with staff numbers and additional expenses. Well, it would only be wrong if they hadn't given me the right information. Anyway, I was told the Geography department would take it from there, so no further action required by me.

'I used to work in industrial chemical production where everything had to be organised to the nth degree, so perhaps I expect too much of schools, but there's a massive gulf between what schools call "organised" and what industry calls "organised".

'To be fair, some of the time schools aren't able to organise things properly because of government policy, though most people are unaware of the issues. I suppose one thing many parents in England do see is the policy on taking children out of school during term time; sixty quid fine for a first offence doubling up to a hundred and twenty if they refuse to pay; and a grand for a second offence.'

'That's higher than the fines courts impose for some quite serious offences.'

'It is high, and it's an extra cost that often falls on those least able to pay. The worst of it is that it could be dealt with to most parents' satisfaction with just a bit of sensible organisation. The government gives schools a bit of flexibility on term dates, leaving them all to micro-manage the issue. What's needed is macro-management, with direction coming down from the government. They could define staggered holidays on a regional basis so that all the schools in a geographical location would have the same holiday dates, and these could be made very different to those in other regions. Taking the country as a whole, school holidays could be spread over several months.

'Maybe schools would have one four-week break and perhaps a shorter one as well, instead of seven weeks together. The first holiday would start just after the last of any exams such as GCSEs. The actual periods could be changed each year so that all regions get a long slot when the weather in this country tends to be at its best. Of course, nowadays, many families go abroad to places where they know the weather will be good, but we should still focus on this country, because that's where the less wealthy tend to stay. At the moment the system penalises poorer families – the ones who can't afford to pay the high prices charged for peak period bookings. And for those who do go abroad it's pointless blaming the tour operators or trying to force them to reduce prices for August holidays – they just respond to supply and demand, like every other business in this country.'

'That's very interesting; it's obviously something you've given a lot of thought to. Anyway, I'm delighted you're here to make these interviews run so smoothly.'

He flashed a brief smile in acknowledgement. 'I heard they haven't been that smooth. Graham Rendel has been inciting rebellion. Frank wanted a solicitor; Bill wants a union rep; and Art won't come without a friend.'

'My colleague was a little over-enthusiastic in his questioning, but I think that's been smoothed over.'

'As in, you've expelled your colleague.'

Plummer reciprocated Collins' huge smile. 'You may think that, Mr Collins; I couldn't possibly comment.'

Collins laughed with the uninhibited vigour of a rugby player after his fifth pint. Plummer thought, 'If I get him any more relaxed, he'll fall over'.

She decided it was time to begin the interview proper. 'Anyway, we need to go through your statement. You listed six people that you're not sure about. That leaves just three that you do know about, plus yourself of course.'

'I suppose it's the way I answered the question. There were people I knew were in front of me or with me, but I wasn't turning around and looking at those who were behind me. Once we were all in the changing room it became obvious who was there, but I couldn't be absolutely definite as to when any of them arrived.'

'That's perfectly understandable. Now, what about from the time that Mr Newhouse left the field until you saw him again?'

'Well, the first thing that happened was the school team took the free kick; one of them whipped it over the wall and another of them headed it into the net. Just like clockwork, tick-tock. From the restart I ignored my position at right back and joined in with the attack. I was on the edge of the penalty area when that little darling Billy Huntsman tackled me like his life depended on it. I stumbled forward, crashed down inside the box and called for a penalty. The referee said no penalty, and I asked him why not. He explained: one, you weren't inside the penalty area when the tackle happened; and two, it wasn't a foul, just a vigorous tackle allowed within the laws of the game.'

Plummer found herself tuning out of this description of the final minutes of the football match, but her antennae were sensitive to a non-PC term Collins had used. 'Little darling? Are you allowed to use that expression?'

'Not to his face, obviously. I was being ironic; Billy's more of a lovable rogue than a little darling. He's really turning out to be a good kid, considering his mother abandoned him.'

Plummer nodded a couple of times before steering the

interview away from any further description of the match. 'Before you go on, could I just say I was really wanting to know about whether you saw Mr Newhouse between his leaving the field and being found in the changing room.'

'I didn't see him after he was sent off; I was focused on the game.'

The remainder of the interview revealed no suspicious sightings, so Plummer concluded it in the usual way.

Oaken arrived with Hart, who looked around the room suspiciously for the alleged "bad cop". On seeing only Plummer, he relaxed visibly as he sat down. Plummer began with the question of order of entry into the changing room, focusing on the one that he was uncertain about – Cullen. 'I'm fairly sure he was there, but I think he must have moved around in the queue because at one point he was near the back, I think, and then he seemed to be near the front, but I could be wrong about that. I'm pretty sure he didn't just queue up like the rest of us.'

The remainder of his testimony was unrevealing, he having noticed nothing and no one beyond the other teachers in the team.

The next arrivals were Hunter and Decker, with no sign of Oaken. Hunter entered ahead of Decker, opening with a very relaxed-looking smile as one without a care in the world. 'Hello,' he began, extending the word in parts until it stretched to four syllables, 'has anyone offered you tea or coffee?'

Plummer showed him her almost empty water bottle. 'A cup of tea would be very welcome.'

'How do you take it?'

'Fairly weak, a little milk, no sugar.'

'Art, would you do the honours? I'll have the same, and don't forget your own.'

As Decker left the room, Hunter switched from his most mellifluous voice to a more business-like version. 'Arthur seems a little nervous about being interviewed on his own, so do you mind if I sit in with him?'

'Do you know of any reason why he might be nervous?'

'I'm sure it's nothing to do with the unfortunate death of Mr Newhouse. May I speak off the record?'

'Anything you say to me is most definitely on the record, Dr

SEND OFF SIR

Hunter, but if it has no relevance to the case and does not relate to criminal activity then it need go no further.'

'Hmmm. What about hypothetically?'

'Hypothetically can work, depending on what it's about.'

'If, hypothetically, someone were attempting to make their name in the field of Street Art by spray-painting, for example, bridges, in an entirely artistic and inoffensive way, having not previously obtained permission from the owners of the said hypothetical bridges, then would you wish to hound them to the ends of the earth, or would you just be happy to know such activity had ceased entirely? Hypothetically.'

'That type of vandalism isn't trivial – the railways alone spend a fortune each year on cleaning paint off bridges. Anyone convicted can expect a significant prison sentence, maybe eighteen months or more. Of course, convictions rely on evidence, and that might be very difficult to come by. So, let me say, in the absence of evidence, if I believed someone no longer indulged in such activity, I'd just be relieved to know that a criminal had mended their ways. After all, there is more joy in heaven over one sinner that repenteth than in ninety-nine who have no need of reformation.'

They were exchanging mutual looks of admiration at the way they had handled a potentially awkward aspect of the investigation, when Decker returned with a silver tray on which were three bone china cups, saucers and plates, and two dishes, all matching in translucent white with gold edges. In the dishes were biscuits of various types: foil wrapped, chocolate coated, bourbons, custard creams, wafers and various plainer types. Plummer looked at Decker with a smile that stayed on her lips until it was reciprocated. 'How very nice; I hope someone isn't trying to bribe me.'

Decker managed to squeeze out a smile, dim by comparison to Plummer's. 'It's all from the reserve store, for honoured guests only.'

Hunter enquired with an apparent innocence, 'Would it be permissible for me to remain while you interview Arthur? I'd like to enjoy this better class of biscuits – we don't see this sort of quality in the staffroom.'

Plummer had already discerned the purpose behind Decker making the tea and ferreting out the biscuits, and was confident

117

Hunter would not feature on the list of serious suspects, so was prepared to proceed with Hunter present for Decker's interview. 'Yes, let's make a start. Now, you were only able to identify two of your colleagues who entered before you, and were unsure about the others. Is that so?'

'That was correct yesterday when I answered the questions that Detective Whittington asked, but since then I've studied the mug shots', he winced at his own words, 'I mean the photographs of members of staff that are displayed outside the staffroom. I can remember the faces of my colleagues well enough to be able to improve my lists considerably.'

'Oh good – please do.'

'There was only one person behind me; that was Mr Rendel. All the others were in front of me, and I'm sure they were all present and correct.'

'Well, that's excellent. Now, could I ask if you saw where Mr Newhouse went after leaving the field?'

'I was doing my bit for the team – I'm not really a footballer but I was getting stuck in – so I didn't look around at all to see where Mr Newhouse was going. I didn't look in his direction at all.'

'So you wouldn't have seen anyone else around the changing rooms, then?'

'No. I just wasn't looking that way.'

'Well, I'll write up your statement, and then, when you've finished on the biscuits, you can check it and sign it.'

Decker now grabbed a biscuit, which disappeared with barely a bite or a swallow. By the time his statement was ready for signing he had managed to consume a further three without giving any impression that he knew he was eating. He signed and made to leave in a single movement, the relief showing in his face and shoulders, a cup still in his left hand.

Hunter let a light smile play on his lips. 'And then there was one. Though I'm intrigued to know why the other two members of the team are not on your list of interviewees. Is that something you can share? I've already worked out where the marijuana came from; is that the reason for one of them?'

'I'm really not permitted to discuss it, Dr Hunter.'

'Do call me Brian. "Doctor" sounds so formal.' He gave a short laugh. 'It's also misleading for half the populace. Someone once called me out of the blue at home about a medical emergency – they lived nearby and knew my name and had looked me up in the phonebook, but I didn't know them from Adam. I had my name taken out of the book after that. I don't think I've had a phonebook since then – I suppose they still do them.'

Plummer showed her appreciation of the anecdote with a short smile. 'Right then, Brian, let's look at the order that people entered the changing room. Is there anything you wish to revise from your earlier listing?'

'No, I'm really quite confident the order is just as I stated previously.'

'You weren't sure about Mr Cullen.'

'Well, I think he was behind me, and then he spoke to me – something about what bad luck we'd had to lose the game – and then I think he went to the front. But I don't know where he was by the time we entered, hence my listing of him as "not sure".'

'So you know he was around there somewhere, it's just his exact position that's uncertain. Moving on, you'll know my next question.'

'Yes. Unfortunately I wasn't looking in the right direction to observe anything relevant to your investigation. But then, you should really be talking to the school team.'

'Why is that, Brian?'

'Well, from the restart after the final goal we were attacking all the time. So we were facing away from John after he'd left the field. The school team were defending, so they were facing the other direction toward the steps and the changing room.'

Plummer felt a hot flush, embarrassed and disappointed at not having realised this earlier. She gulped slightly as she responded, 'Thank you for highlighting that, Brian.'

'Of course, if you're wishing to interview the boys, it'll involve getting the appropriate parental permissions.'

When formalities had been concluded, Hunter departed with the tray of crockery, minus the cup that Decker had already taken, and the dish of biscuits that he left for her on the desk.

Plummer began to collect her papers together, intending to find Dunn and hoping he would not still be in a mood, when there was a knock at the door. Uncertain whether this would be a caller for herself or for Oaken, she offered a tentative, 'Come in.'

Cullen opened the door and walked straight in, resting his knuckles on the desk as he leaned toward her, thrusting his chin forwards. 'I'm Mr Cullen. Why do you not want to interview me? Is it because of the marijuana, or has somebody decided I'm a suspect?' He glared at her as though she must be responsible for his rejection. He lived his angry life imagining himself being repeatedly slighted by anyone taller than himself, which at barely five feet two meant almost all men and most women.

'The marijuana is a complication. I'm following instructions as to whom I should interview.'

Cullen sensed an implied insult. 'Whom? Whom? Are you being especially polite to me for some reason? Was everybody else "Whom"?'

Plummer decided to defuse the bomb before he exploded. 'I could interview you about the football match and what happened after that, if you wish, and then you could be interviewed a second time about the marijuana. How does that sound to you, Mr Cullen?'

It was as though a gale had died in an instant. 'That would be good. Call me Terry.'

She fished out his sheet from the two remaining in the pending file. 'Right, Terry, I have your initial statement here. First of all, you have Mr Cassidy as the only person in front of you as you entered the changing room. You followed with Mr Collins, Mr Davies and Dr Hunter. The other five players were behind you. Did you arrive immediately after Mr Cassidy?'

'I'd just been talking to Dr Hunter, and then I left him behind and went past Mr Davies and then Mr Collins who were walking slower than me. So I thought I was first into the changing room, except that Mr Cassidy was already there. I don't know when he went in, because I didn't see him go in. So I can't say I arrived immediately after him, except in the sense that he was first and I was first of the rest.'

'Well that's clear; and what about the other five? Do you know if they arrived all together?'

'I've no idea. I wasn't looking back.'

'Right. Now, can you tell me what you saw of Mr Newhouse between his leaving the field and you seeing him in the changing room?'

'Nothing at all. I wasn't looking in his direction.'

'So, if I asked about anyone else in his vicinity, you wouldn't know because you weren't looking in that direction.'

'That is correct.'

'Then that's as much help as you can give. I need to complete the details of your statement on this form, and then you can check it and sign it. Would you mind waiting a couple of minutes?'

'Not at all.'

He grew immediately angry with himself for using that expression, with its hidden reference to his lack of height – "Not a Tall". He found the more he tried to avoid that phrase, the more it tended to spill out. By the time his statement was ready for checking and signing, he knew his anger was ready to burst out again. To avoid showing it, he signed the statement and walked out without uttering another word.

Plummer set off for the car park where she discovered Dunn loitering near the squad car; by comparison to Cullen, she thought, Dunn's floods of anger were a relatively mild affliction. She made a valiant attempt at relaxed conversation with him, but he remained stubbornly uncommunicative all the way back to the station.

CHAPTER 11

Cynthia Newhouse talks to Martello

Mrs Newhouse was a divorcée in her mid-fifties, her husband Ken having gone off with a teenage version of her some twenty-five years earlier. He had been a kitchen salesman who had traded on his handsome features and athletic frame to convince many a housewife to "buy the best because that's what you deserve". He had earned sufficient commission to enable him to trade-in each of his latest cars as soon as they showed the least signs of wear and tear. Following the birth of their third child he had applied the same attitude to his wife, who had thought their marriage a happy one up to that point. The irreconcilable difference was that he still retained his good looks and trim body, whereas she had sacrificed hers in the name of motherhood: sagging breasts, stretch marks on her fattened belly, and cellulite on her buttocks and upper legs. Following the divorce, she had been willing to adopt the modern trend for serial monogamy, but with three children in tow the only fish willing to bite were bottom-feeders for whom she had refused to drop her standards. She had grown from being an initially unwilling single mother into a determinedly successful one, the son and both daughters achieving more than she ever had as a wages clerk at a local engineering works.

Mrs Newhouse lived on the outskirts of Chesterfield, where the roads had not yet suffered an invasion of white and yellow lines that restricted parking to designated bays. Witty and Martello parked close to the semi-detached, three-bedroomed house, and were invited into the kitchen. The eggshell blue units trimmed with white edges and handles had been "top of the range" when fitted twenty-six years earlier. Since then, the tall breakfast bar had been replaced with an incongruous though more attractive solid oak refectory table that had now seen active service in the early development of first an accountant and then a solicitor, her daughters. The table looked capable of serving for another century, whereas the "top of the range" units looked jaded, with an assortment of ills from fascia damage to broken handles. Mrs Newhouse explained her preference for sitting in the kitchen. 'This is the warmest room; I use it all the time. We can go into the living room if you like, but the thermostat has been turned down on the radiator in there and it'll take a while to warm up.'

Witty and Martello exchanged glances before he answered. 'It's fine in here. We're sorry to have to meet you under these circumstances.' Mrs Newhouse subconsciously thought she had seen something extra in those glances that she had not experienced herself in decades, but the impression was too fleeting to take root.

Yesterday her daughter Susan had been breathing fire and brimstone down the phone to her, angry at their loss and angry that the police had not informed them properly – a phone call rather than a visit, and lack of a Family Liaison Officer. Mrs Newhouse had listened to instructions on how to make a formal complain about their treatment at the hands of the police, and had agreed to do so at her insistence, even though she had recognised the driving force behind the bitter façade was sisterly love. Now that she was meeting with the police officers she reneged on the agreement and presented a placid demeanour, offering them the choice of tea or coffee. She was having tea, so they accepted the same.

Mrs Newhouse quietly asked why Detective Castleton had telephoned her yesterday and not called on her in person, having been advised later by her daughter that it would have been the normal way. She also questioned why no one needed her permission for the autopsy to take place. Martello and Witty were torn between undermining Castleton and protecting the public image of the police. Witty responded, 'The coroner makes the decision about whether an autopsy is necessary, though people can ask for a body scan rather than a physical post-mortem. That's normally only for religious reasons, and even then it can still be necessary to follow up with the invasive type. Was Mr Castleton just calling to obtain your agreement for the type of autopsy?' Mrs Newhouse looked doubtful but confirmed that may have been the main reason. Witty suggested, 'Perhaps there was a communication error. Maybe he thought someone else had already spoken to you – Mr Verbane perhaps, from the school?' Mrs Newhouse confirmed she had already been informed by Verbane when Castleton had called. Witty apologised on behalf of the police, though left the suggestion hanging in the air that the reason which lay behind it was that Verbane had already broken the news and so they would have been too late to follow normal procedure.

Witty continued, 'John had an injury to his head that the pathologist wished to examine straight away so he could obtain the clearest possible picture of it. For that reason he dealt with John as a matter of the highest importance and urgency and he completed the autopsy in the evening, rather than leaving it to normal working hours the next day. He established that the cause of death was from John's head making contact with a hard metal object, a coat hook that was fitted to a wooden board which was firmly attached to the wall. We believe the contact was not accidental.'

Mrs Newhouse's calmness broke with this revelation. Her voice increased in pitch and intensity as she asked, 'You mean he was murdered?'

Witty knew he needed to downplay the seriousness of the offence, at least for now, without undermining the seriousness of its consequence. 'We're doing everything we can to establish exactly what happened so we can form a view of the underlying offence. We're treating the case with all the seriousness of a murder inquiry, though it may turn out to be something less than that in the end.'

Witty explained there was no need for formal identification of the body as the Headmaster had already completed that procedure. He asked if she would like to view the body, explaining there was no need for the police to be present, but that they would take her there if she wished. She asked 'Do people usually wish to see the body?'

Witty gave an answer that enabled her to feel free to decide for herself whether or not to view. 'There really isn't any such thing as "usually", Mrs Newhouse. It's different for everybody, though if a body has been affected, say, by a road accident, then it can be better not to look.' Turning to Martello he asked, 'Would you say the body looked nice enough not to upset Mrs Newhouse just by looking at it?'

Martello had not admitted to Witty that she had avoided looking at the body in the autopsy room. She responded to Mrs Newhouse, 'You don't need to look if you don't wish to; it was a head injury, after all.'

Witty was confident the head would have been made

presentable for viewings, as the damage was all to the back; he therefore put forward the counter-argument. 'On the other hand, it can be a way of saying goodbye.'

Witty's words struck a chord with Mrs Newhouse. 'I think I would like to see John's body.'

Witty and Martello took Mrs Newhouse to the medico-legal centre where the staff showed all due consideration to the bereaved, their capacity to empathise having been reinforced over time rather than eroded by repetition. One of the staff pulled back the sheet that covered the body, not only revealing the head but also a little more of the upper torso than might have been entirely decent had the deceased been female. Mrs Newhouse gazed in silence at her dead son; Martello felt moved by her calmness and composure, wondering why she had never previously experienced the same degree of empathy for others who had suffered a loss. After the body had been re-covered by the sheet, Martello accompanied Mrs Newhouse back to the car.

Witty had expected to see an incision from the neck down to the pubis, rather than the deep Y known to be favoured in the US; he was therefore surprised to see neither, but instead a Y that was almost horizontal at the top. He stayed behind to talk to the mortuary attendant, asking about the shape of the incision to the upper torso. The attendant explained that the single line method could destroy evidence relating to injuries to the throat such as damage to the hyoid bone that would indicate strangulation, whereas the deep Y is used in the US for cosmetic reasons where the body may be displayed in an open casket. Witty made a mental note to check the autopsy report for any injury to the neck area.

On returning to the car he found Martello sitting in the back with Mrs Newhouse, where she was engaging her in gentle conversation about her other children. He drove to Chesterfield without being invited to join in with their chat. As he parked outside the house and stepped out smartly to open the door for Mrs Newhouse, he wondered if a chauffeur's cap would suit him. Martello climbed out at the other side without waiting for the same courtesy that he was hoping also to give to her.

When they re-entered her home Mrs Newhouse offered them another cup of tea, adding, 'I suppose you're probably too busy with the investigation to stay for long.'

Witty pondered on the correct response to this question: to stay might suggest they were not putting their energies into the investigation; to leave might indicate they were uncaring as to her welfare. Witty asked Mrs Newhouse to give him a moment to confer with his colleague, which they did in the hallway. Witty began, 'I'm concerned she's too calm. She's lost her only son, and yet she's dealing with everything without appearing upset – she may be bottling it up. I think she may need counselling but I don't think she'll recognise that just yet. What do you think?'

'Castleton hasn't arranged for a FLO and I'm not going to mention it to him. I'll give her the list of grief counsellors – though I'm not convinced it's as good to speak to a stranger on the phone as to talk to someone face-to-face. I think she should have a WPC with her for a while; Linda would be ideal but she'll be busy at the school for ages yet. I'm out of favour with Castleton so I'd be happy to stay away from the office. We need to get some background info on her son anyway so leave me here and I'll keep her company. I'll give you a call when I need picking up.'

They returned to the kitchen and Martello re-started the conversation. 'Would it be convenient for you if I stayed and asked you some questions about John? We need to collect as much background information as we can in case it has a bearing on the investigation.'

'Yes, I've no plans to do anything today. I don't feel like doing anything, anyway, so you stay and ask your questions.'

'Good, thank you. And will you call me Lily?'

'Right, Lily, and I'm Cynthia.'

Witty took his leave of them and headed back to the station.

Lily asked questions about John, and Cynthia answered them, more in the style of two friends on first name terms than a police officer and a bereaved mother; in order to create the right impression Martello made copious notes on everything that was said. Cynthia gave a potted history of John from his first day at school through his athletic successes as a teenager and then his attendance at a college that was now classed as a university. Martello believed Cynthia was finding the process cathartic as she appeared to relax while she recounted John's achievements. Cynthia's words dried up when the biography reached his joining the teaching staff at Midshaw School. Martello recognised this was the very part of the life history that could be the most relevant, so she pressed her to continue.

'I have John's date of birth as the eleventh of September 1987. He joined the school straight from college, so he'd been teaching there for several years. Could you give me the names of the people at school who were closest to him during those years, especially those who are still there now?'

'John was a very nice young man, so I'm sure he had a lot of mates, but I don't know of anyone in particular. If you ask at the school I'm certain they'd say he was ever so popular. Maybe more so with the women, I'd guess; he'd have got that from his father, of course.'

'Do you know of any women friends he had at school or elsewhere?'

'He had a girlfriend from college, but they split up soon after John started teaching; they seemed to be heading for something permanent, then suddenly it was all over between them. John never said what had happened. After that, whenever I asked about girlfriends, he was a bit cagey. I suppose it was so he wouldn't be embarrassed if they didn't come to anything. Then a couple of months ago he mentioned he was seeing a woman called Jane, another teacher at the school. I'm sorry, I don't recall her surname. Anyway, they even visited me here a couple of times, so I thought it was serious between them. But then a friend of mine told me, at the Bingo, what she'd heard from somebody else: he'd been seen with a foreign woman at a pub that's miles away from here. She'd said she knew the woman was foreign because she had a funny accent. I said maybe it wasn't John, but she said the other woman was certain it was him.'

After a moment's pause, Cynthia continued. 'I see you're looking down your nose at Bingo, but it's somewhere where women can just sit and chat. There are some men who go, but they're really only there under sufferance.'

Martello was unsure what look she had given that had triggered Cynthia's response to it. She knew she had recently found herself imagining how a life without a man might feel. She thought it could be very lonely, and wondered how Cynthia had handled decades of the same.

'I'm sorry, Cynthia, I didn't mean to give that impression. I was just wondering about myself, and what life will be like for me in the future.'

Cynthia gave a fulsome laugh that belied the feeling of loss she was suffering. 'With your looks you'll not have to worry about that, luv.'

'Looks don't last forever, and beauty's only skin deep.'

'That's just a lie put about by ugly people.'

Martello returned the laugh before quickly coming back to the questions about John Newhouse. 'Do you know anything more about the foreign woman?'

'She told me she looked quite a bit older than John, but that's all she knew. It was probably just some friend, not a girlfriend.'

Martello returned the focus to anyone who would not have appeared out of place near the girls' changing room. 'Do you know of anyone else from the school?'

'No – only Jane. I think I can remember her surname, now; it was something like Leatherette; no, Leveret.'

Martello felt her questioning was running on empty and was just about to go down the "hobbies and other pastimes" route when the doorbell rang. Cynthia stood up, saying to Martello almost as though she were asking permission, 'I'll see who that is.'

Martello heard Cynthia say, in a clearly audible whisper more suited to the theatre, 'It's a police woman.'

First into the kitchen came a woman of about thirty, dressed in a white blouse and black pinstripe jacket with matching skirt. She spoke in an abrupt style, the words shooting out a little too quickly, with the gap between the sentences almost non-existent. 'I'm Janet Henshaw, John's sister. I hope you're not upsetting my mother.'

Cynthia followed her in, quickly apologising to Martello indirectly by addressing her daughter: 'Lily and I have been talking about John. She's been very kind, so you've no reason to be sharp with her.'

'Well, I'm here now, so the police officer can go. We need to sort out the funeral.'

Martello addressed Cynthia, offering her an easy way out. 'I didn't have any more questions, so I'll be on my way unless there's anything you'd like to ask me now.'

'No, I can't think of anything, Lily, but I've got your details if I think of something later. It's been very nice talking to you.'

Martello exited the house, leaving Cynthia to the tender mercies of her daughter. She phoned Witty to let him know she was setting off; he told her he would drive over straight away and pick her up.

CHAPTER 12

Dunn Interviews a Schoolboy

In the afternoon, Witty, Martello and Plummer reviewed and discussed the statements that had been collected. They agreed Cassidy may have had the opportunity to kill Newhouse. They also did not entirely discount Cullen, as he seemed to have disappeared off people's radar for a short time. Witty went to see Castleton to give him the team's collective assessment of the current state of the case. Castleton considered what was needed next.

'Cassidy is the main suspect, but let's clear up this Cullen question first. He needs to be interviewed about the weed; it doesn't look like Dunn's been given much work to do, so send him back to the school to interview him about it. Then we'll pick up the thread in the morning.'

Witty knew better than to dispute the choice of Dunn for the interview; he believed Castleton often favoured Dunn as someone made in his own image.

Dunn arrived unannounced at the school and asked for Verbane, looking slightly annoyed to be redirected to Oaken. He told her he wished to interview Cullen. The last lesson of the day was about to finish, so she left Dunn in her office and hurried to Cullen's classroom where she stood outside the door, peering in through the narrow vertical glass panel; he was organising his class to leave in rows, the sequence being determined by his arbitrary assessment of perceived behaviour during the lesson. As the last of the Year Eights left the room, she stepped inside and informed him that Constable Dunn was waiting in her office to interview him. She picked up one of his two bags that were brim-full of exercise books, and followed him to the staffroom where they deposited them in his large pigeonhole. As they walked to her office she explained how Hunter had felt obliged to inform her about the marijuana. Cullen smiled mirthlessly. 'I can explain all that; it wasn't mine.'

Oaken responded, 'The school will back you if the police try to make something out of nothing.' She delivered him to her office and closed the door behind her.

After introductions, Dunn began, 'I'm here to interview you about the Class B drug you had in your pocket when your clothes were searched at the crime scene yesterday.'

Cullen had recognised the futility of denying possession, though believed he had a sufficient defence prepared. 'It was in my pocket, but it wasn't mine.'

'So, you're admitting possession, but denying it was yours.'

Cullen's first thought was that Dunn must be some sort of moron simply to play back what he had said, changing the words but not the meaning; he immediately censured himself for thinking the non-PC word "moron". His second interpretation was that it was a ploy to lead him into a false sense of security. Then he decided the words "admitting possession" were subtly different, and that Dunn was trying to get him to declare himself guilty; he determined to be wary of everything Dunn said from hereon. 'If, by saying "admitting possession", you are saying I am admitting to a criminal offence, then, no, I am not admitting possession in the legal sense, only that it was in my pocket.' Cullen sat back with a relaxed smile, pleased with his response.

With just a hint of annoyance Dunn asked the key question. 'Well, if it wasn't yours, whose was it then?'

'I can't tell you that.'

'Do you mean you can't tell me because you don't know, or you can't tell me because you are choosing not to tell me?'

'I promised to keep it a secret.'

Dunn's voice shot up to a shout just short of a scream. 'What do you mean, you "promised"? This isn't the Boy Scouts, there isn't a "keeping secrets" badge; it's the police you're talking to.' Dunn realised he may have been too quick at letting his anger show itself. 'I apologise, Mr Cullen, but I'm sure you appreciate the death of your colleague means the investigation of all related matters takes on an added seriousness.'

'But this isn't related to the death of Mr Newhouse. It's just a coincidence that it happened on the same day.'

Dunn responded sagely, with a steady voice as though reciting a given truth. 'Things that people imagine are coincidences often turn out not to be.'

'Well, this was definitely a coincidence.'

'If you tell me how it came to be in your possession, then I can investigate and decide whether I agree with you.'

'I can tell you how I came to have it in my pocket.'

'Please go ahead then.'

'Mr Collins came out of the boys' loos with three students and told me he'd caught them smoking a cigarette that wasn't tobacco. He took them off to the Head's office. I poked my head around the corner and there was a student holding up a little bag of stuff. And that's the bag that was in my pocket.'

'Could you fill in the gap, please. What happened between you seeing the boy holding the bag, and the bag ending up in your pocket.'

Cullen paused for a moment as though getting the story straight in his head. 'He said it wasn't his and that he was just holding it for a friend.'

'Did he say which friend?'

'No, but I guessed it must have been one of the three boys who'd just left with Mr Collins.'

'Well, if I'm to be able to check out your story, I need to know the name of the boy.'

Again Cullen paused before responding. 'I promised him I wouldn't tell. It would damage his trust in adults and in teachers in particular if I told you his name and he found out.'

'I believe you already know my attitude to your keeping it secret.'

'Journalists don't have to disclose their sources. Catholic Priests don't repeat what they've heard in Confession. I believe the same should apply to teachers.'

'Well, Mr Cullen, I can tell you it doesn't.' A hint of anger crept back into his voice. 'So just tell me his name.'

Cullen remained unprepared to release it. 'There's no point in giving you his name, as he'd probably just deny it now that he hasn't got the stuff anymore.'

Dunn looked like thunder as he jabbed a finger in Cullen's direction. 'That's a problem for me to deal with, not you. Now, what's his name?'

Cullen capitulated. 'Billy Huntsman.'

Dunn was in a hurry to get onto the trail of Billy Huntsman, so he wrapped up the interview as quickly as possible, obtaining Cullen's signature on the statement so that there could be no back-tracking.

Dunn found Oaken and asked her about interviewing the boy. She took him to Verbane via the school office where she obtained Billy's file. Dunn filled in the background to his reason for wishing to interview Billy. Verbane looked up from Billy's school record. 'Billy is now eighteen years old, so I understand it's not essential for him to have a parent or guardian present. But the school has a duty of care. I suggest I telephone his home and check what their attitude is to his being interviewed. If no one there wishes to be present at the interview then Miss Oaken and I would offer ourselves to act *in loco parentis*. Actually, Billy lives in a children's home, so the people there are already acting in that capacity.' He looked genuinely troubled as he added, 'I don't know what the Latin is for what our capacity would be in that case.'

Dunn sighed inwardly as he turned to the practicalities. 'Please make the call, Headmaster.' Dunn and Oaken remained seated while the call was made. 'They gave their permission for the interview to take place without anyone from the home being present; I assume it will be tomorrow.'

Oaken interjected. 'Actually, Headmaster, it could be today. Billy is still at school – he does things here every day after lessons have finished. Today it's football practice.'

Billy was none too pleased to be brought from the playing field into the Headmaster's office. The Headmaster was none too pleased to have a boy in muddy kit sitting on one of his clean chairs, but it was too late now to withdraw his offer. Dunn began, 'Mr Cullen told me he found you in possession of a small bag of marijuana.'

Billy's one-word answer stopped Dunn in his tracks. 'No.'

Verbane intervened. 'No, what, Billy?'

'No, sir.'

'No, what I meant was, are you saying no to what Mr Cullen said, or no to having the bag of marijuana?'

Billy blinked rapidly, having no idea how he was supposed to answer this latest conundrum.

Dunn reclaimed his right to ask the questions. 'Did you have a bag or marijuana?'

'No, sir.'

'Why do you think Mr Cullen said you did?'

'He must have been mistaken, sir. It must have been someone who looked like me.' Billy's aim for sincerity and innocence was clearly reflected in his "Angels with Dirty Faces" expression.

Dunn decided this interview was not going to achieve anything. 'I'll need to speak to Mr Cullen again to check how certain he is that the boy with the bag of marijuana was in fact Billy.'

Cullen had left for the day so Dunn returned to the station to brief Witty on the outcome of the interviews with Cullen and Billy. Witty informed Castleton, who instructed him to put the marijuana question aside for now and focus on the main case.

As there was little more they could achieve that day, Witty and Martello finished at their usual times and left the station separately in their own cars, Witty even turning to the right as he exited the car park as though going to his wife's house, rather than taking a left to Hope. He stopped to pick up a local newspaper, something he rarely did nowadays. When he reached the flat, Lily was already consulting a recipe book and deciding what to cook for them that evening. Neil noticed the book, thinking how strange it was to see Lily in a domestic setting; she saw him looking and gave up the pretence with a loud laugh that was edging toward a squeal. With a nod from Neil in the direction of the bedroom they put aside all thoughts of food.

It was more than an hour later when they came out of the bedroom. As Neil admitted to feeling hungry, Lily returned to her one and only cookery book; she found a recipe with a long list of ingredients, a few of which she had available. The pasta with unidentifiable sauce was a disaster in culinary terms; he congratulated her on the excellent and unusual meal.

He picked up his newspaper, the Shawton News. 'There's a lengthy article on an inside page about the death at the school. It begins, "In a dreadful accident the sports master Edward Newhouse was fatally injured when he slipped and fell onto a metal hook in the changing room." It then asks, "How safe are our schools?" It goes on at length about the need for a safer environment for our children to grow up in, and how this government is responsible because of the cutting back of school maintenance budgets in real terms by directing resources to new schools, and that the responsibility for all this lies at the very top. So, I guess that's it then: case closed. We'll arrest the Prime Minister in the morning.' Lily laughed a little too early because she knew there was a joke coming, as Neil always said funny things. She settled in for a comfortable evening.

* * *

In a small, isolated cottage off a single track road that was no more than a wide path between Bonsall and nowhere since the Romans stopped mining for lead, Michael Gough consulted a recipe book and prepared a healthy, nutritious meal full of flavour. The food was barely noticed by his life partner who was reading an article in the Shawton News about the death of someone they named as Edward Newhouse, and was wondering why everyone on the football team had been interviewed except himself.

CHAPTER 13

Witty on the Assisted Dying Bill Debate

Friday

Witty arrived early at the station to find Castleton was already ensconced in his office and awaiting his presence.

'Enter.'

'You asked to see me straight away, sir.'

'You know what rumours are like in this office. Is it true?'

Witty knew better than to offer an explanation about something when the question had been unspecific.

'Is what true, sir?'

'Don't mess about with me, DC Whittington. You and DC Martello.'

'I believe we work well together, sir.'

Castleton knew he would have to push Witty with a direct question.

'Is it true that you have left your wife and are now shacked up with DC Martello?'

'It is true that I'm no longer living with my wife, sir. My colleague has kindly agreed to give me accommodation until the position becomes clearer *vis-à-vis* my wife.'

Castleton's hormones made him wish to believe this line from Witty, though his mind was telling him it was a lie. He tried for the avuncular approach, offering in a softened tone something that was meant to appear as helpful advice. 'Leaving your wife is a big step, Neil, and you have a disabled child to consider. I'm giving you the rest of the day off, to sort yourself out. Go and talk to Theresa, see if you can't patch things up between the two of you. If you don't, you might regret it for the rest of your life. I've known so many officers who have not only ruined their marriages but also their careers, giving everyone a low impression of them by leaving their family just because not everything was perfect.'

'I'll try and sort things out straight away, sir.'

'And don't worry about the case. DI Priestley will be back after the weekend, so it's just a matter of holding the fort for today. I'll organise everything myself.'

Witty left the station at once. He drove half a mile and stopped to phone Martello, who was still at home, and gave her an almost word-for-word replay of his interview with Castleton. He added his assessment. 'It was a pathetic attempt to blackmail me into giving him the chance to get back with you.'

'Neil, it isn't ideal to be having to say this over the phone instead of face-to-face ...' Neil's heart was suddenly pounding; he felt his hearing become acute as it sought to overcome the noise of the blood that was coursing loudly through his ears. He was dreading what would come next; '... but he never was "with" me. I've never let him even touch me. I played every meeting with him as though it was just colleagues getting together.'

Neil exhaled, recognising he must have stopped breathing without realising. 'I would never have asked you, Lily, but I'm glad you've told me.'

'So, what are you going to do with your day off?' It was Lily's turn to feel like life was suspended pending his response to her seemingly innocuous question.

'I'm going to do what he said ...' – Lily shuddered – '... and sort out all my things, and move in with you properly. Is that alright?'

For a moment Lily was flushed with anger at Neil for having given her a fright by choosing his words so carelessly – for not thinking in terms of what she would be hearing. Nevertheless she withheld her complaint and rushed to confirm her agreement. 'The sooner the better, Neil; there's no turning back now.'

The conversation continued with expressions of endearment, neither of them wishing to terminate the call. Lily finally broke the spell. 'I need to be going. It wouldn't do for me to be late for work, especially not now.'

Neil drove to what he already thought of as his old home. There would be no avoiding having that final argument with Theresa before she left for her five hour shift at the local hospital where she worked as a nurse. After the birth of Ollie she had been unable to cope with working. Then, as care provisions were put in place, she was re-employed by the hospital to work "key time", eleven thirty to two o'clock to cover for staff lunchtimes. Soon after, she was able to extend her contracted hours and now worked from ten o'clock to three every day from Monday to Friday. The staff in her department dealt only with patients who attended by appointment, so the problem of the NHS discouraging people from being ill at weekends was irrelevant to them.

Witty parked his car on the driveway. He thought about how to begin, having so far only told her that he was moving out. He could see no easy way of explaining the situation without being entirely direct. He thought of many police officers who would struggle to play that rôle, the concept of honest dealing having been extracted from them over the years like poison. It was as though they had been contaminated by contact with criminals who could be relied on to lie, and consequently they preferred lying to honesty even when dealing with upright citizens; one of the downsides to being in the police force, he reflected.

Though he had his house keys, he rang the doorbell. Ollie had been collected earlier by the social services minibus, so Theresa was alone. She came to the door wearing her neutral face, and began, 'Have you lost your keys?'

He wondered if this was an attempt to suggest he belonged there and should be using his own keys. He reconsidered this, deciding she meant no more and no less than she had said. He spoke quietly through lips that barely moved in his stone-hard face. 'We need to talk.'

They went into the living room and sat down, she on the settee, he on a visitors' chair. She waited for him to speak.

'I'm moving out altogether. I'm not living this lie any longer.'

'What lie is that?'

'Our marriage. We're not married. Not really.'

'Yes, we are. We're married forever. As a Catholic that's what marriage means to me. You knew that when we got married.'

'I didn't know everything, though, did I? You never told me about the problem we could expect if we had children.'

She replied in an even tone, as though they were discussing something mundane, or she were reading aloud an extract from an article in a women's magazine. 'All couples might have children with special problems. We're no different to anyone else.'

He felt a rage coursing through his veins; he had never in his life struck her, but he wished he could right now. He hated her unthinking stupidity, the way she replayed as though in religious incantation the statements offered up by others in different contexts, those words thereby acquiring a status beyond all questioning – like those of her Pope.

'There's a world of difference between being the one in a thousand whose child has some serious illness or other, and the certainty that you knew about but didn't choose to share with me. I thought marriage was about sharing.' He regretted having let his argument descend to her level with this women's magazine-style expression.

'We share the responsibility for any children we have together.'

'That child is your responsibility. If I had known, I'd never have agreed to have a child with you.'

'I have as much right as anyone to have children.'

There it goes, he thought, that same self-centred, ill-conceived argument put about by those who are happy to inflict their illnesses on the unconceived for the sake of their own gratification. He spoke through gritted teeth, 'That's a matter of opinion.'

She snapped back immediately, 'No it isn't.'

He sighed inwardly as his attempt to have a reasoned argument had descended into mere contradiction. 'Well, not everybody thinks like you do. But whatever you think, I'm not living this lie any longer. I'm going to divorce you, whether you like it or not.'

'Have you found someone else, then?'

He was screaming inside his head. The pitch and volume of his voice rose considerably as he fought to keep himself sounding in control. 'You just don't listen. I'm leaving you because I'm leaving you, not because I've found someone else.'

'So you have found someone else.'

'Christ, don't you listen to anything? This is all about you – I thought you liked being the centre of attention.' He knew it was a cheap shot, but in this mismatched bout he had to score any way he could.

'I thought you were saying it was all about Ollie.'

The counter-punch was below the belt, but with no umpire to adjudicate he just had to wince and bear it. 'I'm not discussing this anymore. I'm moving all my stuff today, and I'm going to talk to a solicitor to start divorce proceedings. My boss has given me the day off to sort things out, so that's what I'm going to do.'

He despised himself for giving into lying when he had been so determined to hold the moral high ground. Castleton's words may have been compatible with what he had just said, but his meaning certainly was not. He retreated to his bedroom – the small one that had once been called the box room. He began packing by collecting various items of clothing and squashing them tightly into his suitcase, half of a "his 'n' hers" pair that had had only one holiday together. He waited for the sound of her leaving via the front door before beginning the process of excising himself from the house. He told himself he also would leave through the front door, proudly and with his head held high, though he knew he would have all the sincerity of a defeated mining union man processing to the pit-head and claiming a non-existent victory about mine closures.

In his room Neil sought a portfolio that he had kept hidden from his wife – he knew she would have destroyed it if she found it. He extracted it carefully from underneath the centre of the mattress and began to turn the pages, quickly locating the most closely scrutinised section.

Friday 18 July 2014 Assisted Dying Bill
Debate in the House of Lords – second reading

Neil looked through the copious notes he had made from the television broadcasts. He had subsequently printed the entire debate from Hansard to check against his notes, and then researched each speaker's background. He knew she thought it was obsessive behaviour, yet it was the subject that dominated his life. The first of the hundred and twenty-five speakers was Lord Falconer of Thoroton, the introducer of the Bill. The last was Lord Beecham, not counting Lord Faulks who played a procedural rôle, and Lord Falconer who spoke for a second time to close the debate.

Neil noted Lord Faulks had reminded the House that the Bill related to "*assisted suicide for mentally competent terminally ill adults who are reasonably expected to die within six months.*" Neil had followed the debate closely in the hope that the provisions might be extended so that someone without mental capacity could have the decision made for them, and that the arbitrary time limit of six months would be replaced with an indeterminate period. He had been disappointed to find that the speeches referring to moves in that direction were largely made in the context of "thin end of the wedge" concerns, speakers arguing against the current Bill for fear of future changes in the law building on it to expand the scope. He had found it ironic, as it was that very expansion he hoped for.

He had noted "For" or "Against" next to each speaker, though he felt some of those "Against" had attempted to mask their eventual voting intentions. In the "For" category he had noted with an asterisk those speakers who appeared to be the most incisive or persuasive in their arguments, with a view to writing to them about his own situation in the hope they would support his cause. He was disappointed in himself that he had never actually contacted any of them; or was it because he wished to avoid making his views public, in case he decided for himself that Ollie had a right to die and he should be the one to deliver the *coup de grâce*?

He read to himself some of the asterisked "For" entries.

Baroness Jay of Paddington – clear, focused, and may well be the type of person to make things happen.

Lord Avebury – recognises compassion overrules the Buddhist principle of inviolability of human life.

Lord Blair of Boughton – specifically states the Bill excludes those without mental capacity or who are disabled. As an ex-policeman just maybe he would sympathise with my situation and support a broadening of the Bill, or perhaps extend the scope with a subsequent Bill. He seems to appreciate how unnecessary and unpleasant a task it is for the police to investigate people under the current law when relatives kill themselves.

Lord Baker of Dorking – highlights how the speaker who preceded him, Baroness Campbell of Surbiton, does not speak for all disabled people. He explains how juries ignore the letter of the law and make decisions on humanitarian values. Could I be sure that would happen if I took the law into my own hands?

Viscount Craigavon – objects to the suggestion that we should take comfort in suffering as though it were a virtue, and disagrees with those who wish to inflict their views on others. He highlights the courageous examples of Tony Nicklinson and Paul Lamb, even though their cases are outside the terms of the Bill. Does that mean he would be supportive of an increase in the scope of the Bill?

Baroness Tonge – supports the Bill with reasoned arguments about choice. Additional note dated six days later: cross her off the list of people to write to – she lost her credibility when speaking on TV apparently in favour of people in Gaza lobbing rockets at Israeli civilians.

Baroness Warnock – makes it clear the law needs to be changed. Recognises how self-sacrifice is a virtue. Brilliantly incisive – she should be cloned for the benefit of future generations!

Baroness Richardson of Calow – really gets to the heart of the matter and sees things in a practical way; so unexpected after she'd explained she's an ordained Minister of the Methodist Church. If the Methodists had a pope, she should be it!

Lord Davies of Stamford – said too much relevant stuff to précis – see full speech. Fantastic speaker – crammed masses of content into his slot without any apparent need for notes. He changed from Conservative to Labour – the House of Lords could do with more like him.

Lord Carey of Clifton – used to be the Archbishop of Canterbury. What courage to stand up and say he's changed his mind on Assisted Dying. Quite a contrast to those Lords Spiritual who preferred to maintain suffering.

Lord Brown of Eaton-under-Heywood – recognises that many people are unhappy with the law as it stands. He refers to the peril of people losing respect for the law – just one of many astute observations. (I think there's little enough respect for the law nowadays, and for police officers in particular.)

Baroness Murphy – "one of those members of the medical profession who would be proud to be associated with the Bill." Too good to précis – see full speech. And she was a practising psychiatrist. (cf. Viscount Colville of Culross.)

Lord Graham of Edmonton – gave us a good laugh. His style could be more persuasive than people who rely on facts and statistics to try to win arguments.

Lord Harrison – another humorous speech. He made the point that palliative care isn't sufficient for some. Also, if the Bill fails, "the public will feel cheated yet again by politicians."

Baroness Young of Old Scone – corrects the noble Baroness,

Lady Campbell. "*The Bill is not about pity; it is about power – the power of being in control of one's own death.*" *Would she support the idea of someone in authority, say, the Official Solicitor, acting on someone's behalf if they were unable to claim that power themselves?*

Lord Rees of Ludlow – for forty years he was a colleague of Professor Stephen Hawking. As eloquent and scientifically precise as Lord Rees is, it's Stephen Hawking that people listen to and take notice of. If Professor Hawking is in favour of Assisted Dying, that trumps all the disabled opponents put together. But then, arguments about the right of brilliant minds to make their own choices is the very opposite of Ollie's case.

Lord Finkelstein – in favour of people's right to make their own decisions, even if other people don't think their reasons are good ones. He makes persuasive arguments in favour of individuals rather than the state making decisions, but that doesn't actually help my case – I could do with a system that allows someone acting on behalf of the state to make such decisions for the mentally incompetent. He specifically states, "*The law should not allow anybody to tell anybody else how to die.*" *Does he see that as an absolute?*

Lord Kerr of Kinlochard – suggests Lady Grey-Thompson is not being quite fair when she asks Lord Falconer to quantify the precise number of cases to be expected if the law is changed. I'd have said it's totally disingenuous to demand to know the unknowable. "*The status quo – with respect to the noble Lord, Lord Phillips – is a mess.*" *Too right!*

Lord Low of Dalston – "*The Bill arouses strong passions, but it behoves us to approach it in as dispassionate a manner as we can.*" *If there isn't enough visible passion, people can misinterpret disinterest as indicating lack of interest.* "*One woman told me her dog had had a better death than her mother; another said her grandmother died under harrowing circumstances, palliative care having proved entirely inadequate.*" *I get the impression he would have sympathy with Ollie's condition, but would he support his right to die? He refers to his postbag being four to one in favour of the Bill, so there's clearly a mechanism in place for him to access normal post without my needing to arrange for a letter in Braille.*

Lord Stevens of Kirkwhelpington – recognises "*the police [are faced] with some difficult decisions in sudden and suspicious*

SEND OFF SIR

deaths. As a junior and then a senior detective I went to hundreds of sudden and suspicious deaths, and it was one of the more difficult things that I had to judge and decide on." He's keen to have certainty in the law, and recognises "... it is a nonsense that people can say that someone will definitely die within six months." Does that mean he would favour an open-ended period? If so, would it be enough to establish Ollie is unlikely to last beyond some age that is regarded as very young compared to the population at large?

Lord Vinson – "... doctor forebears applied common sense when coping with life and death. ... Thou shalt not kill; but need'st not strive officiously to keep alive. ... the relief of suffering should trump all other consideration." Mustn't take his words out of context, but could his arguments be extended to include Ollie?

Lord Layard – "If a person is going to die an agonising death, that person is not the only one who will be traumatised. Their family and friends will be traumatised, too. Not only will they lose their loved one; they will be left with horrible memories for the rest of their lives." Again, extending the argument, what about those of us who are suffering horrible memories every day? Do people generally recognise how we suffer, seeing a suffering child?

Lord Pearson of Rannoch – "37 years ago ... had a near-death experience. ... two-hour operation ... anaesthetic steadily failed although the paralysing drug continued to work." His personal experience may make him the most capable of understanding and empathising with Ollie's condition.

Baroness Mallalieu – "the law ... is a mess. It has continued in that form for so long because of a degree of selective blindness on the part of doctors, police and prosecuting authorities..." If only I could rely on such selective blindness myself. "I believe that the law at present is cruel." She made a brilliant speech, highlighting the real issues. If I wrote to her, would she apply her clarity of thought to make a case for those like Ollie?

Baroness Flather – from a much earlier debate, "... if my disabled husband asked me to help him die and there was no legal provision, I would still do it out of compassion and love no matter what happened to me. He received two e-mails the next day to say, "Watch out for that woman." But he is still here... tetraplegic ..." A brave woman to say it, and even braver if she had to do it. She used that key word, compassion. I think she'd understand about Ollie.

Baroness Brinton – disabled and Christian; has a chronic life-limiting illness. She was able to explode myths put about by others, which she did all the more powerfully, being a disabled person herself. "The Bill will allow us to be honest – with ourselves, our families, our doctors and as a society." *I wish I could be honest in the one way that really matters.*

The Earl of Arran – excellent speech, full of facts; side-effect is he undermined the argument for getting rid of hereditary peers! Speech was precisely focused on the Bill, so no way of knowing how he'd feel about extending it.

Lord Mitchell – gave deeply moving personal testimony. Not sure how it might translate into supporting my position. Subsequent note: he's intending to stand down at the next General Election.

Lord Dholakia – cogent, logical arguments. He agreed to the switching off of the life-support machine that was maintaining his brain-dead brother; it's an example of someone making a life-ending decision for someone else. Would his experience of that tragedy encourage him to support the idea of taking it one step further – terminating the life of someone who is almost brain-dead? "Some relatives also face the risk of prosecution for helping a loved one to die." *Very true.*

Neil had initially considered writing to some of those who were against the Bill. He glanced down the pages and read several entries.

Baroness Campbell of Surbiton – "This Bill is about me." *What does that tell us about her?* "However, it is not just about me. My story is echoed by the majority of disabled and terminally ill people in Britain today." *How does that square with the fact that polls indicate almost four out of every five registered disabled people are in favour of the Bill?*

Lord Tombs – claims that "the law as it stands is clear and has performed well." *Were the comments from the Supreme Court too subtle for him?*

Lord Macdonald of River Glaven – finds it "unthinkable ... that there should be no inquiry following an assisted death." *Other people can think such things, so what does that say about his capacity for thinking?*

Baroness Symons of Vernham Dean – the structure of her personal testimony suggests it was deliberately designed to mislead. The effect was probably the opposite of what she had intended – who would wish to agree with someone that has made a fool of them by deception?

Baroness Grey-Thompson – "The Supreme Court urged the Chamber to consider whether the law should be changed; it did not say that the current law does not work." WHAT??? Did she think the Supreme Court was just saying, "Wouldn't it be nice if you people in the House of Lords had a chat about something that doesn't need changing"? "For many people ... they have no choice – and soon they could have less." How does that work – a negative number of choices? How did she come to be in the House of Lords?

Baroness Nicholson of Winterbourne – "Do not use my taxes on the proposed state death department..." Doesn't she know how the taxation system works? Imagine all childless couples saying "Don't use my taxes for schools." It's like protestors with placards saying "Not in my name" – as though they see themselves as so important it's their name on the orders.

Lord Winston – supports unplanned death. Why? Later, he interrupted Lord Sherbourne of Didsbury, having apparently missed the point. I'd expected better of him.

Baroness Butler-Sloss – [the Bill] "... is certainly seen by most people as the first step." So, she definitely knows what other people see, she believes. Is there a medical term for people like that?

Viscount Colville of Culross – seems to believe in psychiatrists. In general he reckons that the mentally ill need two psychiatric assessments a month apart. Has he missed the point?

Lord Browne of Belmont – demonstrates how to lie with statistics. 73% support falls to 43% when there are public safety considerations. Frankly, if the question is phrased like that, I wouldn't expect anybody but anarchists to be in favour of the Bill.

Baroness Kennedy of the Shaws – appears to argue, with reference to our Human Rights and their Gun Laws, that we in Europe are completely different to Americans. In the US, "... the individual right trumps the needs of the wider community. That is not so here." Is she saying that European states override *individual human rights and that she agrees with it? One consequence is that some British people have to suffer painful deaths if they can't afford to go to Zurich. How does she justify bridging to "cruelty to refugees and asylum seekers"? That looks like a bridge too far if ever I saw one. "It speaks to who we are and how we want to be." Isn't that "speaks to" expression more widely used and abused in the US? How different does that make her from those across the Atlantic? It seems to undermine her argument. Was it arrogance that made her ignore the four-minute time limit and take seven and a quarter minutes? That's a lot longer than anyone else. She must have known how long her speech was going to take, so it had to be deliberate; and if she didn't know, then she certainly should have, in view of how the four minute rule was supposed to apply to everybody. Or am I being unfair, just because she's a Criminal Lawyer? Surely not! Marcus said he'd heard someone comment, "It's the behaviour of 99.9% of Criminal Lawyers that give all the others a bad name!"*

Lord Phillips of Sudbury – describes himself as a "long-in-the-tooth lawyer". Quote: "I believe that the status quo is actually not bad." And what about in the real world?

Baroness Sherlock – "unexpected richness of the period before death." What about the soul-destroying poverty of the lengthy period before death that others are suffering?

Lord Morrow – 73% in favour becomes 43% if a loaded question is asked, and yet he admits his own postbag is running at twenty-to-one against. That suggests most people who are for the Bill see no point in writing to him as it would just be wasted effort; they could well be right.

Neil glanced at some statistics he had identified.

1. Breakdown by anticipated voting intentions: sixty-one "For" and sixty-four "Against". That isn't representative of the country as a whole, which would be in the high nineties "For".

2. Breakdown by political party: Conservatives three to one "Against", Labour two-and-a-half to one "For". The country may need Conservatives in the House of Commons for the sake of the economy, but it needs Labour peers in the House of Lords.

3. Breakdown by Religion: not enough representatives to comment on some faiths. Jewish speakers evenly split. Various Christian speakers largely against – notable exceptions are

SEND OFF SIR

Baroness Richardson of Calow and Lord Carey of Clifton.

4. Breakdown of Catholic speakers: one in favour and eight against. Well under two minutes speaking time in favour, compared to about thirty-seven minutes against.

He read through his final comments.

1. They're all so skilled at being polite, with some of them it's difficult to recognise how strongly they support the proposed change in the law, which makes it harder to identify which ones might support extending the scope.

2. No point in writing to people who have entrenched views against, or whose reasoning defies logic.

3. Some peers are now claiming there needs to be more space provided for them, because there are so many of them. Perhaps it would be better simply to reduce the numbers by un-peering any peers who are incapable of rational debate.

4. And let's get rid of the Lords Spiritual while we're about it – what right do they have to be there in a multi-faith society?

He closed the file and squeezed it into a briefcase along with assorted bills and receipts. When all his worldly possessions had been crammed into the car, he put the briefcase on top of the pile on the back seat. Then he went into the living room and turned on the satellite recorder – the sat-box. After it had booted up, he turned on the television and found his two recordings of the House of Lords debate. He had set the sat-box to record the original broadcast, but she had turned off the receiver after he had left the house in the morning. When he had returned at around four-thirty he had set the remainder of the programme to record; he also recorded the earlier part of the debate on the next day's partial repeat showing, thereby giving him the whole session – almost ten hours. He had not trusted her to allow him to keep the recordings, so he had set up coded protection on the files to stop her from deleting them. His final act before leaving the house was to reset the coding system to four zeroes, and to delete the two files; this gave him a stronger sense of finality than even the removal of his personal belongings. He considered leaving the house keys, but decided to keep them in case he later discovered he had forgotten something.

* * *

Martello arrived at the station and obeyed the post-it note that instructed her to go to Castleton's office straight away.

'Enter.'

'You wished to see me, sir.'

'Yes. I thought you ought to know I spoke with DC Whittington this morning. I believe he's considering going back to his wife, Theresa, so I've given him the day off to sort things out with her. That puts you back in charge for now. Priestley's secondment ends today; he'll be back on Monday to take over.'

Martello recognised the lie and the undermining purpose behind the mentioning of the wife by name. She remained silent and unflinching.

'Your investigation needs to make some visible progress. PC Dunn has softened up Cullen about the marijuana, so you need to finish him off; I expect you to get a result today. He can now have a go at that teacher, Cassidy. There was an article in the local rag that was way off target, so I'm going to call a low-key press conference this afternoon for three o'clock to put things straight and bring them up-to-date. Make sure your reports are with me by then. Let WPC Plummer know she's required for the press conference, and make sure she's fully briefed. That's all for now.'

Martello left to consider what was behind the various assignments, speculating variously by numbers.

'One: Dunn couldn't get to the bottom of the marijuana question, yet I've been told to get a result by end of day. Am I being set up to fail? That would give him a hold over me, just in case he still fancies his chances.

'Two: Dunn, not me, to interview Cassidy. Am I being side-lined?

'Three: Plummer to accompany him at the press conference. Am I being side-lined?

'Conclusion: I'm being side-lined.

'Corollary: Plummer may be Castleton's next sexual objective.

'Proposed action: tell Plummer what to expect from Castleton.'

Martello briefed Plummer about the work-related matters, before adding, 'I need to tell you that Bryn the Grin has been pursuing me for months. And getting absolutely nowhere, I hasten to add. He started with asking me to go to places to discuss cases, but it was just a blind. I think he's finally given up on me, and I suspect you may be his next target, which could be why he wants you to be with him at the press conference. I think you should expect the worst if he invites you to a private de-briefing session.' Plummer giggled at Martello's pun, who then discovered it for herself and joined in.

Plummer was confident she would have read the signals, just as Martello had, but was grateful to her for being willing to expose her own position in order to be able to offer the advice. 'Thanks, Lily. I think I'll refuse to attend any off-site meetings right from the start. He's such a creep. I'll have to try not to let him see what I think of him, though – he's not someone I want as an enemy.'

As Martello had shared some personal information, Plummer thought this could be an opportunity to find out more about the latest rumour that was circulating. 'By the way, it has been alleged that you and Neil are an item. Would you care to issue an official confirmation or denial?'

Martello laughed at the way the question had been asked, with its delicate use of that old-fashioned term combined with press-speak, the latter hinting she was already gearing up for the afternoon conference.

'Could you keep it just between us? Neil's moving in with me. He's been wishing to leave his wife for a long time; he just needed a push.'

'I know he's been in love with you for ages, so what changed things for you? What made you give him the green light?'

'For ages? How is it I was the last to know? Why didn't he say?'

'Fear of rejection – you are pretty awesome, Lily.'

The two giggled together like schoolgirls, reflecting the chemistry developing between them – what a chemist might describe as the unique characteristics of girl-to-girl pair bonding.

Martello went to fetch Dunn to join the meeting, which became a formal discussion of assignments. Plummer would begin the process of identifying all the teachers who were present on that day, with a view to establishing if any of them had seen anything relevant. Dunn would interview Cassidy in accordance with Castleton's instruction.

After the meeting, Martello phoned the school and gave Verbane advance warning of their plans, asking that Hugh Cassidy and Billy Huntsman be made available separately for interview by Constable Dunn and herself respectively. She did not mention Cullen, as she intended to try to obtain more information from Billy before considering re-interviewing him.

Martello's car arrived first at the school. Billy had already been singled out from the herd at the sixth form assembly – snappily referred to as the "Year Twelve and Year Thirteen Combined Assembly" – and was now sitting outside the Headmaster's office. Verbane invited her to interview Billy in his office with him present, but she declined and asked for a room where she could interview him on a one-to-one basis. Verbane felt disappointed at being excluded from proceedings, yet wished to be helpful to Martello. He graciously invited her to use his office for the interview, almost tripping over himself in his haste to vacate it for her.

Billy came in and sat down where indicated, looking like the cat that had the cream.

'Hello, Billy.'

'Hello, Miss.'

'You can call me Lily.'

'Yes, Lily.'

'I was wishing to know about what really happened in the boys' loos. And let me say right away, the amount of marijuana in the bag was so small, it isn't going to be made into a big deal, so it would be good of you if you'd just put me in the picture.'

'Yes, Lily.'

Martello realised she would have to ask some specific questions if she was to obtain the whole story.

'Now, yesterday you told my colleague that it wasn't you who had had that little bag of stuff. Were you just winding him up?'

'Yes, Lily.'

'So how did it come to be in your hands when Mr Cullen came in?'

'Somebody just passed it to me.'

'By somebody, do you mean another boy?'

'Yes, Lily.'

'Is he someone I could talk to today?'

'Yes, Lily – but not at school. He's taking a couple of days off.'

Martello recognised there was some hidden meaning behind Billy's laugh. 'Is he away from school for a reason?'

'Yes, Lily. The Headmaster said he could stay at home.' Billy laughed again.

'Has he been excluded?'

'Yes, Lily.'

'So, will you tell me his name? Or should I ask the Headmaster?'

'Mr Verbane doesn't know his name.' Billy laughed once more.

Martello laughed for Billy's benefit, looking him straight in the eyes. She saw his pupils dilate and recognised the accompanying look she had so often received from men, though not normally from one so young. 'You'll have to explain that one to me, Billy.'

'Three boys have been excluded. It's one of them. Mr Verbane won't know which one.'

'But you'll tell me which one, won't you.'

'Yes, Lily.'

'And which one was it?'

'Mickey Blackstone.'

'Why did he give it to you?'

''cos Mr Collins was taking him to see the Headmaster.'

'Let me guess. Three of them had been caught smoking pot in the boys' loos and Mr Collins found them and took them to the Headmaster, and he excluded them for two days. And Mickey gave you his stash as he was leaving, so it wouldn't be found on him if he had to turn his pockets out.'

There was a sense of wonder in Billy's gaze. 'That's totally brilliant, Lily.'

'And then Mr Cullen came in and found you with it and confiscated it. Is that right?'

'No, Lily.'

Martello was taken aback for a moment to hear the word "no" from someone who had been answering "yes" to everything.

'It would be best if you explained what happened, in your own words. Will you do that for me, Billy?'

The look suggested he would do anything he could for her, though he restricted his reply to, 'Yes, Lily.'

'OK, tell me everything that happened in the toilets, right from the start.' She added quickly, 'After you'd been to the loo.'

'OK, Lily. The three of them were passing around a roll-your-own. Then Mr Collins came in and said, "That smells like marijuana. Is it, Mickey?" and Mickey said "Yes, sir. Would you like a puff?" And Mr Collins laughed, only he wasn't supposed to, so he stopped and said they had to come with him to see the Headmaster. And when Mickey was going past me, he slipped the bag into my hand. Then, when they'd all gone, I held it up to the window so I could see it better, and that's when Mr Cullen came in and saw me with it in my hand.'

'So he confiscated it.'

'Sort of, Lily.'

'He said he was taking it off you to hand it in?'

'No, Lily. He said he was taking it off me. But he didn't say he was handing it in.'

'Well, did he say what he was going to do with it?'

'He said he wasn't going to hand it in.'

'Did he say why he wasn't going to hand it in?'

'Yes, Lily. He said he wouldn't tell on me if I didn't tackle him properly in the football match, and let him get past me.'

Martello had developed the capacity to blank out any outward reaction to testimony, a mechanism designed to avoid revealing how much she already knew when interviewing a suspect. Consequently, on hearing this genuinely unexpected revelation, her feigned surprise followed a momentary delay; she opened her large eyes even wider, and raised her eyebrows, holding that pose until she was confident her impression had been clearly recognised. 'So, was it just him that he asked you not to tackle properly, or was it all the teachers?'

'Just him, Lily.'

'And did you let him get past you?'

'Just once, near the start. But I realised it was too late for him to tell on me, so I tackled him as hard as I could after that, and that was dead hard.'

'Well, that's been really interesting, Billy. I think we can leave it there for now.'

He had a look of undisguised disappointment as Martello stood up and opened the door for him to go. She saw he appeared reluctant to leave, so encouraged him to stand by holding out a hand for him to shake, causing him to rise and take it. 'Thank you ever so much, Billy. You've been a great help to me. And if there's anything else you think I should know then do get in touch with me at the police station.'

He held her hand like it was a piece of delicate crystal, not daring to shake it, as he concluded with a final, 'Yes, Lily.'

Martello left open the door to Verbane's office and prepared to leave, collecting together her papers. Verbane, having been loitering nearby, appeared almost straight away; he entered his office and closed the door behind him. Having previously been present for Billy's questioning by Dunn, he assumed this latest interview may be related. He rattled off a few questions. 'Has Billy been up to something? Does it have anything to do with drugs? Do I need to be taking any action?'

Martello gave Billy a clean bill of health. 'Billy has not committed any offence. In fact, he has genuinely been "helping the police with their enquiries".'

'Well, that is a relief. He's a good boy, once you get to know him.'

'I need to talk to another boy, now: Mickey Blackstone. I understand he isn't in school today. Could I have his contact details?'

Verbane obtained Mickey's file.

'There's no telephone number for him. I can give you his home address.'

Martello drove the short distance to the house, which was a narrow, mid-terrace property made of bricks that were essentially red but included large contributions of yellow and grey. Though it may have been pleasing to the earliest tenants of a hundred and fifty years earlier, and could still look idyllic from a distance across the fields on a warm summer's evening, on this cold, grey morning its cracked fall-pipe and dirty windows in rotting frames gave it an air of neglect. Martello pressed a dangling button that she took to be a doorbell, but on hearing no sound inside she decided to knock: just three moderate taps. Receiving no response after several seconds, she upgraded to a repeated loud knocking. A woman appeared at the door, cigarette in mouth, holding a tea-towel in one hand.

'Hello, luv, have you been there long? I was drying the pots.'

'No, not long. Is Mickey Blackstone at home?'

'Yes, he's upstairs. Come in, luv. I'm his mum.'

Martello felt for her warrant card.

'You don't need that. I can tell you're police.'

'How did you know, Mrs Blackstone?'

'Nob'dy like yerself comes knocking at our door unless it's police.'

Mrs Blackstone turned her head and shouted up the stairs that led directly off the small entrance hall. 'Our Michael, get yerself down 'ere.'

She led Martello into the downstairs room. On the wall hung a large television screen; it looked down on a nest of three dark oak tables, a three piece suite that had once been cream-coloured but was now streaked with grey and black, and an old, walnut veneered sideboard that appeared too large to fit through the door and so looked destined to remain imprisoned for many more decades.

'What's he been up to, then?'

Before Martello could offer any response, Mickey strolled in dressed as a US baseball supporter, replete with red and white sneakers, jeans, over-sized jersey, and topped off with a cap that had a long peak placed to keep the sun out of his eyes if only they had been positioned on the left side of his head.

'What've you been up to, Mickey?'

He turned to Martello. 'Is it about smokin' at school?'

His mother looked puzzled. 'Smokin'?'

He answered her. 'Weed.'

Mrs Blackstone turned to Martello. 'I don't know what's wrong wi' kids nowadays. Cigarettes were good enough for everybody when I was young.' As though emphasising the point, she drew deeply on her cigarette, leaving nothing but the filter.

Martello clarified the reason for her visit. 'I'm not here to deal with the smoking issue. I understand the Headmaster has already dealt with that, by rewarding you with two extra days' holiday.'

Mickey laughed like he had never heard anything so funny before. Martello guessed his previous experience with police officers had left him unprepared for her ploy, and she wasted no time in exploiting it. 'It's about the bag of marijuana that you passed to Billy Huntsman, and which Mr Cullen then confiscated.'

Mickey saw an opportunity to repay the humour. 'And you've come to give it me back?'

Martello laughed loudly with her eyes closed to stop him from detecting any insincerity in them. 'No, Mickey, I just need you to sign a statement saying it was yours and you passed it to Billy. Is that OK?'

'Yeah, sure, no probs.'

'And did you really offer Mr Collins a drag?'

Mickey was throbbing with pride, barely able to get his words out. 'Yeah, I did.'

With just a brief pause for reliving the humour of that moment, Martello continued, 'I have to give you a caution first.'

After the first seven words, Mickey recited it with her, looking thoroughly pleased with himself. Martello completed the formalities as quickly as possible in case the *bonhomie* expired too soon. The three gave their goodbyes with smiles all around. On her way back to the school she reflected that she seemed to have caught Neil's wicked sense of humour.

CHAPTER 14

Martello and Plummer Interview Teachers

Plummer sat with Oaken and checked through a complete list of all staff employed at the school, noting reasons for absence against any who were away on the Wednesday afternoon. Three of the teachers were absent due to ill-health, two had been receiving off-site training, and one had been visiting a primary school. There were part-time teachers to be accounted for, and rostered absences to be recorded. The end result was a comprehensive list of all adults who should have been on the premises just prior to the end of the school day.

Plummer remained in Oaken's office when the latter was called away to deal with a disciplinary matter. Martello arrived shortly after, and Plummer gave her a progress report. 'I've put together a list of all staff who were in school at the time of death. I haven't yet started on interviewing them.

'It's a long list; we need to prioritise them. Anyone who was supposed to be in a classroom for the last lesson of the day is unlikely to have been able to slip out unnoticed. We need to talk to Miss Oaken again to find out who that leaves.'

It was just a matter of minutes before Oaken returned; she quickly identified all the teachers who had been engaged in giving final lessons on the Wednesday. Plummer also noted the classrooms they had been in, for possible future reference.

Martello asked Oaken, 'Could there have been anyone else on the premises at the time? Workmen, for example?'

Oaken undertook to check various sources of information, including the Visitors Book on reception and maintenance records in the administration office. She returned and informed them, 'There were no other people in school. There were some bus drivers waiting at the traffic turning loop, though they always sit inside with the doors closed until it's time for the children to board. There were three buses, so three drivers, but I don't imagine any of them would have walked right over to the girls' changing room and left their bus unattended – they'd be too concerned about what they'd come back to.' Oaken provided them with the details of the bus company, just in case they wished to pursue that line of inquiry.

Oaken explained how the system of cover teachers operated: agency staff would be obtained – sometimes at very short notice – to take the place of absent permanent teachers. There had been three agency staff employed on that day and at that time to cover for three long-term absentees, and Oaken confirmed their movements were fully accounted for. She further explained that Verbane, in an effort to minimise expense, sometimes asked staff to give up their free periods and provide cover for unexpectedly absent colleagues. The effect of having ten teachers out of lessons for a whole afternoon had been substantial; the eleventh, Newhouse, had been timetabled to be taking games anyway. Normally this might have been expected to have resulted in a substantial demand for more agency staff, but Verbane, on the grounds that the football match was a social occasion, had asked staff to "volunteer" to provide cover for their football-playing colleagues. The players had therefore prepared lessons for the classes they would be missing, and these were largely delivered by "volunteer" teachers. Two had been delivered by teaching assistants, who would have explained what work had been set, and then monitored the students' behaviour. The end result of all this volunteering was that, in addition to the senior staff of Verbane, Oaken and Clifton, only two teachers had free periods for the last lesson of the day: Miss Jane Leveret and Miss Christine Nunn.

Martello suggested two additions to the list of early interviewees. 'The two administrative staff, Mrs Joanna Jackson and Mrs Margaret Webster should remain on the active list, as their movements are less regulated than the teaching staff.'

Oaken sought a way of disagreeing without usurping their authority. 'Jo and Peggy don't really fit the description of "active" anything. I think everyone would have noticed if they'd stepped out of their office and gone as far as the girls' changing room.'

Martello sought clarification. 'Are you saying their presence would have been thought out of the ordinary or even suspicious?'

'Most definitely – they rarely leave their lair.'

'I'll put them on the reserve list then – the Headmaster has already said he didn't see anyone suspicious in the area.'

Oaken responded, 'I agree – no one, suspicious or otherwise.'

Martello continued, 'It would seem Miss Leveret and Miss Nunn are the ones we should be interviewing first, though we may well need to interview everyone in due course. Could you let them know?'

Oaken checked the school timetable and informed them Leveret would have a free period starting in a little under half an hour, and Nunn one hour later. They agreed there was no need to disrupt lessons by asking them to come for interview any sooner. Oaken undertook to bring them at the start of their respective free periods, and told them they were welcome to continue to use her office for now and for the interviews. After Oaken had left her office, Plummer gave Martello an update on Dunn's movements. 'Dunn started interviewing Cassidy in this room without me, and after just a few minutes he came out and found me and said he'd decided Cassidy should be interviewed back at the station. I had to go with them and then come back here. He said he'd let me know if there's any progress, or any sort of a breakthrough, but I haven't heard anything yet.'

Martello and Plummer used the waiting time to discuss the case and the forthcoming press conference, before Plummer changed the subject and asked about Lily and Neil's plans. Martello confirmed they were going full steam ahead, and that Neil had already arranged to see a divorce lawyer, Manny Gilder, who had a good reputation for achieving the best results for his clients. Their conversation had switched back to the Newhouse case by the time Oaken delivered Leveret for interview. The latter gushed into the room.

'Hi, I'm Jane Leveret. I do Performing Arts here. That includes dance as well as drama. There's nothing quite like a *coup de théâtre* …' she pronounced it "th-ee-ate-r" rather than in the French style, '…to give the students a sense of achievement. So. You'll be wanting to ask about John and me. Well, I wasn't one for keeping it secret, only John said it would be better if we did, otherwise people might say we weren't focusing on the children.'

Martello made a quick appraisal of Leveret while she was speaking. Prettily dressed in light colours despite the time of year; late twenties; fairly short; medium bust; light hair hinting at blonde – probably from a bottle, though with some room for doubt; an apparent innocence of features that Martello decided to take at face value for now, though at the same time knowing a seasoned policeman might read them as indicating the opposite. She responded with, 'I'm DC Martello and this is WPC Plummer. Yes, you're quite right, we are interested in your relationship with Mr Newhouse, though first of all I'd like to ask you about where you were last Wednesday afternoon right up to the time Mr Newhouse's body was discovered.'

'So. I wanted to see John play in the football match, which is why I didn't volunteer to cover for anyone for the last lesson of the day. I went straight out to the playing fields and walked around to stand just behind the net at the end of the pitch that John would be attacking – he was Centre Forward, you know – and I watched him wherever he went. It's a good place to stand if you don't want to be hit by the ball, because it either goes over the top of you, or it's stopped by the net. I talked to some of the boys who were watching the match. All the Year Twelves and Year Thirteens were there, both boys and girls. The Headmaster hadn't given them the choice, as it was their timetabled games lesson anyway, and he'd said it was a good opportunity for them to show their support for their fellow students as well as expressing their appreciation for the teachers. In case any of them didn't understand what they were expected to do and not to do, he also said that he expected to hear a lot of cheering, and that booing would not be tolerated.'

'When did you leave your position behind the goalmouth?'

'So. It was near the end of the match. The score was four each. People say "four all", don't they? "Four all – the Saints" – do you know that hymn?' Southampton Football Club are called The Saints.' She laughed briefly at her cleverness and continued without pausing for any response. 'Anyway, there was nothing happening at my end of the pitch, so I started walking around and then down the side where the boss was standing.'

'The boss?'

'The Headmaster. I'm allowed to call him the boss; I asked him. He was standing next to the half-way line. So I said to him, "It's a very even game, boss." And he said, "You really don't need to call me "boss"." And I said, "No, Headmaster, but you are the boss." And he said...'

Martello interrupted, 'What happened next on the field?'

'So. The ball hit John on the chest, but a lot of the boys who were watching the match shouted "handball", which is why the referee gave the school team a free kick. Five teachers stood in a line between the ball and the goal-line; they call it a wall. Hugh Cassidy called out: "five man wall". The referee stood a couple of metres behind them and told them to step back to where he was, but they only stepped back a little bit, so he went and painted half a circle around the ball and then he came back and painted a line behind the wall. He told them to step behind the line, but they didn't move back far enough for his liking. That's when he showed John a yellow card; it was really unfair, because all five of them were standing in a line but he only showed the yellow card to John. Anyway, he told them again, and this time they shuffled back a foot or so. Then three boys started chanting "Send Off Sir", so that's what the ref did – he showed John the yellow card again, and then a red card as well. After that, the other four in the wall all stepped back to well behind the line. The ref wasn't fair to pick on John like that, and he certainly shouldn't have taken any notice of the boys. Perhaps he singled him out because he was the team captain, or maybe because he was the best player, or perhaps it was just because he was the nearest.'

'Then what happened? I suppose the school team took the free kick.'

'I didn't notice – I was watching John.'

'So what did John do?'

'So. He walked off the field and stood at the top of the steps. Then he turned around and walked down the steps, and that was the last time I saw him alive. Every time I look at those steps now, I think to myself, "That's where I last saw John alive." Because it was, you know.'

'Did you stay next to the Headmaster?'

'Yes, right up until when Dr Hunter came and told him about John.'

'Was anyone else with you and Mr Verbane when Dr Hunter arrived?'

'Yes, Christine Nunn, Vicky Clifton and the Headmistress. Christine came first, then Vicky and Glenda arrived more or less at the same time but from opposite directions.'

'You were watching John as he left the field. Did you see anyone with him? Or anyone else in the area?'

'No, there wasn't anyone around; not even any students –

nearly all of them were standing on the same side of the pitch as the Headmaster, because there was a cold wind blowing and it's always best to stand with your back to it. The bottom corner where John was standing is always the coldest because the wind really swirls around there. I remember thinking, "John, don't stand there, you'll catch your death."'

Leveret stopped when she realised what she had just said, though did not seem so much upset about it as self-satisfied. She continued, 'It was prophetic, don't you think? Me thinking about his death just then?'

Martello and Plummer nodded slightly, waiting for Leveret to pick up her thread again. After several seconds Martello decided she would need to break the silence. 'Would you like to tell us about your relationship with John?'

'So. John and I had been going out together for a few months. We'd been to an off-site meeting of teachers from all over the area, and I asked him back to my little cottage to have something to eat and to talk about what we had learned at the meeting. That's when we realised it was love at first sight.'

Martello could not restrain herself from pointing out the weakness of the statement. 'You had seen him before, so it wasn't really first sight, was it?'

Leveret dismissed this objection as a technicality. 'Seeing someone at school is very different to seeing someone at home. So it was first sight, in a way, as I hadn't seen him at home before.'

Martello smiled inwardly. 'So did he recognise it was love at first sight, as well?'

'He said, "Have you got something nice to eat, then?" So I said, "What about me, am I nice enough to eat?" He laughed at that and we went to bed.'

'And you'd been going out ever since then. How long ago was that?'

'About two months.'

'Right, well thank you for putting us in the picture. We'll let you know if there's anything else we'd like to ask you.'

Martello concluded the interview with the usual formalities.

After Leveret had left, Martello and Plummer managed to hold themselves together until they were sure she was out of earshot, before bursting out laughing. Plummer highlighted her affectation.

'So. Why does she keep starting sentences with "so"?'

'I think it's another fashion that started in the US, like Californian teenage girls making their voices go up at the end of statements so they sound like questions.'

'So. I hope it doesn't spread – it's just so annoying.'

'I didn't think anything really annoyed you, Lin.'

'Lots of things do – I just don't let it show.'

'What about the speed of seduction – do you think it was a world record?' She wondered how it compared with her abrupt invitation to Neil.

Plummer eventually replaced her smile with a reflective look. 'But who seduced whom? Instead of hunter and hunted, was it hunter and huntress?'

They compared impressions about her other testimony, concluding Leveret had probably told the truth as she perceived it. Oaken came to the door and offered them coffee, which the three of them took together in her office. She asked if they had discovered anything of interest so far. Martello was only able to give a non-committal response, 'It's early days, yet.'

Oaken fetched Nunn from the staffroom where she had been sitting waiting, having been given advance notice. Martello and Plummer introduced themselves, Nunn responding with studied formality: 'I am Miss Christine Nunn.'

The woman was dressed soberly: above the tweed skirt that fell to below her knees was a twin-set knitted from green and brown short staple wool and covered with protruding hairs that suggested an outward defensive quality, and inward, scratchy atonement. Her brown semi-brogues avoided the frivolous adornment of the curved design seen on a full brogue. With no jewellery on her fingers, wrists or ears, only the silver chain about her neck gave evidence of some ornamentation. At fifty-plus and without a trace of make-up, everything spoke of an old-maid-in-waiting. Martello thought it may be best to allow her to thaw a little before starting with the interview proper. 'I have you on the list as a Religious Education teacher. I understand you have many years of experience, teaching at this school.'

'I have taught here for thirty years, and bear witness to the many changes in education that have taken place during that time.'

'Changes, Miss Nunn?'

'When I began, I taught Christianity. Now I have to teach about all sorts of heathen religions. But I am not free to speak openly on the subject.'

'Then perhaps we can turn to something you are free to speak about – I mean what happened last Wednesday afternoon. Could I begin by asking where you were from just before Mr Newhouse left the football field up to the time that his body was discovered?'

Nunn carefully drew up the drawbridge chain that lay around her neck to reveal a plain, silver cross. She allowed it to settle a little below her throat, holding it forward for a moment as one who might present it to protect themselves against the forces of darkness.

'I was at the school football match. I was there for the entire final period of the day.'

Martello decided to provoke Nunn with a question to which she was virtually certain there would be a disapproving response. 'Do you have a particular interest in football?'

'Not the slightest.'

'Then why were you there?'

'I had declined to forego my free period and accept Mr Verbane's invitation to cover for other teachers. It is incorrect to think of it as a free period; I normally use that time for marking scripts and preparing lessons. Mr Verbane subsequently made it clear that anyone who was free at any time during the afternoon should make their way to the playing field in order to support their colleagues and the students. If I am forced into retiring, I shall be unable to influence the next generation of children. I therefore have no intention of retiring, and consequently have to avoid giving Mr Verbane any excuse to press me in that direction. Hence, I was at the playing field.'

'Would anyone be able to confirm where you were?'

'You are asking me if I have an alibi for the time of Mr Newhouse's death? I suppose you're obliged to ask everyone on equality grounds, no matter how ridiculous the question. Very well: I was talking with various students, those with no apparent interest in the football match. Then I saw Miss Jane Leveret approaching Mr Verbane, so I hurried to join him and gave him an alternative person to converse with.'

'You make it sound as though you did not wish Miss Leveret to be speaking to him alone.'

'That is a not unreasonable interpretation.'

'Is there some reason why she should not?'

'I am not one to repeat heresy, I mean hearsay, so I suggest you speak to Mrs Barbara Saxon of the history department about the antics of her husband and Miss Leveret.'

'Would you care to elaborate?'

'I would not. You should get it from the horse's mouth.'

'In that case, could we return to the question of where you were, and also what you observed? Is it correct that you, Mr Verbane and Miss Leveret were together at the point in the football match when Mr Newhouse left the field?'

'That is correct.'

'And did you see where he went after that.'

'I saw him walk to the top of the steps. The excitement of the students indicated a goal was scored, and at that point he walked down the steps and out of sight. I turned my head back towards Mr Verbane, who was on my left. I did not see Mr Newhouse again, and never shall in this world.'

'And when the match ended?'

'I continued in conversation for a short time with Miss Leveret. After Mr Newhouse had been sent off, she wandered in the direction of the steps; then she turned and called out to me about how unfair it was that Mr Newhouse had been dismissed. I stepped towards her and began a discussion about the concept of fairness as a movable feast.'

'And were you still talking together when Dr Hunter went to Mr Verbane with the sad news?'

'We were still in conversation.'

'Did you see anyone in the vicinity of Mr Newhouse between the time that he disappeared from your view and the announcement by Dr Hunter?'

'Only those people one would expect to see in the vicinity. The students were milling around in a group, talking loudly. They had not yet collectively decided to leave the playing fields, so none of them had yet descended the steps.'

'Then, unless there is anything else you would like to share with us, I think we can terminate the interview there.'

Nunn carefully returned the silver cross to its secret hideaway before taking her leave.

SEND OFF SIR

Martello and Plummer debated whether they should speak with Clifton next, or follow the Saxon path. They agreed Clifton should be first, though the other route was too intriguing to leave untrodden.

Oaken returned to her office, where Martello asked if Clifton was available to answer a few questions. Oaken went away, returning with Clifton a few minutes later. Martello and Plummer introduced themselves, Plummer mentioning she had seen her in the changing room on the Wednesday. Clifton thrust out a hand and kept it in position until first Plummer then Martello stood up to shake it, while booming, 'I'm Victoria Clifton. Call me Vicky.'

Martello sat down again and hid her hands under the edge of the desk, using her left hand to check that none of the fingers of her right hand had been crushed beyond repair. Martello began the interview while Clifton was still looking at Plummer in the expectation that questions would be asked by the one in uniform. 'I would like to start, Vicky, by asking where you were last Wednesday afternoon up to the time Mr Newhouse's body was discovered.'

Clifton turned to Martello and held her in a steady gaze. 'I was next to the pitch for the entire match, mostly talking to the boys about football. You're probably more interested in what happened starting from around the time Mr Newhouse left the field, aren't you?'

A slight nod from Martello encouraged her to continue.

'I had been on the far side, dealing with a group of three boys who had been calling on the referee to send off Mr Newhouse, and had then switched to yelling out disparaging comments about various teachers. I sent them around to the other side, whilst I stayed there to ensure they didn't come back. Just before the end of the game I went around the pitch and joined the Headmaster.'

'What route did you take around the pitch?'

'I went behind the goals at the far end – the end away from the girls' changing room block.'

'Did anyone see you go around?'

'Maybe some of the players. It's where the action was; they were all at that end except for Hugh Cassidy.'

'So now you and all the boys and girls were along the side where the Headmaster was standing.'

'Yes, all but seven boys.'

'Which seven boys were those?'

'The ones who had been positioned to retrieve the ball. Two of them were away behind the goals at the far end. There was also one each side of the half way line, about twenty metres away from the side-line. Then there were two more behind the goals at the changing room end with a third nearby to make sure the ball didn't go down the steps – it takes much longer to retrieve it if it goes down there.'

'Do you know the names of the three boys at the changing room end of the pitch?'

'Not sure; I can get them for you – I'll have to ask.'

'Please do, Vicky, and let one of us know as soon as you can. Now, who else was with the Headmaster?'

'Miss Nunn and Miss Leveret, and then Miss Oaken. Three misses together – it sounds like the staff team's performance near the end of match.'

She snorted at her allegedly amusing observation.

'And you were all together when the game ended?'

'Not quite. Jane and Christine had set off just before, I think.'

'So, there were three of you together – Mr Verbane, Miss Oaken and yourself – when Dr Hunter came with the sad news.'

'Yes.'

'And did you see anyone near Mr Newhouse from the time he left the field until he went into the changing room?'

'No, no one.'

'Except the three boys at that end, who were there to retrieve the ball if it went their way?'

Clifton stopped for a moment to scan the recesses of her memory. Her eyes narrowed like someone with myopia attempting to squeeze the lubricant into a smaller gap between the eyelids so as to distort their vision in order to focus better.

'Actually, I'm sure they were there when the school team scored the final goal, but I'm not certain they were there shortly after the match ended. I was looking down that way to make sure the boys didn't forget to do the applause thing – I was all ready to shout at … I mean to, them if they forgot – and the three of them weren't there anymore. But then, they could have just left as soon as the match finished. It took a while for all the players to walk from one end of the pitch to the other.'

'We'll sort out exactly what happened to them, though please don't give them prior warning – we'd like three independent testimonies rather than one joint one.'

'OK, message understood. When do you wish to speak to them?'

'Could you give me their names first, and then we'll decide when we can fit them in.'

'Righty-ho.'

'Finally, then, could you just confirm you didn't see anyone suspicious in the area around the changing rooms from the time when Mr Newhouse left the field to the time when Dr Hunter came with the sad news.'

'I can't say what was happening around there while the game was still going on, though I can say I didn't see anyone but the two teams once the match had ended. I saw the school team go down the steps followed by the staff team.'

'Well, thank you Vicky, that's been most helpful. I wonder if you could do one final thing. There's a Mrs Saxon we'd like a quick word with. Could you see if she's available?'

Clifton checked the printed sheets that were on the wall of the office. 'She isn't free, but if it's only a brief conversation you want with her, I could stand in for her for ten minutes when there's a suitable gap in her lesson.'

'That would be great. Thanks very much.'

Several minutes later Mrs Barbara Saxon arrived unaccompanied, and introduced herself. Martello completed the introductions before starting with, 'Would you mind telling us your view of, um, your husband and Miss Leveret?'

She needed no second invitation, launching straight into an explanation. 'They were on a school residential geography trip, ten weeks ago yesterday. If you can tell me how Miss Slut-Bunny from Drama Club got to be on a geography trip then I'd like to know. He said she came into his room and he was too polite to say no. I said if he ever did that again, with anybody, I'd do to him what the mob threatened to do to Eliot Ness in Chicago during Prohibition.'

'Was that castration by any chance?'

'You're on the right track; I said something along the lines of giving him a penectomy with the bread knife.'

'Well, the occurrence on the geography trip doesn't appear to have any direct connection with the investigation, so we can put it aside. Thank you for sharing it with us.'

'Oh, I share it with anyone that asks, and some that don't.' She laughed bitterly before taking her leave.

Plummer turned to Martello. 'I hope I'm never called out to a domestic at her house.' They shared a quiet giggle, like conspirators. 'It wasn't really part of the investigation, was it?'

'Maybe not, but it was interesting. We still have to write it up, though.'

Martello was determined to make a comprehensive report back to Castleton so that he would have no valid excuse to reprimand her. Plummer was keen to ensure she would have plenty of time for the briefing session with Castleton, and to prepare herself mentally and tactically for the forthcoming press conference. They therefore decided to return to the station, putting off any further interviews. As they were collecting their papers together, Clifton called in with the names of the three boys who had been on ball retrieval duty nearest the girls' changing rooms: David Williamson, Simon Green and Zachariah Peck. Martello explained they would have to be interviewed another time, and reminded her not to let them know in advance.

CHAPTER 15

Castleton Gives a Press Conference

Earlier that morning when Dunn and Plummer had delivered Cassidy to the station, he had been left in an interview room with a constable on silent guard duty. Dunn had consulted with Castleton and been instructed to make a start on the interview on his own while he dealt with other matters unrelated to the case.

Dunn entered the interview room and began by issuing a caution. Cassidy declined to be assigned a solicitor. 'I haven't done anything wrong, so I don't need a solicitor. I'll answer all your questions honestly, and then you can let me go.'

Dunn decided he already disbelieved Cassidy, feeling there was something not quite right about him. Perhaps it was the smile he attempted to paste over his worried face. Maybe it was his ploy of claiming honesty, or of refusing a solicitor to bolster the idea of his innocence. Dunn was a believer in the myth that a policeman can tell when someone is lying. He therefore went with his gut instinct and decided he should interview Cassidy based on a presumption of guilt. Having turned on the twin CD-based recording system and completed the identification of those present, Dunn launched straight into the attack.

'The autopsy report states that Edward John Newhouse was killed as a result of being pushed onto a coat hook. His head was caved in at the back.' Dunn threw down a photograph of the injury in front of Cassidy, who turned away, retching without vomiting. Dunn interpreted this as a sign of guilt – a refusal to confront the consequences of his actions. 'There are three things we look for when a crime like this has been committed: means, opportunity and motive. You had the means. You had the opportunity. What I don't know is your motive – why did you do it? He was a handsome bloke – people say he was a ladies' man. What happened? Did he steal your girlfriend?'

'There's no point in asking about a motive, as I didn't do it.'

'You're an educated man, aren't you Mr Cassidy. Now what would be your conclusion if I said to you that the only person who was in the vicinity of a crime was a Mr X. Would you say that it must have been Mr X because there was no one else who could have done it? Well you're that Mr X. No one else could have done it, so it was you. Now, let's have your explanation of how it happened. It could have just been some pushing and shoving and you didn't mean for it to happen. It's not for me to put words into your mouth; you just need to come clean and give a full and frank confession.'

'You must be wrong about something because I was somewhere else when it happened.'

'That means you know when it happened, otherwise you can't say you were somewhere else.'

'Yes, I can. I wasn't there when it happened, whenever that was, so I must have been somewhere else when it happened. It's just logic.'

Dunn gave what he thought was a performance of a hard but fair cop who knew all the facts and was angry with the guilty man for not coming clean; there was a curl to his lip as he responded. 'You're very clever with words, Mr Cassidy, but don't think that's going to get you off. We have forensic evidence that shows what happened, and we have witnesses who have said they saw you go into the changing room before anyone else. There are plenty of witnesses who say there was no one else anywhere near. All the other players from the football team went in together, and there you were, on your own, with the dead body of Mr Newhouse. The case against you couldn't be more open-and-shut. You're standing there near the coat hook, with the dead body, and no one else around. It's what we call the smoking gun … thing. You're never going to get out of this, Cassidy, so it's in your interests to admit it straight away.'

'How is it in my own interests to admit to something that I didn't do? That is completely illogical.'

'That's twice you've mentioned logic. Well, don't think logic will save you, when you're up against solid facts.'

'But the logic is saying that your facts are wrong, which means they aren't facts.'

'So, you're telling me that all these experts are wrong, are you?

Pathologists, Crime Scene Investigators, witnesses – they're all wrong except you? You're like the man in the army who's marching out of step with everybody else, but claims you're in step and everybody else is out-of-step. There's a word to describe people like that. Maybe you're wanting a psychiatrist to say you're not fit to plead. Is that your plan for getting out of this?'

Cassidy was shaking his head slowly from side to side, refusing to believe what he was hearing. Dunn decided to leave him to reconsider his declaration of innocence. 'Interview suspended at …' He stated the time.

Dunn took a recording of the interview to DCI Castleton and played it through. 'You've been very fair with him, Dunn. He's obviously guilty, so we'll leave him to stew for a while – it'll give him time to construct a confession that minimises how bad it makes him look. Then we'll go in together. We'll do it after the press conference.'

* * *

Martello and Plummer returned to the station and informed Castleton they had completed a number of interviews that they wished to report. Castleton arranged a meeting with them and Dunn for two o'clock to review their findings. Castleton kicked off the meeting. 'PC Dunn has interviewed Hugh Cassidy and I've listened to the recording. There's something about him that says he's guilty, but I'm always one to keep an open mind, so let's have your reports and we'll see if there's anything that argues against Cassidy being our man.'

Martello gave a run-through of the interviews in chronological order, beginning with Billy Huntsman and Mickey Blackstone. In one sentence Castleton dismissed the successful outcome and minimised its importance, also including an implication that Martello had failed to focus on the main subject. 'Well, that's a small matter, so you can forget about it now and get back to the main investigation.'

Martello and Plummer went through their interviews with Leveret, Nunn and Clifton. They confirmed they had not found anything to suggest any alternative to Cassidy as the perpetrator, though Martello felt obliged to add that there were three boys to be interviewed who had been in the vicinity. As they were joint interviews and joint conclusions, Castleton was unable to single out Plummer for praise without also implying praise for Martello –

which was something he was not prepared to do. He addressed a curt response to Martello. 'Anything else to report?'

Martello then gave the briefest of summaries of the interview with Saxon. Castleton saw an opportunity to undermine Martello. 'Was it your idea to interview Saxon?'

Plummer interjected, having anticipated what was coming next for Martello. 'It was my idea, sir. I thought it might have had some relevance, but it didn't.'

Castleton had to drop his planned attack on Martello for wasting time, instead directing to Plummer, 'It was clever of you to spot that possible lead. It doesn't matter that it didn't work out this time. Just you keep looking out for things like that. One day it will be a small item that you've noticed which will provide the breakthrough. Well done, Linda.'

Plummer and Martello avoided exchanging any hidden sign that they both knew what had just taken place, for fear of the communication being intercepted. Plummer responded with downcast eyes. 'Thank you, sir.'

Castleton put forward his assessment of the case. 'It's clear we have only one suspect: Hugh Cassidy. It's going to be difficult to nail him without forensic evidence, but I think we can do it if we can establish there was no one else around. Are we all in agreement that he's our man?'

Though it was phrased as a question, they knew he was not inviting alternative views. Dunn came back with full support; Martello and Plummer remained silent.

'DC Martello, do you agree?'

'I'm not sure, sir. There are still some leads to check out.'

'You favour the plodding style, do you? Check out everything before you have an opinion? Sometimes you need inspiration for detective work; perhaps you're not really cut out for it. Maybe you should go back to Traffic.'

Martello flushed with anger. It was one thing to express such opinions privately in a one-to-one and with a right of reply; it was an entirely different matter to say these things in front of other constables. She remained silent, her annoyance with Castleton growing into full-blown hatred. Castleton decided to delay asking Plummer for her opinion in case she also uttered misgivings; it would be too obviously disingenuous if he publicly supported identical views from Plummer for which he had just denigrated

Martello. He dismissed Martello and Dunn, keeping Plummer back so they could prepare for the press conference.

'We need to show a united front, so if you have any misgivings about Cassidy being our man then you need to express them now. If the press see any sign of a split, we're all done for.'

'I haven't met Hugh Cassidy myself, so I haven't been able to form any sort of opinion of the man. I'm in favour of trusting instincts, but only when they don't stem from prejudice.'

'That's exactly how we all should be, Linda. Have you any thoughts about getting out of uniform?'

For the briefest of moments she felt a shock that he was referring to her removing her clothes, before she decided his intended meaning was to invite her to join CID – and no doubt with an obligation to express gratitude to him. 'I'd like to see this case through first, sir, before even starting to think of anything else.'

* * *

Rowland Ryland of the Shawton News, at fifty, had been divorced for sixteen years; his lack of interest in anything but bird-watching and walking in the Peak District had made his wife feel old before her time and so constituted mental cruelty, she alleged. She had raided his investment funds with the help of divorce lawyer Manny Gilder before heading for the rumoured bright lights of London; in contrast, Ryland had remained settled and comfortable, happily living close to open countryside. He had never harboured ambitions to become a hard-hitting reporter on a National newspaper, and had been satisfied with making a modest living for twenty years from reporting local news. He had been born to old parents, and had inherited sufficient property and money early enough in life to make paid work almost unnecessary, which was fortunate as he received just a pittance for his daily effort. The combined effect of low pay and general apathy for his work was that he rarely researched articles in any great depth. Nevertheless, the death of a teacher at a local school was a significant event, and he intended to make a decent stab at reporting it from now on – especially as there had been some negative feedback about his initial article.

At the press conference Ryland found himself in the company of various second-string reporters from the National newspapers. Castleton opened with a positive spin on events. 'Following the discovery of a body at Midshaw School on Wednesday afternoon the police have been making exhaustive inquiries into the circumstances. The body was that of Edward John Newhouse, a teacher at the school.' He looked in Ryland's direction as he gave the full name and then used the middle name. 'John had struck his head on a coat hook, and this had penetrated his skull, resulting in his almost immediate death. The post-mortem report indicates the impact resulted from a deliberate action by person or persons unknown in pushing him into the coat hook. Inquiries are ongoing, and though we are currently interviewing someone who may or may not be implicated in the death, we would ask for anyone who saw anything suspicious in the vicinity of the school between three o'clock and four o'clock to contact the police at Midshaw station.' Castleton rattled off the telephone number before awkwardly reciting the e-mail address.

Ryland remained silent as those around him flexed their reporting muscles by calling out the usual questions.

'Do you have a suspect?'

'It's too early to describe anyone as a suspect.'

'Do you believe it was committed by someone employed at the school?'

'We do not wish to narrow our range of possible suspects at this stage.'

'Could it have been committed by children at the school?'

'We are placing no limits on the range of our enquiries at this time.'

'Did he have any known enemies?'

'That is a course of enquiry we will be pursuing along with others.'

'Was he involved in any illicit activities?'

'We have no evidence to suggest he was, at this stage.'

'Where exactly was the body found?'

'In the girls' changing room.'

This last answer led to a frenzy of questions which Castleton tried without success to subdue.

'Why was he in the girls' changing room instead of the boys' changing room?'

'It was in use for a particular purpose.'

'Were there any girls in the changing room at the time?'

'Not to our knowledge.'

'How many girls were there in the changing room?'

'I just answered that question – none as far as we know.'

'Where had the girls gone?'

'We have no reason to believe there were ever any girls there.'

'Then why was it called the girls' changing room?'

'Because that's what it is, when they are using it.'

'So who was using it?'

'Eleven male teachers.'

'Did male teachers make a habit of using the girls' changing room?'

Castleton felt anger rising in him at this focus of their questions. Plummer saw it change the pigmentation of his neck, leaving it mottled and blotchy like scarlet fever. As it worked its way upward, by eye contact and raised eyebrows she offered to pick up where he had left off, which he accepted with a curt nod.

'Under normal circumstances, the boys use the boys' changing room and the girls use the girls' changing room. This was a special occasion, when the boys and the male members of staff were to play each other in a football match. It was felt inappropriate – and I am sure you will all agree with this – for the male members of staff to share the changing room with the boys. So, for that afternoon only, the girls were excluded from their main changing room, notices were put up outside, and it was used by the eleven members of the staff football team. Now, I am sure you will all agree this was a perfectly good arrangement. Questions about where the girls were are really not at all relevant.'

It was unclear whether the reporters looked abashed or merely disappointed, but it stemmed the flow of questions and enabled Castleton to bring the meeting to a rapid conclusion.

After the room had cleared, Castleton turned to Plummer. 'You did a great job there, Linda – helped me out of a bit of a hole. I'd really like to thank you properly. Perhaps I could take you to dinner this evening?'

Plummer had prepared for this type of question as thoroughly as for those to be expected from the members of the press. 'I like to keep work and other time entirely separate. So, thank you for the offer, but it's enough just to know that you appreciated the contribution I made at the press conference.' As they left the room and set off down the corridor she executed her escape plan; with a quick excusal she ducked into her place of sanctuary through the door marked "Ladies".

Castleton still felt angry with the reporters, and annoyed at the failure of his ploy with Plummer. He met up with Dunn, for whom anger was always under the surface without the need for any particular reason. They set off to interview Cassidy, fully primed to play the bad cop, worse cop routine. After the preliminaries, Castleton began by adopting a disinterested tone. 'I understand you're continuing to deny you pushed Mr Newhouse onto the coat hook. It doesn't really matter to me how you play this, but I feel I should tell you that the courts are much more lenient with people who plead guilty, as it saves them all the time and trouble of having to have a lengthy court case. So, let's just get it over with, shall we? Tell us how it happened, and so long as that fits the facts, you're free to put whatever gloss on it you like. Nobody's going to dispute it if you say you pushed him and he fell back and hit his head and you didn't mean him to get injured. So, what do you say? Let's clear it up now and we can all go home.'

Cassidy had had more than enough time to think about what to do next. He leaned forward and spoke clearly into the microphone. 'I would like a lawyer. I am not going to say anything else.'

Castleton hated losing to this defence. He shouted in Cassidy's face, 'We're going to get you, you little prick, lawyer or no lawyer.'

Dunn added his own carboy of vitriol. 'And when you're inside you're going to meet some really vicious fuckers; your arse won't know what's hit it. So make the most of your last days of freedom.'

Despite Castleton and Dunn being convinced of Cassidy's guilt, the lack of direct evidence to charge him meant there was little point in keeping him at the station before they had prepared a comprehensive case. He was therefore released, which coincided with Ryland walking back from his afternoon tea and cake at the café where the tables were covered in pink gingham and a window seat was unofficially reserved for him. Having been exposed at the press conference to what he perceived to be proper reporters, he determined to try a little harder to be professional about his own work. He took out his smartphone and snapped Cassidy's picture, then set out to discover his identity on the off-chance that he was connected to the Newhouse case.

SEND OFF SIR

In the evening papers there were short and reasonably factual accounts of the death of John Newhouse and of the state of police investigations surrounding it. In the Shawton News there was a longer article, but nothing beyond the information provided at the press conference plus some local flavour. There was no mention of Hugh Cassidy in any of them.

CHAPTER 16

Local Reporter Investigates

Saturday

Neil and Lily were enjoying their shared warmth too much to think about getting out of bed. They were not scheduled to work this Saturday, and there was little they could do on the Newhouse case anyway now that Castleton had imposed his direction. Neil felt the sunlight streaming in through the caramel-coloured curtains and changing the morning inside the room into a summer's afternoon, though he expected the day outside would be frosty and cold. His mind drifted toward wakefulness, not quite giving into full consciousness, as his thoughts wandered. 'The light in this room feels like how it was when I was a boy. The sun was different in those days, white and cold in the mornings, and yellow and warm in the afternoons. At the weekends my father played records during the day; he wasn't allowed to in the evenings in case it kept us awake – my brother, my sister and me. His favourites were Joni Mitchell LPs, "Clouds" and "Blue"; he sometimes joked that "Clouds" had got in his way, but I don't think he meant the songs. Mum didn't like how some of the tracks made him maudlin; she didn't like lyrics that had so much poignancy. She used to prefer the bands that were popular when she was in her teens, but she'd lost interest in them by the time I was little. Now they play music from earlier eras: Nat King Cole, Ella Fitzgerald, songs by Irving Berlin. Mum says she likes whatever he likes – I don't think she's really into music.

'I wonder what types of music today's children will like when they're older. They might remember Rap as the sound of their teenage years, but I can't imagine they'll want that stuff when they become more mature. Rap isn't even music, anyway – it doesn't have all the key elements. Perhaps they'll fall back on other generations' music, like Mum and Dad have. Maybe songs from musicals – they seem to stay popular for ages.

'When I was very young I knew lots of the songs from "Oliver!" by heart. Dad watched the video with me plenty of times. I remember one time Mum telling him not to be so soft, when she caught him looking all teary-eyed when Harry Secombe sang "Boy for Sale". This morning is so wonderful, perhaps I should sing "Who Will Buy?" I could watch "Oliver!" with my own ...'

A thought stabbed him deep within his brain, the pain as intense as any response to physical trauma. 'I can't watch it with Ollie. It would be living a lie to think he was getting anything out of it – he doesn't seem to be able to experience pleasure, though the doctors say he does feel pain. How much longer must it go on for him? The legal system in this country declares that once a baby is born it has a right to life, even if it can't experience what most people would think of as life. British judges try to stop anyone who wants to do anything to put an end to someone's suffering, because they only believe in applying the law, whether or not that law is reasonable. Why don't they change the law? Because they claim they're unable to create, amend or abolish any law. Yet, when they interpret it, if they agree with that law they interpret it widely, and if they disagree with it they interpret it narrowly – even to the point that they appear to be attempting to frustrate parliament. Surely they could interpret the existing law in a way that recognises someone's right not to have to suffer nothingness? I'm sure a majority of MPs would be pleased that it removes the onus from them to have to pass a new law that would see them pilloried by the media because of the small, very vocal minority of the population who are against it. Some of the self-appointed spokesmen – and women – have such strong views; they are trying to be more Catholic than the pope.

'The judiciary refuses to take the lead because they see it as the responsibility of parliament, and the House of Commons fights shy of the subject for fear of bad publicity, so they allow this injustice to continue. Even murderers aren't sentenced to a life of perpetual emptiness punctuated with spasms of pain. I wonder how much longer the system will be allowed to stay this way. Perhaps there'll be a popular uprising, with the revolutionaries on one side and the forces of law and order on the other. I could stand at the barricades and incite my uniformed colleagues to swap their helmets for black berets.' He found himself smiling at the unlikely scenario.

'But if the law doesn't change, how long will Ollie have to continue with his meaningless existence? Jim Kinder looked into Ollie's life expectancy; he said it's such a rare genetic disorder, there aren't enough fully documented cases for him to be able to predict the future with any confidence. I'm sure he knows what I'm hoping for, but he hasn't found any evidence to suggest Ollie won't be condemned to exist for a long time. Ollie has drugs to deal with the pains he gets, but the nightmare will only stop when he's dead, so for him it's an eternity of nothingness or suffering.'

Neil's conscious mind attempted to take control. 'I want to think some nicer thoughts. I want to think about Lily. Her face, her body, her white silk nightdress that reaches down and touches her perfect toes and her beautifully sculpted feet.' He heard a beautiful, slow version of Ewan MacColl's song, "The First Time Ever I Saw Your Face", playing in his mind's ear.

He was jerked out of his reverie by Lily pushing and pulling at his arm. 'You were off in a different place there, Neil. Care to share?'

He knew instinctively that some of the thoughts he was having were best kept to himself. His conscious mind was still trying to find the right way to express what he wished her to hear, when the pressure that comes with remaining silent for too long caused it to be overtaken by his subconscious, which made him blurt out, 'I wish we could have children so that we can bring them up to see how wonderful life is.' As an afterthought triggered by his last words, he added half-musically, 'now I'm in your world.'

Lily gave a spontaneous reply, her conscious mind not being allowed the time to filter her response. 'I'd like to have children as well.'

Long pauses separated their two further, measured statements. 'But it would spoil your figure.'

'I'm starting to realise what really matters, Neil. There's a lot more to life than looks and clothes and work.'

Their conversation ceased as they reflected on the significance of each other's words. Lily decided she needed time to consider things and she could not talk and think properly in parallel. She threw open the silk sheets with the self-focus of someone unused to sharing a bed; she stepped out abruptly, without thinking of the draft Neil would feel.

SEND OFF SIR

As he waited his turn for the bathroom, he looked around the bedroom. 'Clearly designed for a woman – a lady – despite the absence of pink. No hint of mahogany. Light colours based around pale brown mellowing to yellow, like three-hundred-year-old yew or maybe tulip-wood. It could have graced a design magazine – maybe it once did. What a contrast to the tiny box room I've been living in. I wasn't even allowed the second bedroom for the sake of appearances in case someone came to stay; not that anyone ever did.'

* * *

There were no buildings within a mile to intrude on the splendid isolation of the former agricultural labourer's cottage, though there were lines of sight across treeless moorland to two sheep farms. In summer, the paths near the tiny dwelling had been lined with purple, patches of bell-heather displaying brightly amid the swathes of ling that tried to hold back the sea of green bracken. Now, the bracken that besieged the stone building was brown with just an occasional ochre frond, much of it having withered away to no more than short stems. The heathers had one final offering: their grey-brown stems shone silver by the paths where they were exposed to the elements.

When the cottage was being built there had been a plentiful supply of local stone for those who were prepared to risk dismantling the decaying manor house a few miles distant when no one was looking. The result was that the walls of the cottage were thick enough to insulate it against the cold and the warm in equal measure. Outside sounds were also efficiently excluded by the walls. As there was no preservation order on the cottage the current occupants had radically addressed the most vulnerable ingress points – the windows. The quadruple glazing consisted of two pairs of sheets of glass with narrow gaps to block the loss of warmth, fitted a fifth of a metre apart to keep out virtually the only external noise – the wind. Being without mains supplies, the cottage was dependent on a newly installed oil-fired central heating system. Hugh Cassidy and Michael Gough were confident they would remain warm and quiet inside the cottage when facing the howling gales of their first winter together.

Michael had pressured Hugh into declaring their relationship a permanent one by taking advantage of a recent change in the law to allow same-sex marriages. Hugh had conceded, providing the marriage took place far away and in secret – which is why the ceremony had been held in St Ives, Cornwall. Even the honeymoon had been obscured by Hugh's booking of a hotel room, "with twin beds, please".

No evidence was permitted to be put into the public domain. There was to be no joint bank account, though one concession was that on their separate on-line applications for accounts at Midshaw Bank they had each ticked the box which indicated "Married/Civil Partnership". In reality the payment of bills was shared more-or-less equally, though they were all processed through Hugh's account, which thereby looked typical of many heads of household.

No visitors were ever invited to the cottage, which was declared too small for overnight stays and too remote for anything less. Hugh visited his parents frequently to keep them from having an excuse for inviting themselves to the cottage, so they kept his old room permanently ready for him. Just once, shortly after they had returned from the declared "summer holiday", Hugh had taken Michael to meet them; this was strictly as a friend, with Michael using their guest bedroom.

Hugh's thoughts were deeply troubled as he remained oblivious to Michael's presence in the bed next to him. His usual worry was how upset his parents would be if they discovered their only child was Gay. Beyond that was their disappointment if they thought they would never have grandchildren. He had considered surrogacy, but decided the idea of a Gay couple having children was against his personal morality, being focused on the wishes of the couple and not on what might be best for the child. However, this morning his usual fixation with keeping the secret from his parents had been edged out by a more immediate concern. 'Who had said they had seen him going into the changing room alone? Why had no one said they had seen him going in with everyone else? Why did the police imagine he would have attacked John, or anyone else for that matter? Why had they decided it must be him?'

Michael normally enjoyed the warmth of the bed they shared, but this morning he was discomfited by Hugh's uncharacteristic detachment. Michael turned to look at Hugh: he saw nothing but a stone-like mask that had replaced the soft, gentle features that he

182

loved. He stretched out his hand and tugged at Hugh's face to turn it to face him, which Hugh eventually allowed to happen. 'You'll have to tell me about it sometime.' With all the anxiety of one who imagines themselves more loving than loved, he asked the end-of-relationship question that sounds so commonplace and yet to him held the ultimate in importance. 'Have you met someone else?'

'There isn't anyone, Mikey. It's something else entirely.' They sat up and Hugh explained how the police had accused him of killing a colleague. Michael grew red in the face as he shouted with all of the release of an uncontrolled scream but only a tenth of the volume, 'They mustn't get away with it. You need to get a lawyer.'

Hugh agreed, and the conversation circled around asking each other how to go about finding the best one. Eventually recognising that neither of them knew where to begin, they emerged from the bed to face the miserable weather.

* * *

Neil was too happy with the here and now to think of what they might do even for the rest of the day. Lily on the other hand had already arranged to meet George Westmorland at the Black Bull in the early evening before the townies invaded the place. Neither wishing to cancel, nor to exclude Neil from her plans, she asked him to go with her and meet George. His instincts told him not to invade her personal space and time, so he gave an acceptance provisional on an unlikely outcome: he would go if Jim Kinder were available as well. Neil knew how many hours Kinder dedicated to his work, and that left him very little free time for standing in a pub and chewing the cud, so he expected him to have to decline the invitation.

Neil realised he needed to let people know he was no longer contactable by phone on the landline at his wife's house, so decided that gave him a good enough reason to phone Jim. Beth answered; she sounded relieved it was only a social call and not another urgent demand for her husband. Jim came to the phone and was far too intrigued not to take up Neil's down-played invitation. He remembered seeing the goddess-like DC Martello at the school, and tried to avoid sounding too surprised that someone as outwardly ordinary as Neil was now in a relationship with her. He apologised in advance that he would be unable to stay very long as he had another engagement later that evening.

183

Lily phoned George to make sure they were still "on" for the evening. When she mentioned she was now "in a relationship with a guy from work," he expressed his delight for her and demanded to meet him at once, sounding for all the world like a protective father desperate to check the suitability of a daughter's boyfriend – his own daughter would have been about Lily's age, so he sometimes imagined Lily as a surrogate. They agreed to meet at the Black Bull at six o'clock, earlier than usual, to fit in with Neil's friend. Lily was pleased that, arriving with an escort, for once she would not have to be late. George's wife Bridget was not so pleased at having to revise her card-playing schedule for the evening to fit in with George's early meal and trip to the pub – she always took him there, and also collected him if she were available.

After breakfast, Neil and Lily undertook various practical chores, just like the married couple they hoped someday to be. For him, marriage to Lily would overwrite an unhappy recent chapter of his life. For her, the band of gold would act as an amulet to protect her from predators – or at least some of them, maybe.

Lily decided they should agree a shopping list. 'What sort of things do you like to eat, Neil?'

'I haven't had a full English breakfast for ages.'

'Don't you think we should eat healthily?

Neil realised he had said the wrong thing; he knew in future he needed to think more carefully about Lily's eating habits. 'Yes, absolutely.'

Lily wrote out a list, each of them contributing items they believed would be appreciated by the other and would be appropriate for a young, healthy couple who wished to remain so. Fruit and fresh vegetables were "in"; burgers and crisps were "out". Neil drove them to the supermarket, Lily choosing everything while Neil looked around unsuccessfully for people he knew so that they could see him with her. They loaded the car with the shopping that had been packed into newly-purchased reusable canvas bags, before walking the short distance to a shoppers' café, barely aware of the light drizzle, and both of them pleased to be seen together in public.

* * *

Michael fussed around in the kitchen, putting together a

shopping list, calling out to Hugh to ask him about things of which he had not the slightest interest but to which he attempted to give the expected replies. Which brand of olive oil did he prefer? Where did they stand on fried eggs, now that the warning on eggs generally as a source of cholesterol appeared to have been lifted? Should they have large or extra-large eggs? When the list had been completed, Michael headed off to do the shopping; he liked to go early, before the fresh fruit and vegetables had been picked over by the more discerning customers.

As soon as Michael had driven away, Hugh telephoned his mother Gwen and told her about the events at the school, omitting to mention how the police saw him as a suspect. When the conversation appeared to be drawing to its close, she asked the usual question, 'Hoffech chi siarad â'ch tad?' ('Would you like to speak to your father?')

The stock response was, 'Dim ond gair cyflym', ('Just a quick word'), but on this occasion there was some hesitation in his voice before he replied, 'Ie, byddai hynny'n dda', ('Yes, that would be good'). His father Gareth listened in silence as he explained about the death at the school, and then about the police interview, and how he would be phoning around on Monday morning to make sure he found a good solicitor. After the explanation was complete, Gareth suggested, 'We ought to come and help out. I can take time off work.'

Gareth owned and ran a tiny business that provided printing services, its viability heavily dependent on his personal availability. The sign on his office wall bore no relation to the reality of the operation: "Lack of foresight on your part does not constitute an emergency on our part". The advent of home computers and printers had resulted in the loss of many of the smallest printing jobs for individuals and societies. The demand for publicity material by small- and medium-sized enterprises in tandem with the economic cycle now generated the firm's variable profits that ranged from modest to non-existent. Hugh recognised the offer to take time away from work was an expression of love from father to son that the social conventions of rural South Wales discouraged from being spoken more openly. 'That's a really nice idea, Tad, but you have a business to run. I know you can't just drop everything and come up here to the wilds of Derbyshire.'

'Of course I can, Hugh. I have some jobs waiting, mind, but there are more important things in life than printing flyers, I can tell you.'

'Well, you know there isn't room for you and Mam; you wouldn't be comfortable, and I'd be embarrassed to see you squeezed into this little place. You've earned your right to a bit of comfort.'

'You'd have nothing to be embarrassed about, Son. Nothing, I tell you. We'd fit right in there and not get in your way. If you like, I could come on my own.'

'Well, I'll think about it if the police don't drop their stupid accusation.'

'All right then, Hugh. Do you want to speak to your mother again?'

'No, that's all right. I have to go now – things to do, you know.'

'All right then. Goodbye, Hugh.'

As Gareth put down the phone, Gwen asked him, 'What was all that about, Gareth?'

'Oh, nothing, Gwen love.'

'Well it must have been about something, Gareth.'

He explained about the accusation by the police and told her it would all blow over before the week was out. He put on his coat and made the ten minute walk to work to see his two employees and check that the printing was up to standard.

Ten minutes later the phone rang again, Gwen saying out loud to herself, 'Two calls in a morning; we are popular today.' She gave her phone number and added, 'Cassidy the Printers.'

Rowland Ryland responded. 'Good morning. Do I have the pleasure of speaking to Mrs Cassidy, Mrs Gwendoline Cassidy?'

The modulations of her voice supported the claim that the Welsh are a naturally musical nation. 'Well, I'm not sure so many call it a pleasure, and Gwendoline is my Sunday Best name, so I'm Gwen today.'

Ryland laughed gently, not just for her benefit but also out of the pleasure of feeling like a proper reporter. 'My name is Rowland Ryland. I don't know what my parents were thinking of when they gave me the name Rowland, what with the surname being so similar. So I don't have much choice about what I'm called; everyone calls me Rowland.'

'Well, Rowland, what is it I can do for you? Will it be some printing you're wanting?'

Rowland laughed again, seeing a connection. 'I think you must be clairvoyant, Gwen – it is about printing, in a way. I work for a newspaper, the local one in Midshaw where your Hugh teaches at the school. A teacher called John Newhouse has died, and I'm getting together some background information about him from his friends and colleagues. So far, I know that John was the sports teacher, and he was handsome and athletic. I haven't yet been able to talk to Hugh, so do you know if Hugh and John were friends, especially?'

'Oh no, Rowland, Hugh's special friend is called Michael.'

Rowland found himself swallowing hard to clear a large gobbet of spittle that had formed out of nowhere; he knew Gwen had let something slip that needed investigating further, but that he should let it lie for a moment so as not to draw attention to it. 'Do you have a telephone number for Hugh, so that I could ask him some questions about John and the school?'

'Well, I do have a telephone number, but Hugh gave strict instructions that we were not to tell anyone what it is. He's what you call "Ex-directory.'

'Do you have a number for Michael, then?'

'Well, it's the same one of course, so I still can't tell you. And there's no use asking about his mobile phone, because that's not for the telling either. Oh, you newspaper reporters are so sly.' She laughed, pleased with herself at not having given away any confidential information.

'Ah well, Gwen, I don't want to ask you anything that you're not happy to talk about. So, if John is out of bounds, shall we say, would you like to talk about Hugh and Michael?'

'Well, there's not much I can tell. They had a holiday in Cornwall in August, where they made it legal, you know, but he doesn't talk about it to us.'

'And do you know exactly where in Cornwall that was?'

'Oh, I think that's probably confidential.'

'Could you tell me what they thought of Cornwall, then?'

'They liked it very much. I know they enjoyed visiting the studios of more than a dozen artists near to where they stayed.'

'Well, that's nice. It's been a pleasure talking to you Gwen, and would you mind if I called you again if I need to check some facts?'

'Maybe you should talk to my husband next time. He's working right now.'

'That's Gareth, isn't it; could you give me his number?'

'Yes, of course. That one can't be confidential – how would we get any business?'

She gave the number, slowly, to make sure he wrote it down correctly.

'And do you think he would mind if I gave him a call this morning?'

'I don't know, perhaps it's best if you call him and ask him yourself.'

'I'll do that. Thank you, Gwen, you've been a great help.'

Ryland dialled Gareth's work number immediately to make sure Gwen would be unable to phone him first, in case she thought she should.

'Cassidy the Printers.'

'Am I speaking to Mr Gareth Cassidy?'

'You are.'

'I have just been speaking with your wife, Mrs Gwendoline Cassidy, regarding your son, Mr Hugh Cassidy, in connection with the case of the death of Mr Edward John Newhouse at Midshaw School in the girls' changing room last Wednesday at approximately three thirty p.m., and about the investigation regarding your son's movements around that time; I am in the process of collecting together background information on the people who were at the locus, the crime scene, or are known associates of those people.

'Your son was a close associate of Mr Newhouse, so I am investigating people associated with him. Hugh's life partner, Michael ...'

'Gough.'

''... were together on holiday last August in Cornwall for a special event. Can you confirm it took place at St Ives?'

'It was St Ives where they went on holiday, but I can't confirm exactly where they were married.'

Ryland avoided reacting to receiving the confirmation he had hoped for. 'And how long had they been together before that?'

'I don't know; Hugh doesn't speak to us about that sort of thing. We only know about the ceremony because my wife overheard them talking about it when they came to stay with us just after. She was in the… Anyway, they're happy about it, so it doesn't matter to us how long they'd been together, and it shouldn't matter to you either. He's always been a lovely boy, ever so gentle and kind. If you knew him at all you wouldn't have made that stupid accusation.'

'What accusation is that, Gareth?'

'You should know what accusation if you're the police.'

Ryland maintained his silence.

'Are you the police?'

'No, Mr Cassidy. I'm just trying to put together some background information for the Shawton News.'

Gareth raised his voice. 'I'm not talking to any reporters.' He slammed down the phone, with an uneasy feeling that he may have let slip something confidential, though he could not think what it might be – the reporter already seemed to have all the facts.

Ryland phoned Gwen straight away. 'Hello again, Gwen, I've just been speaking to Gareth. Now, he mentioned that Hugh has always been, and I'll give you his exact words, "a lovely boy, ever so gentle and kind". I'm intending to include that quote in today's newspaper article, so that people know what a good person Hugh is. Would you like to give me some more background info on Hugh that I can use as well, maybe some examples of how nice he is to you and your husband, anything like that. We can have a good, long chin-wag if you have the time.'

'Well there's lovely, Rowland. What would you like to know?'

Gwen settled into a chair and proceeded to give a summary of Hugh's life, reminding herself of little things she had almost forgotten and that she still delighted in remembering.

189

CHAPTER 17

Newspaper Article Published

The Shawton News was published every day except Sundays and Bank Holidays. On Monday to Friday the first edition would be on the streets by noon, with revised editions up to five o'clock depending on breaking news and significant corrections. Saturday was a half day for staff, so there was just the noon edition.

The paper had an editor and deputy editor plus four reporters; the total was matched by those employed to sell advertising. Three of the reporters, including Ryland, were responsible for various geographical areas; the other generally wrote the leading article – Ryland's by-line rarely made it from the inside columns. As he believed this time he had the best story, he was prepared to argue his case if the editor decided his article should be bumped to somewhere less prominent. His concern was unnecessary: it was accepted as the main item, and the only alteration she made was to replace his proposed banner headline of "Unexplained Death Investigation" with one designed to grab attention, even if it had little justification.

MURDER AT MIDSHAW SCHOOL?

At a press conference given yesterday by the police, Detective Chief Inspector Bryn Castleton stated that the death of sports master John Newhouse was the result of "a deliberate action" and that they are "currently interviewing someone" in connection with the offence. This paper can exclusively reveal that the person being interviewed is Hugh Cassidy, a teacher of English Literature and Classics at the school. Cassidy was photographed leaving the police station shortly after being interviewed.

[A large, grainy photograph accompanied the article.]

The parents of Hugh Cassidy, Gareth and Gwen, live in a quiet and remote valley in South Wales. They were shocked to hear of the accusation that had been made against their son by the police. In an exclusive interview with staff reporter Rowland Ryland, Gareth described his son as "a lovely boy, ever so gentle and kind". Gwen described him as "the sweetest, kindest, most thoughtful boy any mother could wish to have".

When asked to confirm that they were questioning Cassidy as their main suspect, a police spokesman declined to give an official response. However, in an off-the-record statement, a member of the police force who claimed inside knowledge of the interview described Cassidy as "a clever killer who tried to make it look like an accident".

Interviews with current members of staff at the school have revealed nothing but the highest praise for Mr Cassidy. Any suggestions that he may be implicated in the death of Mr Newhouse were consistently met with utter disbelief.

Attempts to locate Mr Cassidy for comment have so far been unsuccessful. He lives as a recluse with his partner Michael Gough; the couple were married in August at St Ives, Cornwall.

See page two for a related article: Men in Girls' Changing Room.

Men in Girls' Changing Room

Following an exclusive interview yesterday with staff reporter Rowland Ryland, retired biology teacher Dr Andrew Logan prepared a lengthy account of the history of the changing rooms at Midshaw School, with additional comments about the need for more privacy in school changing rooms generally. The article has been substantially condensed, with the salient issues summarised in the five points below.

> 1. *With one per cent or more young boys being Gay, should non-Gay boys be allowed privacy by the provision of separate changing rooms for the two orientations?*

2. *Though the ratio for lesbians is substantially lower, should similar considerations apply to girls' changing rooms?*

3. *Should the presence of a Gay boy in a mixed-orientation changing room be seen as unacceptable as it would be for a heterosexual boy to share a girls' changing room?*

4. *By focusing on the term "Gay", does society discriminate against other groups such as transgender and intersex?*

5. *Should the term LGBT be used as a collective term for Lesbian, Gay, Bi-sexual and Transgender, or should it be extended to LGBTI to include Intersex? Perhaps an acronym such as Legbit should be created before someone unkindly suggests Blight?*

John Newhouse was in the girls' changing room because the boys' changing room is a single, open space and it was recognised as unacceptable for teachers to share that space with boys when they were getting changed. In view of Dr Logan's thoughts on separation for Gay boys, which could be applied equally to Gay men, this suggests there should be four separate changing rooms for males at Midshaw School. If Cassidy, who is Gay, had been in a separate room to Newhouse, who was described by one colleague as "aggressively heterosexual", would the tragedy of John Newhouse's death have been averted? Was there some sort of disagreement between Newhouse and Cassidy regarding their shared use of the changing room? When this was put to the official police spokesman, the response was "no comment".

CHAPTER 18

A Walk at Longshaw (National Trust)

Michael arrived home with the shopping to find Hugh reading a book from the A-level literature list. 'I got most of the things from the supermarket; it's just too convenient not to. I went to that new delicatessen for the cheese; the range was good but they're a bit pricey. How's the book?'

'It's interesting, in a way.'

'That sounds like "damned with faint praise".'

'You're right. I look for something good in everything I read, but there are times when I have to look a lot harder than others.'

'Do you feel like a walk? Maybe before a late lunch – I thought we'd have a cheese salad.'

Michael usually received a look of approval for whatever meal he suggested, but not on this occasion. When Hugh had stopped reading, his mind had turned immediately to the police accusation. He felt it cast its shadow over him, like the giant golden eagle Aetos Dios and he Ganymede.

Michael continued. 'I know it isn't really salad weather. It isn't ideal for a walk, either, but I quite fancy going over to Longshaw and taking a hike over to Bolehill Quarry and round to Surprise View.'

Hugh attempted to look and sound enthusiastic, though not quite enough to convince Michael entirely. 'Longshaw and salad sounds good to me.'

They drove over to the Longshaw Estate, turning off the A6187 at Fox House and then taking another right into the Woodcroft car park. Hugh reversed up to the dry-stone wall, leaving their National Trust membership windscreen sticker prominently displayed in lieu of a parking ticket from the machine by the path. Hugh liked the anonymity that came with putting on hiking boots and waterproofs, making them just another two blokes out for a walk. They strode past Longshaw Lodge and headed toward what was once known as the boating lake though was now called the duck pond; they expected at least to see the resident mallards, though no fish as the water was too acidic. Four walkers were tramping heavily along the path that skirted part of the pond; the mallards, pochards, mandarin ducks and Canada geese appeared to be oblivious to them. After the other walkers had passed by, Michael walked very quietly to the far corner of the pond where the coots and moorhens were; as he approached they took fright and flew away, triggering a chain reaction from the other, previously unconcerned, waterfowl. Hugh had observed before how groups of noisy walkers clomping past often elicited no response from the birds, whereas individual walkers caused them to take to the air. Michael returned, disappointed. 'I don't know what scared them off – I was ever so quiet.'

'Maybe make more noise next time – birds can be perverse.'

They passed by the path to Yarncliffe quarry on their left and continued on to Granby Barn. Michael put his finger through the small circular hole in the door to lift the latch. They went inside and looked around at the displays about the landscape, local birds, ancient trade routes, millstone and grindstone quarrying, and the history of Longshaw Estate. Michael began to read about the landscape while Hugh gazed through the little window that looked out over Burbage Brook. Hugh could remember much of the information displayed, so decided he would leave Michael reading while he took a stroll by himself. 'I'll walk down to Yarncliffe Quarry while you're reading. Shall I stay there and wait for you, or should I come back?'

'You could wait here until I've finished reading, or we could just go together now.'

'There's some interesting details about the place – it's worth you reading through it all. I'd like to see if there's anybody climbing or abseiling – I know it doesn't interest you.'

Michael could see the logic of Hugh's argument, but was nevertheless annoyed at being excluded by Hugh. 'I'll have a quick read. Which way are you going?'

'Down the road – it takes about ten minutes.'

'I'll see you there then, unless you dawdle and I catch you up.'

Hugh crossed the B6521 before setting off down the road, there being no pavement on the near side. As he approached the quarry entrance he saw a van parked in the short space between the road and a large white gate; it displayed advertising that promoted an organisation which sought to inspire young people with climbing, abseiling and caving. He crossed back over the road at the entrance to Yarncliffe Quarry. In addition to the National Trust permanent display there was a temporary notice: the site would be closed for two days after today to facilitate some tree felling. In contrast to the oak trees that had tap roots to stabilise them, some of the short-rooted silver birches had been almost toppled by the high winds of the previous night and were now leaning precariously toward the crag.

Hugh saw how the wooded area near to the crag had been cordoned off as a safety measure, so was unable to go and stand in his favourite position. He walked into the heart of the quarry where he saw two young men in climbing gear standing together at the foot of a fin, a sharp corner that protruded from the centre of the crag. He thought how handsome the blond one was. He sidled over to him and asked quietly, 'How high is that climb?'

The young man was poring over a Rockfax book that identified the individual climbs at the quarry; he showed him the open page. 'This gives lengths of climbs rather than heights. Those abseilers on Ant's Slab are coming down sixteen to eighteen metres. We're going to be tackling this climb here with the undercut corner; it's called Cardinal's Arête. It starts off hard and then gets easier, with a neat finish. It's about twenty metres and pretty much straight up. We have to be careful in the middle section – some of the blocks are a bit loose. Do you climb?'

Hugh smiled and looked him earnestly in the eyes. 'I've tried bouldering, so climbing could be the next thing for me.' He added, 'I'm just out for a walk with my mate.' He was pleased that the ambiguity of his answer had avoided lying. 'We're going down to Sheffield Beach and then up to Bolehill Quarry – have you ever climbed there?'

'Lawrence Field? There's a lot of good climbs up there; we've done a few of them. Where's Sheffield Beach?'

'It's what some of the locals call Padley Gorge. Are you local?'
'Chesterfield.'

The second climber interrupted. 'Let's get going then.'

Hugh smiled at the Adonis. 'I'd better let you get on.'

He took a dozen steps back toward the quarry entrance. Looking up to the top of Ant's Crag, he counted one middle-aged instructor and six adolescents – five lads and one lass, to use his favoured terminology. They appeared to be preparing to abseil down the cliff face. There were a further four lads at the bottom who were calling up to them. The lads at the top called back, sounding like they were enjoying themselves. All the accents he heard were local. He doubted whether the blue helmets they wore would give them much protection if they fell without the restraining effect of the ropes. He watched as three of the lads stepped off in turn, placing their trust in the equipment and the instructor, and maybe God.

Hugh began to walk up the pathway to the left of the quarry to have a better view of those at the top at the moment they took that step of faith. He asked himself if he would have had the nerve at their age to make the descent. The remaining two lads without hesitation set off to walk down the sheer face; he wondered if their display of bravado had more to do with not losing credibility in front of their mates than with how they really felt. The lass, however, who had already postponed her turn several times, sat steadfastly on her bottom and shuffled back up from the cliff edge to the safety of the fence. Hugh reflected she could not have heard that since the advent of feminism lasses were under just as much of an obligation as lads to appear brave. He recalled how so many of the older girls at his school showed all the signs of being backsliding as far as feminist principles were concerned, being fixated on looking good for the boys to the exclusion of things such as academic work.

Hugh heard the instructor offering the lass words of encouragement, but she remained stubbornly against the very idea of abseiling. 'Come on Laura, I know you can do this. And then we'll be off to Dovedale, to do some caving. You never know, we might even find some treasure there – someone found some gold and silver pieces near where we're going. You just have to have belief in yourself; you know you can believe in the climbing gear, because all the lads have just used it, and some of them are a lot heavier than you.'

He clearly heard the remnants of a Welsh voice in the instructor, a small, stout man who in a bygone era he imagined might have mined for Welsh gold. He thought the instructor's

Welsh lilt had probably been watered down over time, drip by drip, and yet it had retained enough of its essence to remind Hugh of his parents and the valleys of South Wales. He had a feeling of guilt and shame that he had discarded his own Welsh accent so readily as he had crossed the border into England; he still failed to convince himself it had been necessary in order to teach in an English school. He tried to assuage his conscience by thinking of others who had similarly chosen to deny their roots: a colleague now unrecognisably from Glasgow who had developed a weird way of speaking, her modulations fluctuating wildly as all her words conjoined; another colleague who was convinced she had been able to remove every last trace of her Scottish accent, yet everyone else recognised it as refined Edinburgh. But, he told himself, the sins of others – if they were indeed sins – did not absolve him from responsibility for his own denial; perhaps worse than losing his accent was that he now rarely uttered a word of Welsh – God's own language, as he had been brought up to believe.

Hugh went to the quarry entrance and waited, guiltily thinking of the attractive blond climber. Within a couple of minutes he saw Michael approaching on the other side of the road. Michael waited until he was directly opposite the quarry entrance before starting to cross, asking before he had reached Hugh's side of the road, 'Anything happening at the quarry?'

'Usual stuff; abseiling and climbing. It's going to be closed for two days.'

'Are we still going down Padley Gorge, or should we go up Tumbling Hill instead, now that we're down here?'

Hugh took his cue for their little shared joke. 'Jubilee Hill, you mean.' Hugh preferred the local nickname that was derived from its use in 1897 for Queen Victoria's Diamond Jubilee; from that time onwards, jubilee and millennium celebrations had been marked with a beacon at the high point overlooking Grindleford.

They took the route through the trees. Hugh explained, 'This is an "Ancient Woodland".'

Michael turned his head slowly to take in the scenery. 'Well, it certainly looks very old.'

'The term "Ancient Woodland" is specific – it means it existed before 1600.'

'How can anyone know these trees are that old? People can't go counting their rings without cutting them down, and then there wouldn't be any left.'

'Well, I think radiocarbon dating could be used, but I wasn't actually talking about the age of the trees we are seeing here right now. "Ancient Woodland" just means the woodland itself has been in existence since before 1600, with some trees dying and new ones growing. There wasn't much planting of trees earlier than that date in England, and last summer we noticed a few indicators that this woodland was here before then.'

'Did we notice? I don't remember.'

'I showed you some wood sorrel – small white flowers with pink tinges or purple veins, and three heart-shaped leaves a bit like shamrock. Then there was the wild garlic – you were the one who remarked on the smell down by the stream. We both saw the bluebells. That makes three indicators to suggest it's an Ancient Woodland. Then there are the coppice stools – mature trees cut down to low stumps. New trees grow from the stumps, using the old root system. The whole cycle keeps repeating and never dies. It's a sort of immortality.'

Michael smiled. 'Not one that works for people though; we still need to find the Philosopher's Stone.'

'Well, having children is a route to genetic immortality, though not one we'll be taking. As an only child, when I'm gone that'll be the end of my line. I sometimes think "The Last of the Mohicans" owes so much of its poignancy to the idea of loss that extends beyond the individual.'

'I won't say "I've seen the film" – I know you're thinking of the book. You don't let go of literature, do you? Not even when we're out walking. It's one of the reasons I love you.'

Hugh turned around slowly, relieved to discover no one was nearby to overhear words that he wished Michael would only express within the four walls of their cottage.

They emerged from the woodland and continued on the path close to its edge, before dropping down to the stream that now had ambitions to be a river, being in spate from the heavy overnight storm. Hugh led the way over the little stepping-stones, careful to test each one for stability. They took the steep incline to the top of the hill rather than the wider, more gently sloping route, before continuing to the viewing point. Hugh went to the brink and looked down at the bare rock. Michael called him back. 'Don't go too close to the edge.'

After taking in the view, Michael led them on the high route, passing through a narrow gate before crossing the A625 close to the Grouse Inn and heading toward White Edge Moor. As they approached White Edge Lodge, Hugh asked, 'Do you recognise this? We saw it on TV.'

'Was it something to do with William and Harry? Didn't they used to stay here when they were in their teens?'

'I don't know about that – it was something else.'

'You'll have to give me a clue.'

'It was in a Jane Eyre film – I still have it on the sat-box.'

Michael looked carefully at the building. 'I don't remember anything as small as this.'

'You're right, in a way. The film people added a whole extension in fibreglass. When they'd finished filming they took it down again.'

Michael laughed at this revelation. 'Things are not always what they seem to be on TV.'

'Nor in real life', thought Hugh.

They continued over the moor and crossed back over the A625 near Wooden Pole, said pole being clearly visible against the leaden sky, before taking the wide, puddled path to Longshaw Lodge. Michael decided to lead them on a side-trip by climbing the steep steps to the Duke's Seat, a stone structure built in 1830 by a Duke of Rutland, where he regularly took his mistress. The Duke had found the presence of packhorses and their drivers spoiled his enjoyment of the view, so within five years he had had the turnpike rerouted. On a clear day the panorama over the estate included Kinder Scout and beyond, but today there was nothing visible through the grey mist. They headed back down the steps and continued along the broad, pitted path past the Robin Hood and Little John wells. As they approached Longshaw Lodge, Michael took them on a final detour to the Plunge Pool, a circular, stone structure that had been dry for decades. Hugh could imagine the bright young things of a bygone era sitting on the edge, splashing water as they drank their "shampoo", "champers", "fizz", "bubbly", or whatever name was fashionable at the time.

They headed for the tea room and stood at the counter where Pauline asked them what they would like to drink, knowing they would both select hot chocolate with cream and marshmallows. There were two types of cake available – sometimes there was only one. Michael chose Chocolate, his favourite. Hugh opted for Lemon Drizzle as it sounded like it matched the weather; he found the bright, zesty flavour quite in contrast with the greyness of the day.

In the car park they changed their muddy footwear while standing at the back of Hugh's Skoda Yeti Outdoor – a four-wheel-drive ready for the snowy winters – before heading back home.

They were not regular readers of the Shawton News, but Hugh wished to see if there was any update on the Newhouse investigation. They stopped at a newsagent's in Chesterfield where Michael jumped out of the car to fetch one, walking back slowly while reading it.

'There's a photo of you on the front page, Hugh; it's very grainy – I don't think anyone would recognise you from it.'

Hugh was dumbfounded as Michael handed him the newspaper. When he reached the end of the front page article he felt a cold shiver pass down his spine, despite the warm air blowing within the car. Michael remained silent, waiting for Hugh to decide what they should do next. Hugh turned to the inside page and read the article under the heading "Men in Girls' Changing Room". He handed the paper back to Michael, saying, 'There's more inside.'

Michael read the article while Hugh sat motionless looking into the distance. After Michael had put down the paper, Hugh stated simply, 'We need to think what to do.'

Michael tried to imagine what Hugh was thinking. He would have welcomed their relationship being brought into the open if it had not been for knowing Hugh's wishes on the subject; now he was afraid that Hugh may be planning a future without him.

Hugh's mind flooded with a jumble of remembrances of things past; unordered recollections and connections burst in on his mind as he looked for a way forward in his life. His thoughts remained unspoken. 'I shall soon be home, but will the cottage continue to be a place of quiet seclusion? I've tried to hide away from the rest of the world, with its prejudices and spite. I fled my homeland, the land of my fathers, seeking anonymity away from the shame. How shall we sing the Lord's song in a strange land?' His lower jaw and larynx fought against his stony face as his muscle memory replayed his singing of William Walton's Belshazzar's Feast, the words an adult echo of boyhood bible studies at the Congregational Chapel: "By the rivers of Babylon, there we sat down, yea, we wept, when we remembered Zion."

He remembered himself as a boy sitting by the river Cynon with two friends, then with the same two boys playing hide-and-seek among the barns; this image reminded him of Dylan Thomas's Fern Hill, which he began to recite in his mind. He remembered his own lost innocence. 'We played happily – I hid for fun, not for fear. We said we would always be best friends, and so we were until something came between us when we were eighteen. In some cultures kissing between men is normal; only, never in my valley.' He played with words in his mind, 'My "How Green was my Valley" valley. How green was I in my valley?'

For a moment he imagined he could smell bread baking, a false scent from the long-lost kitchen of his childhood home in Cwmbach, his little valley. 'As a child I was happy as the hearth was home, but when I was eighteen my friends' parents told me to stay away from their sons. I left in the summer, and knew there would never be a return to my grass roots, no welcome in the hillside. I was cast out of Eden, and my Mam and Tad refused to stay without me, though I never told them why I had to leave; I was still their little prince.

'Now they're bound to find out. Today's newspaper is tomorrow's fish 'n' chips wrapper, but by then the damage is done. A posting on the World Wide Web will inform the global village and the Welsh ones. European court rulings to restrict search engines and give me the right to be forgotten will be no use – people will still find out, and once someone knows, no court can make them forget.

'So, if there's no going back, then the only way is forward, living my life openly, homosexually – a better word than "Gay", that elicits sniggers in class which undermine so much wonderful literature. That word should be given back by people like me. We should say we are sorry, not for what we are, but for stealing that word. We came like thieves in the night and stole the word; that was our only sin.

'How can I live openly while ever my parents are alive? What if they were not alive?' This concept hurt him viscerally before his conscious mind could intervene. 'I hate myself for having that thought; to think of my parents having to die for my sin so that I can live without the fear of discovery. Why should I have to keep it secret, anyway? My whole being tells me what I want and feel is my type of normal. I should be allowed to have the same quality of life as the next man.'

Hugh's rambling thoughts were brought to a halt as he found himself parking the car on the hard standing by the side of the cottage, with no recollection of having driven there. The thought born out of the depths of despair that he had felt on seeing the revelation on the front page of the newspaper now attempted to resurrect itself, but was cut short by his action of turning off the car's engine and with it himself as autopilot. Michael opened his passenger door and went to the rear of the car where he took out both pairs of boots, holding them by their laces. Hugh also went to the rear where he took out all the waterproofs. As they entered the house they went their usual separate ways: Michael to clean the boots before returning them to the car; Hugh to hang the waterproofs to dry and then to sit and read. Except this time, instead of picking up a reading book, he began to mark his students' scripts. Michael noticed. 'Since when do you mark homework on Saturdays? That's always your Sunday job.'

Hugh looked up, for once unsmiling. 'It takes my mind off other things.'

Michael went to create the salad, and poured two large glasses of white wine to numb the effects of the real world that had intruded into their rural idyll.

After lunch, Hugh continued with the marking, devoting substantially more time than usual as he sought to include as much insightful comment as he could on each and every script, determined that all his students should receive the best possible advice on developing their understanding and interpretation of the literature and the classics they had been studying together – The Picture of Dorian Gray, King Lear, Hippolytus and Antigone. He continued through the afternoon and beyond, disappointing Michael by asking him not to make the evening meal he had planned. At a quarter past six Hugh closed the last of the homework books, then packed them neatly into the two bags he used for lugging them between home and car and staffroom and classroom. He stood and walked, as nonchalantly as he could perform, over to the row of hooks that held their various keys. He took his car keys and casually put on his coat, with an over-the-shoulder parting line, 'I'm just going out.'

Michael saw through the performance – Hugh never went out this way on a Saturday evening. His main fear erupted to the surface. 'Where are you going? Who are you going to see?'

'I'm only going out for a breath of air – I just need some time to clear my head.'

'Well, how long are you going to be? Should I prepare the food for when you're back?'

'I'm not hungry so don't do anything for me.'

Michael picked up a bright red Royal Gala apple from the fruit bowl and thrust it into Hugh's hand. 'Take this with you, just in case you get peckish.'

'Yes, that's a good idea.' Hugh wondered if there was any cyanide to go with it.

'So, when will you be back?'

'I don't know; I may be some time.'

Michael accepted this as being as much of an answer as he would be getting, so he unlocked the door, let Hugh out, and relocked the door behind him.

* * *

Lily offered to be Neil's chauffeuse, an offer he happily accepted as it gave him the freedom to have more than just a single pint at the Black Bull. Previously the alcohol had been a way of deadening his senses, whereas now it would be more to do with letting go of past troubles and shaking off inhibitions. They arrived at ten minutes to six and Lily found George Westmorland already seated in the Snug with an almost full pint of bitter. Not wishing him to miss the fact that she was not late for once, she began, 'Well, I'm early but you're even earlier.'

George stood up and would have given her his usual greeting, but decided to forego the customary fatherly kiss on the cheek in view of Neil's presence. Lily introduced Neil to George, who declined the offer of another pint. While Neil was at the bar for his own first pint and a slim-line orange juice for Lily, George opened the conversation. 'So, this is the man who has succeeded where lesser mortals have failed.'

Lily was too forthright to play the coy maiden. 'We're having a great time together, in bed and out. I'm sure he's the right man for me.'

'What's the down side, or isn't there one? You'll have to be quick – he'll be coming back in a minute.'

'He's married, with a mentally disabled child.'

'That doesn't sound so good, Lily. What he's planning to do about it?'

'He's going to get divorced, only she's a Catholic so it could take much longer than normal.' She decided not to add 'and then we'll be getting married', because she realised how it might sound fanciful considering how much had to happen before that would be possible.

'What about the child?'

Lily was relieved not to have to begin on that subject as Neil was now on his way back from the bar. She guillotined the conversation with, 'That would take a lot of explaining.'

Neil heard the closing remarks. 'What would take a lot of explaining? I hope you're talking about me.'

Lily was not one to back away from a subject, so she responded, 'I was telling George that you're getting divorced from a Catholic woman and that you have a mentally disabled child.'

Neil was a little taken aback at how much information had already been disclosed to someone he had only just met and about whom he knew very little. Nevertheless he turned to Lily with a smile and congratulated her. 'Well done officer – that was a succinct summary.'

George recognised how Neil could be feeling put out by Lily's disclosure of his personal circumstances, so he sought to engage him in conversation directly. 'How mentally disabled is the child?'

'Completely and utterly. He's only one step away from being a human vegetable.' Following Lily's lead on being open and direct, he continued, 'There's no point in him living, really. He understands nothing, so he can't feel pleasure, but he can feel pain.'

George decided the conversation had already gone deeper than he was comfortable with for now, so decided to regale them with a farming anecdote. 'Parents normally look forward to the birth of a child, though I remember one of the local farmers – I won't tell you his name – he wasn't quite so fussed about his fifth, or maybe it was his sixth. I was sitting right here, and he was over there standing at the bar.'

Neil made no comment about the unlikely scenario – the farmers always use the Public Bar.

'His wife's sister came in and said she was nearly due and he mun come back home.' George appeared to savour the word "mun", local dialect for "must". 'He said, there's no rush, she'll be alreet for a bit yet. So she went back. Twenty minutes later and she was here again. Message for you, get back right now, you're needed. Response was, I'll just finish me pint, and then I'll be over by-and-by.' George took a slow, deliberate drink of his own beer, with all the timing of a practised raconteur. 'Then the woman comes back again. Message for you. You don't seem fussed about coming now it's lambin' time, but you were happy enough to come when it wa' tuppin' time.' George beamed, first in Neil's direction and then in Lily's to indicate that was the end of the story. They both laughed good-naturedly; though neither of them were familiar with the word "tupping", they could guess the meaning.

With the precision to be expected of a surgeon, Jim Kinder entered the pub at ten seconds before six o'clock. Neil saw him heading for the Public Bar, so excused himself and went to see him. Neil began, 'Hello Jim, Lily's in the Snug. Before I take you through to meet her properly, maybe you and I could have a chat here first.' Neil gave an account of his changed marital circumstances, adopting Lily's style of full and frank disclosure, and ending with, 'The law allows me to get shot of my wife, eventually. The law doesn't allow me to get shot of the child, ever. I'm sure it must be against your code of ethics to want a child gone like I do, but what do you think are the prospects? What's your prognosis?'

Jim had looked into Ollie's background and researched other children with the same affliction as far as he could, but normal rules for gathering data had left him unable to form a definitive scientific opinion, so he had gone outside the official routes. He gave an explanation of his investigation, allowing Neil to interpret it as best he could. 'When I started out as a doctor, I thought the idea of all human life being sacred was one that I could hold onto, no matter what. But I do sometimes waver, especially when I think about Ollie. As to life expectancy though, it's just possible there may be a point when some fatal event could be triggered as the body enters puberty. There are other illnesses that present at puberty and which are always fatal at that time, but this isn't one of those. For Ollie's condition, there are examples where the patient has not only survived childhood but continued into their twenties and even thirties. The unofficial view of the medics that I've contacted in each of the five cases where death occurred suddenly in their early teens is that one or other of the parents had simply lost control and killed the child themselves. There were two cases in Argentina, one in Chile, one in Italy – Sicily in fact – and one in Belgium. There were also a dozen recorded cases around the world where the child never made it beyond their second birthday; all but one of the doctors I was able to contact refused to express an opinion as to the cause of death of the infants, though several of them hinted it was a blessing to all concerned. Just one in Austria put forward a theory; he believed a thin film of plastic sheeting – something like Clingfilm – had been placed over the child's nose and mouth and stretched so it sealed over the whole face, and then as the air supply was blocked off, death by suffocation resulted. I don't know whether the pathologist in Austria should have been able to detect that method, or whether they even chose to look. I have the impression pathologists in many countries choose not to delve too deeply to find the true cause of death in cases where they deem it was a release rather than a crime, though I should expect pathologists in the UK would always look for the cause. Dr Mallory could probably give you a much closer insight into whether the suffocation method should be detectable, or whether different methods could have been used that are just as quick and effective and are less easy for pathologists to recognise. It isn't something I'll be investigating myself – my code of ethics demands I concentrate entirely on the preservation of life.'

Neil had been listening intently and believed he understood not only what had been said but also what had been left unsaid. 'Thank you, Jim; I couldn't ask for anything more. Now let's go and talk to the most beautiful woman in the world; she's sitting with George Westmorland – you may know him, he's the local bank manager.'

They left their domain and ventured into the Snug, which was still only sparsely populated. Sitting around a table they began to fish for something of common interest to talk about. When the performance of the local football teams surfaced, George looked for an alternative topic, knowing Lily's lack of interest in the subject. He picked up the newspaper he had been reading while waiting for Lily to arrive. 'This is quite interesting. A death at Midshaw School – is it something you're involved in, Lily?'

Knowing that careless talk costs jobs, she chose her words carefully as there were people sitting within earshot – if they strained to listen. 'Neil and I have both been working the case, though we might not be next week.'

Despite the possibility of it being interpreted as antisocial, Neil asked if he could have the newspaper to read the article. He read while the others circled around the subject. He then opened the paper and read the inside article that was referenced on the front page. When he had finished, he looked for an opportunity to re-enter the conversation, which he did by saying, 'Lily, I think you need to read this.'

She read the articles as the other three switched back to football, then placed the newspaper on the bench seat next to George. She accepted the moment's silence that followed as her invitation to comment. 'I wonder how much of it's true?'

George offered a minor indiscretion, lowering his voice as he did so. 'I can confirm the part about the marriage.'

Jim had another engagement for later that evening and had been looking for an opportunity to leave without being too abrupt, so he decided to seize the moment. 'Before you say any more, I appreciate the importance of confidentiality. I have to go soon anyway, so I'll take my leave of you now. I look forward to seeing you all again sometime soon.'

Neil asked him to stay a while longer, using just enough politeness and not enough insistence so that he was able to leave immediately but with a sufficient display of reluctance. He accompanied Jim to the door and thanked him again for all his help. Passing the bar, he took the opportunity to buy two more pints of Pedigree and another orange juice.

On returning, George thanked Neil for the pint and insisted he would buy the next round. Lily asked George, 'Could anyone at the bank have divulged the information to the press?'

George looked at her, and then at Neil, as he explained quietly. 'No, I'm the only one there who knew, and I certainly haven't told anyone else. The computer system used to hold such information, but the ability to record that type of detail was taken out years ago. The screen used to show various alternatives that could be selected for marital status, things like single, married, divorced, widower. Long before same-sex marriage was introduced into law, "Civil Partnership" was created; it was provided as an option on the computer system and then suddenly it was merged with married so we couldn't tell the difference. I asked Head Office about it because it had been useful information to have – part of knowing your customer. I was told some civil servant had said it might be embarrassing for someone if it was revealed they were in a civil partnership, and that all the banks were being advised to lose the option for distinguishing between married and civil partnership. I argued back that while ever people are being discouraged from being open about being Gay, we'll continue to have prejudice.

'I also said this to a regional director at a dinner one time, and I mentioned that we'd had some complaints from married customers who were using internet banking, and who'd noticed their own status had changed from "Married" to "Married/Civil Partnership". In fact I'd had a long chat with one chap, who wasn't at all prejudiced about Gays, but at the same time insisted on his right to be registered as "Married"; he was the one who really opened my eyes to the idea that hiding the different statuses was itself playing into a form of prejudice. In his case we agreed to change his status to "Other", though I don't know what was left after all the specific categories had been eliminated. I don't think we've got an option for "Transitional" – man becoming woman, woman becoming man – so maybe that's what's left. Anyway, I asked to have the "Civil Partnership" option put back in.'

Neil recognised George was becoming more voluble as the beer took effect, which he encouraged with a laugh and a question. 'What did the regional director say – did he say he'd think about it?'

George returned the laugh with interest. 'No, but he did say he'd make me his sexual advisor.'

Lily was intrigued by this and asked what it entailed. George reddened a little as he elaborated. 'It's code, a bit of an in-joke. It means, "When I want your effing opinion I'll ask for it." Sorry, I should have stopped myself before I started; that was a bit rude.'

Neil gave enough of a laugh to reduce George's

embarrassment, before asking, 'If the system doesn't differentiate between traditional and same-sex marriage, how come you know about his?'

'Ah, well. The couple were wishing to buy a house and to take out a mortgage with the bank. They also wanted the outstanding mortgage covered on a reducing basis by insurance in the event of one of them dying. This isn't the same as mortgage payment protection that's the subject of a major scandal; it's just life cover I'm talking about. Mr...' He avoided divulging the name in public. '...the man in the newspaper came into my office on his own to deal with some of the paperwork. I knew from the system that he was either married or in a civil partnership, so, as the insurers needed to know, I asked if it was to a man or a woman. It nearly always raises a laugh, but not this time. He said it was a same-sex marriage and that he didn't want anyone else to know. I agreed to do the paperwork myself and keep it in my confidential filing, which is why I know no one else at the bank knew about it.'

Lily interjected. 'Why did the insurers need to know?'

George hesitated for a moment, considering whether he had already been a little too free with his reference to sexual matters. He decided to press ahead. 'I phoned the insurance section and spoke with a chap who explained it's to do with calculating life expectancy so that the premiums are fair for the level of risk. He said that people who are living with the HIV virus and are diagnosed early can live normal life-spans, but people who aren't diagnosed early enough can suffer severe symptoms that can be fatal. Though GRID – Gay Related Immune Deficiency – was renamed AIDS as it came to be understood better, there's still a Gay bias to the stats. There are about a hundred thousand people with HIV in the UK, with maybe one in five of them undiagnosed. There's about the same total number of people who get HIV from heterosexual contact as from homosexual, though of course there's far more heterosexuals than homosexuals, so homosexual contact is maybe a hundred times higher risk. Insurers work with the total picture rather than considering it at individual level, where it's dependent on promiscuity; oh, I didn't mean to sound judgemental, I just can't think of a better way of expressing it.

'Anyway, the population's HIV rate for men is a bit more than twice the rate for women – something over two per thousand compared to one per thousand. So, because of the numbers, the insurance underwriters apply a small loading for Gays, and they also have slightly different weightings for single Gays compared to those in a civil partnership or a same-sex marriage.'

Lily nodded. 'So, single Gays pay a higher premium.'

'Actually, no, it's the other way around; they'd researched the subject and established that, in general, Gays in same-sex marriages or civil partnerships are more likely to be promiscuous than single ones – I was really surprised about that. Anyway, I explained it to the customer. He said neither he nor his partner were in the least promiscuous and that the premium shouldn't be loaded. The guy on the phone from the insurers said he sympathised but he wasn't able to change the loading; I asked if he couldn't just put in an exclusion clause like they already do with "no pay-out to policyholder on suicide", but he said it would be even more impossible to prove the promiscuity question after someone is dead than when they're alive.'

Neil kept to himself his amusement at the idea of degrees of impossibility. 'So, did he go ahead with the insurance in the end?'

'Yes, he decided the small extra loading wasn't enough to miss out on taking the cover.'

Neil felt the evening had turned into a working session, so he sought to change the topic of their conversation to something more amusing. 'That was very interesting, George.' He paused for a moment. 'That's the serious side of your work – is there a funny side as well?'

George was pleased to respond. 'Ages ago, a long way from here, I came across a chap who had an unusual middle name. You've heard of Roger Bannister, no doubt; well, it was nothing to do with him. It was this chap's middle name that was Bannister, and he explained to me his father came up with it when he was born. His mother had refused to let go of the bannister at home while she was giving birth.'

Neil looked suitably amused – having had the story directed at him – though he wondered about its veracity.

George was still keeping Lily and Neil entertained with anecdotes from work when his mobile phone made a squawking noise. 'I'll have to take this.' He scuttled outside to where there was less noise and more privacy, returning several minutes later. With a continuous shaking of his head he declared, 'You're not going to believe this. The man we were talking about earlier – he's been kidnapped.' George responded to Witty's request for more details. 'Midshaw Bank is part of a multi-national banking corporation. Our South American bank's customers have a particular problem: they sometimes get kidnapped! The kidnappers just want to empty their bank accounts, so they demand – with menaces – to know their PIN, that's the Personal Identification Number, and then use it to get money out of a cash machine. Sometimes you hear people call it the PIN Number, but that would mean the Personal Identification Number Number. I suppose we should call it the PI Number. Anyway, the bank places daily withdrawal limits so as to minimise such losses. This led to kidnappers using the card just before midnight and again just after midnight, to get twice the daily maximum. So the bank tried various algorithms to catch such activity, but they were always fighting a losing battle. Then someone came up with a brilliant idea: enable the customer to send out an S.O.S. The usual PIN would operate in the normal way, let's say 4907, and the system would also allow another PIN to operate as normal but actually to trigger the S.O.S. That second number would be the one that results from taking each digit away from nine, so 5092 would also work; they called this the "Inverse PIN". Someone else suggested it would be easier for customers just to reverse the numbers, so 4907 becomes 7094, but various reasons were put forward as to why this was an inferior solution, some mathematical and some practical – dyslexia was mentioned. So we stayed with the Inverse PIN. If you take 4907 as the PIN, then 5092 is the Inverse PIN, and if the Inverse PIN is used then the card works like normal but it means the money's being withdrawn under duress, such as by a kidnapper.

'Now, one problem the South American bank found they had to overcome was that inebriated young men', he turned to Lily, 'and women, thought it was amusing to use the Inverse PIN themselves, just for fun. So the police refused to play ball when the bank told them about any alleged kidnapping, because usually it wasn't. The bank then brought in a penalty clause for misuse – quite a big penalty I seem to remember, and after that the system worked effectively. Recently the same software was introduced into all the other banks in the group, with an option to switch the mechanism on or off for individual customers, or even for each entire bank.

We at Midshaw have just started to use it on a trial basis; a small number of customers have been invited to use the system once they've signed the special terms and conditions, including the part about the penalty for misuse.

'Mr you-know-who signed up to the system and someone has just used his card but with the Inverse PIN. That has triggered some sort of message at the computer centre and they phoned me to decide what to do about it. This is the first time it's happened with a Midshaw Bank customer. Once the system's running smoothly, someone at the centre's supposed to deal with it and I should just get automated messages to keep me informed of progress. But for now I'm the one that has the responsibility to investigate. If I believe it's genuine then I'm obliged to inform the police straight away. I would have thought the size of the penalty for misuse would persuade people only to use the system the way it was intended, so for now I'm assuming Mr Cassidy has been forced into divulging the Inverse PIN to someone who has then used it to get money out of his account.'

Neil had been getting a little irritated with George's digressions and overfull explanations, whereas Lily barely noticed them. When George paused, Neil asked, 'How much money was withdrawn?'

George launched into another detailed explanation. 'I can tell you not only the amount but also the denominations of the notes. Customers used to complain that the cash machines didn't give them any choice about what notes they wanted them to dispense. Some of them even made lots of small withdrawals one after the other just to avoid getting large notes. Of course the machines can only give out whatever's available, and with many customers preferring small denominations these tend to be used up first, which means later customers have less choice. The machine that was used had all denominations available, and yet the kidnapper, who withdrew six hundred pounds, specifically requested it to dispense the whole amount in twenty pound notes. The computer centre people said his daily withdrawal limit is a thousand pounds and his balance meant he had more than eight hundred pounds available. That's particularly strange, as kidnappers and thieves usually take the maximum they can. There is an exception, though; where there's an additional security check linked to a known daily limit for a particular type of transaction such as a cash withdrawal, fraudsters and the like take out just less than the figure that triggers a warn…'

Neil interrupted George in full flow. 'I think we need to make some basic checks before we assume a kidnapping, George. Do you have the contact details for Mr Cassidy?'

'Yes. Part of the system is for the computer centre to provide me with all manner of information on separate texts. They're a bit cryptic, but I know what they mean. So I have both his home landline and his mobile number.'

'Well, would you mind telephoning the numbers and see what response you get?'

George nodded in agreement and phoned the landline, after which he explained what had happened. 'I spoke to his partner, Michael Gough. Not "Michael Cassidy", I noticed. Mr Gough became very upset. I should say very, very upset. He said Mr Cassidy had gone out in his car, and that that was very unusual for a Saturday evening. He didn't say where he was going, only that we wanted to clear his head, and he wouldn't say how long he would be.'

'Best to try the mobile, then.'

George phoned the number. 'I'm only getting an automated response that the phone has been switched off – not connected to the network.'

With a sweep of his hand to encompass Lily in the proceedings, Neil responded, 'In view of the Newhouse case, I think we need to take the disappearance seriously. Could you give us the phone numbers?'

As the other two had been on the beer, Lily had no choice but to nominate herself as the driver, untypically using one of Witty's sporting metaphors. 'We'll all go to the station in my car and get the ball rolling.'

At the station they located the duty sergeant and supplied the background on the missing person. Sergeant Robert Oldham had had a long career in policing and was plodding toward retirement, happy enough to take night duty now that not only his children had left for pastures new but so had his wife. His predilection for sitting reading policing-related material throughout each night-shift had resulted in Oldham developing a slouch and a pot-belly. A positive consequence was that he could be a fount of theoretical knowledge on some subjects, and his years of experience also gave him good sense at a practical level. He offered Witty his assessment. 'It isn't uncommon for men of his age to go missing; the figures are nowhere near as high as for teenagers, of course, but it's still common enough. Seventy per cent of Mispers are found within sixteen hours; only one in ten are still missing after two days, and only one in fifty after a week. Normally I'd say he should be assessed as low risk, but this bother with the dead teacher puts a different gloss on it. You're closer than me to this case, Witty; how do you see it?'

'He isn't a run-of-the-mill Misper, what with the accusation of homicide, and the coded message to his bank to say he's under duress. I really think we should be pulling out all the stops.'

'I think you're dead right. Do you reckon he might be doing a runner? You did say he's taken a lot of cash out of his bank account.'

'Anything's possible. He's originally from South Wales, so he might be heading home.'

'Well, it's better for us to do everything we can and regret the waste of time when he turns up safe and well, than to have cause to regret not doing more. I'll invoke the procedure for high risk Mispers.'

Witty phoned Gough to let him know they were taking immediate action. He asked for a list of Cassidy's haunts, and for a recent photograph to be e-mailed to him at the station. He undertook to keep Gough informed of progress, and asked him to do likewise. Within minutes Gough had sent eight photographs in JPG format, known as J-pegs, each with a smiling subject; Witty selected the one with the least pronounced smile. All police on duty were instructed to be on the lookout for Cassidy's car, with type, colour and vehicle registration plate as advised. Cassidy's car registration was passed to ANPR, the Automatic Number Plate Recognition system. Cassidy's image was uploaded, and those without access to suitable technology were told to collect printed photographs from the station at their earliest convenience.

Oldham, Witty and Martello discussed whether they should be searching specific places associated with the Misper. Martello suggested they could check the school, as they had the entry code to the main door. Oldham responded, 'More than three Mispers in five are found within five miles of where they disappeared, and almost four in five within twenty miles, but that's because many of them don't have their own transport. Your Mr Cassidy is a different kettle of fish; he could drive anywhere. If his car is parked near the school then it should be searched, but if it isn't then it probably shouldn't. I'll arrange for a patrol car to check out the area and let you know.'

Witty phoned Gough again when he felt everything had been done that could be done for now, explaining how tracking down a missing person was something that could take anything from hours to days or even much longer, and often depended on whether the person intended not to be found. Gough agreed he would contact the station immediately if Cassidy returned home. Martello drove Westmorland back to his house and promised to let him know of any developments. As Martello and Witty headed back to their own home, Witty speculated on where Cassidy may have gone. 'He could be going to his parents' home in Wales. Do you think we should get in touch with them?'

Martello was pleased to be asked for her opinion, as Witty normally took the lead on any such matters. 'If he is, I don't think they'd appreciate being given advance warning – it would just give them something to worry about until he turned up.'

Neil was delighted to hear Lily express concern for people she had never met – empathy had never been her strong point in the past. He added this to the long list of reasons why he loved her, as though he needed reasons.

PART 2

CHAPTER 19

A Second Death

Sunday

Sunday morning had long been Lily's favourite time for staying in bed late. Neil on the other hand had never enjoyed such a start to the day with his wife; she had become pregnant at the beginning of their marriage and on the strength of it enjoyed staying in bed and expected him to be up and doing things about the house – quietly – and making her a cup of tea and providing breakfast on a tray and "don't forget the napkin" and "a few flowers in a vase would be a nice touch once in a while". So, as much as Neil wished to stay in bed late with Lily, his conditioning saw him up and about early; he was happy to provide Lily, unasked, with a cup of proper coffee in bed, and not as a chore but as an expression of love.

Witty telephoned the station and was unsurprised to find there had been no developments on the Cassidy missing person case. He phoned Gough to inform him of this, having first checked with him that Cassidy had not returned home in the night.

Despite their agreement to follow a healthy diet, Neil saw there was now some bacon in the fridge; he decided to make a full English breakfast to make the day more special, wondering whether, when it comes to food, perhaps the lady doth protest too much. He grilled the bacon and fried the eggs and tomato, the cooking timed to perfection as Lily showered and dressed. He was pleased with himself as he invited her to sit at the neatly laid table, offering, 'This'll make a nice change for both of us.'

'Great, so long as we don't make a habit of it; probably best to check with me next time, though.'

Neil decided that was a policy he should adopt for everything from now on until he understood her better.

After breakfast he watched the recording of yesterday's Premiership football while she did some ironing. They talked of having a pub lunch. It would need to be a late one after their large breakfast; unfortunately, some of the local pubs that did good Sunday Lunches at twelve o'clock were down to mushy vegetables by one o'clock. The discussion proved academic as Neil's phone rang at eleven fifty-five: a body had been found.

Witty drove without hurrying, Martello giving directions; he smiled inwardly as he reflected on how police in films were often depicted racing to crime scenes when the time for urgency was long past. Besides, he was in no rush to see another dead body; guiltily he recognised he had no wish for Martello to have to see one either, though accepting that such protective instincts were nowadays viewed as sexist. As they approached the specified stretch of the B6521, it was clear where they should stop. There was the usual collection of emergency and police vehicles parked up, and a constable was directing other traffic away from the area.

DCI Bryn Castleton was already at the scene and intercepted Witty and Martello. 'The body was reported at eleven twenty-seven. There was an organised walk that set off at eleven o'clock from the café: three National Trust volunteers and eighteen others. Shelley was at the front and Keith at the back, with the other walkers sandwiched in between apart from Charles who had gone on ahead to check the quarry site – he's the one who reported the body. He tells me normally the quarry would be in use by climbers, but the National Trust had a planned two-day closure to clear some of the trees nearby and to move a pile of logs. When he spotted the body he phoned it in and then went back and spoke to Shelley and Keith to change their route; so instead of going past the quarry and up Tumbling Hill, she led them up the road and across to Padley Gorge. They'll be coming back a different way to avoid this area entirely. Charles is over there if you have any questions. It's National Trust property so we'll keep him involved as much as needs be.

'Mr Cassidy's face is unmarked, so I've no difficulty in confirming that it's him. The forensics people are still processing the area down here and at the top of the crag. I don't know if they'll also be examining the rock face, in which case they'll need to recruit some climbers; it's probably not necessary as it's obvious what happened – there was a suicide note in his pocket. There was also a bottle of White Horse whisky at the top, maybe a quarter full; it was carefully wedged upright with stones, with a proper whisky glass next to it, and a little stainless steel measurer. Seems a bit strange, that; why not just drink it straight from the bottle, and why not drink it all. Anyway, it near as dammit confirms my suspicion that he was responsible for the other death. You and Martello reported this one missing yesterday, so you can stay on the case; start with taking a look at the body.'

Before heading for the corpse, Witty asked Castleton if Michael Gough had been contacted and if they had examined the car. Castleton's response of, 'What car?' indicated they had not noticed the vehicle parked just off the road a little way up the B6521, squeezed up against a dry stone wall close to a white seven-bar gate near the end of a grass track. They walked over together and looked at it from the outside. Castleton instructed Witty, 'Telephone Gough and inform him about his partner's dead body. Ask him to bring over the car keys if he's got any; the pathologist wouldn't like the idea of disturbing the body to search for them, and it seems a bit pointless to break into it if we don't have to.'

Witty had some misgivings about dealing with Gough in this manner, but knew it would be unwise to express his opinions, knowing that Castleton would brook no argument.

After making the call, Witty went with Martello to view the body as instructed. It lay at the foot of Yarncliffe Quarry, spread-eagled except for one leg that lay crooked at an unnatural angle. From a distance the body appeared unmarked, as though he had simply lain on his back to look up at the sky. He wondered if Cassidy had attempted a break-fall like a judoka, once it was too late to stop himself from falling. On closer inspection, Witty noticed the back of the head had some damage; he was surprised that it appeared to be less than he had observed on Newhouse four days earlier. There were signs of blood having seeped into the earth, giving a russet hue to the thin crust of friable brown earth. Witty finished his viewing and turned to speak to Lily, only to find she had gone. He saw her away to the right, by the silver birch trees, throwing up the bacon, egg and tomato. He waited until she had finished before walking over to her, offering a look of concern and sympathy with eyebrows raised and cheeks pushed up by a widened mouth with lips squeezed together at the edges. She began to speak straight away, looking directly into his eyes. 'I can't do this, Neil. I know it makes no sense, but seeing a dead body that looks almost uninjured seems worse than seeing a shattered one – it's as though he should be able to stand up and walk away. It's such a waste of a life. Castleton's threatened to send me back to Traffic; I'd expect to have to see more dead bodies, and it always gets to me. I just can't do it.'

Witty assumed the "waste of a life" meant Cassidy, but wondered if she might also be thinking of her own life if it were spent having to cope with the horror of looking at the dead and injured. He felt this was neither the time nor the place for discussing future options. 'Alright love, we'll talk about it later. Are you OK to carry on today?'

'Yes. I'll not give that bastard the satisfaction of seeing me just walk out.'

Witty returned to Castleton. 'You mentioned a suicide note, sir. Does he give a reason for his suicide? Does it mention Newhouse?'

'Well, it's not an ordinary suicide note, it's more like a poem to his parents, except it doesn't bloody rhyme. Go and take a look if you like, they've got it over there in a plastic bag.'

Witty signalled Martello to look at the evidence with him.

Happy I was to live my life,
With parents who loved me more than the world,
But I had a secret, a man for a wife,
And now that you know, my memory's soiled.

Yet think not of loss
For I grow not old.
My life is cut short
My story is ended.

Witty had had little time for poetry and so felt unable to assess it aesthetically or structurally. He knew it would be left to experts to consider it forensically – checking it against other handwriting by Cassidy and assessing if it could have been composed by him. He believed there was little evidence of it having been written under stress or duress: it was written neatly and the only alteration was that "my trouble and strife" had been lined through and replaced with "a man for a wife". He reread the poem but could find no connection with Newhouse, so he considered it could not reasonably be taken as indicating culpability for his death. He had an uncomfortable feeling in the pit of his stomach that he was reaching the limits of his knowledge and capability on the Newhouse case. He also believed Castleton would be driving it forward irrespective of any evidence that failed to fit with his own view.

He walked Lily further away from the scene, around the back of a large log pile, and asked her about the threat of a return to Traffic. She told him what Castleton had said, and of her view of his motivation; they agreed it would be best to talk it through later. He then switched to the investigation. 'I'm not sure how we should read this suicide note, or what we should be doing on the Newhouse case. I'm going to phone Marcus and see if he's at home. The likes of us can't stand up to Castleton, but Marcus would if that's what's needed.' Martello nodded her approval.

The Detective Inspector answered after just a couple of seconds. 'Marcus Priestley.'

'Hello, Marcus. Are you disturbable?'

'Evidently – you've just disturbed me. But it's not a problem; what can I do for you?'

'There's a case I've been working on with Lily: a death at Midshaw School, teacher by the name of John Newhouse. DCI Castleton suspected another teacher, Hugh Cassidy, who appears to have committed suicide by jumping off a cliff, and Castleton's taking it as having proved him right. There's a suicide note that's a bit weird, but it doesn't admit to anything, so I'm not at all sure he killed Newhouse. I'm feeling out of my depth, Marcus, and I can't argue with Castleton – he's such a bastard, he'll take it out on me and I can't do with that at the moment. He's also picking on Lily, so she's suffering right now.'

'That was a mouthful, Neil. Why don't you come over and talk me through the case and anything else. Is Lily with you?'

'Uh-huh.'

'Good; bring her as well if she's free.'

Witty and Martello waited for Gough to arrive. Castleton intercepted Gough and took him straight over to see the body. Gough's features appeared frozen as he gazed at the face of his dead partner. Castleton returned with Gough to Witty and Martello, who offered expressions of sympathy; Gough accepted them gratefully and yet with some surprise, as though he had never imagined police officers would care about his feelings. The four then went to examine the parked car. Wearing thin, pale yellow, loose-fitting latex gloves, Castleton took the spare keys from Gough and opened the door on the front passenger's side. When he checked in the glove compartment he found an envelope of the type used for depositing money into a bank at an automated paying-in machine. Squeezed in amongst the pre-printed instructions were written the words, 'Michael, I am so sorry for betraying you.'

Castleton teased the contents carefully from the envelope, awkwardly counting the bank notes with gloved fingers; he found it contained six hundred pounds. He informed Gough, 'We'll have to hold onto this until it's been forensically examined.'

Witty invited Castleton to have a quiet conversation to one side. 'Sir, Mr Gough appears to be holding up well at the moment, but I think it may be because this hasn't really hit him yet. I think he'll need someone to be with him; we wouldn't want any more bodies, would we sir?'

Castleton accepted the advice and walked back to Gough. 'Mr Gough, in situations like this we offer someone for you to talk to, to keep you company. Now, you're Gay, aren't you, so would you prefer a man or a woman?'

Witty overheard the exchange and cringed, thinking, 'Subtle, DCI Castleton, very subtle.'

Witty and Martello avoided Castleton as they took their leave of the other officers, arriving fifteen minutes later at Priestley's large detached house in Ecclesall, a leafy suburb of Sheffield. His wife Helen answered the door. She was slim and fairly short, a hint of Chinese in her smiling face that was framed with grey-tipped black hair. Seeing the two together she held the outer door wide open for them to walk in past her. She spoke to them with an index finger to her lips to ask for silence, the final traces of her Northern Irish accent hinting at her Protestant roots. 'Don't tell me, let me guess. You're here for a party but Marcus forgot to tell me about it.'

They responded in kind. 'Hello Helen. We're unfashionably early – the party's set for seven o'clock.'

'Hello Helen. My party frock's in the car.'

Marcus Priestley was sitting in the living room, his tall, muscular frame filling a deep red leather chair. As they entered the room he stood to greet them; Helen followed them in, and behind her appeared two little faces peering around the corner to see who the visitors were. Priestley beckoned Martello and Witty to come in and sit on a sofa, before calling gently to his children. 'Edwin, Alice, come in and meet our guests, Lily and Neil.' They ventured into the room: one small step, a pause, and then another step.

Lily spoke to them in a soft, sweet, lilting voice that Neil barely recognised as hers. 'What a beautiful dress you're wearing, Alice; I'd love to have one just like that. And Edwin, is that a football shirt you're wearing? Who's your favourite team?'

Edwin happily responded 'Sheffield Wednesday and Barcelona', having little knowledge of either of them.

Alice, having no wish to be outshone, offered her own favourites. 'I like horses and cows.'

Edwin switched to Alice's theme. 'I like pigs.'

Helen took them to another room, where they could be heard debating the merits of various animals, before a closing door silenced them.

Priestley knew that Witty's untypical stream of words on the phone suggested there were other matters to consider than just the two dead bodies. 'Start by telling me all the things I've missed that don't involve the cases themselves. I think there was a hint that DCI Castleton is something of an issue.'

Witty turned his head to Lily to invite her to speak first.

'He's been trying to get off with me for ages and now that I'm living with Neil he's really got it in for me.'

Priestley displayed more surprise than he actually felt; he had often wondered how anyone could work closely with Martello and remain impervious to her beauty. He recalled a phrase from therapy. 'Could you unpack that for me?'

Lily explained recent events from her perspective, covering the whole gamut from birth to marriage to divorce, with Neil adding an occasional clarification. She finished with details of the way Castleton had set out to humiliate her, and the threat he had made to send her back to Traffic. In the quiet moment that followed, Helen brought in coffee for the three of them, so Witty tried to provide some light relief while she was there. 'I sometimes had a bit of fun when I was on traffic duty. I had a woman from Dore who wanted to tell me all about child-care facilities; it took me ages to realise it wasn't a crèche she was talking about, it was a traffic collision.' The other three laughed gently, thinking of the pretentious accent adopted by some of the residents of that area of Sheffield. 'Then there was a woman from Fulwood. She'd hit some old bloke with her new car. He'd been halfway across a road when she reached a junction and decided to set off without waiting for him to get out of her way. Her car had catapulted him into the air and he'd landed on the bonnet and put a dent in it. But she hadn't come in to report the accident and admit it was her fault – she just wanted to know how to sue the old bloke for denting her car. I got her to look up Highway Code rule one hundred and seventy on her smartphone, but she said that didn't apply to women from Fulwood because they own the roads in Sheffield. I told her she was wrong, they only drive like they own the roads – it's the women from Dore who actually own them.'

Helen lingered a moment. 'And what do you say about women from Ecclesall?'

'I don't say anything about them, Helen. They're all far too smart for me.'

Priestley joined in. 'Actually, there could be some truth in that. Someone told me they'd been looking at a ten-year census and reckoned there's a higher proportion of graduates in Ecclesall than in Cambridge.'

Helen tarried, having decided she had an obligation to see the score evened. 'Do you have any observations about male drivers in Sheffield?'

Witty racked his brains for something to say that might

possibly be amusing, but could find nothing to satisfy even his own variable standard of humour. He settled for some impressions he had formed during his years on the force. 'I don't know if there are more men than women with personalised vehicle registration plates – I mean number plates – but I've noticed people who have them tend to be more likely to drive without due care and attention. Maybe it's because they've had to pay extra, so they think it gives them more right to the road. There's a lot nowadays – something like seven per cent of households have one. Some of the worst offenders can be those driving cheap varieties – a letter, three numbers, three letters – where you have to spend a minute working out whether the cars are personalised or just old.

'I suppose the most inconsiderate tend to be those with personalised number plates on expensive cars or big four-wheel-drives – what they call Chelsea Tractors, in London. I saw one incident not far from here. It was a Friday lunchtime. A Range Rover from a marketing company stopped in the middle of the street outside a cocktail bar just off Ecclesall road, holding everybody up while the passengers got out, with the back car in the queue sticking out dangerously into the main road and blowing his horn to warn people. It could easily have caused an accident, but I'd been called out to one that had already happened, so I didn't have time to stop and deal with it.

'I remember a funny thing happened just after that. I was rushing up Ecclesall Road with lights and siren going and approaching a T-junction at the Prince o' Wales pub; the lights started to change against me, but I saw this couple in matching cags had stood in the middle of the side road and were giving signals to stop all the traffic until I'd got past, as though they'd always wanted to be traffic police.'

After a pause he added, 'You get some very strange people in Ecclesall.' He saw an opportunity for humour. 'I didn't mean you, Helen; but Marcus is another matter entirely.'

A smile flickered across Priestley's lips before he offered an observation of his own. 'In the past, when most people had smallish cars, drivers could see down a line of traffic, and that made it easier to anticipate problems. Nowadays there's usually a Chelsea Tractor in the line – their driver gets a good view but they block everyone else's. If there's a collision between a small car and a big one, the small one comes off worse, so people buy big cars to keep themselves relatively safe. It's often women who use them to take their children to school and to keep them safer on the roads compared to other people's children.' A frown crossed his brow and he spoke more vehemently. 'We use the Range Rover for driving the nippers about, so I suppose that makes us as guilty as the next mm – person.'

Helen looked concerned at his growing agitation. 'If something upsets you, don't forget you have to stop and think "Is this really what's troubling me, or is it just an echo of something that happened before?" You've always done your best to keep people safe, and mothers in four-wheel-drives are doing the same, even if there is an implied self-centredness.'

She turned to Witty to explain, 'Marcus sees moral hazards everywhere, and although I agree in principle with what he says, it wasn't enough to stop me buying the Range Rover. Besides, I need something to cope with the snow.'

Priestley retorted, still with a sharp edge to his voice. 'That's for the two days of snow we average each year.'

Helen decided she needed to close the subject. With an air of serenity she spoke slowly and quietly. 'We discussed this before, Marcus, and if you remember correctly you'll recall you agreed I was right. It's probably better not to continue with a debate you know you're not going to win.' She headed out of the room, not quite closing the door behind her.

Priestley recognised his guests were feeling a little uncomfortable and were waiting for him to break the silence. He asked Witty to brief him on the investigation. Witty responded, 'A suspect committed suicide this morning. He left a strange note.' He read out the words from his notebook.

Noticing the door was slightly ajar, Priestley suspected Helen had stayed within listening range to check he had been able to drop the subject of their debate. He thought she sometimes looked for symptoms of PTSD when he was simply expressing a strongly-held opinion – a downside of being married to a psychiatrist. He called out, 'Helen, could you come in?'

She covered her tracks by stepping away lightly before calling from a distance, 'Yes, my lord and master?' She stepped in heavily to complete the unsuccessful deception.

'Have a listen to this, will you? It's a suicide note.'

Witty read it again.
Happy I was to live my life,
With parents who loved me more than the world,
But I had a secret, a man for a wife,
And now that you know, my memory's soiled.

Yet think not of loss
For I grow not old.
My life is cut short
My story is ended.

Witty added, 'There was one alteration: he originally wrote "my trouble and strife", but put a line through that and replaced it with "a man for a wife".'

Priestley asked Helen, 'What do you think?'

'About the alteration? Cockney rhyming slang replaced with an indication that the relationship was one of husband and wife rather than husband and husband; the suggestion that's he's the male half of the couple is perhaps intended as a sop to the parents – it'd indicate he thinks that's what they'd prefer, but I'm just speculating.'

'What do you think of the whole thing, though?'

'Interesting use of dissonance: the last word's meant to invite the reader to substitute the obvious alternative word, maybe implying the writer had chosen a path less trod. At the risk of literalism, I'd say the message itself is clear enough: a Gay man has committed suicide because the secret that he kept from his parents has now been exposed.'

'Right, Helen, that's enough. Get back to the kitchen where you belong.'

Marcus and Helen laughed at this deliberately non-PC order; they both knew who really wore the trousers in their home. At the doorway she turned and added one final observation. 'Do you know how much time he had to compose it? It's good enough in its way, but far from brilliant. I suppose the limited poetical quality may reflect the stress he was under.'

Witty indicated by a nod in Helen's direction and a finger pointed at the case file, that he would like to offer another piece of cryptic evidence for her assessment. 'There was also an envelope in the glove compartment of the car.'

Priestley authorised the disclosure. 'Go ahead.'

'It was a bank paying-in envelope with six hundred pounds in it. The words "Michael, I am so sorry for betraying you", were squeezed into a bit of space between the envelope's pre-printed words.'

Helen asked, 'In twenty pound notes, by any chance?'

'Yes, all of it.'

'Thirty notes representing the thirty pieces of silver that Judas accepted as payment for betraying Jesus. What we aren't told in the message is what form the betrayal took. The fact that it was written on a paying-in envelope suggests lack of preparation. Maybe a practical element to it as well: cash for Michael – I assume that's his partner – to cover routine bills until his bank account's been sorted out. If so, then the intention to kill himself had probably formed in his mind by the time he withdrew the money.'

Priestley invited Witty to offer up any other facets of the case that might benefit from Helen's expertise. Witty turned and looked directly at Helen as he explained, 'There was a bottle of whisky left at the scene of the suicide. It was a quarter full, and there was a glass tumbler with it.'

Helen's brow furrowed and her eyes narrowed, as though she were looking back over past experiences. 'Better whisky than paracetamol. I've only ever had one patient, thank God, who went the paracetamol way. What do you say to someone who now feels OK and is glad he didn't actually kill himself, when you know he'll be dead within a couple of days and there's nothing you can do about it? At least the whisky route is unconsciousness before death, so they don't know how stupid they've been.'

Witty clarified the cause of death. 'Actually, Helen, it wasn't the whisky that killed him; he leapt off a cliff.'

'Even more immediate if the cliff was high enough.'

'The fall was about twenty metres onto solid rock, so I'd assume death was instantaneous.'

'Sadly, that may not be true; the brain can keep working for a minute or more even if the rest of the body's shattered, unless the shock blacks it out.

'Anyway, why the whisky, you ask? Dutch courage is the usual reason. He didn't drink it all, you say. What size bottle was it?'

'I saw it but I didn't notice the exact size. It was between a half-litre and a litre, so seventy or seventy-five centilitres.'

'If the bottle started out full, he may have taken a fatal dose of alcohol, but it takes longer to work than gravity. You'll be having to ask yourself if he was still conscious and capable of throwing himself off a cliff after that much whisky; it comes down to timing – how quickly he consumed it all.

'As to the tumbler, if someone's going to die anyway, they might like to leave this earth doing something they enjoy; a whisky lover would find it more pleasurable to drink from a glass than a bottle. Was it a top quality whisky? Twelve-year-old single malt, say?'

'No, it was a fairly standard tipple – White Horse.'

'Well, it could still have been his favourite. How many drinks would that be?'

Priestley observed, 'Home-sized measures tend to be bigger than in pubs, and more variable.'

Witty responded, 'Actually, he had a thimble with him – a stainless steel spirit measure; I didn't notice the size of that either.'

Priestley drew on his extensive personal past experience of whisky. 'I expect the bottle will have been seventy centilitres. Pubs generally dispense twenty-five to thirty-five millilitres, so a bottle would give twenty to twenty-eight shots. Three-quarters of a bottle would be fifteen to twenty-one.'

Helen reflected, 'The number sixteen is in that range. I've had more than one patient who was fixated on the number two and any powers of two. Was he into maths?'

Witty replied, 'He wasn't known to be – he was an English teacher; well, Literature and Classics.'

'We know he wrote a poem. He wasn't Welsh by any chance, was he?'

Witty's voice reflected his amazement at her question. 'He was indeed.'

'Could it have been an *hommage* to Dylan Thomas? His final drinking session was eighteen whiskies at the White Horse Tavern in New York.'

Priestley looked at Helen for a moment, with the reverence they both agreed was her due. Turning to Witty, he declared, 'That's entirely speculative and I ask that it be stricken from the record.' He added, with an angled nod in Helen's direction, 'Don't let anyone in on the secret of how I solve cases, will you?' Helen left the room, laughing a little in appreciation of the implied compliment, and closing the door behind her.

Witty and Martello briefed Priestley on the Newhouse investigation, Witty holding back whenever he was confident Martello could explain a facet of the case as well as he; both admitted to being unable to see how the Newhouse case bridged to Cassidy. Priestley asked if they knew how the newspaper found out about Cassidy being Gay. Neither of them had a theory, though Martello added that the bank manager knew but swore he had not revealed it. Priestley put this on his list of items to be investigated. At the end of the briefing session he told them he would go to the station to work his way through the files and interviews and would phone them if anything came up that they could help him with. Barring interruptions, he wished them an enjoyable evening.

As Witty and Martello headed for home, she immediately began a conversation about her future on the force. 'This isn't the first time I've struggled with police work, Neil. Usually, somebody helps me out, and not just men with ulterior motives – I get on well with women, you know. I suppose you think I've been trading on my looks, and I suppose I have, but they won't last for ever. I was desperate to get out of Traffic after I saw that lad that had driven through a wall – it's a vision that's stayed with me ever since. Something about Cassidy's face reminded me of that first lad, and it just brought it all back.'

This latter expression conjured up an image of her vomiting, but he wisely held his tongue, for once suppressing his urge always to try to be amusing.

'I don't think I can stick it much longer. I'm happy with the good bits, the investigations, but I just don't want the bad bits, the bodies and the blood. And now with Castleton on my back, I can't even look forward to being in the office.'

Witty was trying to listen while remaining focused on driving. He found himself wondering about the expression "on my back", and about the similar-sounding expression with opposite meaning, "on my side"; and what about "on my backside" he mused. He felt he was trying to think of anything but what Lily was saying; it was too difficult to have an in-depth conversation with her while driving. He thought of a way of putting it off. 'What we need to do is write down an entire list of the pros and cons of being on the force. We'll do it as soon as we're home.' Lily recognised the proposal as a request for her to be quiet, so they travelled in silence for the remainder of the journey.

On arriving home, Lily decided to take her turn at making a meal. Yesterday they had bought plenty of fruit and vegetables, both equally determined to suggest they were fully committed to a healthy lifestyle. The reality for Neil was that he had often cooked for himself and eaten alone, his staple diet consisting largely of pizza, fish finger sandwiches, and beef burgers in a bun. Lily on the other hand had maintained her figure by cutting her food intake down to an absolute minimum, with two poached eggs on toast representing her concept of a binge. They dutifully ate their way through cottage cheese with pineapple, multiple varieties of lettuce, grated carrot, celery and rocket; something about the pack of baby beetroot had made Lily decide to leave it unopened. They drank chilled tap water from a bottle kept in the fridge – Neil had drawn the line at buying bottled water, instead introducing Lily to the system he had known since childhood. They agreed with each other that it was an excellent, healthy meal. Neil wished inwardly for another course, preferably something that included meat.

The civilised meal was followed by an equally civilised discussion, plusses and minuses recorded with little expression of emotion as they went through the reasons why Lily should stay on the force or should leave it. Neil understood the strength of the pent-up feelings that Lily was suppressing; Lily hoped Neil recognised it. Castleton appeared to be an insurmountable obstacle, as he could have so much influence on Lily's immediate future. Their final conclusion was that Lily should avoid doing anything hasty, and that she should try to see the two cases through to their final conclusions. Neil reflected on how his past experience had taught him that some of the most emotional problems have to be dealt with unemotionally.

CHAPTER 20

Priestley Takes Over the Investigation

Monday

Priestley reviewed the Newhouse case notes into the early hours of Monday morning. The fingerprints on the envelope that contained the fifty pounds were those of Newhouse, with no evidence of anyone else having handled it. Though he considered it may prove irrelevant to the inquiry, nevertheless he still wished to know the reason for the money being in an envelope rather than a wallet, even if only to discount it from the investigation.

The interim post-mortem report detailed how the absence of trauma to the front of Newhouse's brain indicated the head had struck a stationary object, rather than a moving object having struck a stationary head. It also stated that the damage to the skull was consistent with Newhouse having impacted with considerable force, which indicated a deliberate act. However, it also left the door open to a defence of accidental injury resulting from Newhouse slipping while moving backwards at great speed, as the report stated the force was just within the upper limit for that scenario. Priestley thought a jury would be unlikely to believe someone had deliberately run backwards and had then slipped on the soapy water that was recorded as being present on the floor, but he was concerned that a defence lawyer could present a theory that Newhouse had been moving forwards quickly in the direction of the hook when he had slipped on the water and turned in the air before striking the back of his head on the coat hook. The counter-argument that the edges of the impact site on the skull showed no evidence of a turning movement could well be lost on a jury. He foresaw a need to obtain further forensic evidence, or a confession that was consistent with all the known facts.

On hearing the recording of Cassidy being interviewed by

Castleton and Dunn, he decided there was a need for action against the two officers, at the same time recognising how the police force as a whole could be besmirched if the details entered the public domain. He decided to refer the matter upwards, so returned home and set his phone alarm for six fifty, ahead of the radio alarm that was permanently set for just before seven a.m. Chief Superintendent Barbara Watt, Commander of Derbyshire's Shawton Division, had approved a number of circumstances under which officers of Priestley's rank and above were permitted to phone her at any hour, one of which was where the force could be in danger of suffering substantial reputational damage. He felt the current situation may qualify, but decided to hedge his bets by aiming for a mildly unsociable seven a.m.

Priestley was already half-awake when his phone alarm began to beep. He quickly turned it off and carefully edged out of bed. At seven o'clock on the dot he made the call and briefed Watt succinctly. She instructed him to stay at home until she contacted him after she had met with Castleton.

Priestley phoned Detective Constable Anthony Beresford, instructing him to collect the Newhouse case notes from his house and then go into the office and familiarise himself with both the Newhouse and Cassidy cases. Tony Beresford, aka Berry, was a twenty-five-year-old who had just returned from a secondment with Priestley. He had scraped a first class honours degree in mathematics at Sheffield University, having carefully calculated the exact amount of work needed to achieve the minimum mark for that classification.

Berry was something of an enigma to many, a combination of sheer brilliance and utter stupidity. After university, he had begun working locally for a major financial institution, first as a programmer and then as a systems analyst, ending as a senior systems analyst on the world's largest commercial customer database – according to the Japanese hardware supplier. This came to an end when he plucked up the courage to ask out a fairly plain, single girl who appeared to be available, only to be rebuffed with an emphatic, "No, I won't go out with you – you're too boring." He had immediately looked around for something to reduce his Boring rating, culminating in his applying to join the police force.

The induction and assessment process had discovered his strengths, so he was accepted as a graduate and potential high flyer with no requirement to begin in uniform, and was told he might expect to be an Inspector within three years if everything went well. Since he had joined on the first of April, some of his weaknesses had been revealed, so his progression was not now expected by many to be quite so rapid.

Berry was proud of his critical thinking capacity as indicated by his high negative construct ratio – he could find flaws in witness statements, discussion points, proposals for action, the metric system, foreign languages that arbitrarily associated genders with nouns, in fact just about anything. He had been assigned to Priestley by upper management as a fast track mechanism to give him earlier exposure to higher ranking work than would normally have been considered appropriate for someone of his inexperience. Priestley believed he understood Berry well enough to enable him to play to his strengths, and Berry was confident that Priestley represented his best practical learning resource.

DCI Castleton arrived at his office on the Monday morning to find his computer screen almost entirely obscured by a sheet of A4 paper attached with clear tape to the top edge. Scrawled across it in thick black ink was the message "See me now. Watt". With a feeling of trepidation Castleton went directly to the Chief Superintendent's office. Seeing Watt on a good day could be scary enough, but on a bad day it would be the stuff of nightmares. He knocked on her door. A contralto called out, 'Wait.'

Two timed minutes later the same voice issued a curt invitation.

'Enter.'

'Ma'am.'

'Don't sit down.'

'Ma'am.'

'This comes from the very top. Sexual harassment.' She pronounced the word in the English way, avoiding emphasis on the "ass".

Castleton remained silent.

'We do not tolerate it.'

'No, ma'am.'

'You have been complained about.'

'DC Martello is making it up, ma'am. It's because she's underperforming and she knows I want her out.'

'The complaint did not come from DC Martello.'

Castleton rushed to correct his mistake.

'DS Ogilvy is mistaken, ma'am. I was just being friendly.'

'It was not DS Ogilvy.'

He assumed it must be the next name in his reverse chronological order.

'PC Tucker was giving out signals to everyone. How was I supposed to know she meant everyone but me? … Ma'am.'

'It wasn't PC Tucker either. Christ, man, just how many victims are there?'

Castleton remained silent, believing another wrong guess could leave him sunk without a trace.

Watt was satisfied he was already holed below the waterline. 'There's plenty of evidence that you're a serial offender. You're suspended with immediate effect. Give me your warrant card.' She held out her hand and waited; he took it from his jacket pocket and dropped it gingerly onto her outstretched fingers, not daring to approach close enough for a firm handover. 'You can expect a full investigation and I expect the outcome to be Dismissal with Disgrace.'

Castleton noted the reminder of her service in the Royal Navy – she had never adopted "sacking" from the vernacular.

'You may be able to avoid further proceedings if you voluntarily resign today.'

'That's a big step, ma'am. Dismissals are very rare; only the highest standard of proof would be acceptable and I don't believe you'll find any witnesses who are credible.'

Watt bellowed at him without the slightest suggestion of restraint. 'Because they're women? God Almighty, man, you condemn yourself out of your own mouth every time you open it.'

'I'll need to take advice from the Federation, ma'am.'

'You can take advice from whomever you wish, but if I don't have your resignation in writing by end of day I'll be initiating an investigation, and I expect your name will eventually end up on the struck-off list – the Public Register of Disgraced Officers.'

He whined, 'Doesn't my past record on investigating crimes count for anything?'

'Do you really wish to bring up your crime-handling ability?

SIO on the Newhouse case but you never even visited the crime scene. Now, get out of my office and out of my station!'

Castleton returned to his office, on the way looking for anyone on whom he could vent his anger. The place was virtually deserted; he reviewed the options and decided none of those who remained would make suitable targets for a rant. He jealously looked at Berry: privileged because he was a fast-track entrant, sacrosanct, protected from harm by a company of angels, his place reserved at the right-hand of God. Next to him he saw a constable known for his highly developed muscles and less well developed brain, currently jabbing a keyboard with one finger; he was the type to demand a private interview, then hit him hard a few times and claim he walked into a door. He recognised a woman who had set out to emulate the men, or was that emasculate; she had recently started to advertise herself as a lesbian, perhaps as part of her drive for social manhood, so two forms of jeopardy there – she might claim sexual harassment at the same time as kicking him in the balls. That only left two others, both women; he decided it would be unwise even to acknowledge their existence in view of the threat from Watt.

With only a few years to go to a full pensionable retirement, he felt unwilling to roll over, despite the viciousness of the dog – the bitch – that had just savaged him. However, if his dismissal were to be published by the College of Policing, it could affect his chances of finding other work. As he left the office he turned off his phone to stop Watt from badgering him for a decision.

Watt phoned Priestley, getting down to business without any preamble. 'I suspended Castleton and demanded his resignation over sexual harassment. I'm sure if I asked them, every woman on the force would recall something damning that would bolster the case against him. I didn't need to use the issue of his interview with Cassidy; I'll keep my powder dry on that one, though if it turns out Cassidy wasn't responsible for Newhouse's death then that alone is enough to blow him out of the water.

'I've also been contacted by the National Crime Agency. You obviously made a good impression on them, because they're wishing to poach you. Well, so you know how much I'd rather you stayed on my team, I'm making you Acting DCI with immediate effect.

'Now, get the Newhouse case moving; start with proving the

case against Cassidy one way or the other.'

'Yes, ma'am.'

The line went dead.

Priestley contacted Martello to let her know that for now she had nothing to fear from Castleton, as he had been suspended. She thanked him for his part in arranging it, though he insisted it was Castleton's own actions that had led to his downfall. He mentioned his new status, trying to sound as blasé as possible about it. He asked her to go to the school with Witty to deliver the news of Cassidy's death to the Headmaster. She asked if he would first accept a call from Witty, who was wishing to take some time out of the morning to talk to the solicitor Manny Gilder. Martello passed on Priestley's news to Witty who in turn phoned Priestley and was given the permission he requested.

With Witty having an appointment elsewhere, Priestley phoned Plummer to check if she was available to go to the school to assist Martello, and to let her know about Castleton's suspension and his own elevation; she confirmed her availability, and added, 'Everyone already knows – even good news can spread quickly.' After a pause, she asked, 'Should Dunn go to the school as well?' Priestley told her Dunn would not be required.

Martello went alone to the school, only to find that Verbane was fully aware of the suicide. She also found his attitude had changed substantially – he directed his growing anger and frustration at her.

'Ah, DC Martello, I had a call late last night from Michael Gough. He told me he was working his way through Hugh's personal phone book and was contacting everyone in it, starting with Hugh's parents and then working alphabetically, so I must have been one of the last to know about Hugh's suicide. I want to know what drove him to it. Having lost two members of my staff within a week, I believe the time has come for the police to do much more to get to the bottom of things. I want someone new, someone senior, to take charge of the investigation. I want to speak to the Chief Constable.'

Martello would have liked to agree wholeheartedly about the need for a new SIO, but felt the best way of avoiding any escalation of emotion would be to undertake to refer his request upwards rather than enabling him to make waves directly at the highest level.

'I don't have his telephone number, Headmaster, though he's not normally involved in the day-to-day work so I wouldn't expect him to have knowledge of either case.'

'Then who is the highest ranking officer who is involved in investigating cases?'

'That would be the Chief Superintendent, sir.'

'Well give me his number.'

'That would be her number, sir.'

Verbane fell silent for a moment; finding himself guilty of sexism, he felt his arguments were now weakened.

Martello seized the opportunity to handle things her preferred way. 'If you'll trust me, Headmaster, I shall ensure your concerns are expressed at the highest relevant level, and ask for someone suitable to contact you directly.'

Martello's large eyes had opened wider as she asked for his trust; Verbane was not immune to their influence.

'Well, of course I trust you, Ms Martello. But do please hurry them along.'

Martello phoned Priestley to let him know the outcome of her meeting with Verbane. He asked her to let him know he was on his way. She hurried back to Verbane. 'I've relayed your concerns and they've been acted on immediately. Detective Chief Inspector Marcus Priestley...', she used the lengthy title but omitted the word "Acting", in the hope that it made Priestley seem more important than a DI temporarily covering for a higher rank, '...has spoken to the Chief Superintendent...', she omitted Barbara Watt's name to minimise the risk of direct contact by Verbane, '...and he's taking over the investigations with immediate effect. He's on his way here right now to meet with you. And may I add, Headmaster, that DCI Priestley has the reputation for being the most capable officer on the force, and that his assignment reflects the seriousness in which these two cases are regarded at the highest level.' She was pleased with her wording, even though she knew not everything she had said would have stood up to forensic examination.

Verbane was pacified. 'Thank you, Lily. I knew you were someone who could be trusted.'

* * *

Priestley arrived at the school and spoke with Martello. 'I know it may not turn up anything useful, but you need to start house-to-house enquiries. I've asked Linda to come over so she can share the load.'

'Anyone else, sir? PC Dunn?'

'No, I've put him on special duties today.'

'Sounds interesting.'

'Oh, believe me, it isn't.'

'What exactly should I be doing?'

'Ask anyone who lives near the front gates if they saw someone – anyone – entering the school grounds between three and three thirty or leaving between three fifteen and three forty-five. I'm going to have a tête-à-tête with the Headmaster.'

Verbane received Priestley in his office and, after introductions, began the discussion in earnest. 'First of all, may I ask why you were not assigned to this case earlier? DC Martello says you're the best person for the job, so why were you not put in charge sooner?'

'DC Martello was very generous to describe me in that way. In fact, I've just returned from a secondment that had to be seen through to a conclusion. Now that I'm back, let me assure you I'll be giving these two deaths a hundred per cent of my attention.'

Verbane interpreted the use of "a hundred per cent" as suggesting Priestley possessed an innate honesty; far better than using one of those expressions he saw as crass, such as "I'll give it a hundred and ten per cent."

'Where do you propose to start?'

'I know that the nine other players in the football team have already been interviewed, and I believe there's nothing more to be gleaned from them. Also, yourself, Miss Oaken and Ms Clifton have provided evidence, though less formally. I'd therefore like to begin by interviewing you formally, whilst accepting you have an alibi for the time of Mr Newhouse's death.'

'I'm not sure there's any more information I have to offer.'

'I'd like to ask you what significance there is to the sum of fifty pounds.'

Verbane looked surprised. 'In what context?'

Priestley decided to keep the question as vague as possible while sounding as though it related to something specific. 'What might someone in the school see as significant in the sum of fifty pounds?'

Verbane hesitated. He felt he ought to know what was being

asked, and was certain Priestley knew something that he was trying to avoid revealing by structuring the sentence in that way. There had been an issue over that precise sum of money, and Mr Collins was one of those who had been interviewed. Putting two and two together, he decided Priestley must know about an issue Collins had raised at a staff meeting. 'I assume this relates to the objection Mr Collins made about the funding for a school trip.'

Priestley had no idea what Verbane was talking about. He nodded sagely as though he had hit the nail on the head, encouraging him to continue.

'Mr Collins is a great organiser in many respects; very thorough. He calculated the cost of a school trip, made an allowance for variances in expenditure, and proposed a figure that should be charged out to the students. I felt there were reasons for increasing that estimate by fifty pounds.'

'And what reasons did you have for increasing the estimate?'

'The staff give freely of their time to make trips happen, so they're not expected to pay for the privilege; their costs are charged against the funds obtained from students. There are rules for how many staff are needed as a ratio against the total number of students on a trip. Sometimes trips are slightly over-staffed if it's felt a member of staff may benefit from the experience. For some trips it's hard enough to find enough staff prepared to take the students, so a willing volunteer may be accepted on a supernumerary basis.'

'And that was what happened on this particular trip?'

'Yes.'

'And were there any other factors? You did refer to "reasons" in the plural.'

'I was speaking in general terms. Generally, there may be reasons.'

Priestley recognised the scent of mendacity, so pressed on. 'What were all the reasons relating to that trip?'

Verbane knew it was too late to turn back. 'The school has social responsibilities to all the students. If the parents or carers of a student cannot afford to pay for a child, then I have a discretionary fund that can pay for them. But it isn't a limitless supply. To supplement the funding for certain students on that particular trip is was necessary to inflate the amounts charged out to those parents and carers who were more capable of paying, as evidenced by the fact that they had initially agreed to pay for their own children without requesting support from the Headmaster's fund.'

Priestley remained silent to see if there was any more to be revealed. Verbane offered up an excuse of sorts. 'Lots of headteachers use this same flexible approach, so I'm sure it's alright.'

Priestley went in for the kill. 'Correct me if I'm wrong, Headmaster, and I realise I'm paraphrasing what you said, but, if a teacher wants to go on a "jolly", you charge that to those you perceive to be the wealthier parents, and if a student wishes to go on a trip that their parents won't pay for, then you also charge that to the wealthier parents. So, does that mean you know the true financial status of every parent? And can you be sure that wealthier parents don't just play the system? And what about poorer parents who are too proud to admit they can't afford to fund their child? And then there's those who are so determined to make sure their child doesn't miss out that they go and borrow money at massive rates of interest and end up paying more than anyone else? Frankly, what you have just admitted to is fraud, similar to the kind of thing that would earn a member of parliament six months behind bars. Before you respond, let me ask you a more forward-looking question. If I asked you about this subject in, say, one month's time, what answers would I receive from you about funding for trips?'

Verbane saw a glimmer of light shining between the bars of his impending incarceration. 'You would find that wealthier parents were no longer being asked to fund the inclusion of poorer students or additional teachers.'

'Actually, Headmaster, the problem with your current system is something you've not appeared to acknowledge. The allegedly wealthier parents never were asked to over-contribute; you simply took the money from them without informing them and without giving them the chance to opt-out.'

Verbane's head hung low, employing the strategy of avoiding eye-contact with the Alpha Male. Priestley decided he could now afford to ease down the pressure, having not only established himself as a worthy interrogator, but also learned something that would be likely to keep Verbane from bypassing him and complaining to his superiors if any issues developed in the future.

'I'll leave the interview details on record, though I don't currently foresee any need to pursue the question of fraud any further, especially as there are much more important matters to investigate here. On which front, I understand Miss Oaken has been acting as liaison with the detectives; may I ask if she'll continue to be available in that capacity?'

'Yes, certainly. She'll be pleased to assist you in any way possible. If you need anything from anyone, just ask her and she'll arrange it. She also provides her office as a base for interrogations.'

Verbane felt like adding, 'Ask her. Ask anybody. Just don't ask me anything else.'

Priestley suggested, 'I think you mean interviews.'

Verbane answered, 'Yes, of course.' He thought, 'No, I mean interrogations.'

Priestley departed, thinking, 'If he had known anything about the fifty pounds in the changing room he would have mentioned it long before going down the road of admitting to fiddling the books and defrauding parents.'

Priestley met with Oaken so that he could begin another line of inquiry. 'All the teachers who played in the football match have been interviewed, but none of the boys from the school team. It may be necessary to interview all of them, but for now I'd like to start with one you believe could give me some clear facts about the game and what happened at the end.'

'I suppose the team captain could be the right starting point.'

'As he's the captain?'

'That, amongst other things. Alex Peveril is one of our brightest students, with a tremendous memory for detail.'

'When could he be made available?'

Oaken consulted her wall charts and then took out a buff file that contained a thick wad of papers. 'Alex will be available in a quarter of an hour. He starts a slot of self-study in place of going to maths lessons.'

Priestley phoned Berry and asked what he thought about DCI Castleton's suspension. He said he was unaware of it. Priestley wondered if Berry generally failed to pick up on office gossip. He instructed him to finish reviewing the case notes and then to join him at the school to assist with the investigation.

CHAPTER 21

Witty on Justice and the Law

Witty contacted the office of divorce lawyer Manny Gilder and asked to make an appointment. He was relieved to be invited to come for an immediate meeting, as he now wished to press ahead as quickly as possible with the process of obtaining a divorce. He found Gilder to be a small, wiry man in his late fifties or early sixties, with a high, bald dome and an armilla of silver hair. Witty knew Gilder only by reputation, yet Gilder welcomed him as though they were old friends. 'Come in, come in, it's good to see you, come and sit over here. You must call me Manny. Let's have a chat about things and you can tell me what's happened already.'

Witty wondered if this positioning of "already" at the end of the sentence, something that was once seen as a Jewish linguistic trait, though had now been adopted more widely by the under-educated, was a deliberate way of asserting his religious origins in order to engender confidence in clients; he knew many people who believed Jews made the best lawyers, whether or not they were aware of their long history from the time of the Crusaders when they were restricted to belonging only to the two most despised professions – banking and the law.

He expected to be paying through the nose for the consultation time, so had prepared to deliver his information as succinctly as possible. 'I'm Neil Whittington. My wife's name is Theresa; I want to divorce her as quickly as possible. We have a severely disabled child. I'm in the police force – a Detective Constable. My...'

Gilder interrupted the torrent of words. 'Not so fast, my friend. We need to get to know each other better. I should also check how definite you are with your wish to divorce your wife.'

'Absolutely definite, Manny.'

'Very well, then. Now, as a detective in the police force you know something of the law and how it works.'

This phrase triggered thoughts of various frustrations. 'I know how it doesn't work, as well.'

Gilder took the opportunity for them to talk over common ground. 'Tell me about it.'

For a moment Witty was uncertain whether this was use of one of his most hated contradictory Americanisms asking him NOT to tell him about it, that ranked just ahead of "That can't happen" meaning it most definitely can happen. Gilder's eager expression indicated it was intended in the English way, with meaning as stated. 'We in the police have to uphold the law, but this often appears to have nothing to do with natural justice. We have to concentrate on rules of evidence, knowing that even the slightest slip-up can let in some smart-arse lawyer to get their client off on a technicality. No offence.'

Gilder roared with laughter as though it was the funniest thing he had heard all year. 'And no offence taken, my friend. Though, as a smart-ass lawyer myself, you'll see the benefits of having me on your side. Now, what else do you see as wrong with the law? When I know what you know, it could save time when I explain to you what else you need to know.'

Witty was unsure about the underlying logic, suspecting it may be just a way of increasing his chargeable time, but decided to give him a comprehensive response anyway as it could be a cathartic experience. 'Evidence obtained illegally is inadmissible. But there should be two distinct aspects to such evidence: one, it's evidence and should be allowed to be used as such; two, the method of obtaining it was incorrect and the officer should be reprimanded for getting the procedure wrong. There's a similar situation with awarding of damages. A newspaper may be fined millions of pounds for hacking into someone's phone, but should the person whose phoned was hacked receive those millions of pounds? I don't think it's at all reasonable that the two figures should be even remotely related; the excess should be taken by the courts as a fine for the newspaper's improper behaviour.'

'As far as the obtaining of evidence is concerned, how would you avoid police abusing your system? Someone could deliberately break the rules of evidence collection and simply choose to accept a reprimand. There could even be people approaching the end of their career who volunteer to accept a reprimand on behalf of someone else.'

'Even so, I'm sure some mechanism could be put in place. Too many breaches could result in demotion, or dismissal with loss of benefits. Almost anything would be better than the current system that allows criminals to get away with something even though there's loads of evidence against them, just because the jury aren't allowed to see it... which brings me onto my next grouse. Why are members of a jury not allowed to know about someone's past criminal behaviour?'

'There are some circumstances where the jury is allowed to know someone's history, for example where the accused employed a non-smart-ass lawyer who then facilitated disclosure by asking the wrong question, or where a judge decides it indicates the character of the alleged perpetrator. Other cases may be included if someone is using what may be called a "system" – something identifiable with a particular perpetrator.'

'I thought you were a specialist in divorce law?'

'I used to be a Criminal Lawyer – not to be confused with a criminal lawyer.' Gilder's emphasis made the distinction clear to Witty. 'Then I discovered how much more money there is in Divorce Law.'

'Well I'm sure you're right, but generally juries aren't allowed to know about other offences. I'm told the official line is that it might prejudice them, but let's be sensible for a moment. If someone has past convictions for a comparable offence then the burden of proof should be reduced; if the level of proof required for a first-time offender was ninety-nine per cent, then the level of proof required for a twenty-first-time offender could be, say, eighty per cent. It makes sense for the jury to be able to take into consideration the existence of the previous convictions when they're deliberating. That brings me onto another objection to the law in this country.

'There are other things that a jury is often kept in the dark about: pieces of evidence, opinions, background details and the like. It would make far more sense for a jury to be given all the facts and opinions with suitable *caveats* so that they can reach their own conclusions about the evidence and its reliability; instead, they're kept from knowing things that can be crucial to an understanding of a case.'

'What you say would have had resonance in the past, Neil. The first known trial by jury in this country was in twelve twenty, and back in the thirteenth century there would have been no such restrictions; it could be said there was no weighing of evidence back then – jurors were expected to use their local knowledge and their beliefs to decide on guilt or innocence.'

'Well, speaking of jurors, I also have an issue with the jury system itself. Take twelve people of unknown capacity for understanding and let them try to follow all the complexities of a case. It can be like a random throw of a dozen dice.'

'Many people would say the jury system was a good choice back in the thirteenth century, when a different route was being taken on the continent: the Inquisitorial system, with its methods of proof such as torture, as had been used in Roman times.'

'Back then, trial by jury could well have been a good choice, but now it's often used by criminals who use…'

'People like me.'

'Well, yes, clever lawyers, to manipulate the juries into making decisions that sometimes defy all logic. In fact, I think there's a good case for getting rid of juries as we know them, either entirely, or by having professional jurors who are experts in sifting information.'

'You're trying to put the legal profession out of work here, Neil.'

'Perhaps current lawyers could become professional jurors, or maybe judges in a system based on unbiased investigation.'

'Aye, there's the rub. Where would we find unbiased investigators?'

'Perhaps lawyers could be retrained to become part of an investigation-based system; change criminal courts to work more like coroners' inquests.'

'Even with an investigation-based system such as in France, defendants would still have a right to their own defence lawyer, so it isn't quite so different to the British adversarial system as it appears at first glance. And coroners' inquests are not simply investigation-based when you scratch the surface and see what lies beneath; where someone has a vested interest in the outcome they may hire a smart-ass lawyer in the hope of obtaining a persuasive verdict to support subsequent litigation.

'I remember being at a coroner's court for one such case where the deceased's family was represented by a substantial legal team. A surgeon had performed an operation that appeared to have been successful, but the woman patient was failing to recover within the expected timescales; the surgeon weighed the option of repeating surgery for which there was a predicted fifteen per cent mortality rate, against initially monitoring the subject closely during which time there was a predicted five per cent mortality rate. He chose the lower-risk option, but unfortunately the patient died during the monitoring period. Clearly the family could not expect the deceased woman to be brought back to life, so their interest was very largely financial with the NHS as the *milch* cow, though no doubt they will have convinced themselves they were acting from higher motives.

'The lead barrister was a quite attractive woman as I recall – she looked as though butter wouldn't melt in her mouth. She remained seated – being a coroner's court – from which position she interrogated the surgeon for well over an hour. She harassed the surgeon, subjecting him to loaded questions that she supplemented with subtle nods and shakes of the head designed to mislead him into agreeing with her statements even though these were clearly at odds with his testimony; a lesser witness could quite easily have fallen into the traps she was setting. I would say I was witnessing an adversarial rather than an investigative system in operation in that particular case.'

'I'm more familiar with the criminal courts where I see opposing teams of lawyers playing the adversarial system as a game, with the aim being to win rather than to produce a fair result. It's like when Angelo Dundee pretended there was something wrong with Cassius Clay's glove to give his man a breather against Henry Cooper; it wasn't to get a fair result – it was to help his man to win. Barristers are the Angelo Dundees of this world.'

'You may be right about that, my young friend. A top barrister gains his reputation and his high income by being someone who can pull a rabbit – a win – out of his blue brief-bag when the evidence suggests he should lose the case. Gone are the days when there was a "get out of jail" card, such as reciting the first verse of Psalm fifty-one and claiming the Benefit of Clergy.'

Witty had not previously heard of this historical defence; he felt it supported Gilder's reputation for omniscience. 'That's a new one on me.'

'Though actually a very old one.'

'Well, what really gets me is that defence lawyers not only do everything they can to get their clients off, but actually believe they're morally right to do so. It often amazes me how intelligent people can allow themselves to be brainwashed into believing that the rule of law should override the morality of natural justice.'

'Ah, morality and natural justice. If only witnesses would also believe in morality and natural justice, and would always tell the truth, then there would be no need for lawyers to resort to adopting an attitude of not wishing to know the truth.'

'Well there's another thing that needs changing. The penalties for perjury are significant, but they exist largely in isolation from the underlying cases. To my mind, if someone commits perjury in a murder trial then their sentence should be the same as is given to a convicted murderer. Perjury where the offence was minor would not simply get a correspondingly minor sentence, though; there should be a minimum level for perjury, maybe five years, so that people aren't prepared to lie because they don't fear the consequences of being found out. And that brings me onto another complaint about sentencing.

'If three men – sorry if that sounds sexist, but I'm being realistic – if three men commit an armed bank robbery and only one of them is identified, then the other two should be tried without them being in court...'

'*in absentia*'

'... right, and the convicted one should be invited to disclose the identities of the other two; if he doesn't then he should also receive their sentences, to run consecutively. If at some point in the future he decides to give them up, then he doesn't have to serve any more of their sentences himself, and they have to serve their own entire sentences. A safety feature would be that the first criminal only gets out of serving the others' sentences once they've been caught and convicted; otherwise there would be lots of loopholes, such as passing the blame onto someone who's beyond the law, either because they're somewhere with no extradition, or because they're dead.'

'Are there any flaws that you see closer to home?'

'Something that's affected me when I've been arresting someone is that they've incited others to help them by shouting out and lying about what's happening. I'd like it to be permissible for duct tape to be put over the mouth of someone who's been arrested if they refuse to shut up.'

'I can see how that would help you in your work, though I was thinking even closer to home – money and divorce. And believe me, divorce is all about the money.'

'I don't have masses of money, unlike various criminals who have mega-bucks from their nefarious activities. There should be a simple system for confiscating it.'

'The tax-man did take a billion pounds from convicted criminals last year.'

'Well, that's a small step in the right direction. I think the law should make it easier for the courts to take all their money off them, without having to prove where any of it came from. Reversal of burden of proof, if you like: it isn't yours unless you can prove it is yours.'

'You're familiar with the Proceeds of Crime Act, of course.'

'I know something about it – criminal confiscation and money laundering, but it seems like so many of them get away with it. I remember one master-criminal got his lawyer to get him bail, and she then helped him to get out of the country; she went with him to help him spend his billions of drugs-money – a young, blonde, female lawyer.'

'Well I'm only one of those four things, so I hope you'll find I'm more trustworthy. We need to think about your money now. Perhaps we can focus on your particular circumstances.'

Witty had enjoyed venting his spleen to a willing listener even if he was paying for the privilege, but took the hint that it was now time to focus on his divorce. 'There's a house that's jointly owned and with a joint mortgage. There's a bit of equity in it, but not much.'

'We need to go back in time. How did you meet your wife?'

'In a Nativity Play; she was Mary and I was Joseph. She gave me nits; my mother said they must have come from her because they were orangey-red, just like her hair.'

'And how old were you at the time?'

'We were both seven.'

Gilder applied his dry sense of humour, choosing to treat the story with more reverence than was intended in the telling. 'And was this the start of your relationship that culminated in your marriage?'

Witty was the first to crack, laughing at the deliberate

seriousness. 'No, Manny. We went through the same schools together, but we never went out with each other. She was part of a group of Catholics that tended to stick together, so we weren't even part of the same set.'

'Her group was not actually segregated, I assume?'

'No, but they didn't socialise much with other groups. I did sometimes see her around town, always the centre of attention of her crowd. Her long, red tresses made her look like a Botticelli Venus – she was always out of reach for the likes of me, and not just physically because she was so tall.'

'So when did your romance start?'

'I'm not sure we had time for romance. Totally out of the blue I received a phone call from her. First of all she said she was thinking of organising a reunion for everyone who finished at senior school in the same year we did. She asked if I'd be interested, and I said yes. Then she said, actually, she was especially interested in me, and regretted we'd never got together at school, because she'd always fancied me. Well, I was completely gob… taken by surprise. She made it obvious she was waiting for me to ask her out, so I did. On the very first date, which was a meal at a very nice restaurant the next evening, she said she was wishing to settle down and, basically, she'd like me to be the one she settled down with. Now, you have to remember that she'd always been the unreachable type at school, so when she took me back to her flat afterwards I just couldn't believe my luck. But then she explained that as a practising Catholic she didn't believe in sex before marriage, or contraception for that matter. Before I knew what was happening, we were arranging a super-fast wedding; I was desperate to get stuck in – sorry, I'm not sure what sort of detail I should be giving.'

'Please have no qualms about giving me the full, explicit version.'

'Well, I was definitely thinking with my hormones and not my brain, so the marriage went full steam ahead.'

'Concupiscence has been the basis for many a hurried marriage but is not a good indicator of long-lasting bliss. Err in haste, repent at leisure. Was the marriage initially satisfactory?'

'The first time we had sex was a bit of a fumble for both of us. I'd had some experience but she was a virgin.'

'And you know that how?'

'Because she was a Catholic. And she told me she was, as well.'

'Did you find any resistance to penetration?'

Witty looked unsure how to respond, so Gilder clarified. 'Did you discover any evidence of a maidenhead, Neil?'

'No, but she explained that. She used to go riding horses when she was younger.'

'Exactly how long was it between your wedding night and the birth of your child?'

'Just over seven months; Ollie was premature.'

'Do you have any reason to believe Ollie is not your child?'

Witty found himself becoming angry at Gilder. 'Of course not; Theresa was never unfaithful to me – I'd have known.'

Gilder looked kindly at Neil. 'You're probably right, but we lawyers do like to check our facts. Now, can you obtain a DNA sample from the child?'

'That's already been done. A friend of mine – a doctor – has been researching his genetic condition. I've already supplied Ollie's DNA to him.'

'Then may I suggest you have it compared with your own DNA, just to be certain.'

'I could get someone at work to do it for me as a favour.'

'May I suggest, Neil: not on this occasion. We need everything to be above board. I can recommend a private laboratory. Now, where was the child born?'

'At Midshaw Hospital.'

'You should have them check their records regarding the duration of the pregnancy. Or perhaps it would be easier to obtain the details through the doctor who researched the child's condition if he can access them – sometimes hospitals are reluctant to provide information even to those who have every right to it.'

'If it's essential I could try him now.'

'Go ahead; it may clarify our strategy for the divorce.'

At Gilder's invitation Witty phoned Kinder from his office; the call was answered by a receptionist who put him through having established his *bona fide*. 'Hello, Jim. It's me, Neil Whittington. I'm with a solicitor and he's asking about Ollie and how premature he was.'

Kinder sighed inwardly as he reflected on how so many people nowadays looked for a scapegoat when they had the misfortune to have a severely disabled child, and how lawyers often fed that compensation culture. He knew the National Health Service paid out a phenomenal amount of money every year where there was even a whiff of negligence; contact with Witty had started to lead him to believe that the funds would be better used for treating all manner of illnesses instead of being dedicated to the preservation of sometimes barely sentient beings. 'I'm sorry, Neil, but there's no question of negligence by the hospital. I've already reviewed the records in some detail, and I can tell you that the pregnancy was entirely normal and went to full term.'

Witty felt the blood drain from his face. 'It wasn't to do with negligence, Jim; it's to do with who's the father. Are you quite sure it was a nine-month pregnancy? You see, we'd only been married for not much more than seven. I'll need to get a DNA comparison done to prove it, but it must mean that Ollie isn't mine.'

Kinder confirmed Ollie's DNA was on record and that he could supply the details to enable a paternity check to be made against Witty's DNA.

Gilder understood enough of the situation from hearing Witty's side of the conversation to begin formulating a game plan. When Witty terminated the phone call, he began, 'That changes things considerably, Neil. Once we have the DNA confirmation we can proceed on an entirely different basis. You mentioned Theresa is a practising Catholic, so would I be right in thinking she'll be opposed to the idea of divorce?'

'She's always said so, though I don't know if she'll change her mind once she's confronted with the proof that Ollie's not my child.'

'Oh, I think we have a better option than that. You see, the courts tend to award everything to the wife and mother; to put it simply, they apply the rule from the woman's perspective as "what's yours is mine and what's mine is also mine". This is irrespective of what the woman has been up to – it's to do with the idea of "no blame" divorce. We should consider it from a more fundamental position. You were tricked into the marriage so she could cover up the fact that she was already pregnant. We should go for an annulment. Your marriage is voidable as she was pregnant by another man at the time you married.'

'Have you handled many cases of annulment?'

'A nice round number.'

'How many, exactly?'

'Well, none actually, but I'm sure we can put together a solid case.'

'Does it help my case that she lied to me about being a virgin?'

'Ah, Neil, if the courts had to consider all the cases of girls unjustifiably making that particular claim we would need seven times as many judges as we have now; no, seventy times seven.'

CHAPTER 22

A Review of the School Football Match

Oaken arrived at her office with Alex Peveril. Alex was a smiling, confident young man, six feet tall, almost triangular shaped from broad shoulders to narrow hips, muscular, handsome, olive-skinned, with a look that said he had it all. Priestley decided to dent his wall-to-wall charisma in the hope of making him more amenable to answering questions. 'I hope you're alright taking time out of self-study. I understand you're unable to do the usual maths lessons.' Alex laughed with a confidence Priestley felt was entirely unsuited to someone in what he assumed was his situation of having difficulty with the subject.

Alex explained, 'I went through most of the A-level course in the summer before last – I needed something to do – school holidays are way too long. My father spoke to the school and said he'd tutor me at home for maths so that I didn't get bored with it at school. He had to come for a meeting with the Headmaster and Mr McGovan, Head of Maths. Mr McGovan said it was against his socialist principles for a student to have private tutoring. Mr Verbane told him not to look a gift horse in the mouth, seeing as the school had a shortage of maths teachers, so he should be glad to have one less student. Mr McGovan said he didn't want me to suffer from not getting the best teaching available. My father said, "The proof of the pudding is in the eating", and that's why I took all the exams last year, maths and further maths, which is why I haven't any more maths exams to take here. That's why I get to study whatever I feel like in my free slots.'

Priestley tried a different tack to see how reliable his testimony might be. 'Were you at that meeting?'

'No. My father told me it was about me and for me but not with me.'

'Then how do you know what was said in the meeting?'

'My father told me afterwards.'

'And that was over a year ago.'

'Yes.'

'How can you remember all the details about what your father said?'

'I have an eidetic memory.'

'What's one of those – is it like a photographic memory?'

'That's a misleading expression – there has to be some conscious thought to lay down the details of a photograph, so in the end it's not so much a photograph as a collection of facts about the photograph. That doesn't mean it isn't possible to retain an image of a photograph by imprinting it on the mind; it just means no one can look at a photograph of something and simply store away the image without laying down the details in some way. It's obvious really.'

'Well, if you've also retained all the details of the School versus Staff football match, would you like to explain to me what happened?'

'Yes; sure. Would you like the long version or the short one?'

'How long is the long one?'

'An hour and a half plus stoppage time, unless you also want the half time break as well.'

'I'll go for the short version.'

'We won five-four.'

Priestley knew he had met his match about the match, so gave him a good laugh at this. 'OK. Could I have a medium version, with just the bits that you think I might be interested in. Obviously the goals, plus any incidents that caused a stir; if in doubt, include it. I understand Mr Newhouse was sent off – events leading up to it would be of particular interest, and whatever you noticed after that to the end of the game.'

'Right, then; edited highlights. We won the toss and I chose to kick towards the far end. The wind blows across the field but it also blows a bit from the top down towards the girls' changing room block, so if ever we win the toss I always choose to play into the wind in the first half; statistically our team scores more goals with the wind at our backs, and there are more goals scored in the second half of school matches when players are tired, so it makes sense to play into the wind in the first half.'

Priestley hoped the edited highlights would not be too detailed, but allowed Alex to continue without interruption despite feeling the digression about wind direction would be unlikely to help his investigation.

'Our goalkeeper Robbie Henderson positioned himself between the posts at the changing room end. The teachers took the kick off and they were straight into the attack. There was a through ball and Robbie came to the edge of his penalty area to retrieve it, but it was just outside so he couldn't pick it up. Mr Decker flicked it past him and just about ran it into the net – he shot into the empty goal from around the penalty spot. So we were one down in the first minute. We went for an attack that broke down when Gazza Talbot tried to dribble past Dr Hunter and had the ball taken off his foot by him when he anticipated Gazza's next swerve. They kept the ball pretty well and we couldn't get it back off them. The ball was passed to Mr Cullen out on the wing; he ghosted past Billy Huntsman like he wasn't there. He took it to the edge of the penalty area and then passed it to Mr Finlay who made like he was going to blast it into the right-hand side of the net, so Robbie dived that way and Mr Finlay kicked into the other side. That meant we were two down straight away.

'Before the restart I shouted to the team that we all needed to get stuck in and not be afraid of tackling them; Billy's normally good at tackling but he'd let Mr Cullen get right past him –it was like he was afraid to tackle a teacher. After that we had an attack, but Deano Bonsall did a really weak shot at the end and Mr Cassidy just bent down and collected it. He belted it down the wing and Mr Cullen had the ball again. We were all shouting at Billy to tackle him, and he did; he played right through the ball and the man, and Mr Cullen was really annoyed about it, lying on his back and trying to tell Billy off. Nosher Smith, standing just off the field – he was a substitute – shouted to Mr Cullen, "get up, you wuss", so Mr Cullen then tried to tell him off, but we all started laughing so Mr Cullen ran back to their end.

Nothing much happened after that for quite a while; lots of unforced errors on both sides, several throw-ins. Then, just before half-time, Jacko Stanage brought down Mr Decker on the edge of the eighteen-yard box – the penalty area. Mr Collins came up from defence to take it. We formed a four-man wall: Marco Hope, Deano Bonsall, Bobby Bolsover and me. The ref told us to get back to where he was standing, so we did, and got ready for Mr Collins to shoot – you know, protecting our tackle. But he didn't shoot; instead he played it across the goal to Mr Offial who ran with it a couple of steps and then smacked it into the roof of the net. That made it three-nil to them. There wasn't time to restart, so we went back to the changing room – we didn't want to stiffen up in the cold.'

Priestley checked on what happened to the staff team. 'Did the teachers go back to their changing room as well?'

'Yes, theirs was closer, so most of them were already inside by the time I went past.'

'OK. Anything else before the second half?'

'Not really. I did a pep talk, said we were fitter so they'd weaken towards the end, that we needed to make the ball do the work, not try to beat the opponents single-handedly, keep possession even if that meant passing back to our end. I reminded them that Liverpool had come from three-nil down against AC Milan to lift the European Cup, so there's no reason why we couldn't get back into the game, especially with the wind at our backs. Tommy Thompson asked if that meant Gerrard would be coming on as a substitute. We laughed at that, but it made me remember our own subs might be wondering what the plan was for them. So I said, "We're in this game to win it, but at some point three of us will have to give way to let Kenny, Jimmy and Nosher have a go, so don't take it personally if it's your turn. That's the plan unless there are any injuries. Danno and Bobby, keep running at their defence and if you're feeling knackered then let me know and you can go off.'

'When you were heading for the changing room, or coming out after the half-time interval, did you see anyone that you couldn't recognise anywhere around there?'

'No, just students and members of staff moving between classrooms. I didn't notice anyone I wouldn't have expected to see.'

'OK then, the second half.'

'Right. Well, we came back all fired up to give it a good go. It was our kick-off and we went straight into the attack; we'd agreed earlier what we were going to do. I tapped the ball to the side for Marco to run onto it and belt it down the wing for Danno, who had set off as soon as I first touched it. Marco and I sprinted down the centre of the pitch, Danno crossed it, Marco collected it just in front of Mr Rendel and played it for me to run onto and knock it past Mr Cassidy. A brilliant plan that worked to perfection.'

'Was it your plan, by any chance?'

Torn between appearing immodest and not taking credit for his own work, he settled for, 'We worked it out as a team, though it began as something I suggested.

'Anyway, I'll skip some of the detail about how we wore them down, to the point where we had two corners in rapid succession. Danno took the first corner, which was cleared by Mr Hart – but only by putting the ball out for another corner. So Danno took the second one and crossed it right onto my forehead – all I had to do was connect with it and it was always going to end up in the net.'

'So, you're just three-two down.'

'And looking like the stronger team, I have to say. We kept pressing, and they couldn't break out to launch an attack. Eventually – and I'm skipping a lot of the match here – we launched a three-pronged attack straight down the middle. I passed to Marco to avoid being tackled by Mr Davies, and he passed to me to avoid being tackled by Mr Rendel. I was inside the penalty area on a line with the right post as I see it, what they'd call their left post, and I could have had a shot at that point for a hat-trick, but Deano was completely unmarked on my left so I passed it across to him to score, only he didn't shoot; Mr Cassidy had been trying to cover his left post when I could have shot, so he ran back to cover his right post when Deano could have shot, only Deano passed it back to me and so I put it into the net. I told Deano off about that. If I'd kept running forward I'd have been offside when he returned the ball, and we'd have blown it. He said he hadn't been expecting me to pass in the first place, and I said yes, I'm sorry for not signalling, but he needs to be ready and if it happens again he needs to shoot. The thing is, you see, Deano had fluffed a few chances earlier in the match and I didn't want him losing confidence.'

Priestley broke into the monologue. 'Are you saying that you were prepared to miss out on a hat-trick for the sake of helping a team-mate's confidence? Adults don't generally have that type of maturity. Are you seeking beatification?'

'You aren't the only person who can be "Priestley".'

They shared the joke with a brief laugh.

'Actually, it comes back to when I was thirteen years old. There was a pre-season practice, with various years' teams involved, but not playing as full teams. Instead, we had players from different years all on the same side. There was a Year Thirteen lad – what you might know as Upper Sixth. Everyone looked up to him; he was great. He did five years ago what I did in the match: he crossed the ball to me so that I could score, when he could have scored himself. And I thought at the time, that's how I want to be. So, ever since then I've always tried to play for the team. That's probably why I was made Captain. Did anything like that happen to you when you were young?'

'Ouch!'

'Sorry, I meant young-er.'

Priestley frowned in thought for a moment. 'Not really, not with older and younger players together – I think the school may have thought that too dangerous. I do remember a Boys v. Girls match, though. I was in my last year of prep school – I was at a boys' school. We had this match against the nearby girls' school. We had to play the ball with our wrong foot – left foot if you're a right-footer like me – and we weren't allowed to tackle them properly but they could tackle us. On top of that – and you'll probably not have come across this before – we had to run with our stronger hand on the thigh of the other leg, so for me that was right hand on left thigh. It was a farce – none of us could play properly like that.'

'So you got thrashed.'

'Not exactly. When we went nine-nil up they stopped the match so that we didn't go into double figures.'

'I don't think that would happen nowadays.'

'Because girls can play better?'

'That's not what I was thinking.'

Priestley decided not to invite Alex to take the digression any further. 'Anyway, back to the match. It's now three-all.'

'Right. Well, I brought Kenny on in place of Bobby. Kenny had fresh legs and he was running just inside the touchline when Mr Cullen tripped him. He kind of crumpled into a heap, but jumped back up again and I thought he was going to go after Mr Cullen, who was running away, so I called Kenny back to take the free kick. He placed it superbly into the penalty box and I brought it down with my chest, and I shouted "Deano" and played it along the ground to him. He hit it hard enough to beat Mr Cassidy at his near-side post. So that put us into the lead for the first time. Before the restart I subbed Deano, bringing on Jimmy. After that, the teachers got themselves together a bit better, with Mr Newhouse organising them, yelling at them to do this, do that, get over there, come over here – he was really keen to get them going. They used the width of the field to make their next attack, finishing with a cross to Mr Newhouse; he was really going for it, like a juggernaut – he brushed aside Vinnie and Jacko like they weren't there. He shot hard, low down to Robbie's left hand corner. Robbie got his fingers to it but he couldn't stop it. I remember Deano shouted "Mr Newhouse has scored again", and Bobby, who was standing next to him shouted, "He scores every week".

'After that they really turned up the pressure. Mr Finlay attacked through the centre and was brought down by Tommy a few metres outside our penalty area. It was a direct free kick and Mr Hart came up to take it. We formed a four-man wall. Mr Newhouse stood well offside five metres behind us. Mr Hart shot and it looked like it was heading straight for Mr Newhouse's head until he moved out of the way; the ball flew into the corner of the net without touching him. The teachers were shouting well done to Mr Hart, but the referee disallowed the goal as he said Mr Newhouse had been interfering with play in an offside position. Mr Newhouse complained at the ref; I heard him say they do that standing offside thing at free kicks all the time in the Premier League, and the ref said he wasn't responsible for what they let them get away with in Premiership football. Then the ref threatened to book him if he didn't move off, so Mr Newhouse got on with the game.

'The disallowed goal seemed to fire up the teachers even more. Mr Finlay made a run into the box and Vinnie came in to tackle him, but he was just too late. He didn't get the ball but he did get the man, so the ref gave them a penalty. Mr Newhouse stepped up to take it. The ref told everyone to stay outside the box and the "D", and then stood to one side to blow his whistle. The ball went into the bottom corner at Robbie's right-hand side; he'd moved to the right but got nowhere near it. The ref blew his whistle again and pointed to the penalty spot, saying "no goal". He then pointed to Mr Cullen and said it was disallowed for "encroaching" – Mr Cullen had run into the box way too early. Mr Newhouse took the penalty again. The ball smacked the crossbar and bounced back into play, and Marco cleared it up-field.

'I was still intending to give Nosher a game, but at four-all we couldn't really afford to weaken the team. He's a bit overweight – rather more than a bit – and he isn't fast enough, so I couldn't bring him on just yet. We were all fired up to get back into the lead, so I got Jacko to come into the attack as well. When Jacko got the ball he went straight for their goal, even though I was shouting to him to pass it. Just outside the penalty area he played the ball through Mr Cullen's legs, and I heard Jacko say "megs" to Mr Cullen, who then tripped him while throwing his hands in the air as though to say "I never touched him". Danno shouted "book him ref"; the ref turned to Danno and said "that's my decision, thank you". He did show Mr Cullen a yellow card for the trip, though, and I saw him pointing back to where he'd done the earlier trip to remind him it wasn't his first offence.

'They set up a five-man wall, holding onto each other's sleeves. The ref told them to step back to where he was standing, and they sort of shuffled but didn't actually move back. Then he whipped out his can of vanishing spray…'

'His what?'

'Foam for showing how close they could stand – like they did in the World Cup. He went back to the ball and sprayed a semi-circle around it, then paced the distance again, striding past the edge of the wall. He did a long line behind them and told them to step behind it. He drew the line a bit too straight, really – it should have been an arc of a circle of nine point one five metres radius with the ball at its centre. Anyway, they were holding onto each other so tightly, they could hardly move.

'Mr Newhouse was at the end of the wall, so the ref warned him that if the wall didn't move back, he would book him. They took a tiny step back, but nowhere near enough. So the ref booked Mr Newhouse. That made them step back a bit, but then they dragged each other forward again. So the ref gave Mr Newhouse another yellow card followed by a red one.' Alex paused momentarily. 'It's really sad, Mr Newhouse having that accident. He was a good football coach.'

After a longer pause for reflection, he continued with the account of the match. 'After that, the ref said to Mr Decker, who was next in the wall, that if the wall didn't move back to where he said, he'd be the next to go. So Mr Decker screamed at the other three still in the wall to get back, and they all stepped right back until they were behind the line – they didn't even dare stand on the line, like they do in Premiership matches. After that, I took the free kick and flicked it up to Marco who headed into the corner – more of a cush shot really, not much strength behind it, but very accurate.

'There were probably only five minutes left, so I decided we should concentrate on defence. I needed to give Nosher a game, so I took Gazza off, switched Marco to defence – he's very fast – and put Nosher on in midfield. From then until the end of the match is was non-stop attack by them. Mr Finlay tried to place the ball in the corner but shot just wide. Their next chance went to Mr Offial, who hit it over the bar. Then he had another chance and shot well wide. Straight after we took the goal kick, the ref signalled for the end of the match.'

'Well, that's been very informative, Alex; I could imagine myself having been there. I'm also interested in some of the things that happened off the field. Did you notice any boys being sent from one side of the field to the other?'

'Yes, of course, they were the three players who'd been substituted: Bobby, Deano and Gazza. Ms Clifton objected to some of the encouragement they were giving our team.'

'I heard they were chanting "Send Off Sir" until Mr Newhouse was shown a red card, and then they started throwing insults at the other teachers.'

'I don't believe the ref was influenced by the chant – he made his own decision. As for the insults, it's a well-established tactic for undermining the opposition – a traditional activity that takes place in league grounds every Saturday afternoon up and down the country.'

'So, do you condone it?'

'They were still hyper from playing in the match. I think it was understandable.'

There was a knock at the door; Priestley introduced DC Tony Beresford and invited him to join them. 'Alex here has been giving me a run-through of the football match. We've just reached the point where I'm going to ask about what he saw of Mr Newhouse from the time that he was sent off, and what he saw of Mr Cassidy after the match.'

Alex took his cue. 'After Mr Newhouse left the field I really didn't see him at all; I was much too focused on the game. At the end of the match I organised the school team to form two rows for the teachers to pass between us as we applauded them. But all the action had been at the far end, so Mr Cassidy was a long way from anyone else, and he walked straight towards the changing room. As he reached the bottom of the steps I shouted "Mr Cassidy", and he turned around and stopped. I signalled that we were going to applaud them, by pretending to clap in the air a couple of times. He gave me the "thumbs up" sign and stayed where he was. So we applauded the teachers at the edge of the pitch, and they formed two rows at the top of the steps and applauded us, with Mr Cassidy applauding from the bottom of the steps rather than walking back up them again. I was the last to leave the field and go down the steps – more like what a ship's captain's supposed to do than a football captain, I suppose, except that our ship didn't sink. Once I'd passed Mr Cassidy I noticed him turn and walk into the changing room, just as the other teachers started to come down the steps.'

'And how long was it before the first teacher coming down the steps went into the changing room after Mr Cassidy?'

'However long it takes to walk down the steps. Just a few seconds, I suppose.'

'Would other players from your team have been able to see Mr Cassidy?'

'Probably those next to me on the same line – the other line would have been facing away. I'll just have a think about that.'

Alex paused for a moment, half-closing his eyes as though imagining the scene. 'Right, I was at the far end of the line; next to me were Marco Hope, Deano Bonsall, Gazza Talbot, Danno Harris, Kenny Derwent and Billy Huntsman.'

'Could you tell me their proper names – when they're not playing football.'

'Mark Hope, Dean Bonsall, Gary Talbot, Daniel Harris, Kenneth Derwent, William Huntsman. When we play football we need names that can be shouted, so two syllables and a long sound on the end are always best. I'm Aaaaa-liiiii-ks. Not ideal, but it has to do. Hmm, I think "ks" might be a letter from the Ukrainian alphabet; do you happen to know?'

Priestley shook his head slightly. 'Sorry.'

'Not to worry – I'll look it up.'

'Right, well that's been brilliant, Aaaaa-liiiii-ks. One final thing, and it has nothing to do with school or football; Detective Constable Tony Beresford, here, was telling me in a bar last week that the metric system is fundamentally flawed, and that there are much better numbers to use. Now, I think he was taking the Mickey out of me, so I'd like you to interrogate him and see if you can make any sense of what he says. I'll be making some notes about the football match while you're doing that, so let me know when you're finished and tell me if you think he was just having me on.'

Alex laughed at the idea of interrogating a policeman; Berry looked shocked at the thought but knew to go along with it. Alex began, 'I assume you were talking about number bases.'

'Yes. Half of ten is five. Of the four numbers from two to five, only two of them are exact divisors of ten. Compare that to twelve: two, three, four and six are all divisors, and only five isn't. So that's four out of five. Which means twelve would have been a much better number base than ten, as people like to be able to take half of something, or a third, or a quarter.'

Priestley looked up and asked Alex, 'Are there any problems with that idea? Wouldn't it make it harder to do multiplying? Twelve twelves are a hundred and forty-four, and that's harder to work with than a hundred.'

Alex replied without hesitation. 'In the base-twelve number system ten tens would still be a hundred, but it would be worth as much as twelve twelves in the metric system. Of course there would have to have been two new single-digit numbers created, so people would count one to nine, first new number, second new number, ten.'

'So, he wasn't pulling my leg, then. And do you agree that twelve would have been a better number?'

'It's probably the most practicable. The only other contenders would be two, or perfect powers of two such as four, eight or sixteen, though twenty-four would have been fun for those of us who can do twenty-four times tables in our heads.'

'Right, well, thanks very much, Alex – you've been a great help.'

Priestley acknowledged Alex's grown-up status by thrusting a hand out to him, which Alex shook with a firm, adult grip. Alex hesitated at the door. 'We've been told that Mr Cassidy's died; the rumour is it was suicide. He was a really good bloke – I liked him a lot. He was very intellectual, but nice with it. He never talked down to anyone – and that can be quite difficult when you're as brilliant as he was.'

'Do you find that a problem yourself?'

'It's something I'm aware of – I suppose Mr Cassidy has shown me how it's done. I'll think of it as his legacy to me.'

Alex appeared subdued, so Priestley waited a moment before continuing.

'I looked at the team sheets; I see he was nicknamed "Butch". Who came up with the names?'

'We did them together – all of us in the school team. We all thought the name "Butch" was just too good a fit – you know, the film, but also because he wasn't butch. I feel pretty bad about that, now.'

'Mr Newhouse was given the nickname "Nobby" – would you like to explain that one?'

'Not really.'

'Does it mean what I think it means?'

'Very likely.'

'Beginning with a capital K?'

'That would fit.'

'Girls? Teachers?'

'Both.'

'Could you give me their names?'

'Sorry, no.'

'Because you don't know them?'

'Because it would be behaviour unbecoming a gentleman. Anyway, I can't see how it's relevant.'

'Well, I won't press you for now, but if it starts to look like it's critical information needed for the investigation, then I trust you'll reconsider.'

'I hope it doesn't come to that.'

'We'll leave it for now, then. I'm sorry I put you in an awkward position, Alex. Thanks very much for your help.'

After they were alone, Berry asked Priestley, 'What was all that about the maths? You didn't seem interested last week in the bar.'

'I was trying to assess whether Alex is the real deal. Can we rely on what he says, or might he make things up if he isn't sure about them?'

'I can only comment as far as the maths is concerned: he's the real deal.'

'So should I rely on what he said about Cassidy having gone into the changing room just seconds before the other teachers?'

'I can see no reason why not.'

'I agree entirely, but we still need corroboration. Let's get hold of some of the others who might have seen Cassidy.'

Berry opened a briefcase and took out a sheet of paper which he handed to Priestley. 'By the way, when I reviewed the interviews of the staff players, I put together what they seem to suggest is the likeliest order of entry into the girls' changing room after Newhouse. I've printed it off.'

1	Cassidy
11	Cullen
2	Collins
5	Davies
4	Hart
6	Hunter
8	Finlay
7	Offial
10	Decker
3	Rendel

Priestley asked, 'How confident are you about this list?'

Berry looked offended. 'I'm confident this is the likeliest order based on the testimonies, though I can't comment on the actual order as this is derivative data I'm presenting to you.'

Priestley was not entirely sure what Berry meant, but decided not to delve further as he recognised the inquiry had moved on since those statements had been taken.

Priestley instructed Berry to ask Oaken to bring Mark Hope to them. Mark confirmed Alex Peveril's explanation of Cassidy's movements. Next was Gary Talbot, who had not noticed Cassidy. When Daniel Harris confirmed Alex Peveril's view, Priestley decided he had enough corroboration to proceed.

CHAPTER 23

Dr Logan on Communal Changing Rooms

Priestley phoned Watt to let her know he was confident of Cassidy's innocence.

'Watt.'

'Priestley, ma'am. Cassidy didn't do it. He only entered the changing room seconds before the other teachers, and Newhouse had been dead for several minutes by then.'

'Right. I'll send my adjutant to pay a call on Castleton, to insist on his resignation.' She terminated the phone call. Priestley wondered if she had used the army's designation because of his own background, hers being the Royal Navy; the meaning was nevertheless clear.

He relayed her information to Berry. 'She's sending Superintendent Yelland to see DCI Castleton. He accused Cassidy of killing Newhouse, and that has to have been a factor in Cassidy's suicide. She wants him out.'

Berry responded with a sigh. 'As do we all.'

Priestley phoned the Shawton News and obtained a number for Rowland Ryland.

'Hello Rowland; Marcus Priestley.'

'Inspector Priestley, how nice it is to hear from you. What can I do for you on this bright, sunny morning?'

Priestley glanced out of the window to see if the weather had changed from the cold, drizzly day that it had been earlier; it had not.

'Acting Detective Chief Inspector Priestley to you, Rowland.'

'And that's why you telephoned me. Well, congratulations. Cheerio.'

Rowland waited silently to discover the true purpose of the call.

'I've read your articles in the paper. Not entirely accurate I have to say.'

'Not an egregious fault for newspaper articles generally, Marcus.'

'You mentioned Dr Andrew Logan wrote something that you summarised for your second article. I expect it'll be a waste of time, but I'd like to read it – I mustn't leave any stone unturned, you know. Could you e-mail me a copy of Logan's original submission to you, in case there's anything relevant to the inquiry that you cut out of your piece?'

'And in return I receive…?'

'What you normally receive, Rowland.'

'Absolutely nothing; a most generous offer.'

'You know I sometimes give you a head start when information is due to be made public anyway; I see it as a handicap allowance, what with you being older and slower than the other runners and riders. And if information is released at a time that enables you to make it into that day's edition, but too late for the Nationals, that's just a chance event.'

'You make a convincing argument, Marcus; it's on its way.'

'Thanks, Rowland. Are you going far today? Just in case there's anything announced later this afternoon?'

'If I were before, I'm not now. I look forward to hearing from you.'

The document arrived within minutes. Priestley forwarded it to Berry and the two of them read through it.

Changing Rooms by Dr Andrew Logan

The Midshaw School girls' changing room block is quite some distance from the main school building, and is completely separate from the boys' changing room block. Originally the building had contained a small changing room for girls and an even smaller one for boys. As the number of children at the school had grown over the years, a series of decisions had to be made on how to increase capacity for lessons generally, including the changing facilities for sports lessons.

The original changing room block was separated from public land by a tall, metal fence in which was set a small gate that was kept locked except when staff let cross-country runners in or out.

The beautiful Derbyshire countryside that extended beyond the fence began with a footpath, with an area of deciduous woodland close by. The local Lib Dems had sanctioned the erection of the tall fence, in support of the safety of children at the school; illegal entry by intruders was made difficult by erection of the fence, though not impossible. When complaints were received that the tall fence spoiled the view of the countryside, those same councillors then claimed the fence had not been authorised in practise, but only in principle, and that samples of the proposed metal fence should have been provided to the relevant sub-committee for final approval or rejection of the plans. The subject disappeared from the council's agenda following the loss of their seats by those Lib Dems who had back-tracked on the plans; there was a widespread belief that the silent majority had spoken through the ballot box.

The single entry point to the playing fields was behind and to one side of the changing room block, where steep steps had been cut into the hill. The steps were made of wood embedded in heavy clay. The wooden timbers were a recurring expense, as they needed repair or replacement every spring. More than a decade ago there had been a proposal to replace the wooden steps with concrete ones. The danger of children slipping and injuring themselves had been discussed at length. One particular issue had been that the long, aluminium studs favoured by the rugby forwards would be especially lacking in grip on concrete. The idea of banning metal studs was deemed infeasible, as plastic studs had just been banned due to a Health & Safety initiative that had identified plastic as being more likely to cause cuts to opponents in football matches.

The continuing debate led to various suggestions being made. One proposal was that children should remove their boots before going up or coming down the concrete steps; another was that competitive sports should be banned entirely, thereby removing the need for the playing fields. In the final analysis, it had been accepted that sport would continue at the school, and that the wooden steps would remain in situ.

In view of the difficulties with the local authority concerning the fence, it was assumed permission would not be forthcoming for the school to build an extension on the side that would encroach onto the adjoining public land as it would impede the public right of way. Also, it was deemed infeasible to extend at the back of the block, as this would be directly into a steep hill. It was further declared unacceptable to extend at the other side or at the front, as this would have limited the options for possible future expansion of other school buildings. It was therefore accepted that there was no space to increase the changing room footprint. There was a fierce debate among the staff about whether the existing block should be extended upwards, or whether a new block should be built on the closest available plot, which was some fifty metres away. Also, if a new block were to be built, there was the question of whether it should it be for use by girls or by boys.

An argument in favour of making the existing block multi-storey was that the users of a new block would have to walk an extra fifty metres to reach the playing fields; this seemed to overlook the fact that the children would be there to do exercise anyway, in one form or another. Walking down steps within a building while wearing football boots was declared an unsafe practice by the Health and Safety representative, as was changing into boots at the door where other children would be coming in and out. This extinguished any further debate on the option.

An argument in favour of a new block being built for the girls was that they needed more modern shower facilities whereas boys would be better able to continue to cope with the Spartan conditions of the old block. Another argument was that boys walking past the girls' block would be invading their privacy, notwithstanding the fact that they had up to that time always shared the same block.

An argument in favour of boys using the new block was that they do more extra-curricular sport and therefore they would make more use of modern shower facilities. Additionally, it was argued that the boys already needed more showers than the old block could provide. It was agreed that, if the new block were to be used by the boys, then the old block should have a sign placed on it with the words "Only Girls Allowed".

The arguments raged back and forth for weeks. The "New

Changing Rooms for the Girls" camp within the teaching staff eventually wore down the opposition. When a deputation of them put this to the headmaster, Mr Gilbert Verbane, he explained the decision had already been taken by the school governors. Their decision was that the new block would be for boys' use only, and as the plans had been drawn up and approved, the building work would start straight after the end of term.

In response to the shower of complaints through the staff suggestion box that the Headmaster and Governors had failed to involve the staff in the consideration of what some alleged was the most important development of the school in decades, Mr Verbane provided a copy of the plans and arranged a staff meeting for early one Saturday morning at which attendance would be voluntary. The plans showed that the new block was to be built as one large changing room with communal showers for boys, and that the old block was to be converted along the same lines, combining the existing boys' and girls' changing areas into a single changing room for girls.

Despite the choice of day and time, the meeting was very well attended. I took the opportunity to raise an issue from my own schooldays. Shortly after my eleventh birthday I had suddenly grown tall and muscular and had developed significant amounts of body hair; this was before any other boys in my class, or even my year so far as I remember. One boy made me very uncomfortable in the school changing room by the way he watched me dressing and undressing. He often contrived to go into the communal shower at the same time as me. Similarly, when my class had our weekly swimming lesson at the local baths, the boy always observed me uncomfortably closely. As I needed more time to dry myself than the other boys – a large, hirsute body takes much longer to dry than a small, smooth one – some of the teachers who failed to understand this, complained at my being slow, even accusing me of "hanging around" when the reality was I could not get myself out of there fast enough, and sometimes I even put on my clothes without properly drying myself. Anyway, the boy in question always waited until I had finished getting dressed before he would leave. Many years later I saw his name in the local newspaper: he had been sentenced to a substantial prison term for assaults on young boys.

SEND OFF SIR

At the meeting I argued that boys often understood their own sexuality and that of others from an early age, and that therefore the building plans for the boys' changing rooms should be revised to enable boys to have some privacy. I did not argue for individual cubicles for all, as I recognised the additional expense would be too much of a drain on school finances. My proposal was that "boys with homosexual inclinations" could request the use of a separate changing area, and non-homosexual boys could request, anonymously if they so wished, that any particular boy should be required to use the separate facility; also, staff could insist, if it became clear someone's behaviour may be deemed unacceptable for them to use the shared area. The first reaction was from a female colleague who demanded to know why I was not also arguing that girls should have a similar arrangement. My response was along the following lines.

'There is a widespread belief that a significant proportion of boys are born with a genetic predisposition to homosexual orientation. Some of the more outlandish claims are ridiculously high and fly in the face of everyday experience. Data collected more dispassionately indicates one and a half per cent of young men identify themselves as homosexual. This figure declines rapidly with age, which may be explained by increasing reluctance to disclose true orientation, or that the idea of homosexuality for social reasons is far more prevalent in younger men who are at an age of experimentation. There are also regional variations, with London as a whole having a far higher proportion than elsewhere in the UK, with just a few notable exceptions where targeted inward migration of homosexuals has resulted in higher concentrations, for example in certain seaside towns.

'As far as genetic predisposition is concerned, the true figure for boys of school age may be substantially lower than the apparent figure for, say, twenty-year-olds. For the sake of argument, a figure of one per cent of boys of school age may be considered reasonable. For this school that suggests an average of one boy per six classes, say, one per school year. For girls who are born with a single-gender genetic sexual predisposition, estimates are less than half of the estimates for boys. For a school of our size, the expectation is that there may be none, or perhaps just one, such girl in any school year. With such low numbers for

271

both boys and girls, it may be deemed sufficient simply to arrange for a few private cubicles to be built away from the communal areas. My suggestion therefore is that the plans for a single communal area in the new block should be revised to provide some privacy for the heterosexuals who would use the main area.'

At that point another female colleague demanded the right for there to be equal numbers of lesbian women as Gay men in society at large, a claim that received murmured support from many other female colleagues, though my impression was that most of them appeared to be struggling to hide a degree of ambivalence. The colleague also claimed that the proportion of lesbians in this country is far more than one in a hundred. My response, which I backed up with data from the World Health Organisation, was that the explanation lay in social and socio-economic factors that tended to become much more significant beyond school age. I was accused of "bringing facts into a debate that should be all about women's rights", an allegation to which I made no response.

A male member of staff then questioned the accuracy of the figures relating to men. He argued that my figures greatly underestimated the proportion of Gay men in this country. My response was as follows.

'First of all, I do not like to use the word "Gay", as I believe it to be singularly inappropriate. Though, increasingly, homosexual men are happy to reveal their sexuality, there remains a significantly high proportion who remain uncomfortable with it, and consequently it makes them quite unhappy, just the opposite of Gay; evidence for this is the number of men who undertake bogus, so-called "cures", often paying large sums of money for private, psychological and chemical quackery, or even, less expensively for them, undergoing treatment through the NHS. Secondly, I referred to genetic predisposition. With the broadening acceptance of homosexuality, the figure of one per cent being those who are genetically predisposed from childhood may be increased to as much as three per cent in adulthood by the inclusion of those who choose a homosexual lifestyle for social or socio-economic reasons. But, just as for women, these factors are not generally present at school age. Thirdly, the teaching profession has a higher proportion of homosexuals than the population at large;

one factor is that those males with ersatz-female, nurturing characteristics are welcomed onto teaching courses by universities, as they view these as being important to the care of children. Indeed, for so many years the emphasis has been on nurture, at the expense of academia, that this selection bias may well have been a factor in the sharp decline in mean academic standards in schools over my working lifetime.'

As I recall, the debate did rather degenerate from that point onwards. I will attempt to reproduce it here.

A young male teacher called out 'So, you're homophobic'.

I fear he had failed to grasp the details of some of the arguments I had put forward.

I replied, 'No, I am not; quite the opposite.'

He countered, 'So, you're homosexual.'

I responded, 'No, I am not.'

He argued, 'But you said you were the opposite.'

I explained, 'I said I am the opposite of homophobic. I believe everyone should have equal rights, regardless of their sexual orientation. It is for this reason that I believe any action taken to suppress that equality should be actively blocked by the whole of society, though, I have to say, there are members of the so-called "Gay community" who generate considerable antagonism by their pursuit of cultural dominance and their determination to take from the hetero-sexual community rather than to give to society at large. For example, the estate of "marriage" has always meant the union of a man and a woman. Rather than taking existing words such as "marriage", and indeed "gay" itself, it would have been better to have created new words, thereby avoiding alienating the heterosexual population. Also, I would mention that the term "Gay" as indicating homosexual may itself be seen as discriminatory as it focuses on one specific group and may do so at the expense of other non-heterosexual groups such as transgender and hermaphroditic. The term LGBT seems to be used increasingly – Lesbian, Gay, Bi-sexual and Transgender. Perhaps an acronym should be created that can be pronounced as a new word, such as Legbit, before someone creates a negative-sounding alternative such as Blight. "Non-heterosexual" could be used in the meantime – though not just the initials, as NHS is already in use.' This latter observation failed to raise even the slightest *appreciation of the intended humour.*

I recognised I had wandered somewhat from the original matter for discussion, so I returned to the subject of the layout of the new changing room block and to what changes should be considered to the existing block. I suggested there should be a survey to find out what the sixth formers thought, on the basis that the arrangement should receive the children's approval and that the sixth form should have the maturity to make a rational assessment.

Perhaps the meeting taking place on a Saturday morning had led to opinions being expressed more openly than might have been expected on a normal school day. Perhaps the Headmaster had grown uncomfortable with the increasingly personal nature of the debate and feared it may create rifts amongst his staff. Whatever the reason, his action was to suppress further debate at that point by standing up and stating, 'I believe we have just heard some illuminating facts and a very good idea from our renowned Head of Science. May I have your support in asking him to get together with our Head of Maths to create a survey for completion by the sixth form, both boys and girls, and let us include the fifth form also?'

Following a general nodding of heads and murmurs of agreement, he asked that the survey be prepared early the next week and distributed on the Friday morning. The two of us did as he bid, having the survey ready by the Thursday. On the Friday morning, all fifth and sixth formers present on that day completed the survey anonymously, with no apparent refusals. Unfortunately, as a very large majority of the boys contrived to tick the boxes that indicated they should share the girls' open plan changing room on the grounds of their (unspecified) sexual orientation, the survey was declared to be more informative about the development of hetero-sexual boys in their teens than about the finer points of sexual equality. The headmaster therefore declared the survey should not influence the decision-making process, which would continue to be under the auspices of the school's governing committee.

The headmaster subsequently confirmed the original decision of the committee for development of a new block for boys with a single changing room. On the other hand, the proposal to combine the old girls' and boys' changing rooms into a single communal room was dropped. The boys' room now became the Second Changing Room for Girls, with various options to suit the occasion; for example, visiting teams would be given the use of the Second Room.

I was disappointed that an opportunity had been missed for giving privacy to heterosexual boys from the attentions of homosexual boys. I chose to retire at the end of the following term, so have no knowledge of anything that occurred on this matter subsequent to that time.

Priestley read the article quickly, waiting until Berry looked up before asking, 'Anything in there of interest?'

'There was a reference to cultural dominance by the Gay community. Do you remember John Barrowman kissing another man at the opening ceremony of the Commonwealth Games? Some people objected afterwards; they said it could offend those countries taking part that have laws against homosexuality.'

Priestley nodded agreement. 'There were also people who said it wasn't appropriate when small children are watching. But is there anything directly relevant to the inquiry?'

'Not that I could see, though perhaps we should inspect the second Girls' Changing Room as well as the main one.'

'There's a second one?'

'Yes, the one that used to be the Boys' Changing Room.'

Priestley admitted his oversight. 'Damn, I didn't pick that up. The style of the article is so dry, I just skimmed through it. I don't suppose it matters, but I'll take a look anyway.'

'I could have a look as well.'

'OK, but don't get excited – we won't be looking when there's any girls in there.'

CHAPTER 24

Maths and English Misconceptions

Superintendent Richard Yelland knocked loudly and repeatedly on the door of Bryn Castleton's semi-detached house on the Uppershaw edge of Midshaw, ignoring the illuminated bell button. Castleton came to the door still dressed in his usual suit, not yet believing his working day was over.

'Come in, Richard.'

'Better keep it formal, DCI Castleton.'

Yelland followed Castleton into the living room, ignoring the offer of a soft-cushioned three piece suite, preferring to perch himself on an upright wooden chair that was one of a pair which flanked a peeling veneered table under a picture window.

'I've heard your interview with Mr Hugh Cassidy. You accused him of the killing of Mr John Newhouse. As a result of that accusation and the manner in which you made it, he took his own life.'

Castleton decided the best form of defence was attack. 'And that proves I was right. He did it and didn't want to face the consequences.'

'If only that were true; but it isn't. It's been established that Cassidy was entirely innocent. He entered the changing room just seconds before several other people, and minutes after the attack. You got it wrong, and now he's dead because of you. At the moment this problem is being contained. If it goes public you can expect to have a very hard time. Watt is prepared to try to avoid that happening, but you have to give her your resignation right away. I understand there's another issue that has earned you a suspension, so it makes sense to bail out while you're still over dry land.'

Castleton had already been weakening in the face of superior forces; he now capitulated, agreeing to sign a declaration of total and unconditional surrender.

Yelland left with the piece of paper in his hand, immediately phoning Watt who informed Priestley who in turn told Berry.

Priestley phoned Martello. 'Lily, I bring you glad tidings of great joy.'

'You're a little early for Christmas.'

'Castleton has resigned.'

'Thanks, Marcus. I don't know how you did it, but thanks ever so much.'

'I'd like to take the credit, but like I said before, it was his own actions that brought him down.'

'And you're sticking to that story?'

'Well, maybe I gave a shove in the right direction. Anyway, let Neil and Linda know.'

'I'll pass on the good news. Suddenly the day seems much brighter.'

'Much brighter for just about everyone. Bye, Lily.'

Priestley phoned Dunn at the station and gave what for him was less welcome news. 'DCI Castleton has resigned over that interview of Hugh Cassidy you and he did together. As I'm now Acting DCI, it's my responsibility to consider what action should be taken against you for your contribution, now that it's been established Cassidy was entirely innocent. See me this evening in the office at seven o'clock.'

'I go off shift at four...sir.'

'You may be going off shift permanently if you're not there.'

Priestley hit the "end call" button before Dunn could terminate the conversation himself. He realised an advantage that old-fashioned, heavy landline equipment had over mobile phones: Dunn had probably been able to release some of his vast supplies of anger by crashing the heavy receiver down onto the cradle, whereas he himself was limited to flipping the protective cover.

He turned to the next item in his notes: David Williamson, Simon Green and Zachariah Peck had been positioned to retrieve the ball from the end of the pitch near the changing rooms, but all the action following the final goal had been at the other end of the field. So, what were they doing and did anyone notice them in those last minutes?

Berry located Oaken and returned with her to the office where she consulted wall charts and files about the three boys. After closing the third file, she addressed Priestley. 'They're what might be called some of the less athletic students. They're in class right now; after lunch they're due to take part in a special session that I'm sure they'd be very disappointed to miss. Would it be possible to see them some time later?'

'What's the special session?'

'It's a cross-curricular Maths and English session that started out as a PSHE lesson.'

'PSHE?'

'Personal, Social, Health and Economic education. This particular session has been hijacked by that maverick Anthony Ashbourne from Maths. He's joined forces with Graham Rendel from English to do a joint lesson that's intended to scotch popular misconceptions in Maths and English, except they've been allowed to broaden their brief. Now, it's anything they think will help students with preparing for the real world – essentially, if they think something could be beneficial for Year Thirteens, then they can include it.'

Priestley considered whether it might be deemed beneficial for Year Thirteens to have some knowledge of practical policing included in the session, and whether he in turn might benefit from seeing and hearing the three boys in a group context before speaking to them individually. 'Perhaps I could volunteer myself and DC Beresford to give them some information about policing? It's one aspect of the real world they may come across in the future, if they haven't already. I could offer a few insights perhaps, or at least be there to answer any questions.'

'Mr Ashbourne and Mr Rendel may have already prepared their lesson to a strict timetable. You could ask them if they'd be willing to include you in the session. They'll probably be in the staffroom in ten minutes time – I'll take you there then.'

'Just before that, would you give us a tour of the girls' changing rooms? I need to check all the ways in and out for both of them.'

'We'll do it now if you like. Obviously I'll check there's no one in there first. They should be empty during lessons, but since we had hairdryers installed we find girls sometimes pop in even when they're not doing PE.'

'Is it just the girls who have hairdryers?'

'Yes. It's supposed to make PE more accessible to girls – being able to do their hair afterwards.'

Priestley went to the changing rooms with Berry and Oaken; he noticed the new hairdryers and the old coat hooks – one of which was now missing. He decided not to suggest the money spent on hairdryers might have been better directed toward making the girls' changing rooms safer by replacing all the broken hooks.

Oaken brought Priestley and Berry to the staff room. Priestley had seen no mention of Anthony Ashbourne but had already come across the name Graham Rendel when reviewing the case notes. He phoned Plummer to ask her perception of Rendel from the interview she and Dunn had conducted. Plummer explained how he had been given a hard time by Dunn. Priestley decided he should begin by offering an apology on behalf of the police force before broaching the subject of joining them for the joint session.

Rendel was sitting in the staffroom with a single exercise book open directly in front of him on the large table and with piles more to the left and right of it; as Priestley and Berry were brought in by Oaken, Rendel completed the marking of the open book, closing it and placing it on the smaller pile and taking the top book from the larger pile. Oaken made the introductions without reference to rank, having been advised of the title "Acting DCI" but being unsure what the "Acting" meant. 'Graham, this is Mr Priestley and Mr Beresford. They're detectives who wish to talk to you about your joint lesson with Anthony this afternoon.'

After the usual pleasantries, Oaken departed and Priestley restarted the conversation. 'Actually, first of all I'd like to offer you an apology on behalf of the police force. As you're a witness and not a suspect, you were interviewed in an inappropriate way.'

Rendel had been interviewed at a time when all the team were suspects, but Priestley chose to overlook this, instead making it plain that Rendel had been cleared of any involvement in Newhouse's death. The look of relief on Rendel's face as he gave the stock response suggested this approach may have worked. 'I'm sure they were just doing their job.'

Priestley took this as an invitation to confirm good relations. 'Well, it's very generous of you to take it that way. I'm the Senior Investigating Officer, Acting Detective Chief Inspector Priestley – call me Marcus, if you will. My trusty side-kick is Tony, a Detective Constable.' The conjunction of the offer of use of his first name and the delivery of his lengthy title was intended to suggest friendliness and power, an attractive and often irresistible combination; the jokey reference to side-kick was to suggest bonhomie while emphasising relative rank. 'Miss Oaken told me you have a special lesson planned for some of the Year Thirteens after lunch. It sounds very interesting. I was wondering if we might come to the session, to offer ourselves for answering questions anyone may have about the police, perhaps?'

'It's a joint session with Mr Ashbourne; it would be best if we discussed it together.' Rendel turned in his seat and waved to someone at the far side of the room who stood up and began to walk toward them. Priestley saw a tanned, slightly overweight, fifty-something man, dressed in an expensive-looking suit, with white shirt and bright, multi-coloured tie. 'Anthony, meet Marcus and Tony. Marcus is the senior police officer in charge of the investigation. He's interested in joining our cross-curricular session this afternoon.'

Priestley proffered his hand which Ashbourne took with an usual grip, the thumb exerting pressure on his second knuckle. Priestley recognised the sign. 'I'm not a mason, Mr Ashbourne.'

'Call me Anthony. I thought all senior police officers were masons?'

Priestley felt he needed to express an opinion on this subject, even if it offended Ashbourne. 'Not all, Anthony; just far too many.'

'That's a relief. I'll come clean, guv'nor: I'm not either, now. That was in my earlier life.'

'Earlier life?'

'I used to be a banker. Reached a point where I had more money than I'd ever spend. Didn't want simply to retire and fade away. Bankers were getting a lot of bad press at the time. Thought I'd put something back into society. Teach children about maths. Teach them about life as well. Your average teacher knows nothing about the real world – no offence Graham. That's why I suggested life lessons; not the PSHE stuff – I'm talking about business life and practical stuff like office politics. Senior management here didn't know whether to be pleased or shocked with my proposals. We settled for a watered down version; a joint enterprise with the English department. Graham and I have come up with some interesting facts to kick it off, and then it's over to the boys to ask questions. Did he say it's an all-boys affair? There's meant to be an equivalent session for girls, given by women teachers, but suitably worldly-wise ones are a rarity. Having said that, I did meet one worldly woman on my course at Sheffield Hallam – she stole an idea of mine. She spoke non-stop, telling the tutor how she'd seen a solution to a problem and she did this and she did that and not letting anyone get a word in edge-ways to expose her lie. Blatant theft of intellectual property; she'd have been ideal for Merchant Banking.'

'So you studied maths at Sheffield Hallam?'

'No, I read maths at Oxford a lifetime ago – Hallam was for the teacher training. I'd spent a year familiarising myself with school maths as it's now taught, before applying to Sheffield Uni. To say I was unimpressed with their maths teacher training department is something of an understatement – they had no idea how much I knew about the subject and they didn't take the trouble to find out. They invited me to do a year's study with them to learn the maths that I knew like the back of my hand. When I tried to put them in the picture, they wouldn't talk to me or answer my e-mails; I felt quite offended at the time. With hindsight I'd say I was still thinking with the status attitude of my old life; I should have realised that to them I was just another would-be student rather than a fully prepared expert – perhaps they're too institutionalised to believe in the power of home study.

'Anyway, I declined their offer and applied to Sheffield Hallam. I was initially much more impressed with them, though I did eventually discover some weaknesses – particularly male lecturers that hadn't grown up and probably never would. Actually, the biggest weakness I found is something I suspect applies to all colleges: the meek acceptance of the views expressed by what are officially leading academics. I was castigated for one of my dissertations where I followed through a logical argument to establish that a supposedly leading maths educationalist favoured neglect of the brightest to make them underperform while pouring additional effort into the weakest to enable them to overachieve, thereby increasing the homogeneity of the standard achieved by the set of all students. I suspect the author imagined it would reduce divisions in society – there was no doubt some crypto-communist principle underlying it all, or at least ultra-socialist.

'Did you know, something like three out of every five teachers vote Labour? Of the rest, there are not many Conservative voters – about the same number as Lib Dems and Greens combined. Anyway, I managed to suppress my "Conservative with a big C" views just long enough to get through the course, and now I'm simply another teacher like all the others – if you don't count the Bentley and the country house.'

Priestley was too intrigued not to risk poking the bear with a stick. 'So, as an ex-banker with no financial need to work, do you see yourself as paying off some debt to society, or is it your own conscience that you're trying to assuage?'

'I was very fair in my financial dealings compared to many, but my conscience demands more of me. What's your conscience demanding of you?'

This hit home with such force that Priestley felt himself wince; he wondered whether this had been just a shot in the dark, or if Ashbourne had read something into his question that had given him an insight into his own troubled conscience. He quickly put aside the flashback of his final action in the army before his honourable discharge, rushed through by the military who hoped the incident would never see light of media day. He realised his quick shake of the shoulders was to cast off those old thoughts, like a dog that had just come out of a stream and treats everyone to a shower, though he hoped his own shake had been less noticeable. He realised his eye contact with Ashbourne had now lasted too long to deny there was something hidden, so he escaped with an unspecific acknowledgement and a change of subject. 'I'm sure we all have something in our pasts that our consciences could take exception to. But may we talk about this afternoon's joint session? Will you give me a list of all the boys, and get them to introduce themselves, so that I can put names to faces?'

Ashbourne smiled. 'Mr Rendel and I will be happy to give you the low-down.'

Priestley and Berry arrived early for the afternoon session and found various scrums of boys and girls outside the locked doors, with a boys-only scrum outside their own intended classroom. Priestley indicated to Berry they should look busy with their lists rather than engaging any of the students in conversation. 'The last thing we want is someone reporting a couple of perverts chatting up boys.'

SEND OFF SIR

Rendel arrived with a large bunch of keys and let everyone in; he wrote "Misconceptions" on the whiteboard in a fair imitation of Copperplate. The detectives were invited to sit at the back; they had lists of all the boys who would be present, and had each used their own discreet codes for noting the names of the three in whom they had a particular interest. They were asked to introduce themselves, which they did as "Mr Priestley" and "Mr Beresford". For their benefit, as agreed with the teachers, the boys stood up in turn and gave their names. Priestley noted that Dave Williamson, Simon Green and Zach Peck were all seated together near the front, which he interpreted as indicating they were friends, and may explain why they had chosen to stay close to each other for ball retrieval duty. He wondered if they had already concocted a story – if they had anything to hide.

Rendel explained to the students that they would start the session with some common misconceptions before moving onto other matters. By agreement, and to bring him fully into the session, Priestley walked to the front as Rendel invited him to 'kick off with the first question.'

Priestley did his best to make his Spanish sound authentic. 'When I was on holiday in Tenerife with my wife, we noticed the title of a television programme on channel *Cuatro*: "*Mi madre cocina mejor que la tuya*". She had a go at translating this, and came up with: "My mother cooks better than yours". What is wrong with that statement?'

Various boys suggested possible flaws.

'My mother is a really good cook so yours probably doesn't cook better.'

'We can't know if it's true unless we know how well they both cook.'

'It's a matter of opinion about whether something is cooked well. We like crunchy vegetables but my granddad likes soft, mushy ones so his have to be cooked for longer.'

'The translation isn't accurate, maybe. But I don't know what it means.'

Rendel asked them to consider it another way. 'How does the meaning differ from: "My mother is a better cook than yours"?'

Simon offered, 'The translation is about cooking the mothers.'

Rendel nodded vigorously. 'Well done. The program title

should perhaps be translated "My mother is a better cook than your mother".'

Rendel continued. 'A quick question: what's wrong with this? Leeds United won two games in a row.'

Zach, not himself the sporting type, saw an opportunity to gain credibility with those who were. He jumped in straight away with, 'They lost at the weekend so they can't have won two in a row.'

Several boys offered derogatory opinions of Leeds United, so Rendel stopped the flow and turned to Ashbourne, who began, 'Is it possible to have two points on a map that are not in a row?'

After general agreement that it was impossible, Ashbourne asked, 'So, how many dots – or anything else for that matter – would you need to justify using the term "in a row"?'

Dave called out a definitive "Three".

Rendel responded, "Correct. So, use three in a row but two in succession.'

Ashbourne asked, 'Why did the chicken cross the Möbius strip?' ... 'Quickly.' ... 'Too late. To get to the same side.' There followed a variety of groans and some tutting.

He then started a longer conundrum, writing "24/7" on the whiteboard.

'I'm sure we've all seen advertisements that refer to "24/7". Would anyone like to explain what is meant by that term?'

Zach offered, 'It means they're open all the time.'

No one had any alternative answer, so Ashbourne led them through a number of steps.

'What does the twenty-four indicate?'

They agreed it was twenty-four hours a day; he wrote "24 hours per day" on the board.

'What does the seven indicate?'

They agreed "seven days per week".

Ashbourne then converted the "24/7" by including the units.

(24 hours per day) / (7 days per week)

(24 hours / days) / (7 days / weeks)

Numerator: 24 hours weeks

Denominator: 7 days days

Result: 24/7 means three and three-sevenths hours weeks per day squared.

Zach objected, 'That can't be right.'

Ashbourne invited them all to work through "24x7".

Simon gave his answer: '24 x 7 hours per week.'

Dave suggested, '168 hours per week.'

Ashbourne asked, 'Which do we think is mathematically correct, twenty-four divided by seven or twenty-four multiplied by seven?'

Though all the boys voted for the latter, Zach looked as though he remained unconvinced.

Rendel invited the boys to consider a number of words commonly misused in English, with Ashbourne then explaining their mathematical significance. "Decimate" was equated to one-tenth, "possible" as less than fifty per cent likelihood, "probable" as greater than fifty per cent, and "more probable" shown to be variable depending on other possible outcomes. As "almost never" and "nearly always" were being considered in various contexts, Priestley found his attention waning; he glanced across at Berry, who appeared fully engaged if not riveted by the subject.

After various other English-to-maths quantifications had been explored, Priestley was relieved to hear Ashbourne announce the final item for scrutiny: the expression "fifty-fifty". Ashbourne divided it into two usages: one where there were two outcomes of genuinely equal probability, and the other where someone was pretending to express an opinion but was really avoiding doing so. Priestley decided he would in future avoid using the term "fifty-fifty" within Berry's hearing, for fear of falling foul of the Ashbourne-Rendel analysis.

During the twenty-four times seven conundrum, Rendel had connected up a laptop computer and "taken the register", a process required at the start of every lesson; by recording the presence of every student scheduled to be in each class, any truants could be identified quickly. He now used the computer to direct the overhead projector to display a statement onto the whiteboard; the paragraph was intended to be sufficiently convoluted to force the boys to concentrate. He read from the board, 'You may come across books from widely-read or widely-respected authors, and sometimes both, and other publications, where the writer steadfastly refuses to place a comma before an "and", and so fails to provide a clear meaning. This may be a result of their blindly following the UK-English convention of breaking a simple list with commas with the exception of the join between the last two items in the list, as opposed to US-English that includes a comma before the last item. That rule applies to simple lists; it should not apply to longer statements, where a comma should generally precede the "and". The other side of the coin is that some authors imbue their work with a plethora, comma, or surfeit, comma, of punctuation, comma, that interferes with the flow of the words, full stop.'

Rendel began a debate on the relative merits of different styles of punctuation by giving examples from various authors. Out of the three boys of interest to the detectives, only Zach contributed to the discussion. 'People don't use punctuation now though, or not as much as they used to.' He paused before continuing, 'And text messages don't even need to have whole words.'

Rendel responded. 'Thank you, Zach. If it was your intention to highlight a similar construct – that of a full stop followed by an "and" – then you did it brilliantly.'

Zach glowed with pride, having little idea what he had just done to earn such praise.

Rendel continued. 'However, there is always a danger of misinterpretation when words are not spelled completely and exactly. Imagine the difference between being invited for a scuffle or a soufflé, for gauging or gouging.'

Zach replaced his look of self-satisfaction with one of bewilderment.

Rendel invited Ashbourne to join him in considering whether the singular or the plural form of verbs should be used with the word "none". Ashbourne began, 'Computers are now so essential to our lives that we would all struggle to live normally without them. At the most fundamental level they operate by recognising the difference between off and on, which we can interpret as yes and no, or one and zero. For a computer program, it's the fundamental building block that makes their DNA.'

Rendel took his cue. 'As humans developed language, the importance of the "singular" concept was recognised. For example, the verb "to be" has a specific conjugation for each personal pronoun: I am; you are; he is; she is; it is; one is. Imagine using "am" with anything other than "I": you am; he am; it am; they am.

So it has long been recognised that the singular form is special; we could say sacrosanct. Now, does anyone think that "none" is singular?'

Simon showed he had been paying attention. 'Do you mean "none is singular" or "none are singular", sir?'

'Excellent question – so what's the answer?'

'Only "one" is singular, so "none" isn't.'

'Quite right; you've earned a bonus question. "One in five apples in the orchard is red." Or, "One in five apples in the orchard are red." Which is it?'

'Well, "one" is singular, so it ought to be "is"; but I think there's more to it than that, so I'm going to go for "are" instead.'

'Mr Ashbourne, would you like to explain?'

'Certainly.' Ashbourne turned and addressed the entire class. 'If we assume the reference to an orchard indicates the total number of apples is not just five, but a much higher number, then "one in five" is a ratio where the "one" relates to a much higher number than one, and the "five" represents a number that is five times higher. For example, there are one thousand red apples out of a total of five thousand apples. So, the "one" represents an unspecified number that is clearly greater than one, and so it is not singular. Hence the correct form is, "One in five apples in the orchard are red." However, don't expect your word processing package to support this construct – it's too subtle for the average designer.'

Priestley made a mental note of how Simon had avoided falling into the traps laid in the questions – something to be aware of when interviewing him. He considered his initial impressions of the three boys: if they are responsible for the death of John Newhouse, and if there is a conspiracy to cover it up, then Simon Green would be the ring-leader, Zach Peck would be the one most likely to fail to keep it hidden, and Dave Williamson could be the one least capable of telling a direct lie. As he was mulling this over, Rendel called out to him, 'Are there any misconceptions about the police you would like to offer, Mr Priestley?'

This had not been scripted; he wondered if Rendel was setting him up to fail, as a way of getting his own back on the police. After a moment's hesitation, he was relieved to find something suitable sprang to mind. 'Yes, I would like to mention the misconception that the police are truthful. In fact, they lie all the time.' Dave and Simon were among the earliest to laugh, whilst Zach maintained a confused look.

Next, Ashbourne introduced a topic that was directly relevant to many of the boys. 'Now I'm going to talk to you about student loans and the government scheme. You may think you've heard it all before, but I doubt whether you'll have heard what I'm about to say. You may know I'm an ex-banker, and there was a time when the word of a banker was accepted by everyone as the honest truth.'

Rendel *ad libbed*, to a murmur of obligatory groans of appreciation, 'You could bank on it.'

'Nowadays too many bankers have let everyone down by being dishonest or deceitful. But ask yourself this: do you think politicians are any more reliable? Those of you with an interest in business or politics may remember the lies politicians told about the Royal Mail privatisation, arguing against the findings of the National Audit Office and the Business Select Committee who concluded the taxpayer had lost roughly a billion pounds by pitching the price too low. A Lib Dem politician talked of "froth" – a temporarily high share price – but the price should be what you can get at the time, based on full disclosure of all relevant factors. Did they not disclose all the factors? If so, that's something else that should be investigated, but I don't expect it will be. And who gained from the low issue price? Big businesses were given a sweetheart deal whereas private investors had their allocations scaled back by a factor of twenty-odd times. The claim that the sixteen sweethearts would be long-term investors proved to be a massive lie; twelve sold out and the other four scaled right back, such that their combined holding reduced from twenty-two to twelve per cent in double-quick time.

'So, if you believe a politician told a barefaced lie about the Royal Mail privatisation, you might like to consider whether politicians are capable of putting out a massive lie about student loans. Ask them how much a student loan will cost you and all you'll get back is, "you won't have to pay anything back until blah, blah, blah." Well, let's take a reality check. I'm going to put a lot of information your way in a short time, but don't try to take notes – this is more about giving you a flavour of the subject in the manner of a *tour de force* .' He noticed Zach putting his hands out and moving his head from side to side as though riding a bicycle. 'No Zach, it's nothing to do with that famous French cycling competition we were all delighted to witness passing nearby last summer. I'm going to be talking about inflation – and not the type relating to bicycle tyres.

'The way inflation works on the economy, prices and wages go up with time, and the pound in your pocket won't be worth as much in the future as it is now. Inflation at a low positive rate is seen as beneficial for the economy as a whole. The opposite, deflation, is seen as a major problem for a country as it sucks the life out of an economy by suppressing demand; Japan is a recent example. High inflation is often the sign of an economy on its knees. The historians amongst you will know about the German Weimar Republic, and may have seen a picture from 1923 of someone pushing a wheelbarrow full of paper money, all of which was worth less than the price of a newspaper. Their economy was in freefall from hyperinflation – that's extreme inflation. A less extreme example comes from the recent World Cup hosts, Brazil; in the first half of the nineteen nineties their inflation rate reached into the thousands of percentage points. We in the UK haven't suffered such high levels, but what we have seen here and across the western world when nations' economies have been faltering, is that governments have been happy to use inflation to make us poorer, letting prices rise rapidly while pay scales fail to keep pace. Now, how does this relate to student loans, I hear you ask?'

He cupped a hand to his ear and looked directly at a boy near the front until he dutifully responded, with exaggerated politeness. 'How does this relate to student loans, sir?'

Ashbourne continued his performance, employing a parliamentary-style response. 'I am glad my right honourable friend asked me that question.'

He turned to the others and in a stage-whisper added, 'Otherwise I wouldn't have had any justification for continuing.'

Returning to his normal voice he picked up the threads of his argument. 'You can expect inflation to make your wages higher in the future, so a salary of twenty thousand pounds now would equate to thirty thousand pounds in, maybe, somewhere between ten and twenty years. The threshold that triggers when you have to pay back the student loan is something that the current and future governments can set as they think fit. There's a principle of

English Law that no future parliament can be constrained by the actions of any previous parliament. This means there can be no guarantee of what will happen to that threshold in the future. It's entirely feasible that even workers on the minimum wage will be paid more than the threshold for paying back student loans, providing they're working full-time. So, if you take out a student loan, you have to think that at some point you will have to pay it back.

'From another perspective, when you hear a politician saying "blah, blah, threshold", you should also be asking yourself, "What's the point of going to university if I'm going to end up with a job that pays next to nothing?" Now, I'm not saying there aren't good reasons for going to university that have no connection with future earnings, but let's be realistic: what value does your degree have to you personally if you come out of university unable to get a job that pays more than a pittance? The number of students out of a thousand who would be happy with that outcome could be counted on your fingers; well, maybe fingers and toes.

'If we assume that your degree was worth all the effort you put into it, not to forget the three or more years of your life, and you now have work that pays more than the repayment threshold, then you can see the student loan system operating just like a traditional bank loan. At least it's meant to, but whereas with a bank you can order a statement and receive one a few days later, with student loans you can ask every month for a year and they still only send one when they think fit; and finding your actual balance can be impossible because of the timing of interest calculations and payments via the tax system – I'll come onto that later. If a commercial bank put together a system like the student loans setup, it would be deemed unfit for purpose – they'd have to scrap it and start again.

'But the main point is this: you pay back your student loan with interest. So – and this is the key question you should then be considering – is the loan worth the interest rate that you're being charged? If you had no alternative source of funds then you will have had to take out a student loan, in which case you should consider paying it off when the rate you are being charged on it is more than the rate of return you are earning on your own capital.

'Let's get practical on this. If you have money in a building society that's paying you just two per cent, taxable, and if you're paying five per cent on the student loan, non-tax-deductible, then the difference of three per cent plus tax per annum is something that you can avoid. On the other hand, if you know you'll need all your savings before long, maybe to put down a deposit on a house, then you need to hold onto it. But if you don't need to sit on your pot of gold, you have to consider what rate you would have to pay to borrow money in the future, and that may or may not be higher than the student loan rate. If you're confident you won't have such a need, then you should just reduce your debt.

'Here's another consideration. If you have parents with money in savings that are paying a low rate of interest, and you know they intend to bung it your way in the future, then get them to give you the lolly straight away. It's the same argument as before, though from a family-wide perspective – why receive two per cent while paying five per cent.

'Another thing that politicians have been speculating about is the number of students who won't pay back their loans. There are those who won't make any repayments; this may have less to do with students not reaching the earnings threshold and more to do with them disappearing off the grid, perhaps going to live in countries where they can happily ignore their agreement to pay back their loans, knowing that the British government can't reach them there. Current official estimates are that only one-in-three students will pay back their loans in full, though I doubt that figure will prove to be accurate. However, the key argument in favour of the loan being written-off rather than repaid is not that the earnings threshold will fail to trigger repayments, but rather that the substantial amounts of interest charged will prove so large that former students will end up paying massive sums of money just to cover the interest payments and so will never reduce the outstanding capital to zero.

'One concern is that if the student loans system is to be largely self-financing, then those with loans will have to pay more to make up for those who aren't paying enough, or anything. There are two aspects to consider: one, if you're staying in this country and expect to get a decent job, then you may find yourself paying an awful lot of interest to make up for those who aren't paying any; and two, if you're not staying in this country, can you get away with it, both practically and morally? This last question is worth a whole session in itself.

'Finally, you may be wondering why the government is so keen to maintain the lie. That's a socio-economic question worth at least a whole term, and you can be sure the expression "social engineering" would feature prominently. The government doesn't wish to see those in society who are capable of a high level of academic achievement missing out on a university education solely because they lack sufficient funds. That's an excellent reason, but doesn't justify the way politicians of all shades lie to us about the expected cost. Why do they not trust us to know the truth?

'And finally, finally, in adult life you'll come across a branch of the civil service known as Her Majesty's Revenue and Customs – HMRC, aka the Tax Man. For individuals, the tax year, or fiscal year, runs from the sixth of April of one year to the fifth of April of the next. Most of the time, tax is taken straight away during the fiscal year by an employer, bank or building society, but after the end of the fiscal year you may have to submit details to the tax man for a final reckoning, for example if you're self-employed. If so, you can complete a tax return online and it all looks very efficient and immediate – you may get a rebate straight away, or you may be given a bill for more tax with time to pay.

'But that efficiency doesn't carry forward into the student loans' system. Let's say you were due a tax rebate of a thousand pounds and you were also due to pay off a thousand pounds of your student loan. Whereas the tax man would give you the rebate straight away, the student loans system doesn't give you the credit for it until the next calendar year, and it may not even start to show on your student loan until the following fiscal year. The same applies if you were due to pay a thousand pounds in tax: you could pay it straight away, let's say at the end of April, but it won't be shown as a reduction on your loan until the following April, perhaps backdated to the end of January. So for nine months you'd be paying interest on the thousand pounds on your student loan that you'd already settled with the tax man.'

Ashbourne put on a pretend-angry face and shook his fist in the air in an actor's performance of annoyance at the student loans' system, raising smiles around the room. 'That has been a whistle-stop tour and I've no doubt it's too much to take in at this pace; the point is, there's complexity and there's lies out there, and there's very few people apart from yours truly who're prepared to bring the facts to light. So I'll arrange a fuller explanation if anyone would like to hear it, and the invitation extends to your parents as well. Let me know if you – or they – are interested, and I'll see about giving an extended version of "Students Loans – The Big Lie".

'And a final word of warning: just because it's a government scheme that the Student Loans Company is administering, don't expect them to be transparently honest. In 2010 the Payday Lender Wonga stopped sending out misleading letters that pretended to be from a separate legal firm, but they still had to pay out two point six million pounds in compensation. Bank of Scotland pulled a similar stunt when they made up Blaire, Oliver, Scott; notice the matching initials, BOS. Student Loans did the same with their invention of Smith, Lawson & Company, and they didn't stop sending out letters until mid-2014. So, remember you're not dealing with the most moral of organisations; be alert … we don't want a shortage of "lerts".'

A few of the boys groaned; others looked too overwhelmed by the presentation to recognise the intended humour.

Priestley used the call-back mechanism on his phone to cause it to ring. He spoke as he walked quickly to the door, indicating to Berry to follow him. 'I'm so sorry – I have to take an urgent call. Perhaps I could come back another time if there's something you think your students would like to know about how the police operate. Thank you, Mr Ashbourne, and Mr Rendel, for inviting us here to your fascinating session.'

They left the room and stepped outside. Berry was puzzled when he saw Priestley close his phone and put it back into his pocket; he asked, 'The urgent call – who was it from?'

Priestley gave a single laugh. 'Ha. There wasn't one – didn't I say earlier that the police lie all the time? I just wanted to exit the lesson politely; I'd heard enough from the three boys. I was going to leave earlier, but that explanation about student loans was really very interesting. My own children are a dozen years away from university age, so it could all be different by then, but it's worth knowing how the system really works. Was it any use to you?'

'It'll give me something to think about in the future, but for now it's entirely academic – I needed a student loan and I can't afford to pay off any more than the minimum.'

CHAPTER 25

Priestley Gives a Press Conference

Priestley checked with Martello on progress with the house-to-house enquiries. After first mentioning Witty had joined her and Plummer following his appointment with the solicitor, she went on to describe their findings. The pattern of activity on the previous Wednesday appeared to have been the same as any normal school day. Cars, mostly with women drivers, had been parked in the vicinity of the school gates from around three o'clock onwards. Most of the drivers had stayed in their cars, though a few women had stepped out to talk to each other. Children had emerged from school and then been driven away. Buses had departed with children who had boarded while still on school premises. Nothing suspicious had been noticed.

Priestley asked Martello to pass her phone to Witty, and then inquired about the meeting with the solicitor. Witty explained there was a lot to relate and it was too good just to say over the phone, so he would like to give him a full account later. Priestley returned to the investigation, asking if any pedestrians had been noticed, suspicious or otherwise. Witty replied in the negative, suggesting that walking children home from a senior school was something no child would appreciate if they cared anything for their reputation. Priestley expressed his interpretation, 'Not cool.'

Witty responded, 'I'm not sure "cool" is a cool word anymore.'

The conversation returned to the house-to-house enquiries. 'Have you many more to do?'

'We're already at a point we could stop – I don't believe we're going to get any more out of this.'

'What about other entrances?'

'There's a side gate but we've already done the houses that would have seen anything there. Just one old lady reckoned a slip of a girl had skipped out of school a few minutes early, otherwise nothing – the drivers all picked up their children near the main gate because cars can't get to the side gate.'

'What about the back entrance?'

'I didn't know there was a back entrance.' Witty realised this was not a good response, so he added a delayed 'sir.' Then he continued 'I thought I'd better give you an occasional "sir" now you're an Acting DCI.'

Priestley remained business-like. 'Much appreciated, I'm sure. There's an entrance in the fence at the back of the sports field. I remember there was a public spat between the school and the council about the fence. Send Plummer back to the station, and you and Martello find a way to the rear entrance by road. I'll walk with Berry from the school side and we'll meet up there.'

Priestley and Berry were first to arrive at the rear entrance; they found a small gate fitted within a solidly-constructed high fence and securely locked with a good-quality mechanism that required a key inserting from the school side. They discussed which houses might be able to see the entrance; they agreed that the curve of the path meant very few could see the actual gate, but perhaps a dozen could see the path close by. They saw Witty and Martello emerge on foot and begin walking along the path toward the gate. Priestley and Berry walked toward them, meeting half-way. Talking through the fence, they agreed which houses should be checked for any activity between two thirty and four o'clock last Wednesday. Priestley sent Berry to collect his car and drive around to meet up with Witty and Martello and assist them with interviewing the occupants.

Priestley made a phone call as he headed for his own car.

'Rowland Ryland.'

'Priestley. Will you be attending this afternoon's press conference?'

'Is the Pope Catholic?'

'Are you running anything in your early editions?'

'Just a small article on an inside page, "police enquiries are continuing", nothing much.'

'You'd better be wearing a groin guard, Rowland; I'm going to be gunning for you.'

'Shouldn't that be "bullet-proof vest" instead of a boxing guard if you're gunning?'

'Very smart, but I'm serious about this. I'm going to have to have a go at you for revealing Cassidy's same-sex marriage when he wanted it kept secret. His suicide note blamed you, in effect.'

'Christ, Marcus.'

'But I'm offering you an escape tunnel. Do you wish to take it? You're going to owe me big-time if you do.'

'Go ahead.'

'After I've had a go at you, you're going to come back with something like: "this simple revelation could not have been the real cause. My unofficial sources told me he was the police's prime suspect in the death of Mr John Newhouse; that is more likely to have been the cause." Then I'm going to be at your throat with, "you should know better than to listen to unofficial sources. I'm Acting DCI on these two investigations and the only sources you should listen to are those authorised by me. And I can tell you categorically that Mr Hugh Cassidy was in no way responsible for the death of Mr John Newhouse; he was entirely innocent." You need to be suitably silenced for a moment by that revelation. Am I correct in thinking one of your unofficial informants was DCI Castleton?'

'You know I can't reveal my sources.'

'Bollocks. I'm not telling you the rest of your escape route unless you're straight with me.'

Ryland thought for just a moment before revealing, 'It was Bryn Castleton.'

'Any others?'

'Elias Dunn. There weren't any others.'

'That's what I expected. You need to come back with "Where is DCI Castleton? I understood he was leading the case." And at that point I say, "DCI Castleton resigned from the force earlier today." After that we can go through the motions of asking why he resigned, which I'll refuse to answer. Now, have you got all that? I'm saving your hide here.'

'Why are you doing this for me?'

'Because I don't believe the suicide would have happened if it hadn't been for Castleton accusing him of being responsible for Newhouse's death. So I'd rather your paper prints something that equates to the truth despite there being evidence that points the other way. Plus I want Bryn Castleton dead and buried in the papers before he tries to claim his resignation was under duress; I want him to have no way back. And one final thing: this will only work if you don't let any earlier version of your paper let it slip that you know what's coming. So make damn sure, even if you do prepare your article in advance, that you don't let anyone even smell the story before we've had our row at the press conference.'

'You have my word, and I don't mean my word as a reporter because we all know that counts for nothing. I mean you really do have my promise on this. And I'll put on a good performance, Marcus.'

'OK. Don't panic if I climb over the table to get at you. I'll release my grip on your throat within a minute; that's a promise.'

'Would you like it if I suggested a bad egg has been replaced by one of the best?'

'I hope that isn't a bribe, Rowland, but I shall look forward to reading it.'

Priestley was surprised to find Yelland would be at the press conference. The Superintendent explained, 'The Chief Super said I should let you run the show, but if it turns nasty I should give you all the support you need.'

The last thing Priestley wanted was for Yelland to intervene when things got nasty – as he was sure they would. He asked, 'Would it be alright if you gave me my head on this one, sir? I'd like to prove myself. I'll make a specific request for you to intervene if I feel it's necessary.'

'Trying to make that "Acting" into "Permanent" are you, Marcus? Well, good for you. I'll just sit back and let you get on with it.'

Priestley thought, 'DCI isn't the only thing I'm "Acting" today.'

The press conference largely followed the script. Ryland put on a performance he could be proud of, even managing to put a snarl into his voice at one point. Priestley thought it was a little OTT, but could not fault it for effort. He in turn played it calmly at first, building up to a crescendo of damnation against the irresponsibility of the press and the need to report accurately from now on. After the fireworks were over, Ryland scuttled out of the room at top walking speed, even breaking into a jog for a few steps. Yelland walked out with Priestley. 'Well done, Marcus. Did you see Ryland shooting out at the end – I think he imagined you might be coming after him. It's good to show you've got the balls for it, but I do think you may need to be a bit gentler with the press in the future. Ryland might try to get back at you.'

Priestley tried to look concerned, while feeling justifiably confident that the Shawton News would make the evening deadline and that he would come up smelling of roses. The herd instinct of the nationals meant they would be very likely to follow the line taken by the local press, at least until they decided they had waited long enough for a result.

Witty, Martello and Berry began the new set of house-to-house enquiries. There was no one home at several of the properties, and those who were home had seen nothing of interest. They looked for signs of people arriving by car and ticked off all but three of the initial absentees by four o'clock. Berry suggested, 'There's no point in all of us waiting. I'll stay, if you two want to get off.'

Witty wondered if Berry had made a joke, but the look on his face suggested otherwise.

'We'll stay for now. You can head back to the station.'

'It only needs one of us, really. If you wish to stay, Lily and I could head back.'

Witty thought Berry may be the only person still not in the know about them being a couple. 'Maybe we should all stay until half past, and then we'll call it a day.'

At twenty past four a dark green Volvo estate turned into the road and onto a driveway. They walked over to the man who was getting out of the car. Witty introduced all three officers to him before explaining, 'We're investigating a death at the school just over the way.' He indicated Midshaw School with a swing of the arm and a pointing finger. 'We're interested in any activity you may have observed last Wednesday afternoon, especially anything between two o'clock and five o'clock.'

He had expanded the range out of boredom, in the hope of avoiding another negative response. The man, who appeared to be in his early sixties, tall and slim, dressed in outdoor gear and wearing a genial expression, felt the need to introduce himself. 'I'm Steve Nugent. I may be able to help you.' Witty felt euphoric at this positive reply. 'I was sitting in my back garden, looking over there with my binoculars at the small copse.'

Witty released the earlier frustration of an unrewarding working day with a touch of humour. 'Diminutive policemen, sir?'

Nugent smiled appreciatively. Berry interjected, 'I don't think that's what Mr Nugent meant.'

Martello flashed a smile at Nugent as she took Berry's arm and led him away a few steps, saying quietly, 'It was a joke, Tony.' She was pleased to realise she had been the one to recognise a joke and tell a colleague – she was usually the one needing the explanation.

Witty and Nugent continued their conversation. 'If I'm at home I often look over yonder. I've noticed there's regular activity on Wednesday afternoons – lots of children go running along the path.'

Berry decided to re-establish his stake in the witness. 'Do you often look at schoolchildren through your binoculars, Mr Nugent?'

Nugent smiled at Berry as an indulgent grandfather might to a misbehaving child. 'You're heading in the wrong direction, DC Beresford. I took early retirement when I came into some money, exchanged my flat in town for a house in the country, and now I'm a twitcher.'

Deciding to avoid any further misinterpretations, he quickly continued, 'I've graduated from being just a birdwatcher – a simple watcher of birds. I like to spend some of my spare time in the pursuit of rare birds – I'm just back from one such excursion. Maybe in future I shall devote even more time to the subject and travel further afield; then I might qualify for the term "birder". The birds around here are not especially rare, but I like to keep my eye in – practise looking through the binoculars to see how quickly I can spot the birds. The children run close to the area that I focus on – over in the trees.'

Witty decided to bring the conversation back on course. 'So, could you tell us everything you saw last Wednesday afternoon. Not so much the birds as the people.'

'There were more than a dozen children who came out of the school through the gate at roughly one thirty and set off running along the path. Actually, I can't quite see the gate from here, but I know it's there. It's the same routine every Wednesday afternoon. I wait until they've gone before getting out my binocs, as birds tend not to settle close to the edge of the woods when there are children running about. Most of the children returned together at around three o'clock. You might be thinking that an hour and a half is a long time to be running, but in fact many of them soon stop running and just turn the afternoon into a pleasant walk. There were two boys and a girl who kept running when the others started walking; the boys returned virtually together at about three-fifteen, trying to out-sprint each other at the end, and the girl came in on her own maybe five minutes later.

'At about a quarter to four a couple with a dog walked along the same path, and they returned sometime after four. Now, as well as looking for birds, I was also reading a book, and I kept popping back indoors for a drink and a warm – it was quite a cold afternoon. That means I may have missed someone, but as the route's visible for a good half-mile, I think I'm unlikely to have failed to spot anyone who stayed on the path.

'As to anyone who was not on the path when I was looking in the direction of,' he replayed both the humorous reference and the accompanying smile, 'the small copse, I would only have been able to see them if they were on the near side of that clump of trees. What I wouldn't have been able to see was anyone who was walking in the hollow-way that runs down to one side, or anyone hiding further into the coppice.'

Martello noted down the details as Witty thanked him for his help.

After Nugent had gone indoors, the three officers stood together in a tight triangle, in the area of the drive illuminated by the motion-activated outdoor light. Witty opened, 'If all that was accurate, we know what activity there was at this side of the school last Wednesday.'

Berry suggested possible weaknesses in the testimony. 'What if his timings are wrong? What if he missed somebody? What if he made the whole thing up? What if somebody stayed hidden in the wood and got into the school when he wasn't looking? What if someone crept along the edge where he couldn't see them? It isn't possible to see the gate from here, or the fence up by where the gate is, so how can he be sure people didn't come and go through the gate without him ever seeing them? What if he's the perpetrator and has made up a cover story to give himself an alibi?'

Witty responded, 'All valid considerations, Tony, but we've done enough for today. We'll report everything to Marcus in the morning and let him decide what we do next.'

Priestley grabbed a bite to eat at the canteen before stepping out to pick up a Shawton News Late Final at twenty to seven. The headline article contained all the details he had hoped to see, and a little more besides. Ryland had evidently door-stepped Castleton at his home. When asked if he had resigned due to his activity regarding the deaths of the two teachers, he had denied there was any connection whatsoever. Ryland therefore felt justified in speculating that Castleton had other activities to account for, and the article demanded to know just what he was hiding. As he turned the pages waiting for the appointed hour, he checked the obituaries and found a tribute to John Newhouse whose funeral was due to take place tomorrow afternoon. He wondered who at the school had written the piece, replete with its coded references.

John was much-loved at Midshaw School by colleagues and students alike, willingly devoting much of his own time to the more athletic students, both male and female. He was good company to many, an uncompromisingly direct ladies' man who would regale friends with colourful accounts of his exploits. He will be sorely missed by all.

Dunn arrived early for his anticipated dressing-down. Priestley took him into a vacant office and allowed him to sit. Holding his copy of the Shawton News in both hands so that Dunn could see the front page, he began, 'Have you read this story?'

Dunn looked suitably downcast as he admitted he had.

'I've listened to the interview you and Castleton had with Hugh Cassidy last Friday. You've seen the suicide note, so you may think it was the revelation of his same-sex marriage that drove him over the edge, but I say it was your accusation and that interview that took him right up to the brink. You had no basis for threatening the man in that way.'

'Sir, DCI Castleton was the ranking officer; I was just following his lead. He has nearly thirty years' experience, and he said his gut instinct told him he was guilty, so it wasn't for me to disagree.'

'First of all, let me make a distinction between thirty years' experience, and one year's experience repeated thirty times. There are people who gain experience over time and become better at what they do as a consequence; and there are others who don't develop, but just become more dogmatic in the beliefs they started out with. You'll have heard plenty of officers quoting how long they've been in policing, as though long service and simple repetition has somehow increased their depth of understanding; you can often spot them by the way they talk about gut instinct when the facts don't support what they say. You need to see police investigations as fact-based, so if there aren't any facts to support a point of view then there isn't a basis for proceeding along that line. Any comment?'

'Sir, you have a reputation for going with gut instinct, so how am I supposed to know whose gut is reliable?'

'I don't go with gut instinct; I work entirely off the facts. If I say I'm following my instincts, I'm really talking about extended logic – considering all the possibilities and deciding which is the most probable. I see myself as sifting information and using deductive reasoning to reach logical conclusions, getting from the general to the particular, from the facts to the specific conclusions. Other people may have the same facts available to them but lack the capacity to put the pieces together, and because they can't themselves see the route through from the facts to the conclusions, they assume no one can, which is why they imagine I've made some leap of the imagination – which they then call "gut instinct".

'Learning from past cases involves getting from facts to general principles that can be applied to future cases, and this has a connection with inductive reasoning – the ability that's measured by IQ tests. So, if you have confidence in someone's standard IQ-type intelligence, then you have a basis for being confident in what you might think of as their gut instinct. Having said that, I'm sure I'm not saying anything you don't already know when I tell you DC Beresford has a high IQ but hasn't yet had the experience to apply it in context, so for now his gut instinct isn't something to be relied on – though in time it could be. However, there are several types of intelligence that make up the whole person; it would take too long for me to explain that subject properly to you, though you could investigate it for yourself in your own time. For now I would simply say, don't just count on someone's years on the force, because they count for nothing.'

'I never understood that before, sir.'

'So, it was ex-DCI Castleton's gut instinct that led you in the wrong direction, was it?'

'Yes sir.'

'Then can you explain to me why you were already accusing Cassidy in the first part of the interview before Castleton even appeared on the scene?'

Dunn realised he had been caught lying; he grimaced and frowned as he responded. 'I'm a bit confused, sir.'

'I'd say you're a lot confused. I suspect you went with your own gut instinct and your gut was wrong. In future I'd recommend you only listen to simple messages from your gut, like "I'm hungry".'

Dunn remained silent.

'In the second part of the interview you were still supporting the accusation. It's one thing not to interfere when a DCI is taking the lead, but it's quite another to join in like you did. It may be a cliché about the good cop, bad cop routine, but it often does work; the suspect sees the good cop as the one they can turn to when the bad cop is giving them a hard time, and sometimes that means they'll reveal things to the good cop to try to make them their friend. With two bad cops the suspect has no one to turn to, so they don't reveal anything.

'If you didn't feel you could be the good cop then you should have remained neutral. I appreciate that would always be difficult with Castleton, and doubly difficult because you'd already started out as the bad cop. However, I ask myself, what was it that made you do more than stay silent, and to throw in some real nastiness; my answer is that it's part of your persona. You have a reputation for being moody and sometimes angry or hostile for no apparent reason; you need to change fundamentally.'

Dunn maintained his silence.

'OK, we'll continue. As you say, ex-DCI Castleton was the ranking officer; well, he's paid for his part in the interview with his immediate resignation, which he'll feel in his pocket with his pension pitched at the minimum the scheme allows – because nobody's going to be supporting any enhancement. What I need to consider is the price you should be paying. The obvious one would be your resignation, just like Castleton. Do you wish to resign?'

'No sir.'

'An alternative is to have you dismissed for gross misconduct, but that would mean making the whole thing official, which wouldn't be good for the reputation of the force. So you have a lifeline, which will prove to be your last if there's any further cause for complaint.'

Priestley picked up the buff folder that had been lying directly in front of him on the table.

'I've been looking through some of the previous complaints against you, and I have to say you've done things that are quite staggering. I'll start with an old guy who was a victim of an assault. That's victim, mind you. His assailant came up with a counter-allegation that was obviously bogus, but you decided to take it upon yourself to keep crime figures down by not logging either allegation as assault; you processed the incident through the Restorative Justice route even though it was clear who had committed the criminal offence. I know there's pressure from on high to massage the crime stats, but you can't just ignore the facts and go your own sweet way. When he said he wouldn't sign the form because the wording indicated he was admitting to having done something wrong, you threatened to arrest him. So, let me run through that again: someone is a victim of an assault, but you threatened to arrest him. For what – being a victim?

'However, that's nothing compared to the *Tour de France* fiasco.' Priestley extracted a wad of papers, the top page being a print of a spreadsheet, replete with coloured boxes, orange and red. 'I have here a detailed report from South Yorkshire's Headquarters at Carbrook House. On the sixth of July 2014 there were PCs and WPCs from other forces assisting the Community Officers from South Yorkshire. There were some from West Midlands, some from Humberside, and you representing Derbyshire Constabulary, East Midlands. You were assigned to Sheffield East, area KA. You were standing on Jenkin Hill, opposite Sandstone Road. At three fifteen someone was stabbed in the back at the fairground on Wincobank Common. There were several ambulances already stationed nearby, so one of the crews attended to the injured party. To allow the ambulance off the common at about three thirty, the Show & Event Crowd Safety people unfastened the tape that was between the barriers on *Côte de Wincobank Hill* – where's that?'

'It's what they called Jenkin Road during the cycle race, sir.'

'Right. Well, according to this report, you arrested an oldish bloke for not smiling, thereby making South Yorkshire police a laughing stock, as everyone assumed it was one of their own who'd done it. You took him to Ecclesfield Police Station, thereby causing him to miss seeing the race; he was a bit annoyed about that, but nowhere near as annoyed as he was with you for arresting him. The report states he tried to explain but you just wouldn't listen.'

'But sir, …'

'I haven't finished. It seems that South Yorkshire were also annoyed with the way you recorded that arrest, as it pushed one of their stats from the orange into the red. It says here why all charges were dropped. Now I'm going to give you the chance to explain what happened from your perspective.'

'First of all, sir, after the ambulance had gone, the Crowd Safety people – they're private Security – put the tape back in place, but decided to stop anybody from filling the space next to the tape. The crowd was two or three deep behind the barriers above and below the stretch of tape, with a lot more standing further back behind the path, so people wanted to spread into the taped area to be closer to the road for a better view. This bloke was standing just at the edge of the taped area and was trying to take a photo of the crowds on the other side of the road, but one of the Security people pushed him in the back and wouldn't let him stand there even for a couple of seconds to take a quick snap. I noticed he looked quite annoyed – some of those Security people can be really petty, you know, using their little bit of authority.'

Dunn conspiratorially leaned in toward Priestley. 'Do you remember what happened to Sir Chris Hoy at the Commonwealth Games? The Security people there demanded he show his ID. Fair enough, you might say, except he was entering the …' Dunn paused for effect, 'Sir Chris Hoy Velodrome.'

Priestley refused to be amused. 'Get back to Jenkin Road.'

Dunn quickly wiped away the grin with the back of his hand. 'Yes sir. The bloke was standing at the edge of one of the end barriers, and I was watching him closely because he didn't seem to be enjoying the occasion – he wasn't smiling like other people, and he didn't even join in the Mexican Wave that kept coming down the hill – so I was wondering why he was there. Then I took my eyes off him for a moment, to look at a couple of French police motorbikes coming past. When I looked back, he was down on the ground with his hands stretching through the barrier and into the road. I bent down and grabbed him, and pulled him back. That's when he told me to get off him, as he was just picking something up off the road, but I thought he might have been intending to put tacks down to give the bikes flat tyres – that's happened on the continent in the past, you know, so it could have been what he was going to do.

'Earlier, I'd noticed there was a journalist just up the road, so I decided to get the bloke away from the area as quickly and as quietly as possible, to avoid any bad publicity getting into the papers.'

'How did you know there was a journalist? Who was it?'

'I'd seen his Press ID around his neck – it was Jonathan Liew from The Telegraph.'

'OK, carry on.'

'Well, the bloke wouldn't budge; he said he didn't want to miss the race, and that he could explain everything. He was getting all het up and talking loudly, so I told him he could explain it all back at the station, and that I was arresting him. That's when he came over all uppity, telling me I should check with my superiors because I was making a big mistake. I said I didn't need to check because I had the authority to arrest him myself. He took out his mobile to make a phone call, but I stopped him – I said he could do that at the station. He didn't say anything else after that, so I took him to a van and we went over to Ecclesfield.

'When I interviewed him under caution, the first thing I asked him was why he'd been looking so miserable. First of all, he claimed it was because he wasn't able to smile; he said it was a symptom of his illness – Parkinson's disease. Then he admitted he'd felt a bit annoyed with one of the Security people for pushing him in the back, and for not letting him stand still a moment to take a picture, especially as a minute later they allowed everybody else right into that area.

'But he denied any intention to throw tacks onto the road or disrupt the race in any way whatsoever. He said he'd been using his iPad to check where the riders had reached, and then he'd dropped it and bent down to pick it up.

'When he said again he wanted to make a phone call, I let him.

'He phoned a friend of his – a Chief Superintendent; and that's when the shit hit the fan.'

'You really should have listened to him and checked with a superior, shouldn't you?'

'Yes sir, though I can honestly say it won't happen again – not in South Yorkshire. They told me if ever I crossed the border into their jurisdiction again, they'd think of something to arrest me for – like not smiling.'

'Really?'

'Well, I'm sure they didn't really mean it, but they weren't happy.'

'I need to consider how you'd handle a similar situation in the future. Would you still get it wrong? According to the complaint from the assault victim that you threatened with arrest, you seemed to lack the capacity to see things from his point of view; he complained you were devoid of "soft skills" – how to relate to other people. And the guy with Parkinson's complained that you didn't seem to be able to recognise the difference between honest citizens and villains.

'If we measured what my wife would call your Emotional Intelligence Quotient, you'd be down at the bottom end of the scale – you just don't seem to be able to empathise with anyone. Empathy is something that women are often better at than men, and I'm not being sexist – it's a case of what they lose on the swings they gain on the roundabouts. Men can be much stronger at having a single focus and ignoring distractions, and women stronger on relating to other people. There are times in this job when single-focus deductive reasoning is the key to solving a case, but when you're dealing with members of the public you need that empathy.

'I wouldn't normally draw a comparison with an actual colleague, but I think it's justified in your case because you need a rôle model. You often work with WPC Plummer; she has excellent inter-personal skills, so I want to see you developing yourself to be more like her when you're dealing with people. If you can't actually BE like her, then you need to work at imitating being like her.

'Now, how familiar are you with the College of Policing's Code of Ethics publication that they brought out last July?'

'I read it thoroughly, sir.'

'And do you recall the nine policing principles listed there?'

'Yes, sir.'

'Well, list them, then.'

'Accountability, Integrity, Honesty.' Dunn frowned heavily as his recitation petered out.

'You're not required to know the whole Code of Ethics document word for word, but unless you're familiar enough with the principles you're unlikely to realise when you're failing to apply them. For that reason, you need to learn the principles' nine key words, so they can act as reminders. At some time in the future, I'll be checking you know them. Here's how I remind myself of them: "I, RASH FOOL". I for Integrity, R for Respect, A for Accountability, S for Selflessness, H for Honesty, F for Fairness, O for Objectivity, O for Openness, L for Leadership. You could make up a different acronym if you prefer, such as,' he flicked his index and middle fingers in the air to identify where the quotation marks should be, 'You "R A FOOLISH" officer. But don't just learn the nine words; you have to understand what's behind them – they need to guide how you think and behave.

'The Code of Ethics also describes ten Standards of Professional Behaviour that you need to abide by, and I'm applying the same approach there – I might ask you about them at any time. For now I'll just draw your attention to Standard Two: Authority, Respect and Courtesy. It applies to colleagues as well as to members of the public. Your use of insulting language in respect of – in disrespect of – female colleagues is something that you need to address right away. So, with immediate effect, you must treat all colleagues with respect, whether they're ordinary blokes or Aphrodite incarnate – what do you refer to her as?'

'Who's Aphrodite?'

'The goddess of beauty.'

'Oh, you mean Lily.'

'I mean DC Martello.'

Dunn perceived a chink in Priestley's argument. 'So it's alright for you to refer to her by some different name, but how am I supposed to know what's allowed and what isn't?'

'I didn't initially mention DC Martello by name, to see what description you came up with – I was giving you some rope to hang yourself, but you don't appear to be familiar with Greek mythology.'

'It wasn't a subject taught at my school.'

'We're wandering off the main path; let's get back to the heart of the matter. I'll be assessing the progress you make on improving your behaviour, and I'll also be looking out for complaints against you. If I find one that's fully justified – and I say that because we can all get unjustified complaints – if there's even one valid one, then you'll be subject to full disciplinary procedures.'

Dunn felt sick inside, just wanting this to be over, but could see Priestley had more to say.

'You're at a crossroads. If you continue as you are, then I don't see you as having any sort of a future on the force. You need to adopt a modern attitude and to come back tomorrow morning a new man. The visible difference needs to be immediate; gradual change just doesn't work in your situation. Now, go away and reflect on what I've said. You either come back as a reformed character, or your days here are numbered.'

Priestley's jerk of the head in the direction of the door indicated to Dunn he should now leave. He stood up and gave a 'Thank you, sir' without any sense of what he should be thanking Priestley for, thinking only of how he had just been threatened with dismissal.

Priestley thought the reprimand, no matter how well-intentioned, could make him the latest focus for Dunn's anger; he made a mental note to be on the lookout for any backstabbing.

He collected together the Cassidy case notes and interim post-mortem report, taking them home for after-dinner reading.

Dunn left the station without another word and drove to his father's house. He needed someone to talk to, and his father, Samuel, was the only current contender. Elias Jobs-Dunn felt permanently embarrassed about his surname and kept promising himself he would have it changed officially to his father's surname, Dunn. As PC Elias Jobs-Dunn, he had to use the full surname on official documents, but dropped the 'Jobs-' whenever he could. He felt a slight burning at a point on the back of his neck whenever he had to introduce himself as 'Jobs-Dunn', and prickled at the thought of his mother who was responsible for his surname. She had retained her own surname on marriage, to avoid any suggestion that loss of maiden name indicated subjugation. She had also argued that the surname of any offspring should reflect her contribution. Elias was grateful that his father had insisted his own surname, Dunn, should come after her surname, Jobs; after all, Dunn-Jobs was open to multiple interpretations and all of them bad. Elias would still laugh with his father about how Jobs-Dunn made him sound like a boy scout, though they knew there was a shared hidden resentment about the ex-wife, and to all intents and purposes ex-mother, now Ms Jobs, who was even more proud of her name since the death of the unrelated Steve Jobs of Apple fame.

Elias parked on the road outside the small, end-of-terrace property in one of the less run-down areas of Nethershaw. On the concreted area at the front of the house, Sam Dunn had arranged a tightly-packed array of deep wooden boxes to create the effect of a front garden. Elias expected soft plants and shrubs would be growing even at this time of year, though everything currently remained invisible to him in the absence of a working street-light. He rang the doorbell and immediately opened the door using his own key. Confident that his father would be at home, he stood in the hallway and called out, 'Dad – are you in?'

Sam opened the door to the downstairs room and stood back to invite his son inside. 'I thought today was Monday?'

Elias visited every week on Thursday evening and Sunday afternoon, an arrangement almost unbroken in five years and enjoyed by both, mutually dependent as they were for their vestiges of family life. Sam never drank alcohol alone, though he enjoyed his home-brew so always took the opportunity to share a glass or two when Elias visited. He offered one straight away, Elias responding, 'Yes, I could do with a drink. I'm having a hard time at work.'

The beer was dark brown, almost black, and with little head. Sam refused to use carbon dioxide to pump the beer from the five-gallon barrel, so the creaminess of the head varied depending on how many glasses had been drawn since it was last primed. Sam waited for Elias to tell him his troubles, a habit maintained from childhood. 'The force has changed such a lot, and I'm being told I haven't kept up with it. There was a time when a policeman was expected to clip kids around the ear, get out the truncheon if there was a bit of bother, and give criminals a working-over in the cells.'

'It sounds like that's what you wish it was like now.'

'Well, it would be simpler sometimes just to mete out a bit of immediate justice.'

'Rules and regs getting in your way?'

'You could say that. I accused someone of being responsible

for a death, and I was sure he did it. But it turns out he was innocent.'

'Well, mistakes can be made, can't they?'

'Yes, but this time it turned into something else. The guy killed himself.'

Sam remained silent, knowing there was more to come.

'I've been told I'm moody and I sometimes get angry about nothing.'

This time Elias waited until Sam responded. 'Well, you aren't like that with me, son. Do your colleagues think you're a boor?'

'Yes, Dad, I think they do, and I've been told I've got to change, pronto, otherwise I'm out. There's an Acting DCI who's read me the Riot Act. He says I've got to become a new man if I want to remain on the force.'

'Do you want to stay as a policeman? If you're not happy, maybe you should look for something else.'

'I think being a policeman is the best job I'll ever get. You know I'm not exactly brilliant.'

'Don't knock yourself son – you're bright enough. You're brighter than me, and certainly a lot brighter than your mother.'

Elias knew the subject of his mother, Belinda, would surface at some point. Sam and Elias shared the pain of her desertion in their different ways. At the age of ten he had become a single-parent child; though there were several others in his class at school, he was the only one without a mother. 'If I'm honest with myself, even though there's quite a few thick policemen, there's also plenty of smart ones nowadays as well, and I'm never going to get beyond being a constable in uniform.'

'Is that enough for you?'

'I suppose it is. But I've been told I have to start tomorrow as a new man.'

'Well, do what you keep saying you'll do: get your name changed. "Elias Dunn." Make it official. I sometimes think you're still angry with your mother; maybe it'll flush her out of your system.'

'You're right, Dad. It's something I can say I've done to help to make me a new man. I can say "I'm Dunn".'

'Whoa, was that nearly a joke? I think you've already started to change.'

'I've never really done jokes.'

'I know a good one. Your mother was so intelligent, when she left Sheffield and went back to Leeds the average IQ of BOTH cities went up.'

'You've told me that one before.'

'Well, I thought it was dead funny – once I'd worked it out.'

CHAPTER 26

Priestley and Martello Interview More Staff

Tuesday

It was a little after midnight when Priestley had finished reviewing the Cassidy case notes and interim post-mortem and forensic reports. The level of alcohol in Cassidy's blood was high, though not so high as to render him unconscious and make him incapable of stepping off the crag; his stomach contents indicated much of the alcohol had been consumed quickly and had not been absorbed into his bloodstream at the moment he made the fatal fall.

There were calculations relating to the distance fallen. To allow for the possibility of his having jumped from a different position close by, or having climbed some distance down the rock face from the top before falling, a table of heights and terminal velocities was included that extended either side of the value for the vertical distance to the ground from the top of the crag closest to the point of impact. For heights of 16 to 22 metres the terminal velocities were listed in metres per second: 17.7, 18.3, 18.8, 19.3, 19.8, 20.3, 20.8.

The injuries were deemed consistent with an impact velocity of between eighteen and twenty metres per second, (forty and forty-five miles per hour), which indicated a fall of between sixteen and twenty-one metres. This finding was stated to be compatible with the deceased having started at or near to the top of the crag close to the point directly above the climb known as Cardinal's Arête, and that the convex curvature of the crag had caused the body to be deflected and to turn in the air, with the final, prone position not being indicative of a smooth, backward fall, but merely the chance orientation at the moment of impact.

Based on the high blood-alcohol level, the possibility was discounted of Cassidy having fallen accidentally while climbing from ground level up the arête to near the top and there was therefore no need to consider his climbing ability or lack thereof. Taken together, the forensic evidence led to the conclusion that Cassidy had been alive at the moment he descended under gravity from the top of the crag, and that massive internal injuries were the cause of his demise. The limited damage to the back of the head was deemed consistent with the torso having taken the brunt of the impulse on impact.

Taking other evidence into account, Priestley recognised the only reasonable conclusion was that Cassidy had committed suicide. He anticipated in due course the coroner's verdict would be – avoiding using the "S" word – "The deceased took his own life."

When he felt there was nothing more he could glean from the files, he crept silently into bed, trying not to disturb Helen. She lay on her right side, facing away from him. Her warm body radiated heat; he edged closer to her, matching how she lay, and carefully placed his left arm around her so as not to wake her.

Though she appeared to him to be sleeping, she was only acting the part. They enjoyed making love when the time and place was right, but she needed her sleep too much to welcome his advances in the early hours of a working day, and she knew he was too considerate to wake her. Still, she was relieved he was now able to lie calmly on his side. For months after leaving the army he had violently fought enemies in his sleep, before she had convinced him to adopt a *gisant* pose; stretched out flat on his back with hands crossed on his chest like an effigy on the tomb of a Norman Knight, he had appeared to aspire to saintliness, which reflected his new attitude to life.

* * *

Priestley fell asleep with the case notes passing and re-passing through his conscious mind; it was a mechanism for solving problems he had often found effective in the past – while he slept, his unconscious mind would deliberate on a problem and seek a solution. He woke before the radio alarm and was disappointed to find he had not been blessed with any overnight revelations.

Marcus found himself thinking of a mechanism he employed to deal with any upsets Edwin might have. The method was for Daddy to talk to him about something nice, keeping up the gentle conversation until he fell asleep; the hope was that his boy's dreams would be filled with those happy thoughts. He remembered he had first used the method when, aged four, Edwin had been deeply and repeatedly scratched down the full length of both sides of his face by a boy at the nursery. The boy's mother was the entirely self-focused type who had not bothered to trim his razor-like fingernails, and had no discernible conscience to be troubled by the consequence. Edwin himself had been very upset, but it was nothing to the degree of traumatisation he and Helen had felt, that their perfect boy had been disfigured; though the damage had diminished with time, it still upset them even now, two years later, whenever they noticed his permanent scarring. Marcus reminded himself not to keep looking too closely at Edwin's scars – for his own sake as well as Edwin's – and wished it was something that could have been fixed as easily as another trauma Edwin had suffered, four days after his fifth birthday – the loss of his new teddy bear. It was the eighteenth of August 2013, a date etched on Marcus's mind; he had been driving the family home from a Sunday picnic, when Edwin had discovered the absence of Conrad the Bear. With Edwin sounding louder than a police siren, Marcus had driven them back to the area they had just agreed was a happy place. Though he had organised the four of them to undertake an extensive fingertip search – even three-year-old Alice had helped – they eventually had to accept that Conrad the Bear would not be returning from the teddy bears' picnic. Two days later, Edwin had been given another Conrad the Bear by Mummy, with the ambiguous invitation, 'Look who's here.' Despite there being no discernible difference to Mummy and Daddy, Edwin had responded 'That's not my Conrad.' For once, Mummy had been unsure how to react; Daddy had stepped in with, 'It's his brother, and he's also called Conrad.' Edwin had then happily accepted the replacement, thereby putting an end to his bedtime tears and disturbed nights.

He wondered if the method would work as well on Alice as it appeared to work on Edwin; but Alice didn't do "upset", at least not on Edwin's scale. He wondered if Helen had researched the happy end-of-day method as he had once suggested she should – he thought it could be helpful in the treatment of PTSD in infants. He decided to ask her. He shook her shoulder very gently. 'Helen, sweetheart.'

'No, you can't.'

'But I haven't asked you a question yet.'

'And the answer's still no. It's nearly time to get up.'

'Well, I was only going to ask if ...'

The radio alarm gave a short burst of static which was followed by a few spoken words and then Radio Four's seven o'clock time signal. Before the final pip had sounded, Helen had pulled back the duvet and stepped directly into her red leather slippers, bending to ease her heels into them with an index finger. After replacing the duvet she headed for her bathroom, which was through his bathroom and far enough away from their bedroom for her shower not to drown out the low-volume words on the radio.

Priestley usually stayed in bed for ten to fifteen minutes, to hear the news and maybe the first featured topic. Sometimes he was so irritated by a presenter badgering a so-called guest and stopping them from speaking – non-labour politicians were often the target of such treatment – that he would stretch out an arm and track down the correct button with his fingers to shut him up. "Him or her" he knew he should say, though it was almost always the same "him". Today he went into his bathroom straight after the last news item.

He was confident his coffee, cereal and toast would be ready by the time he reached the kitchen. As they both worked fulltime, they had agreed they should take it in turns to make breakfast; his turn was now at least three years overdue, and Helen had no expectation of his ever making breakfast other than on Mothers' Day and her birthday. They always aimed to have breakfast together before getting the children out of bed. Edwin sometimes chose not to follow the script, getting up early to wander about the house, but today his roaming remained within the land of Nod; Alice, as usual, stayed in her bedroom, sleeping serenely.

While eating breakfast, Priestley worked out his plan for the day. Before finishing his second mug of coffee he began to put it into effect. First he phoned Berry – always ready and willing to pick up the phone and to do his bidding. Then he phoned Witty with the same instructions: dress for a funeral. Witty responded, 'Black tie, or perhaps something brighter? I could try to put the "fun" into "funeral".'

'I must have words with you sometime about when to put the

"fun" into anything.'

Witty echoed, 'Any fun thing.'

Priestley sighed deliberately audibly. 'Is Lily available to come to the phone?'

'Yes. She's right here trying to listen to our conversation.'

'Well, put her on.'

'Hello.'

'Lily, this morning Neil and Tony will be going to the school to check a few things, then visiting John Newhouse's mother and going to the funeral in the afternoon. I'm wanting you to do some interviews with me at the school; could you be there by, say, eight thirty?'

'Yes, that's no problem.'

'Good. I'll see you in the school car park.'

Martello arrived at the school at eight twenty-two to find Priestley just getting out of his car. She parked in the adjacent place and was quickly followed by a Ford Focus driven by Ashbourne, who parked in the next slot. After a quick acknowledgement to Martello, he addressed the teacher, 'Good morning, Mr Ashbourne. Is that a Bentley? It looks like a Ford to me.'

Ashbourne allowed a smile to flicker across his lips. 'Do call me Anthony. I see you embody the powers of observation for which our police force is so rightly admired – this is indeed a Ford. I've decided to be more "of the people", so I've borrowed the little woman's Focus for today.'

'So there's a Mrs Ashbourne?'

'Not at present. The little woman is a friend; a ship that may pass in the night. I am, however, always on the lookout for the next ex-Mrs Ashbourne.'

'How many current exes are there?'

'Just the three, and I don't really count the second one as she only stayed long enough to put together a believable case for alimony; believable by the judge, that is – no one else would have been naïve enough to swallow her story. Which reminds me, that's something else I was wishing to talk to the boys about – always getting a signed and witnessed pre-nuptial contract; Mr Verbane, bless him, suffered the most severe apoplexy at that idea.'

Priestley found himself warming to Ashbourne; he sensed there was a good man peering out from behind the pompous exterior.

'We're here to do some interviews. You're not on our list, though.'

'What does one have to do to qualify making it past the honourable selection process?'

'One set is those who are young enough to have made the staff football team but didn't play. I'm fairly certain you're the wrong side of forty so I don't believe you qualify.'

'I shan't be seeing fifty again, either. You won't find many youngsters avoided the draft. In the staffroom I overheard only two: Jeremy Benn, who I believe declined for political reasons; and Monsieur Étienne Platini whose excusal was based on his having a square foot, whatever that means.'

'A square foot of what, I wonder. I remember in my student days I worked on a building site and a popular joke was, "What's a cubic foot?" The standard response was, "I don't know, but claim for it." Does he have any sign of a disability?'

'Nothing externally apparent.'

'I'll ask him about it. I'll also be talking to anyone who was out of lessons and unaccompanied between three twenty and three forty.'

'Then it was remiss of you to have left me off your list.'

'I was told you were giving a lesson at that time.'

'That's only half true. Two of us were giving a joint session – something of a luxury to have two teachers, but I don't charge extra for my voluntary involvement in the lessons of others. My part was finished by three fifteen, so I headed for the staffroom.'

'In that case I think I'll interview you formally this morning, if you don't mind.'

After Ashbourne had left, Priestley asked Martello, 'What do you think of Mr Anthony Ashbourne?'

'Letting you know he was out of lessons could be a bluff if he thinks you'd find out anyway.'

'True, but what do you actually think?'

'He isn't like a normal teacher, what with his way of speaking, but I like the way he always looks me in the eye and doesn't let his gaze wander any lower.'

'So, you don't like people looking too closely at your body?'

'It depends. If I want them to look then it's alright, but if I don't want them to look then it isn't.'

'You expect people to know what you're thinking, then. Well, thank you for clarifying that, Lily.'

'No, what I mean is, if I'm dressed up for men to look at me, then I expect men to look at me.'

'So, if you're wearing something with a plunging neckline, it's alright for men to look.'

'Obviously; I'd be pretty stupid to wear something that's meant to make men look at me, and then object if they do. If I don't want someone looking at my bust, then I don't wear something that shows off my bust.'

'I do like your straightforward way of seeing things. It's a pity not all young women have your clarity of thought. Anyway, what do you think of Mr Ashbourne in relation to the case? Could he have done it?'

With no apparent pause for reflection, she responded, 'Yes, given the right reason.'

A shadow crossed Priestley's visage. 'We all could, given the right reason.' His mind flashed back to his last action in the army, a memory that now only invaded his waking hours. He no longer recalled experiencing dreams of any sort, though Helen told him theorists generally agreed he must still have them; he believed he had replaced nebulous dreaming with off-line examination of facts that would be sifted and processed in readiness for the next on-line day.

Priestley and Martello headed for Oaken's room, where they remained after Oaken had left for the staff meeting. He asked Martello, 'What do they teach new detectives nowadays about finding perpetrators? Do you still look for MOM?'

'Means, Opportunity, Motive. I'm not sure how much that helps in this case, though.'

'I agree, Lily. The means were there for anyone who was in the right place at the right time. We haven't yet found a sufficient motive, though we could maybe come up with something on the theme of philandering. But really, we're stuck with opportunity. That's why we need to interview everyone who was not in class in that period of about ten minutes. I'm not getting any hint of an outsider being present, so, unless we come up with some new evidence, I'm thinking we should focus on insiders only.'

On Oaken's return, Priestley asked about the use of two

teachers for one class.

'It isn't something we normally do, except where we have a student on teaching practice.'

'Mr Ashbourne told us he was in a joint lesson.'

'Ah, Mr Ashbourne: a law unto himself. He's always volunteering to give an alternative viewpoint to other teachers' lessons; a few of them have even complained to me about it. The trouble is, he knows so much about so many things, that he's forever pushing himself onto teachers so that the students can receive the benefit of his wisdom. So far, he's taken part in combined lessons with English, Economics, History, Music – he's a brilliant classical singer by the way, but knows even less about pop music than I do. Business Studies have absolutely refused to have anything to do with him – they say he undermines their credibility. I'm not surprised to hear he was in a joint lesson.'

'Are there any others?'

'Any others like Mr Ashbourne? Not in this school – one is as many as we can cope with.'

'So, no other joint lessons, then?'

'Only the ones with PGCE students, and the staff all know the rules say they're not permitted to be left alone – though I can't guarantee they always abide by them. Of course in theory any teacher, with or without a trainee, could slip out of a room during a lesson if the students were fully occupied. Would you like a list of all the teachers and their lessons for that last period of the day?'

'Yes, thank you; it could be useful.'

Oaken went to her laptop and printed off a list of all teachers, teaching assistants, foreign language assistants, lab technicians and admin staff. 'Here's a list of all adults who were in school that day. I could also provide you with an entire list of students, if you wish.'

'By students you mean pupils? How many would that be?'

'Well over a thousand. I could obtain the exact figure for the Wednesday afternoon if you give me a little time.'

'No, that won't be necessary for now. Could we just see three of the children, in this order: Zachariah Peck; David Williamson; and Simon Green.'

Oaken checked their details. 'They're all under eighteen. They should have a parent or guardian present.'

'These are not formal interviews, Miss Oaken.'

'Well, perhaps if I remained in the room?'

'Yes, that's a good idea. You'll see we just have a few simple questions at this stage.'

When Oaken had returned with Zach Peck, Priestley opened the questioning. 'Toward the end of the football match, after the final goal had been scored, you were at the opposite end to the action, I believe.'

'Yes, we were standing at one end and the teachers were attacking the other end.'

'We?'

'I was with Dave Williamson who was near the steps, and Simon Green who was near the other corner.'

'And did you leave your corner in the last few minutes of the match?'

'No sir, we stayed where we were supposed to be, right until the end.'

'Did you see anyone else in that area?'

'No sir, no one at all.'

'Right, well, that's all I wanted to know.'

Oaken took away Peck and returned with Williamson.

'You were near the steps, I believe. Did you stay there until the end of the match?'

'Not quite the end. I couldn't see what was happening from down there, so I agreed when Simon Green suggested the three of us on ball duty at the bottom end should go up the field to see better; anyway, there wasn't any point in staying down at that end when the ball was at the other end.'

'So where were you at the final whistle?'

'Standing on the side-line, nearly up to where everybody else was.'

'Everybody else being?'

'Y12 and Y13 students, the Headmaster and a few teachers.'

'Right, well, that's all I wanted to know.'

While Oaken was collecting Green, Priestley observed, 'Total disagreement from our first two witnesses of the day. Let's hope the third one doesn't come up with yet another version.'

'Perhaps one of them just misremembered?'

'Maybe – and maybe not. I'm going to ask Miss Oaken not to stay in for the next interview, so be careful to avoiding reacting, or she might refuse to leave.'

Oaken returned with Green. Priestley asked her, 'Now that you've heard the simple questions we're asking, I feel guilty about you having to waste your time sitting here with us, so please feel free to leave us to it.' Priestley showed no sign of starting the interview, so she took the hint and left the three of them alone.

'Where were you at the final whistle?'

'I was standing on the side-line, about half way between the corner flag and the half-way line.'

'And when did you move to that position? You'd previously been behind the goal line, I believe.'

'That's right. It was obvious the teachers were on all-out attack, so all the action was at that end, which meant there was no point in being at the opposite end.'

'But if the action had switched to the end you were supposed to be at, there would've been no one to fetch the ball.'

A grin spread over Green's face. 'Right.'

'Come on; tell me why you walked up the side-line.'

'Well, it was near the end of the match, and we were just one goal up. If our team managed to break out of defence and knock the ball right down the field, and then off the end of the pitch, it's as you said: there'd be no one to retrieve the ball. That would waste some time, and so we'd have more chance of holding onto our lead.'

'Isn't that sort of cheating?'

'Sort of. I saw a Welsh ball-boy time-wasting in a match on TV, and he not only got away with it but the ref booked one of the players as well. Result!'

'Does this school do lessons on morality, by any chance?'

'No. Why?'

'I might just suggest the idea to the Headmaster.'

Priestley asked Martello to find Oaken and ask her to take Green away and invite Ashbourne to attend. When they were alone, waiting for Ashbourne, Priestley asked, 'How do you read the three witnesses?'

Martello replied immediately, 'Two against one. Go with the majority.'

Priestley waited a moment before responding, 'There's a bit

more to it than that. Remember MOM. For this little bit of the investigation we now have a motive – time-wasting. I think Peck may have lied because Miss Oaken was there and he thought he might be accused of dereliction of duty; he even started calling me "sir" at that point, which at the time I thought was interesting, though I didn't know how to interpret it.'

'Do we want Peck back for a second round?'

'I don't believe that's necessary – certainly not at the moment.'

Ashbourne arrived and seated himself comfortably in the available chair, pushing it back in order to give himself more room to stretch his legs. 'Greetings, again. You'll be wishing to know exactly where I was and who I saw in those key moments. I've had time to think things through.'

'Right you are, so please go ahead.'

'Three fifteen I headed for the staffroom. The only unaccompanied person of any age that I saw on the way there was David Pratt, NUT union rep.' Ashbourne put on a strangled-sounding voice in a higher register: 'Wot abaht the workers?'

'You don't sound like you're a fan of Mr Pratt.'

'Pratt by name, if you know the expression. It's the whole union thing as well. The world's now a global village, so trying to maintain restrictive working practices is like putting your finger in the dyke to stop the water.'

'If I remember the story correctly, the Dutch boy was successful in holding back the water.'

'Hmm, I should have considered that analogy a little more carefully. Thinking of the Netherlands suggests a further argument you could use against me: that children in this country cannot readily obtain their education abroad. But nevertheless, I believe unions should be consigned to history. They may have done some good things in the dim and distant past, but now they often do harm – just look at how the threat of industrial action led to the Royal Mail privatisation price being pitched very low, at considerable cost to the taxpayer. But it isn't just the unions themselves; it's a broader union mentality that exists amongst teachers that's a factor in maintaining the breath-taking inefficiency of the school system in this country.'

Priestley doubted whether something relevant to the investigation might be revealed if he invited Ashbourne to have his say, but decided to let it play for a little while – just in case. 'What exactly do you see is wrong with the school system, and in particular what's wrong with this school?'

'Did you know that every teacher prepares their own lessons? Not just at this school but throughout the country. There are some common learning resources that can make that process a little more efficient, but essentially the wheel is re-invented half a dozen times every day by every teacher up and down the land. It's crazy. Politicians bleat on about the need for consistent standards, and yet they lack the vision to see that consistency of output is a function of consistency of input. I know teachers build up their own supply of prepared lessons over time so that their effort's reduced, but that can work to the detriment of pupils who can end up receiving tired, out-of-date lessons which were first developed years ago.

'I do maths, which is one of the most stable of subjects along with classics, and there are others that are just a short head behind, but even for these subjects the effort needed to create a lesson plan represents a substantial waste of time. If the government is serious about improving standards of education, it should put its money into providing entire off-the-shelf courses – like the highly successful Open University set-up. Then it could change its recruitment focus onto people who can deliver in a way that pupils can access. I find the most academic of pupils often prefer an academic style of delivery, whereas less academic pupils are looking to be entertained, and for them the trick is to educate them while entertaining them. So the choice facing pupils should be much more focused on how much detail they wish to get out of a lesson, and consequently how they would like that lesson to be delivered.

'The government should provide sets of lessons for every level of every subject, which it should keep up-to-date so that they continue to match current requirements. Every teacher should be able to take such sets of lessons off the shelf when needed. In the end, if teachers had no need to prepare lessons themselves, then they could do a much better job because they would have so much more time to do that job. But anyone suggesting this can expect to be hit with a barrage of fatuous arguments as to why it wouldn't work, and of course the unions would be at the forefront of the objectors with their threats of strike action.'

'It sounds as though you should be in government rather than teaching in a school.'

'Well, Acting DCI Priestley…'

'Call me Marcus. And this is Lily.'

'Well, Marcus, Lily, you have stumbled upon my cunning plan. Once I've proved the limitations of trying to fix the system on a local basis – proved as in tested – I intend to bang the drum at a higher level. I just hope someone will be listening.'

'I can imagine you'll make them listen, Anthony. I really wish we had more time, but we need to get back to the investigation. You mentioned seeing Mr Pratt alone.'

'Yes. He was delivering an IT lesson through a large bank of terminals that were in one room, and he was entirely isolated from them in another room; I could see him through the window, so I know he was there at three fifteen. The nature of many IT lessons is that they enable each pupil to progress at their own pace, so, once the lesson has been prepared, the teacher can just let the pupils run with it. Mr Pratt was therefore able to sit apart while delivering his lesson.'

'That's interesting. We'll speak to him after we're finished here. And you saw no one else alone?'

'I saw no one else alone, though I expect there will be two others who I didn't see.'

'And who are they?'

'Jo Jackson and Peggy Webster. Peggy sits on reception at start and end of day, plus whenever needed during the day if anyone calls in. When Peggy leaves the admin room, Jo is no doubt alone. Peggy's normally on reception well ahead of the end-of-day bell.'

'Right. Well, that's another two interviews we'll have to do. Thanks very much, Anthony, you've been a great help.'

'It's been a pleasure.' He turned to Lily, 'And if you have the time, I should like to talk to you on another matter.'

Lily was taken aback, her body movement revealing the shock.

'I'm sorry, I should have been clearer. I was merely thinking, "Why are you a police officer?" Forgive me, I imagine myself to be an expert on all things, whereas the reality is that I'm only an expert on…' He gave a fulsome smile, '…most things.'

Handshakes were offered and accepted all around. After Ashbourne had left, Priestley turned to Martello. 'Phew! What did you think of that?'

'He's very driven, isn't he?'

'I wonder what he was wishing to talk to you about?'

'Probably the usual, but maybe something else.'

Oaken was found in her familiar place around the corner from her office, and was asked about any male teachers under thirty-five who might normally have been expected to play in the football match. She suggested only Benn and Platini, confirming Ashbourne's contenders. Priestley asked her to invite what he hoped would be the final five interviewees: Pratt, Benn, Platini, Jackson and Webster, in that order. After consulting with her timetable, she asked if they could take a break for half an hour before interviewing Mr Pratt. They exited the school for a breather and grabbed a coffee and some sandwiches from a post office *cum* convenience store, returning in good time for Pratt.

Priestley began, 'I understand you were delivering a lesson in the IT suite last Wednesday afternoon.'

'Correct.'

'You're entirely invisible to pupils if you go into the separate control room. Is that correct?'

'Yes.'

'Where were you between three fifteen and three thirty last Wednesday?'

'In the control room.'

'Entirely unseen by the class throughout that period of time?'

'Correct.'

'So you have no alibi?'

'I don't need an alibi; I haven't been accused of anything.'

'Did you kill Mr Newhouse?'

'No.'

'Is there anything you would like to add?'

'No, except I'll be demanding a solicitor if you ask me any more questions.'

'Well, thank you Mr Pratt. I don't have any more questions for now.'

After Pratt had left the office, Priestley asked Martello of her impression. She replied quickly, 'People who demand solicitors may have something to hide.'

'Or sometimes they're just people who've been pissed off by the police in some way in the past and now hate us all and want to piss us off back. Let's not read too much into it just yet.'

Next up was Jeremy Benn, a young man from the maths department. Priestley began, 'I understand you chose not to play for the staff team in the football match last Wednesday. Could you explain to me why not?'

'Simple. Mr McGovan still fancies himself as a footballer, but he's way past it. He had his nose put out of joint by Mr Newhouse when he didn't invite him to play in the match.'

Martello interjected, 'Do you mean Mr Newhouse hit him?'

'No; it's just a figure of speech. In a Maths Department meeting Mr McGovan said he felt the football match was a waste of teachers' time and so was against our students' best interests. His message was clear: don't agree to play. Everybody knew it was just sour grapes because he hadn't been asked to join the team.'

Martello usurped Priestley's position as lead interviewer by responding spontaneously, 'It all sounds a bit childish to me.'

'And you're surprised? It's one of the biggest downsides to the teaching profession; so many of them have stayed in environments all their lives where everyone is a child, or at most an adolescent. I've come across plenty of fifty-odd-year-olds who haven't grown up yet, and I don't expect they ever will.'

Priestley intervened, 'So what does the future have in store for you? It sounds like you don't feel entirely committed to teaching.'

'While I'm doing it I'll do my best to do it well, but I'm already looking for something in the big wide world. It's just not easy finding anything suitable at the moment.'

After Benn had left, Priestley and Martello agreed he had no motive, whereas McGovan had a slight motive but one that was insufficient to justify further consideration for now.

Oaken announced the next interviewee with just a hint of *je ne sais quoi*. '*Monsieur Étienne Platini.*'

'*Bonjour, Monsieur Platini.* May we hold this conversation in English?'

Priestley was relieved to hear the response, '*Bien sûr, certainement, mais oui.* Of course.'

'Excellent. I understand you were invited to play in the School versus Staff football match, but you declined – chose not to.'

'Yes, I was invited to play it, but I am no good.'

'No good at playing football?'

'Yes. I play the tennis.'

'Someone suggested a problem with your foot.'

'There is no problem with my foot.'

'A square foot? Was it a joke?'

'A square foot is no joke. It means I am no good at playing the football.'

'So, you did not wish to play football?'

'Yes…no, I did not wish.'

After Platini had left, Priestley imitated a Gallic shrug with downturned mouth. With *faux* French emphasis he commented, 'I would 'ave asked 'im if 'e was related to Michel Platini, but I thought 'e would 'ave been *pas amusé*.'

Martello enquired, 'Who's Michelle Platini? I've not heard of her.'

Priestley let out a short laugh. 'It's a "him". He used to play football; now he's president of UEFA – that's the European football organisation. Some think he's a dinosaur when it comes to modernising the beautiful game.'

She gave him a withering look. 'And what makes you think I'm even remotely interested in that?'

Priestley attempted to look contrite; he raised his shoulders and held out his hands with upturned palms. '*Je suis désolé*.'

Oaken delivered Jackson, who began without invitation. 'I don't know what you think you're doing interviewing me. It's nothing to do with me. I work from my office all day. I have far too much to do to be walking about, and I don't have the time to talk to you today either, so let me go back to the office and you can stop wasting my time and get on with your job.'

Priestley saw her pause for breath so he jumped in quickly. 'I'm just wishing to know where you were between three fifteen and three forty-five last Wednesday.'

'I was in my office with Mrs Webster.'

'For the entire time?'

'For the entire time.'

'I've been led to understand that Mrs Webster left to attend reception, leaving you alone.'

'Oh, that's very clever, tricking me into making a mistake. Well you shouldn't be trying to trick people like me, you should be out there looking for the person who did it, instead of sitting here in this office all day wasting your time and theirs and …'

Priestley interjected, 'You have the right to remain silent.'

Jackson clammed up. Priestley continued, 'You can go, but don't leave town without informing me first.'

When Jackson had left, Martello turned to Priestley. 'What was that all about – a bit of a US caution?'

'I only did it to shut her up. I was thinking, "You have the right to remain silent, but I doubt whether you have the capacity."'

'Well, it was a bit naughty. And what about the "Don't leave town" bit?'

'Have you never seen cowboy films where the sheriff says "Don't leave town"? Of course, it has no validity without a court order.'

Martello looked down and shook her head from side to side, first tutting, then muttering loud enough for Priestley to hear, 'Naughty, naughty.'

Priestley laughed gently, thinking, 'This isn't the DC Martello I know – she's poking fun at me.'

Oaken arrived with Webster, who sat meekly with her hands on her lap.

'I'd like to know where you were between three fifteen and three forty-five last Wednesday.'

'First I was in the admin office. Then at three twenty I went to reception. I keep the signing-in and signing-out books; one for staff, one for visitors. I have to be there before the first member of staff goes home, ready to remind them – if they forget to sign out I have to chase them up the next day.'

'And did any of the staff forget to sign out last Wednesday?'

'No; I stayed on reception and made sure they all signed out. Not like the referee – he just left without a by-your-leave.'

Priestley and Martello immediately turned to look at each other, both of them feeling blushes starting; hers began with the ears, his developed outwards from the centre of the cheeks. Priestley attempted to look composed as he turned back to Webster and asked, 'Would you mind bringing me that signing-in book, please?'

Webster returned with the book and showed them the entry for the referee, one Keith Oxley, signed in but not signed out.

Priestley asked, 'Do you know where the referee can be contacted?'

'Yes. He's the father of one of our students. Would you like the details?'

'Yes please, Mrs Webster.'

Martello wrote down the information: student's name, Paul Oxley; father's name, Clive Oxley. Address, home telephone number, mobile number for use in case of emergencies.

After Webster had departed, clutching the book tightly, Priestley turned to Martello. 'I'll not tell anybody if you don't.'

Martello laughed a little nervously. 'I'm sure we'd have worked our way around to the referee eventually.'

Priestley tried the two phone numbers but received no reply on either, and neither had an answering service for him to leave a message. 'Nobody home. Is there anyone else we've missed, do you think? Anyone else we should talk to?'

'Not that I can think of, though Anthony Ashbourne has rather intrigued me about wishing to talk to me.'

'I thought you'd just got yourself fixed up, Lily.'

'I have, and that's not going to change. Could we talk to him together, maybe?'

'I will if you wish, though I doubt whether it's necessary for me to be there. Why don't you see if you can have a word with him here, while I go to the ref's house – if he's not in, I'll leave a note for him to contact me. Then I'll come back here and we can do a tidy-up. After that, we'll need to have an end-of-day session with Neil and Tony to see if they've come up with anything interesting.'

Priestley asked Oaken to invite Ashbourne for a brief meeting; the message returned was that it would have to be after the last lesson, which was another twenty minutes away. Martello suggested Priestley should head back to the office once he had visited Oxley's house, and she would see him back there after her meeting with Ashbourne. Priestley accepted, taking all the files with him to relieve Martello of the burden.

Ashbourne arrived, still bouncing with energy after a full day.

'On your own now, Lily?'

'Yes, Marcus has another meeting to deal with. What was it

you were wanting to talk to me about?' She laughed lightly, delightfully. 'If you're about to confess to something, you'll have to come with me to the station.'

Anthony gave his own most delicate laugh, not his usual unreserved one. 'Tell me one thing: why did you join the police force? Be honest with me.'

Though she knew the reason, she hesitated to reveal it to someone she only knew slightly, however easily he appeared to invite confidences. But why not, she told herself. 'I was so fed up of having lads leering at me all the time, I decided I'd become a policewoman so that I could arrest them, or get some strapping copper to do it for me.'

'Well, it isn't a bad reason, but it is a bit negative. Have you ever thought of doing something entirely different?'

She felt a little suspicious of where this question was leading. 'Just what are you suggesting?'

'I'm not actually suggesting anything, but I am saying that someone with your looks should consider using them while you still have them. If you're happy with police work then carry on by all means. It's just that earlier I thought I detected a look that suggested you're not full of unbridled happiness with your work. Maybe you were just turning off when Marcus was asking the questions.'

'As it happens, I've been very unhappy with some of the work, but then I had some good news: an utter bastard of a colleague had to resign, so I was feeling a lot better about things. But actually, I'm still not keen on some of the stuff I have to do.'

'Have you considered other sorts of work? Something that makes use of your looks? It may be a very unfair world out there, but the good-looking ones get all the breaks.'

'Are you suggesting I should look through job vacancies and send off applications with my photo?'

'Good Lord, no. For the type of work you should be considering, you need to get an introduction. I would suggest Marketing and Event Management, PR, advertising, fashion, something like that. Use your current position to enhance your application. Imagine you're fronting an exhibition or a conference; you have to be a promoter's dream with your combination of appearance and the skills you've developed in the police force. I'm thinking head of security at business events with a visible presence for the VIPs. You'd need to learn some foreign languages to go international, at least French and German. I could look into arranging some introductions for you.'

'And you're offering to do this for me in return for what?'

'You're right to remain vigilant – to be suspicious of offers that appear too good to be true. I gain the impression you may have been bruised in the past; at the very least, too much attention from men with ulterior motives. Perhaps it would be better if you were able to find some contacts for yourself through a friend you can trust to look after your best interests; someone who would really push you case. Do you have anyone who fits the bill?'

'The best I can think of is the bank manager in Midshaw. He's in his fifties, and mostly deals with farmers and local people. He's a good friend and I'm sure he'd do his best for me, but I doubt if he knows any companies suitable for me to apply to.'

'Well, if you're seriously considering getting out of the police force, you need to do it ere long. The bird of life has but a short time to fly, and all that, so I say *carpe diem*. Think about what you might like to do, and then talk to your friend. If it's a no-go with him, then do feel free to get back to me. Here's my card.'

'You know you said you're driving a Ford so that you're more like an ordinary teacher; well, I have to tell you, ordinary teachers don't hand out business cards.'

They had another quiet laugh together. As they prepared to exit Oaken's office, Martello asked one final question. 'You haven't said why you'd go out of your way to help me.'

'My answer may make you think I'm as shallow as the next man. The fact is, men like to be able to say, "you see that beautiful woman over there – I know her"; it massages our egos, makes us self-satisfied. I can imagine having that conversation with someone about you. I like the idea of having a beautiful friend, platonic though that friendship may be – and as I get older, platonic friendships are in many ways to be preferred.'

'So, what do you propose I do?'

'In business we talk about "sweating our assets" – making best use of them.'

Martello's voice took on a sharp edge. 'Are you suggesting I sweat my body for the sake of a new career? What exactly do you mean?'

'Oh, I am sorry; I haven't explained myself at all well. I think

I've embarrassed you – I do sometimes get it wrong.'

'That doesn't sound like you.'

'Getting it wrong? Or admitting it? Well, I'll even the score by telling you something embarrassing that happened to me. In my earliest days of teaching I was giving a private lesson to a teenage girl who I felt was showing rather too much cleavage for my comfort in a one-to-one situation, so I looked at her eyes and then looked down, twice, as I way of telling her this. For the next lesson she was wearing a dress that came right up to her neck, so I thought to myself, "she got the message all right". But as soon as I had that thought, it occurred to me she may have misinterpreted my meaning, and that she may now be thinking of me as a dirty old man. At least I had the sense not to ask her about her interpretation – I always say, "When standing in a hole, stop digging." I don't know if I got it wrong or not, but I may have, and I feel embarrassed about it when I remember.'

Martello wondered if that incident was why he now always looked her steadfastly in the eyes. She paused before continuing, 'So just explain what you do mean about "sweating my assets".'

'You simply need to believe – or at least to behave as though you believe – that every man is just waiting to do whatever you ask. If you display confidence on the outside irrespective of what you feel inside, most men will be happy to obey your every command; or even better, to try to anticipate your wishes.

'One final consideration, though. Using your beauty may make you start to feel you're becoming shallow, selling out your principles; that's the hidden trap of the beauty game.'

Lily found her mind churning, unable to put her thoughts together in any coherent way. She stood up and prepared to leave, triggering Ashbourne to do the same. He stepped to the door quickly in order to be able to hold it open for her. She frowned a little as she passed him, commenting, 'You've given me a lot to think about, Anthony.'

CHAPTER 27

The Funeral of Edward John Newhouse

Witty and Berry followed Priestley's instructions. They met up at the station and travelled together to the school, where, without asking permission – as it may have been refused – they began by photographing the photographs of the teachers that were displayed on the wall. This precaution proved unnecessary as Webster, who was on reception, then proved happy to provide them with the file of all staff photographs.

Witty asked Webster about school representation at the funeral. She explained an e-mail had been sent to all the staff by Mr Verbane which stated he would be representing the school, and that any member of staff wishing to attend should first ask his permission. This was followed by an e-mail from Oaken who stated no students would be permitted to attend, as requested by the family, so that they would not themselves be overwhelmed by numbers.

When asked about staff absences, Webster consulted the signing-in book and identified only two unanticipated absentees, Miss Leveret and Madame Dupont.

Next, Witty and Berry visited the crematorium where the funeral was due to take place in the afternoon. The block was surrounded by hectares of grassland, occasional trees, formal gardens, and pathways with kerbstones to which were attached commemorative plaques. Witty regarded the whole effect as radiating peace and tranquillity. Berry saw the absence of woodland in the immediate vicinity as its main virtue, providing nowhere for anyone to hide.

They returned to the office to deal with general correspondence and other work-related matters, before Witty phoned John Newhouse's mother, Mrs Cynthia Newhouse, to offer his condolences, and to ask for an opportunity to speak to her before the funeral. At the appointed time they arrived at her house in Chesterfield and were invited into a room where members of the family were assembled.

After introductions, Witty addressed Cynthia. 'We've been to see where the service is to be held. It's a very nice place – quiet and peaceful. We've no wish to intrude on this family occasion, so we can remain as distant as you wish at the funeral, but we do need to be present to check on who attends. Would you prefer it if we both stand outside, or would it be acceptable for one of us to come inside the chapel?'

'I don't mind if you both come inside the chapel.'

'Do you know how many people are likely to be present?'

Miss Susan Newhouse, John's sister, answered for her. 'It was in the paper, so there could be people we don't know who just come along without telling us in advance. I assume you're wanting to know who's there that we don't know. You stay next to me and I'll point out any strangers.'

'That's very kind of you Miss Newhouse. I really don't wish to intrude.'

'It isn't kindness, DC Whittington. I'm going to help you with your investigation, and you're going to answer any questions I have.'

Witty and Berry left the family to their private grief. Berry opened, 'I think you've pulled, there.'

Witty gave him a withering look, 'Have you any idea how bad taste your comment is?'

'Pretty bad, I guess. But I didn't expect Miss Susan to be inviting you to cosy up to her.'

'It's obvious that it's just because she's really cut up about losing her brother.'

'So she's vulnerable, right now?'

'You really need to get yourself a girlfriend, Tony. But today is not the day for that.'

'Of course it isn't – I know that. But if I could leave it a week, I could give her a call and ask how she's bearing up. You never know, she might want some support.'

'Just make sure you're on your best behaviour today. After that, all I'd say is tread very carefully – you do know she's a solicitor, don't you?'

'Yes. I don't suppose we could swap places could we? Me inside with her; you outside with the camera?'

'I think you need to take some advice from your mentor. Don't mess up your career progression for an indiscretion.'

'Are you interested in her yourself?'

'Christ Almighty, Tony, you have to be the last person on the planet that doesn't know I'm now living with Lily.'

Berry looked incredulously at Witty, 'You and Lily Martello?' After a short pause, he continued, 'So you won't be interested in Susan Newhouse, then. You will try and give me the chance to talk to her, won't you?'

Witty sighed, 'If you promise to behave, Tony.'

Witty and Berry arrived half an hour before the funeral was due to take place. There was another funeral already in progress, so they did their best not to look lost, eventually settling for a walk to where three large black funeral cars were parked, each registration plate bearing the same three letters followed by a single digit number. Witty spoke to the first driver, 'Afternoon. What time are you due to be leaving?'

'Probably about ten minutes. Are you with this party?'

'No, I'm here for the two thirty. I don't suppose you've noticed anyone hanging around, have you?'

'Are you the police?'

Witty took out his warrant card; there was nothing worse for a detective than being reported for loitering with intent, he thought.

The grounds had an in-and-out route for cars, so those leaving never met those arriving. 'You went past the woods over there on the way in; did you notice anyone in there?'

'No. It's all quiet as the grave.'

Witty wondered if this was undertakers' humour. 'You will call it in if you see anything suspicious, won't you?'

'What are you expecting? A mafia hit?'

'You've watched too many gangster films, my friend.'

Witty wandered off, still trying not to look out-of-place.

A score of cars of assorted colours were in the car park that lay a little under a hundred metres from the main building. The front doors of one car opened and two people emerged, she in a full-length black overcoat, he in a dark suit that almost concealed a grey V-necked sweater which in turn nearly obscured a black tie. As though it signalled the arrival of the main performers, the other cars disgorged the supporting cast. However, Witty knew the leading players were yet to make their grand, though sombre, entrance.

Timed to perfection, a hearse drew up directly outside the chapel, immediately followed by a large black car with matching registration except for the number "2" to the hearse's number "1". Again performing with synchronicity, the people assembled in the foyer fell silent, as there emerged from the second car the mother and the two sisters of the deceased, together with the man Witty recognised as the husband of the elder sister. The silence held as four men slipped the coffin from the hearse, raised it onto their shoulders and then bore it into the chapel. Witty positioned himself so as to be available for Susan to invite him in, remaining stationary to leave her the option of reneging on their earlier agreement. She stepped to one side and took his arm as though he were a genuine consort, following the coffin into the chapel.

Susan remained oblivious to those around her, with no thought of identifying interlopers. Witty saw her set her jaw to harden herself for the moment that the last physical semblance of her brother would be consumed by fire. The eulogy brought tears from her mother and sister, but Susan remained unmoved. The strains of Abide with Me failed to break her resolve to keep her eyes dry. She had hardened her heart against her brother's killer and was angry at being unable to put a face to the object of her bitterness.

After the ordeal was over, she stood in line as a principal mourner as people shuffled along to shake hands and say a few words; Witty stood directly behind her so as not to be mistaken for family. They emerged into the hard, cold afternoon. She turned to Witty and informed him, 'Now's the time for me to look around and tell you who I don't recognise. We've arranged for everyone to have tea at a local hotel. If you'll take me there, I can let the car go and we can spend longer looking around.'

Witty's response was the one expected of him, 'Yes, of course I'll take you there.'

She went over to her mother and exchanged a few words, and then car number two drove away with one less occupant than when it arrived. She returned to Witty and looked at the mourners who only now began to disperse. 'I don't know that man. There's a woman over there that I don't recognise. There's another woman over there that I haven't seen before. Those three girls that are standing fairly close together and look like they're pretending they don't know each other: I haven't seen any of them before today. Everyone else is family or a friend, as far as I know.'

Witty begged to be excused for a moment and walked over to Berry. 'There's six that she doesn't know, but one of them is the headmaster and two of them are teachers. That leaves those three girls: make sure you get photos of them all, but don't let them notice that you're doing it if you possibly can.'

Witty returned to Susan and thanked her for her help. As Verbane appeared to have a rock-solid alibi, he saw no reason not to divulge his name to Susan. 'The man you identified is Mr Verbane, the Headmaster of Midshaw School.'

She nodded in acknowledgement, and then asked, 'Do you know who the others are?'

Witty had a strong suspicion of the significance behind the presence of the two female teachers at the funeral, and had an inkling that the three girls were students at the school. The five were all potential suspects, so he decided he should not release their names. 'Any information such as that has to go through official channels, Miss Newhouse.'

'It doesn't feel like you're keeping your side of the bargain.'

'I'm sure you understand the importance of keeping certain information confidential, so that any future trial isn't compromised.'

'So you're saying they're suspects?'

'Only persons of interest, for now.'

'Couldn't you let me know under solicitor-client privilege rules? I wouldn't tell anyone else. It's just that I'm so desperate to know what happened to my brother; now he's gone I don't have anyone else to turn to.'

'Are you saying you're an entirely single woman, Miss Newhouse?'

She turned to face him directly, her eyes burning into his, 'Yes, but I hope you're not trying it on, 'cos I'll have your balls on a plate.'

Witty blinked heavily at her and moved his entire head backwards before opening his eyes widely, in a display of shock that was rather less than genuine and verging on the overacting.

'I'm sure I never meant to give that impression, being very happily in a relationship myself.'

'I'm sorry; it's just so frustrating not knowing what's going on.'

'You can always obtain the latest official information through the head of the investigation, Acting Detective Chief Inspector Marcus Priestley.'

'And where can I obtain the latest unofficial information?'

'I'm not prepared to divulge any information about the case that hasn't been authorised. But there's another piece of information that I could release to you on a solicitor-client type basis, with the strict understanding that you permit me to speak freely whether or not you like what I say – I'm saying no comebacks, no reporting me to my superiors.'

'You have my word.'

'Very well, then. You see Detective Constable Tony Beresford over there? No, don't look – he's gazing in your direction right now. I'm sure he'd be very happy to let you know the up-to-the-minute position on the case so long as it didn't breach any secrecy rules. He was asking me how he might get to know you better, but he's a bit wet in that direction. Perhaps if you invited him to accompany you to the tea at the hotel, you could discuss things with him?'

For the first time, he saw her hardened features give way to the slightest of smiles. 'I don't know what to say, Detective Constable Whittington.'

'You can call me Neil. Shall I call him over?'

'Very clever, Neil. I'll borrow him for the afternoon if I may.'

'He's all yours. Excuse me a moment, I need a word with him before he goes.'

Witty walked over to Berry, who set off to meet him halfway.

'You owe me the biggest favour of your life, Mr Beresford.'

'Do I? What for?'

'I've arranged for you to accompany Miss Newhouse for the afternoon. And so that there's no delay and no chance of a change of mind on her part, I'm going to let you have my car – here's the keys. That means I'm going to be walking back, at least until I can cadge a lift. Give me the camera, and tell me anything I need to know right away about what you've seen here. Don't forget you need to be back at the station by five to give a full report to Priestley.'

'I took photos of the man and the two women. I took several photos of the three girls, first when they were standing apart as though they didn't know each other, and then when they were holding onto each other like they were best friends and with their waterworks turned on. Strange creatures, girls.'

'Not as strange as you, Tony. Now, off you go. You need to be polite with Susan, but stay attentive, and don't push it with her – just behave like you're trying to be professional but at the same time you find everything she says to be absolutely fascinating.'

'Is that the secret of your success with women, Neil?'

Unsure whether Berry was being sarcastic or serious, he settled for, 'Don't knock it until you've tried it. Look at me: the quantity may be low, but the quality couldn't be higher.'

* * *

At five o'clock, Priestley, Martello, Witty and Berry assembled in a small conference room to go through their findings and discuss how the inquiry should proceed. Priestley opened by explaining how he had attempted to contact the referee, being the only known adult whose movements had not yet been examined. The casual way he mentioned this was meant to imply they were all aware of the need to talk to the referee. Witty and Berry felt uncomfortable they had not realised this before, but had no intention of highlighting their own shortcomings. Martello knew the inside story but had no wish to undermine Priestley. Their collective oversight was thereby allowed to pass unacknowledged.

For more than an hour they shared comprehensive explanations of their interviews and investigations. Witty provided prints of various photographs taken by Berry: one he introduced as Verbane; another Martello identified as Miss Leveret; and a third Berry stated was Madame Dupont. None of them could identify the three girls; Priestley suggested they may be pupils at Midshaw School, and undertook to show them to Oaken in the morning.

When the meeting was about to wind up, Witty decided to wind up Berry: 'We haven't yet been given an account of your investigation into Miss Susan Newhouse, DC Beresford.'

Priestley looked at Berry to rectify this oversight, being unfamiliar with the background.

Berry looked first at Witty with eyes that asked him why he

had done this to him, and then at Priestley with an uncertain look at how to proceed. Witty turned his head smartly to Priestley who looked in his direction and received an exaggerated wink.

Priestley immediately guessed the nature of the missing report, and decided to have a bit of fun at Berry's expense. 'I assume your unreported time was spent with Miss Newhouse, in working hours, so you're obliged to account for them with a full and comprehensive explanation of exactly what happened.'

Berry found himself in stasis, frozen in time and space and unable even to begin to respond. Priestley relented. 'It's OK, Tony, we'll settle for the bare bones – just enough to gossip about and start a few rumours.'

Berry finally grasped they were having a bit of fun. 'I went with Susan, Miss Newhouse – along with a lot of other people – to a hotel for tea.'

'And crumpet?' suggested Witty.

'Miss Newhouse was wishing to know about progress on the investigation. I didn't tell her anything she wasn't permitted to know.'

Priestley asked, with reference to the photographs in front of them, 'Did you tell her who Verbane is?'

'She already knew – Neil had told her.'

'And the other two teachers?'

'I told her their names.' He added, with a hint of satisfaction, 'I'd recognised them from their school photos.'

Priestley adopted a more serious tone. 'Actually, that information wasn't public knowledge – it should have been cleared through me.'

Berry looked crestfallen. 'I'm sorry, sir.'

Priestley took pity on him. He smiled as he asked, 'How did she wheedle their names out of you?'

Berry recognised his kindlier expression and responded accordingly. 'She just looked at me with her great big, blue-grey eyes, and asked me. What could I do? Anyone would have done the same.'

'Yes, Tony, any love-struck fool of a Detective Constable such as yourself would have been powerless to withstand that sort of inquiry. Don't let it happen again.'

Berry was unable to stop himself from smiling as he responded, 'No, sir.'

Priestley nevertheless decided Berry should do penance. 'If I don't hear soon from the referee, Clive Oxley, I'll need to go to his house again this evening. You can accompany me, Tony, unless you've already had a better offer.'

'I'm available, sir.'

'And Lily, I assume the lack of report about your meeting with Anthony Ashbourne means it was not for sharing?'

'I'll be sharing it with Neil, first. It may be nothing in the end, but it isn't connected to the inquiry.'

'Alright. Well you and Neil go and do whatever it is you do in the evenings, and Tony and I shall scour the neighbourhood in search of Mr Oxley. We'll congregate here in the morning at eight if that's OK with everyone. Goodnight Lily, Neil. Tony, you stay here a minute.'

When they were alone, Priestley offered some advice. 'You'll find in this job there's lots of women who'll use their wicked wiles to wheedle information out of you. Take journalists for example: some of the women are dead 'ot. You have to recognise what they're after and don't let them have it – confidential information, I mean.'

Berry offered a defence. 'But she was so desperate; so vulnerable.'

'It seems to me you were the one who was vulnerable.'

'She promised not to let anyone else know. She said it was just like solicitor-client privileged disclosure.'

'And are you anticipating any further solicitor-client privilege?'

Berry was unsure whether the question was serious or otherwise. He settled for an optimistic answer of, 'I've got my fingers crossed.'

Priestley and Berry were well into their mild chicken curries in the canteen – Berry having decided to follow his mentor's choice – when Priestley's mobile phone rang. The voice sounded hesitant. 'Is that Inspector Priestley?'

Priestley settled for a simple 'Speaking', despite his title having now expanded.

'I'm Clive Oxley. My son sent me a text message to say you left your card at my house and you're wanting to speak to me.'

'Yes. I assume you've heard about the death of Mr John

Newhouse?'

'Of course; I'd just sent him off in a football match – I feel bad about it now.'

'I need to interview you about what happened after you sent him off.'

'You don't mean what happened in the match, do you?'

'No; what happened to Mr Newhouse.'

'Then I don't believe I'll be any help to you there, Inspector. After the match, I picked up my kit bag from behind the nets and headed straight for the car park. I was in a hurry to get off; I didn't want to be late for the youngsters at the floodlit training ground – I was doing football coaching with them.'

Though Priestley's instincts – his logic – told him Oxley would not prove to be the missing link in the investigation, he knew the importance of leaving no stone unturned. He decided an informal discussion may be the best method for discovering Oxley's character, and could even help to uncover any other snippets of information that tended only to be revealed in a relaxed atmosphere. He suggested, 'Are you busy this evening?'

'Football training's just finished – that's why I've only just picked up my son's text about you wanting to see me. I was intending to walk to the pub; there's a darts match that I'm down to play in.'

'Well I wouldn't want to disrupt your plans, but I do need to talk to you. How would it be if I were to see you there? Is there somewhere quiet we could talk?'

'If I set off straight away, I'll be there in ten minutes.' Oxley specified the name and location of the public house and Priestley confirmed he knew the place.

After the call, Priestley informed Berry of the planned meeting, continuing, 'He says he was in a hurry to go to football coaching after the match, so there were probably people waiting for him there. That means very little of his time would be unaccounted for, from the end of the football match to his arriving for the coaching; if he'd had any blood on him, he may not have had the time to clean himself up. My instincts tell me he's not our man – what's the likelihood of someone giving up their time to referee a match for schoolchildren, then killing someone, and then going to help other children with learning the beautiful game. It seems illogical.'

Berry looked thoughtful. 'So you're saying your instincts are really your logical conclusions. I trust your logic, but some people think they're being logical when they really don't understand something enough. Would you like to think about this bit of alleged logic?'

'Go on – try me.'

'Let's say the likelihood of someone having a bomb on a plane is a hundred thousand to one, and someone having a tortoise in a bag is five thousand to one, then the probability of both those things happening on the same plane is five hundred million to one. So, if you want to reduce the risk of someone having a bomb on a plane that you're travelling on, from a hundred thousand to one down to five hundred million to one, you should always carry a tortoise in a bag. Do you agree?'

'I hope you're not taking the mickey, DC Beresford. I sometimes wonder if I should demand more respect from you – and others.'

'Don't worry, sir – you get all the respect you deserve.'

'Are you still taking the mickey?'

'No sir; I meant you're fully deserving of respect... I think I should stop talking.'

'I agree. Let's go.'

CHAPTER 28

A Football Referee on Cheating

Priestley knew the "Dog & Hair" by reputation only. It was a Real Ale pub that included its own small brewery – what they called a micro-brewery. Many people assumed the name was spelled "Dog & Hare". The landlord came up with the name based on the idea of people returning for "the hair of the dog that bit them", and was not opposed to the thought of picking up additional trade from anyone into greyhound racing, or members of the country set who were weak on spelling. Though the pub had been in existence for less than five years, its discoloured cream ceiling and dark brown wooden pillars adorned with horse-brasses suggested it had existed for much longer. He and Berry looked into one room and found it empty; they tried a second room and saw a man in his thirties dressed in a dark tracksuit, holding an almost full pint of golden brown beer. Priestley enquired, 'Mr Oxley?'

The man responded with a nod of the head. Priestley handed a twenty pound note to Berry and asked for a pint of the pub's own best-selling brew, and to get something non-alcoholic for himself as he would be on driving duty all evening.

Oxley stood up. 'You must be Detective Inspector Priestley.'

Priestley proffered a hand while adding, 'Actually, I'm now Acting Detective Chief Inspector; I'm using up my old cards – I wouldn't like to be accused of wasting the taxpayer's money.' He glanced briefly around the room. 'It's a while since I've been in a Real Ale pub.'

Oxley sat down again behind a circular table and to one side of the elbow of the red velvet right angled bench seat that ran the length of two sides of the room. Priestley sat on the adjacent side, sufficiently far removed that they would be equidistant from Berry when he occupied the single chair that had been pushed up against the table.

Priestley hoped that chatting in a pub would put Oxley off

guard if he had something to hide, and would make him comfortable with giving as much detail as possible if he had nothing to hide. He decided to kill time with small-talk until Berry was back. 'I tried the mobile number that the school gave me, but it wasn't working.'

'What number was that?'

Priestley recited it.

'That's my old number. I'd better let the school know my new one. I use pay-as-you-go, and when the old phone stopped working, the shop insisted I had to put money on the new number as part of the price, so I couldn't just use the old SIM card. It's a real bind, but what can you do?'

Berry arrived almost immediately with the pint and the orange juice, the landlord having no one else waiting to be served. Priestley introduced him as Detective Constable Beresford; he then re-introduced him as Tony and himself as Marcus. Oxley responded by offering his first name, Clive.

Priestley put off beginning the interview, taking a long pull on his pint and offering his drinking credentials. 'This looks quite a light beer, but it has plenty of body.'

Oxley gave his own assessment. 'I think of it as an autumn pint. Not as light as a true summer beverage, but a long way from a mid-winter variety. I'd say more of a September beer that's been stretched into November. There's a definite hint of apple and a smidgeon of pear in it. The next brewing should be moving onto something heavier and more malty; perhaps a treacly one would be good for December.'

Priestley had never thought of seasonal beers as being sub-classified by months; he decided he needed to move onto the investigation to avoid displaying his relative ignorance of the subject. 'Shall we talk about last Wednesday? On the phone you mentioned you picked up your kit bag and headed straight for the car park. How long did you stay after the match?'

'I went just about straight away. I needed to get off as soon as I could, to do my coaching, but I waited until they'd finished clapping. There's nothing worse for a ref than following a team and for the clapping to stop as soon as he arrives. I didn't think the staff team would have wanted to applaud me for anything, having disallowed them two goals and sent off their best player.'

'So the staff team went into their changing room before you

went down the steps.'

'Yes – I saw the last of them go in. I followed the school team before they turned off to go to their changing room, and I carried on to the car park.'

'Did you see anyone else on the way to your car?'

'No one. The supporters were still by the pitch. It wasn't like a professional club match, where they sometimes drift off before the end to beat the rush when they reckon they know which team's going to win. They all stayed where they were. I assumed they had to wait for the school bell before they could go home.'

'Is there anyone who'll have seen you go?'

'Well, yes and no. A lot of them will have seen me, but your guess is as good as mine when it comes to how many registered that they saw me. It's the same on a football field – a good ref is one who's invisible.'

'Do you see yourself as a good ref?'

'I try to be. It's because there's so many bad refs that I took up refereeing in the first place.'

'Yes, I know what you mean. Match of the Day seems to be more often about the refereeing than the football.'

'Well, you're right about that, but it isn't what I meant. I do find it quite ridiculous that the Premier League doesn't make better use of cameras to put a stop to refereeing errors. They should get rid of traditional referees and assistants and just relay decisions to the players from a small team of umpires who watch the action using cameras and who can do action replays. Instead of stopping games when there's a possible offside, they should let it continue and then decide from an action replay whether it really was offside. It's stupid to let so many results be affected by bad decisions, especially offsides. There's loads of things that could be changed, like having an independent timekeeper and stopping the clock whenever the ball's out of play – waiting for a corner, a throw-in, a free kick, an injury, a substitution – some of which take minutes that refs hardly ever add on in full. I'd even have the clock stopped when somebody's trying to waste time with the ball in the corner. We could have, say, forty minutes of genuine playing time each way, instead of forty-five minutes plus stoppage time. It might put an end to substitutions when there's just seconds left, if they know they're not able to run the clock down that way.'

'It'd look very different to the traditional game, wouldn't it?'

'Changing how the system works can be a good thing, especially if it stops cheating. I really hate it when cheats get away with something. Did you know, in the nineteenth century each team had their own umpire and it was only if they disagreed that it would then go to the referee for a decision? The problem with that system was that the umpires could be really biased; I think it was one named Ibbotson who was probably the worst – he was Blackburn's umpire.'

Priestley remained silent, inviting him to continue by nodding and opening his eyes wider.

'But that wasn't what I meant. I was thinking of my son, Paul, who plays in the local Sysands League.'

Priestley was unsure he had heard correctly. 'Sissons?'

'South Yorkshire, Shawton and North Derbyshire Sunday League, S Y S A N D S League. It goes up to age sixteen. I used to watch my son's team being cheated so many times and I just got more and more annoyed about it. I'm not talking about the players cheating, though there's too much of that; I'm talking about the referees. It isn't like Premiership or Championship matches where the refs look like they're doing their best but sometimes make mistakes. I'm talking about out-and-out cheating.

'What's supposed to happen is that the home team manager arranges an independent ref and pays him a fee. Over the season the cost evens out, as each team plays every other team once at home and once away. One problem is that there's a shortage of qualified refs in the Sysands League, so nobody queries it when a team manager says he couldn't get one. In theory they're supposed to inform the other team manager in good time, to give him the option of arranging one himself. Of course, if they leave it late enough, there's next-to-no chance of finding a spare ref. So the home team manager then says, "We'll let our coach do the reffing." Big problem there: a coach that doesn't referee a match in a way that favours his own team is as rare as rocking-horse shit. I've seen lads know they can get away with anything when it's their coach that's the ref. I once saw a goalie run way, way out of his area and then jump up with his arms outstretched to block a lob. There was nobody else anywhere near the attacker, so the lad would have only had to run the ball into the net. The goalie had clearly denied a goal-scoring opportunity, but the coach – a very small bloke, as I remember – didn't send him off. That sort of cheating is just so obvious, though the ref cheated all through the game in other ways that weren't quite as blatant but were still pretty easy to recognise. I'm surprised the away supporters didn't lynch him at the end.'

Oxley paused to take a long draw on his pint, as though he was washing away his annoyance with that particular irritation. He started again. 'Sometimes the ref's an unqualified supporter of one of the teams, and you can imagine the bias that can come from that. But what I find particularly appalling is that sometimes it's a qualified ref who's doing the cheating. Before the match they all start out with the official statement about declaring their interest in the club, such as brother-in-law of the manager, father of one of the players, and so on. It's as though that declaration somehow means they're intending to do the job fairly, because they've volunteered the information, but the reality is nothing like.'

Priestley thought he saw a flaw in this argument.

'Doesn't that mean that matches you referee for your son's team leaves you open to an allegation of cheating?'

'It would leave me open to an allegation of cheating, Marcus; you're right, it would. Except that I never referee matches that Paul's playing in. I decided that right from the start.'

'Well, what about matches for other teams at your club?'

'You're right again, that also could lead to an allegation of cheating, which is why I don't referee matches for any of the Midshaw teams – that's my son's club. It'd normally be quite inconvenient for ferrying him to his matches and me going to mine, except there's a lot of really good pitches all together at Midshaw, so plenty of clubs hire them for their own home games – you can play much better football on a good pitch. That means I can referee another club's game while Paul plays on a pitch nearby, so I don't usually get any allegations against me about being biased, though I do sometimes get other allegations, like, uh, I must be blind, deaf, stupid – things like that.'

Priestley discovered he was running on empty and Oxley was getting close. He lifted his glass to Oxley. 'Ready for the next one?' Oxley nodded. Priestley turned to Berry. 'Two more, in clean glasses.' Returning to Oxley, he enquired 'Are there many genuinely independent refs like yourself?'

'It depends on what you mean by "genuinely independent". For some refs, the match fee makes a difference to them. They're faced with the prospect of refereeing fairly and not being invited back by the manager, or reffing to favour the team whose manager hired them and so be likely to be asked again. It takes away their independence.

'I said there's a shortage of refs, but it doesn't mean you can always get a game when you want one; sometimes it means a long drive, which you might not want to do, or you might not even be able to do if you've already got another match just before or just after it somewhere else. So refs like to do games near their homes, which of course can be a cause for favouring the home team.

'Some refs cheat in clever ways, trying not to show their bias. One method is to give a few wrong decisions in favour of the away team early on; maybe a couple of throw-ins, perhaps a goal-kick instead of a corner, but nothing that makes a big difference. The away supporters then think the ref's unbiased but accidentally making wrong decisions. When a big decision goes the other way and it's worth a goal to the home team, the away supporters think it's just because he makes lots of wrong decisions, but they don't assume he's actually cheating.'

Priestley barely noticed Berry place the pint glasses in front of them, though his hand automatically found its way to his own.

'Does it make that much of a difference, though? Surely, if one team's quite a bit better than another then they're going to win anyway.'

Oxley's increased animation suggested he was warming to the task of explaining what he perceived were the shortcomings of local football refereeing. 'Listen; let me tell you about one of the matches I saw, that my lad played in. You won't believe me. You'll say it's too far-fetched. But I saw it with my own two eyes.

'The ref was a big bloke, more than just a bit overweight, he must have been six foot two and eighteen stone – the type of bloke that no one's going to argue with, never mind skinny kids. He wasn't very mobile with his knees bandaged up, and he just stood still in the middle of the half where the home team were attacking. I know for a fact that he was the club manager's brother-in-law, because he declared it himself before the kick-off. Let me tell you what he did to get his team to win four-three. He gave them THREE penalties that were all just ridiculous, and the one that they missed he let them take it again because he said the keeper had moved – yes he did move, but only after the shot had been taken – he moved to save it. The goal they scored that wasn't a penalty came from a free kick on the edge of the box, and I could live to be a hundred and still have no idea what he was supposed to have given it for.'

Oxley drained his old glass and started on the new, before continuing. 'Now, do you remember where I said he was standing? He was in the middle of the away team's half. That's because he had just one linesman – they're supposed to be called "assistant referees" nowadays, but everybody still knows them as linesmen. Well, the linesman was also from their club. So every time Paul's team attacked, he flagged them offside. And you wouldn't believe the way the ref screamed at Paul's teammates when they were about to put the ball in the net after each one of the ridiculous offsides had been flagged; he shouted and whistled like his life depended on it. You see, afterwards, if somebody says "we had eight goals disallowed", then everybody smells a rat. But if somebody says "we had eight clear goal-scoring opportunities denied by the offside flag", then people don't realise what was really going on – it's not as obvious, you see, for anyone who wasn't there.

'Our lads scored three goals near the end when they realised their only chance was to do individual attacks starting from inside their own half. They were all scored by one player or another running on his own with the ball and slotting it past the 'keeper, with the rest of the team standing still for fear of the ref coming up with some reason for disallowing it. Now, you say to me, "surely the better team will still win". Well, I tell you Marcus, if that match had been refereed fairly, Paul's team would have won twelve-nil, instead of losing four-three. And that was the match that finally made me decide to become a referee, for the sake of all the kids that deserve a fair deal and aren't getting it. The only problem is, I can't do anything for my own son, as I won't referee his matches, and it's so difficult to find another unbiased ref.'

Oxley stopped and took a long drink, his eyes blazing with the injustice his son had suffered. Priestley took another pull on his own beer, wondering if that was the end of the rant about refereeing, but Oxley had only been pausing for breath.

'I can tell you about other matches where the ref has been cheating.'

Priestley found himself tuning out as Oxley listed the many

examples he had witnessed. He realised Oxley was waiting for him to speak, or at least to nod agreement. 'Say that again, Clive.'

'I was saying another problem is that referees try to apply the rules of the game instead of doing what's fair. Like that Brazilian fourth division match last year when the physio ran on and stopped the other side from scoring; he did a few saves and the ref couldn't award a goal because of the rules. I was talking to somebody in here a while back about it and he said it's like when he was at school in Ecclesfield in the nineteen sixties and some boy who wasn't playing stuck out a foot at an inter-house match and stopped the green team from scoring, and the ref – a teacher – didn't award them a goal; he told it like it was yesterday – he was on the green team. If I'd been the teacher I'd have found some way of getting them a goal to make up for it. What's needed is a wide-ranging rule that says if somebody – even a spectator – cheats in a way that hadn't been thought of in the standard rules, or that applying those rules don't produce a fair result, then the ref can award any decision he likes.'

'That's a lot of power to give to the ref, Clive, though I can see it makes sense. Would it be used very often, do you think?'

'Well, you'd hope that once a ref spots some new type of cheating, they'd fix the rules; I don't see any evidence of it happening, though. Take for example the so-called "professional foul"; you hear ex-players on TV talking about "taking one for the team" when they get a yellow card for doing one, as though a professional foul is something honourable. I can't help feeling there's a lack of morality in some of these ex-players; I don't think ones like that should be allowed to commentate on TV, because they set a poor example for young people. If I see a professional foul, I give a yellow card every time – unless I've a reason to give a red card.

'Then there's top players who're targeted – opponents taking it in turns to crash into them or trip them up; well, instead of the usual let-offs and then yellow cards based only on the players who're committing the offence, I'd also apply a rule that looks at the victim. A first tackle on any player produces a warning, but when there's a second tackle on the same player even if it's by a different opponent, it's a yellow card offence. After that, any player that deliberately smacks into the same opponent gets a red card. I wasn't sure if Howard Webb took that line in a match at the

World Cup when he gave someone a yellow card after their first bad tackle on a star player, but if he did I don't think it was official policy.

'Another thing that annoys me is where someone looks like they're about to take a free kick, but they step over it or run past, and then someone else takes it. I think the Germans set a record in the world cup, with three of them pretending to take a free kick before the fourth one hit it; they looked like they were dancing around their handbags. He fluffed his shot, so it made them look even more ridiculous. That kind of thing could be stopped by having nominated free-kick takers.

'I'm sure there are more things that could be fixed with specific rules, but in the end you can't predict everything that might happen. That's why a rule that gives wider powers to the ref is the best one to have – it could be used to stop any new type of cheating before it takes hold.'

'Maybe every sport should have a rule like that. Take Formula One for example, when somebody's on pole and "accidentally" takes a wrong turn and interferes with everybody else's practice laps so he stays on pole; there's no point in saying he hasn't broken any rule, because that just means they haven't been clever enough at putting the rules together. They should put the driver on the starting grid down to last place out of the current qualifying round, say tenth. They wouldn't even need to prove he'd cheated – it would be enough to say that he'd benefitted from something he did that he wasn't supposed to do. It's the same when someone crashes into an opponent and knocks them out of the race, deliberate or not; the all-powerful rule could be used to transfer a lot of the culprit's points to the victim, say twice twenty-five if the other driver was in the lead at the time. I reckon that general type of rule should be used to deal with any new types of cheating in any sport.'

'That's spot on, Marcus. If they'd had that rule in football it could have been used at the 2010 World Cup finals when Suárez handled for Uruguay against Ghana in extra time; instead of just sending him off and giving them a penalty, they could have given them an actual goal. His action had a big impact in South Africa by getting Uruguay through to the next round, though he made an even bigger impression four years later in Brazil.'

'You mean his two goals against England?'

'I mean his gnashers on Chiellini's shoulder.'

After a round of grins, Oxley continued. 'Maybe we should have official penalty goals for when the ball's on its way into the net, and ordinary penalties for when it isn't. They have penalty tries in rugby, don't they? Rugby has some cheating, like a hand up the jumper to make it look like a ball and then complain to the ref when they get tackled because somebody really thought it was the ball; and they could do with better checking for forward passes, but they're still much smarter than the football authorities when it comes to using cameras. I say cameras rather than technology.

'There was all that palaver about having goal-line technology to fix just one particular problem – checking if the ball has crossed the line. For Premier League matches it's looked reliable, but remember France's second goal against Honduras in the World Cup? I don't believe for one moment it fully crossed the line. The French pundits on the TV programme said it was a goal, but that's hardly surprising; the other commentators weren't convinced. Only FIFA could bring in a computer system that people don't believe.'

Berry interjected. 'In Brazil they were using some German technology, not the British Hawk-Eye system that's used for Premiership matches. The German system had fourteen cameras working at five hundred frames a second, so it ought to have been reliable, but in the end it comes down to humans who program computers. The FIFA spec only required accuracy of plus or minus three centimetres, so what was the accuracy they were actually working to? It wouldn't usually make sense to build something substantially better than the contract specified. Were people really able to claim accuracy down to millimetres? I bet they didn't take into account distortions to the shape of the ball when it collides with something hard, like a goalpost or a boot, but then I don't think the system was built to anywhere near that level of accuracy anyway. Normally, I'd be voting for the technology, but I have to agree with you – I replayed it over and over again on TV and on my computer at home and I just don't believe what the system said – I'm sure it got it wrong. If they fixed the system after that non-goal, I don't expect they'd have announced it wasn't right before.'

Oxley nodded repeatedly. 'Sometimes you just have to believe your eyes, don't you? And my eyes were like yours – they said France shouldn't have been given a goal. It wasn't like in 2010 when Lampard's goal against Germany was disallowed – I think the technology would have got it right in that case, 'cos it was so far over the line, and if it had been two-all at halftime we could have gone on to get a good result.'

Berry laughed. 'If it was the same system they used in Brazil, it might not have given a goal to Lampard. I said it's a German system; they could have programmed it to interpret the data like this.' He spoke in a monotone, in a mock-German style. 'If zee goal is against Chermany zen do not award zee goal; if zee goal is by Chermany zen award zee goal.'

Priestley and Oxley laughed in recognition of Berry's performance, Priestley being especially appreciative, recognising Berry was stone-cold sober.

Oxley quickly resumed his earlier theme. 'The goal-line stuff does nothing about the more common problem of offside errors that also affect the score-line. It does annoy me that the football authorities are proud that ninety-eight per cent of decisions are correct in top matches; instead they should be dissatisfied with themselves for allowing two per cent of decisions to be wrong when it's within their hands to fix all the errors using cameras, especially as that two per cent often includes mistakes that affect the result.'

Priestley was aware Oxley was continuing to elaborate on some aspect of use of cameras, mentioning judo, weightlifting, boxing and badminton, but found he had lost track of Oxley's argument. He told himself to make an effort to concentrate.

Oxley continued, 'But back to football, another thing that could be fixed is when someone gets injured in a foul tackle and has to go off for treatment, or to have blood cleaned up. The innocent team can be left a man short. There should be a rule that says while ever he's off the field, the other team have to lose a man as well. Then, if a team has no substitutes left, they don't end up playing a man light because of what the opponents did, because the other team would also have to lose a man if the injury came from a foul, even if it wasn't a red card offence. I'm not sure how they'd decide who the other team would have to part with, though.'

Priestley saw a parallel and decided he should contribute to the one-sided conversation. 'They could do it like they do in parliament. An MP in the government's party is paired with an MP in the opposition's party, and if one of them can't vote – let's say he's really ill, or away on government business – then the other one in the pair doesn't vote either.'

'I never knew that; it sounds pretty good.'

'Of course, it's voluntary, really, so they could renege – they could go back on the deal.'

'It's a bit dicey, then. In football we have that performance with a drop-ball when someone's injured and the other side kicks the ball out of play to let them get treatment. The ref then directs a player to return the ball, maybe by kicking it out of play, or perhaps knocking it to their 'keeper. When it's left up to the players, sometimes they don't play nice, and that can leave the other team in a poorer position than when they put it out. Occasionally it makes a big difference – do you remember somebody booting the ball to the opponent's 'keeper and it went in the net, so the goal had to stand? Was it Chesterfield in a cup match?'

'That one passed me by.'

'It passed the 'keeper by, too! Anyway, it's ridiculous, a ref having to organise a drop-ball and saying who should do what. I've even seen players take it into their own hands to decide who gets the drop-ball – remember Scotland's opening Euro 2016 qualifier away to Germany? James Morrison and Christoph Kramer did Rock, Paper, Scissors after Marco Reus was injured.

'Whenever there's a stoppage – whatever the reason – the rules should simply allow a ref to award a free kick to either side from where ever he thinks is fair. The ref should be allowed to use his judgment and stop the game any time, whether or not there's a head injury. That's the trouble though, isn't it? Refs are supposed to apply the rules, rather than doing what's fair or sensible.'

Priestley found this struck a chord. 'It's the same with the legal system. The Police and Criminal Evidence Act specifies rules for how to do things right, but if something hasn't been done perfectly it shouldn't mean the evidence has to be thrown out. Lawyers spend their time trying to find the tiniest fault with the way evidence has been collected, and then object to it in court, and the judge has to apply the rules, rather than doing what's fair and reasonable.'

'Well, at least it sounds like the judges are trying to follow the rules. It's not like referees who ignore the rules. I reckon more than half the matches in the Sysands league are refereed by cheats; sometimes they cheat a bit and sometimes they cheat a lot, but you don't find anyone on TV saying there's cheating by referees in grass roots football, do you?'

The term "grass roots football" triggered Priestley's memory of a case where a linesman died of a heart attack as he lay on the grass, having collapsed after being pursued by angry fathers.

Oxley was continuing unabated. 'Commentators on TV don't say what they think when it comes to professional matches, either. I've heard them say things like, "he was just onside" meaning "he was just offside", or "he was clearly onside" meaning "he was clearly offside", or "that's a close decision" meaning "he got it wrong". That's men commentators. I don't know what women commentators say – I always turn off the sound if there's a woman commentating on a live men's match.'

Priestley had previously overheard male colleagues making similar statements about women commentators. Helen used to berate him if he hit the mute button at home, because of the suggestion of sexism it represented. They had reached a compromise: he could mute the sound so long as the children were absent. He decided it would be safer not to reveal his own attitude in front of Berry. He cast around in his mind for something that might counterbalance the gender negativity. 'Some of the men commentators say things that women might be more sensitive about, such as referring to the Iranian players' Christian names at the World Cup. There's also men commentators – usually ex-players – who say that an attacker has a right to go down and claim a penalty if they get even the slightest contact in the box; to me that's not a moral attitude – it's just another form of cheating, and they're encouraging it.'

'Maybe women commentators would be less cynical, but it's only men who've played at the top level that really know what's possible when it comes to conning the ref.'

'Perhaps the men know the top level, but they don't seem to know much about what really happens when it comes to grass roots football. I've never heard anyone on TV talking about cheating by refs like you've just explained it, or by linesmen either for that matter.'

Oxley switched to this aspect of football with barely a pause for breath. 'Don't get me started on linesmen. I don't have them unless they're genuinely independent and there are two of them I can trust. Very few refs in the league use linesmen: the fair refs don't, because the linesmen are likely to be parents who're biased; and the unfair refs don't, because they can interfere with how the ref's manipulating the game.

'The worst I ever saw – and you'll think I'm going back on what I've just said about parents being biased – was one match where I saw a ref who was probably trying to be fair; he had his young teenage son running one line, and let an away team father run the other. I knew the father, and he was someone who was always completely fair whenever he was asked to run a line – you see, there are parents who don't cheat, but the chances of getting two fair ones together aren't high enough for me to risk it for my own matches. Anyway, the referee wouldn't allow this parent to signal offsides. The ref said he'd do them himself for the half of the pitch that he'd camped himself in, whereas his son was allowed to flag for offsides in the other half of the pitch.

'Now, for a start, I think that was really insulting to the father, to say he wasn't to be trusted to flag offsides, whereas the young lad was allowed. But it was worse than that. The ground had what's called "technical areas" marked off, and only the team coaches were supposed to stand in those areas. Well, we all saw this lad flag for an offside that clearly wasn't, so one of the other fathers from Paul's team walked up to the technical area to see what was happening. Not long after, it happened again. What it was, you see, was that their coach was telling the lad to flag for offside when it wasn't, and being just a lad he didn't like to argue with the man – the coach – so he did as he was told. So the father tried to tell the ref what was happening, and the ref refused to listen, and then sent HIM off for complaining – except he wasn't so much complaining as trying to explain. The ref told him he had to leave the area otherwise he wouldn't restart the match.

'So, we had a lad who was doing as he was told by their coach, which meant in effect their coach was being the linesman, and was cheating like mad with it. We had a ref who I think may have imagined himself to be fair but had no idea what was happening and wouldn't listen, and wouldn't correct the wrong offsides because he'd never overrule his son – because it was his son. We had an away team father who wasn't allowed to do the proper job that he could have done. We had another away team father banished to the car park. And after that, we had the lad's mother spitting venom at the father who'd been sent off. I mean sent away, really – it isn't a proper sending off unless you're a player. She was angry at him for complaining about her son for giving wrong offside decisions; maybe she didn't understand the offside rule, otherwise she'd have recognised her son was wrong with his flagging. And all the time their coach was manipulating the lad and the ref and getting away with it. They ended up winning by two goals and should have lost by three.'

Priestley was impressed with the level of detail Oxley was able to recall, as though every moment was seared into his memory. He was also impressed with the beer, and asked if there was a different Real Ale that might be worth trying.

'There's the Nutty Brown. It doesn't do for everybody, but it's a nice pint when you're in the mood for it.'

Priestley took out another twenty pound note and handed it to Berry. 'I'll try a Nutty Brown.' He turned to Oxley. 'Would you like one as well, Clive, or would you prefer another Golden Meadow?'

'I'm supposed to be playing darts in a bit.'

'Tony, do you know how to play darts?'

'Yes, M... Yes, sir.'

'Right, it looks like you're on the team. Clive and I have more to discuss. Is that alright with you Clive?'

'Yes, Marcus. I'll have another Meadow.'

Priestley recalled his earliest childhood football memory, reinforced by repetition over the decades. 'You know the World Cup? There's been some obvious cheating in that, hasn't there? Remember Maradona?'

'Do you mean "Hand of God"? Argentina, 1986.'

'Yes. Because of that one incident I grew up believing football is all about conning the ref. Even now I'd be hard pressed to come up with many names of players who didn't cheat in some way at some time. Off the top I can only think of Gary Lineker.'

'Well, there are plenty of ways of cheating, and not just by individual players. Matches can be fixed by governments, football officials, gambling syndicates, even whole teams. I doubt whether the Algerians will have forgotten – or forgiven – West Germany conveniently beating Austria in a one-nil kick-about in 1982 to get the pair of them through to the second round.'

'Maybe they've stopped doing the Nazi "*Anschluss*" chant, though. It means "union" – they were saying the Germans and

Austrians had joined together to fix the result, just as Hitler had engineered their union in 1938.'

'*Anschluss*? That's a new one on me; I'll add it to my little collection of obscure footballing facts – you never know, it might come up in a pub quiz. There was one good thing came out of the match-rigging, though: FIFA had to change the system for the next tournament, making them play the final matches in any group at the same time. Algeria came pretty close to getting their own back on Germany in Brazil, which is amazing considering what Germany did to Brazil after that, before they went on and won the final.

'I've little doubt there's been plenty of fixes of one sort or another, down the years. You could start with Uruguay in 1930 and probably find something suspicious in every one since then. Some have looked quite blatant, such as in West Germany, Argentina, Spain, Mexico, Italy, South Korea, Brazil. And it can't be a coincidence that so many times it's the host nation's team which benefits.'

'How do you know about any sort of cheating in tournaments that happened before your time? Is it hearsay evidence?'

'You mean am I relying on other people's opinions? Well, I've come to my own conclusions about some of the incidents by watching films of the matches. I've watched a lot of the old World Cup games, and it's amazing what you can see going on in them. Like Gerd Müller in West Germany in the 1974 final, when he ran and jumped on the ground near the ref; appalling cheating really – I'd have sent him off for it, and I reckon the Netherlands would have gone on to win the match. I don't blame the ref for that one, though, and I'm not saying it because he was an Englishman. I think he proved he wasn't biased when he gave Holland a penalty in the first minute, though I think the penalty he gave later to Germany for an attempted trip wasn't quite so clear-cut – maybe he was feeling some home-team pressure; I personally wouldn't have given it. Anyway, the problem with the Müller incident was the stupid rule that said he couldn't do anything about something he didn't see, even though it was caught on camera well enough.

'Nowadays, almost everything's spotted on camera, but the refs still can't use the information. It's ridiculous that there could be a billion people watching a match on TV and they all know what happened because they've just seen the incident from lots of different camera angles, but the one person who isn't allowed to know is the ref – and of course he's the one who really needs to know if he's to make a good decision. You'd have thought that in Brazil, having put the effort into fitting up the goal-line technology, they'd have taken the obvious next step of using cameras to relay to the ref all the information they have available, so he could know about all the things we see at home.'

'What sort of things?'

'To start with, there was the opening match in São Paulo: Brazil v. Croatia. If the ref saw what Neymar did in the first half, why didn't he send him off? Was it because he was trying to favour the home team? Did Neymar think he could get away with anything, because he was Brazil's star player? If I'd been reffing the match, I'd definitely have sent him off.'

'Do you fancy yourself as a World Cup referee then? Isn't there a vacancy? I heard Howard Webb's retired from actual refereeing.'

'He has, though he's still heavily involved in the game. I'd like to be a World Cup referee, but I'm not qualified to anywhere near that level. Our Howard's going to be a hard act for anyone to follow. He did very well in Brazil; he didn't see everything of course, but he was a strong enough ref to be able to make the big decisions. I remember he wouldn't let the Colombians get away with some cheating, where it was their corner and one of them tapped it forward and then conned the other team's players into thinking it hadn't been taken, and then another player sauntered over to take the corner but just ran in with the ball as though the corner had already been taken. Mr Webb gave them a good finger-wagging for that performance and sent them back to start again – for me it was the best single bit of reffing in the whole competition. The Colombians tried it again against Uruguay, and the Dutch ref wasn't having any of it either. Maybe they should have been penalised first time – that way they might not have tried it again. The ref could say the second player took the corner and touched it twice, so it's now a free kick the other way; problem with that is they could claim it hadn't been taken at all in that case, because it wasn't on the quadrant. Anyway, it was Howard who was first to say they couldn't do it.

'He also did really well in the Brazil v. Chile match, though if it had been me I've have given more yellow cards; I suppose he was following FIFA policy, which is why Brazil's Fernandiñho was allowed to get away with four bad fouls without getting booked. The linesmen were faultless – Mike Mullarkey and Darren Cann. Mullarkey was the one who spotted the ball had hit Hulk's upper arm, so Brazil's second-half goal was disallowed. They tried to complain, but the English officials weren't having any of that malarkey.' Oxley chuckled as he added, 'I always say that.'

Priestley asked, 'You've talked about the match before, then?'

'Of course; just after it happened it was one of the things that everybody talked about, until something else came along to talk about.'

'You mean something other than football.'

Oxley looked startled at the idea. 'I mean something else to do with football.'

Berry took the momentary lull to make a contribution. 'I saw that match and I called it a foul by Hulk as soon as it happened, but the other guys I was with didn't believe me at first. It was all to do with the trajectory of the ball. The change of direction could only be achieved by the ball striking a surface that was positioned ahead of the player's chest, which meant it had to be the upper arm. The player would have had to have turned to face the ball more acutely to cause that angle of deflection by contact only with the chest. Maybe someday computer technology will be able to work out that sort of thing and let the ref know.'

Priestley looked at Oxley with raised eyebrows and a nod of the head in Berry's direction, before turning to address Berry. 'You can go back to sleep again, Tony.'

Oxley took his glass in his right hand. 'Here's to the English team – the best team in the tournament. It's just a pity it was the officials and not the players.' He took a long pull, Priestley replicating the action despite his upbringing reminding him that toasting in beer was bad form. After a short pause, Oxley bent down to extract a small black notebook from the sports bag at his feet. Priestley noticed the pages looked well-thumbed. Oxley opened the book near halfway and then turned back a few pages. 'This is what I call my International Refereeing Diary. I recorded and watched all sixty-four World Cup matches and made notes on them. I came up with my own scores based on correct decisions – with the benefit of cameras and slow-motion action replays. I adjusted the scores based on actual events; I subtracted one for an offside goal that was given, and added one for a wrongly disallowed goal, and one for a penalty that should have been given. I couldn't do anything about the scores to register the effects of other wrong decisions such as players not being sent off, goal kicks that should have been corners, and so on. Even without those unknown consequences, you'd be amazed at how different the competition would have been with proper decisions.'

Oxley consulted his notes. 'You know in Brazil v. Croatia, if Neymar had been sent off for his foul on twenty-six minutes, obviously he wouldn't have scored his first goal, which came just a bit later. I wouldn't have given Brazil a penalty either, when Fred slipped or dived – he appealed to the Japanese ref who seemed in a big hurry to award it; somebody described the ref as "inexperienced", in which case why was he given such a big match? I wonder why he was really chosen. Anyway, neither Neymar nor anybody else would have scored for Brazil from that penalty if it hadn't been awarded in the first place.'

Oxley noticed Priestley frowning as though concentrating hard. 'You did see the match, didn't you?'

'Yes, though I didn't keep notes so I can't remember all the details.'

'Well, if Neymar had been sent off like he should have been, the Croatians might have dominated the game and ended up with a big win. But even with just fair decisions based on what actually happened on the pitch, Brazil would still have lost the match. I couldn't see any proper reason why the ref stopped the Croatians from scoring a second goal in the eighty-third minute. The TV commentators were left guessing. Was there a push on the 'keeper? Was there an offside? For me, the answers were no and no, and the ref should have overruled the linesman's flag whatever he claimed had happened, and the goal should have stood. Then it looked like Brazil's third goal came from them getting away with a foul, so I wouldn't have given that either. Anyway, by my reckoning, instead of Brazil winning three-one, they should have lost two-nil – and that's not taking into account that it would have been eleven men against ten from the twenty-sixth minute onwards.

'At the end of the group stage, Mexico would have been top with seven points, having scored five goals and conceded one. Croatia would have been second with six points; seven goals for, two goals against. Brazil in third would have had only four points, three goals for, three goals against. The other changes to the table came from reducing the goals scored in the last two matches – Brazil and Mexico would have had one less each. Cameroon had that dispute about bonus payments, which may have led to match-fixing; but the other three teams would probably have beaten Cameroon anyway, so there would have been no effect on their positions as they were separated by points rather than goal difference. If you take away the three Cameroon results, it would still have been Mexico top, Croatia second, Brazil third.'

'Reducing the goals scored in the last two matches – does that mean you think those games might have been fixed?'

'Not fixed – I didn't see any clear evidence of deliberate bias, though it can be hard to tell if TV doesn't show enough close-ups of particular incidents. I scored the teams of officials out of ten in every match in the tournament – refs and linesmen together, overall performance, but also taking into account score-changing errors such as offsides and penalties that they might not have been able to get right without the help of action replays or other camera shots. For the Croatia v. Mexico match I only gave the Uzbekistan officials a six, mostly because of the offside goal; apart from that they seemed to be just about faultless. For the Cameroon v. Brazil match I only gave the Swedes a six, for the same reason. In both those matches I think the officials did as well as anybody could do without the benefit of replays, so I'm definitely not suggesting they were fixed – quite the opposite, really. Take the Swedish ref: he's a very wealthy guy, so he's never going to be bribed with cash.'

Priestley recalled working with several Swedish Army officers in 2006, part of NATO's International Security Assistance Force that took over responsibility for Mazar-e-Sharif in Afghanistan. He tried unsuccessfully not to remember his subsequent move to Camp Bastion, and an action that led to his swift return to blighty in the August – events that in an older theatre of war might have resulted in a VC, but now qualified him as dangerously reckless. He blew out his cheeks and expelled air slowly to clear that reminder from his head, untravelling the flight from Mazar-e-Sharif to Camp Bastion. After breathing in untarnished air, he responded, 'I think a lot of Swedes are very strong on integrity, anyway, irrespective of wealth – from the ones I've met personally it seems like it's a national characteristic.'

'I don't know any Swedes myself, but you could be right.

SEND OFF SIR

Anyway, what do you think of Brazil finishing third and out of the
competition before the knock-out stage?'

Priestley half-closed his eyes and nodded slowly to indicate he
was giving the matter some thought. 'There'd been lots of people
protesting about the government spending billions on football
when there's so much poverty in the country. Before the first
match kicked off, police in São Paulo were baton-charging
demonstrators, firing rubber bullets and arresting dozens of
protestors. Maybe at that time the authorities believed there could
be riots across the country if Brazil didn't win their first match.
Perhaps the match officials had been instructed in advance to make
sure Brazil won, even if it meant ignoring the laws of the game.
Inter arma silent enim lex – in times of war the law falls silent.
Remember the *Zeitgeist*: there were civil wars developing around
the world – Ukraine, Iraq, Syria.'

'Remember the what?'

'Oh, sorry, the *Zeitgeist* – it's German – it means the spirit of
the age.'

'And what was the other stuff?'

'A bit of Latin – based on something Cicero said.'

'He was born in São Paulo, wasn't he? I think he played for
São Paulo before he went to Santos; I don't know who he plays for
now.'

'I meant the ancient Roman bloke.'

'I knew that – I was just joking.' Priestley chuckled lightly,
thinking it was expected of him, but was uncertain whether Oxley
really knew. Oxley paused to allow Priestley's chortle to run its
course. 'So, are you saying it's alright to fix matches if you think it
might prevent rioting? Does it mean the authorities thought the
Brazilian people didn't have enough moral fibre to be able to take
a first round defeat without turning to mob violence?'

'I wouldn't like to say, really – some people are very intense
when it comes to football. Just look at the country's reaction as a
whole when they were thrashed by Germany. And there was some
mob violence in Buenos Aires after Argentina lost the final; the
police had to use water cannon, rubber bullets and tear gas, and
made dozens of arrests.'

'Well, when you put it like that. I've met quite a few people in
this country who're really intense about football.'

Priestley remained silent as he thought, 'And you don't include

365

yourself in that category?'

Oxley proposed another theory. 'Maybe it was just a matter of keeping the hosts in the tournament to keep ticket sales high – that'd fit with how the second match in their group went. Mexico should have been two-nil up against Cameroon in the first half-hour – a linesman flagged two offsides that weren't. If it stayed nil-nil then that would keep Mexico's points down, and if they eventually won the match like they were expected to, then at least it would have kept their goal difference down. Brazil only won their group on goal difference, so you have to wonder whether FIFA rigged the first two matches for Brazil's benefit, which is funny if Cameroon were trying to rig their own games to lose them – it would show a ref's rigging trumps players' rigging.

'Brazil's second match was against Mexico and it was a nil-nil draw. There weren't really any opportunities to make game-changing decisions; I don't know what might have happened if there had been.'

'Surely, FIFA wouldn't ever rig matches?'

Oxley grinned. 'Not while ever they're headed up by Sepp Blatter, Mr Integrity himself.' Priestley joined Oxley in side-splitting laughter. Berry attempted to appear just as amused, wondering if they had reached that state of inebriation where everything seems hilarious.

Priestley suggested, 'Perhaps Mr Blatter sees match-rigging that favours the host as a reward for them paying out billions to prepare for the tournament. It's hardly as though anyone can do much about it. FIFA officials have something akin to diplomatic immunity; any country bidding to act as hosts has to sign away their sovereignty as far as the officials are concerned, so they can get away with anything.'

'I wonder if we'll have to wait until Blatter's dead before people can say exactly what they really think of him.'

'Waiting until he's dead is the best way of avoiding libel, but it can often leave injured parties feeling like someone got away with something. I don't know how committed FIFA are, as a whole, to stopping match-fixing by organisations other than FIFA. I was told FIFA employ just a handful of people to investigate match-fixing, which isn't many, considering the size of the problem. I wondered what we – the police – should have been allowed to do about Nigeria's World Cup warm-up match against Scotland that everyone knew in advance had been fixed. Maybe the game should have been cancelled.'

'I remember the Nigerian goalkeeper threw the ball into his own net. Wasn't it interesting that the ref disallowed the goal and awarded a free-kick? It did occur to me the ref might have been cleverly unfixing a fix.'

'That sounds like you think there can be good reasons for referees to ignore the rules and do some fixing of their own: to stop players from fixing matches.'

'Well, when it coming to fixing matches, referees are in a league of their own.' Oxley laughed at his perceived pun, Priestley joining him, with Berry trying to sound amused.

Berry asked Oxley, 'How many of the last World Cup's matches do you think might have been fixed?'

Oxley consulted his notebook. 'We all know about Cameroon. I didn't see any obvious fixing in any of the other group stage matches apart from Brazil's group.'

Priestley asked, 'What about biased refereeing?'

'A bit of bias is much harder to recognise, because it can be just a difference of opinion or interpretation of incidents.'

'What sort of bias do you think you might have seen?'

'Well, there's the question of giving yellow cards; Brazil seemed to live a charmed life as far as they were concerned. FIFA's guidelines may have resulted in fewer yellow cards for all the teams, but sometimes it seemed like Brazil were allowed to get away with an amazing number of fouls that I'd have given yellow cards for. Take Brazil v. Colombia for instance: I'd have given three yellow cards to Brazilians in the first half, two of them to Fernandiñho. I'd have given another six to Brazil in the second half, except that two more were for Fernandiñho who obviously would have been sent off in the first half. When a Brazilian finally received a yellow card in the sixty-fourth minute, I wasn't sure if it was for the foul or for kicking the ball into the net after the whistle had gone – if it was for kicking the ball, you have to ask whether the ref and FIFA shouldn't get their priorities sorted out.

'It was ironic that the Colombian James Rodriguez was booked for a slightly mistimed tackle in the sixty-seventh minute, as he'd been targeted for heavy tackles right throughout the game because he was Colombia's best player; I'd say he was probably the best player in the whole tournament, even though the Golden Ball went to Lionel Messi – perhaps that was a sympathy vote for losing the final. Rodriguez won the Golden Boot despite Colombia going out in the quarter-finals – otherwise he might have scored even more goals.

'The ref had no real choice but to give Colombia a penalty in the seventy-seventh minute, though he only yellow carded the goalie, whereas some refs might have red carded him. If the ref was trying to help the Brazilians by letting them get away with so many bad fouls, then you'd have to say what goes around comes around, as it was one by a Colombian on Neymar that took him out of the tournament, and could even have put an end to his playing career. If it was FIFA's policy that led to so many Brazilians not being yellow carded, and if a reaction to that was the foul on Neymar, then the policy was obviously wrong; but if it was home-team bias, then that's a different FIFA issue.'

'With views like that, I don't see FIFA inviting you to referee any of their matches, Clive.'

'Too right.'

'Did you notice any incidents where it wasn't down to interpretation of the rules or FIFA guidelines – things that were definitely errors by officials?'

'Well, there were some errors that came about because the officials didn't have the benefit of seeing slow-motion and action replays, so you can't necessarily blame the referees for those – though you could blame FIFA. If I applied the same principle to World Cup matches as I do to the Sysands League, I wouldn't allow myself to referee the matches in England's group – to avoid any allegations of bias. But when I watched matches from England's group I reffed them anyway – and came up with some good news. I'd have given England a penalty against Costa Rica, which would have meant England would have come third, above Italy on Goals Scored – always assuming they actually converted the penalty, which isn't something you could say for definite in view of the team's past record. I'd have made three different decisions affecting Costa Rica's goals against Uruguay, two for and one against, so that result would have been four-one instead of three-one to Costa Rica. I was OK with the other four matches, so Costa Rica would still have come top, but on Goal Difference.

'If I include all the forty-eight first round matches, I reckon there were twenty-eight where I agreed with the goals awarded. In the other twenty, one had the right score because of two compensating errors, and eleven had the wrong score but the right result in terms of win, draw, lose. There were three draws that should have been win-lose, and three win-lose that should have been draws. That leaves two where the winning side should have been the losing side: Brazil should have lost to Croatia, and Ecuador should have lost to Honduras.'

'Have you any idea what effect all of that would have had on positions in the tables and who would have qualified for the next round?'

'I've worked out all eight revised tables, so I know what all the alterations would have been. There were two changes to minor places: England overtaking Italy, and Honduras going above Ecuador. The only definite change to qualification was that Brazil would have dropped to third and been out in the first round. Apart from that, Bosnia and Herzegovina might have qualified – they'd actually have had to draw lots with Nigeria for second place in Group F. They would have had the same Goal Difference, the same Goals Scored, and their head-to-head I scored as a one-all draw.'

'Are you saying that, apart from Brazil's group, there weren't any fixed matches? That other wrong results were just down to mistakes by officials?'

'It can be difficult to recognise the difference between honest mistakes and biased decisions.' Oxley turned several pages. 'Brazil v. Germany started like there was some bias in favour of Brazil. It was on just thirty-six seconds that Brazil was given a corner when it was clearly only a throw-in. In the eighth minute, a free kick to Brazil could have been given the other way as a penalty to Germany. In the ninth minute there was a tug by a Brazilian, then there was a slip, but a free-kick was given against Germany. When Germany scored in the eleventh minute, there was nothing contentious about it so it had to be allowed. In the seventeenth minute a Brazilian dived in the German penalty box, but the referee only gave a corner, so I think that indicates he wasn't blatantly intending to fiddle the result. There was a foul by Brazil in the twentieth minute that wasn't given, so it still felt like there could be a bit of bias.

'But then the German onslaught came, and it was four-nil just after twenty-five minutes into the game, so the officials and anyone watching would have known what the eventual result was going to be. In fact, in the twenty-eighth minute there was another Brazilian dive, just outside the penalty box; the referee didn't buy it, though I think he should have started booking players for diving. But he wasn't even booking players for red-card offences – in the half-time review on TV it looked like David Luiz had got away with two of those. With another German goal in the twenty-ninth minute, making five-nil by half-time, I wondered what the Brazilians would do in the second half. Their only tactic seemed to be to dive in the box – I counted three more, and again the referee was right not to give them penalties, but he still wasn't giving yellow cards; I'd have given Brazil another four yellow cards in the second half, as well as the one he actually gave.

'After the match, with the score seven-one, pundits were saying how totally unexpected it was. But if you look back, they shouldn't have made it out of the group stage, and they only squeaked past Chile in a penalty shoot-out. When they played against Colombia, it looked like a bit of bias when they were given a very doubtful free kick outside the penalty area in the third minute, but the main benefit they had was not getting yellow cards. By the sixty-second minute they'd racked up nine unpunished yellow card offences, and the Colombians were clearly getting increasingly frustrated with the referee. Then a Brazilian stepped across the goalkeeper in the sixty-fourth minute; it was as though they thought they could get away with anything. What with that and then putting the ball into the net after the whistle, Brazil could have had another two yellow cards, but they only collected one. When Rodriguez was booked in the sixty-seventh minute it certainly had all the smell of bias. If you also consider Colombia's disallowed goal for offside when the ball had actually come off David Luiz's back, and in the eighty-first minute a linesman flagging for an offside that wasn't, you'd have to seriously consider whether at least one of the officials was determined to stop Colombia from beating Brazil. So, was it a genuine interpretation of FIFA guidelines that benefitted Brazil, and were there honest mistakes or biased officials? All I can say is, I gave the officials a collective none out of ten. If I'd been reffing the match, Brazil wouldn't have been able to get away with their bully-boy tactics, and I expect Colombia would have won the match.

'So, to my mind, Brazil didn't deserve even to get through the first round, and certainly not through to the semis. When they came up against a well-drilled team, should everyone really have been surprised they got thrashed?'

Priestley hesitated a moment. 'Well, perhaps a lot of people were like me, and had some niggling feeling that home teams do sometimes get benefits from officials, so they didn't expect any other team to be allowed to put so many past them.'

'At least those benefits didn't enable them to make it to the final, which would have really spoiled things for me, so in that sense it's a big improvement compared to certain previous tournaments. Take 1978 for example. Anybody with even half a brain – half a footballing brain – knows that the 1978 tournament in Argentina was fixed, and I don't just mean Argentina six Peru nil – though it's obvious when players have been ordered to lose.

'In Brazil, apart from Cameroon's Alex Song deliberately doing something to get himself sent off against Croatia, I didn't see any clear evidence of players trying to pick up yellow or red cards – though that might have more to do with FIFA's guidelines on issuing cards and knowing what they might get away with. In that same match, I thought it looked a bit suspect when the Cameroon goalkeeper pushed the ball to a Croatian for an easy goal. I thought it was very interesting that two Cameroon players had a physical disagreement during the match. Was one trying to win the match and the other trying to lose it? I'm just guessing, really.

'On the whole, I'd say players showed their passion and desire to win throughout the tournament, though obviously the Ghana team didn't look quite so committed when they demanded three million dollars be flown in to pay them before their final group match; but that might have had more to do with stopping other people from skimming off some of the money they were due. Cameroon and Nigeria were also demanding money up front, and Nigeria may even have been up to their old match-fixing tricks as well. But if you look at the other teams, you could see tons of passion on the field; it's what makes football such a great game. Sometimes there's a bit too much passion, like Suárez for example, but generally, the players looked like they were doing their best.

'When you have players who're committed to winning, the only way a match can be fixed is through the referees. You'll know better than me, Marcus, what methods can be used.'

371

'Bribery, blackmail, coercion – there's plenty of varieties.'

'Try this for size. "There'll be a massive grain shipment to your country if we win by at least four goals." Or what about, "You won't get out of the country alive if you don't make sure we win." You can guess where they came from.'

Priestley sang the first five words of 'Don't cry for me Argentina', *sotto voce*, Oxley nodding repeatedly in agreement throughout the performance.

Oxley waited until he was sure Priestley had finished singing. 'There are more varieties. "We know where your family live and we'll be paying them a visit, unless!" Or, "Here's the number of a Swiss Bank Account, and all you have to do is give us a bit of help." A similar one I've heard of is, "I'd like to lend you a lot of money, and you don't have to pay it back unless you want to." Or perhaps the most subtle, "You know why you're being appointed to referee this particular match – prove to me you understand without us having to talk about it." I'm sure there's plenty more varieties.

'If FIFA want to make every result fair – and that's a big "if" – then they need to drop the idea that a few refs and assistants can spot everything that happens. They need to invest in a system for refs to view the game on monitors with access to multiple camera shots and slow-motion replays. It would help to stop bribery and the like if the ref's identities weren't known; they could be chosen at random, and could view matches away from the stadium so no one sees who they are. They could even change the refs every ten minutes if they liked, so that no one ref could engineer a match result.'

'I noticed in the Commonwealth Games they had five judges in the boxing but only three counted, and they were selected randomly by computer. I'm pretty sure I spotted some bias, though it could mostly have been down to judges favouring boxers that kept coming forward irrespective of how many punches they received compared to how many they landed. But the system appeared to work most times, with the difference being the better boxer won on a split decision instead of three-nil. With football they could select at random from a huge number of judges instead of just three from five. All the viewers who were independent of the teams could see action replays on television and vote for what they think the decision should be.'

'Just when I thought I'd heard every idea there is, I hear a new one. That's brilliant, Marcus. You can't bribe millions of people.'

'Well, you can try, but you only get the chance once every five years – they're called General Elections. Just look at what Gordon Brown's tactics were.'

Priestley turned to Berry. 'Keep 'em coming, Tony. And when you come back, you can give us your analytical assessment of the World Cup.' He handed over his empty glass.

Oxley put his hand over the top of his glass, signifying he was declining another pint. He then stayed silent, not wishing Tony to miss out on the fascinating topic they were discussing.

When Berry returned with the beer, Priestley took it straight from his hand rather than waiting for him to place it on his beermat. After a long swallow he turned to Berry. 'Now then, Tony, give us some of that relentless logic of yours.'

Berry sat down before beginning. 'Have you heard of Philippe Blatter? He's the nephew of Sepp Blatter. He runs a company called Infront, which is a shareholder in Match Hospitality. Match Services is one of FIFA's ticket and hospitality partners; you remember its boss Ray Whelan and the ticket tout scandal that broke in Brazil, where the police claimed it also related to four previous tournaments. How many do you get when you put two and two together?'

Priestley gave a single nod to the rhetorical question, so that Berry would continue.

'Then there's the fact that FIFA awarded some TV rights to Infront for the next two World Cup tournaments, though I don't know if their 2022 contract will be scrapped – there's a different type of corruption allegation relating to Qatar. FIFA claim to have investigated, but they're not going to let anybody know their findings. So, hands up anybody who thinks there's no corruption at the top of FIFA?'

Priestley slowly and deliberately folded his arms, Oxley following suit. Berry continued. 'Hands up if you think there won't be any corruption in the next tournament?' The audience of two remained unmoving. 'So, the only question is: what type of corruption? Clive has already explained about past ones, which leaves the question of what varieties we might expect in the future. Clive, how has Russia done in the past?'

'They've never made it out of the group stages, though the Soviet Union reached the semis back in 1966.'

'So, based on past performance, you wouldn't expect to see Russia make it out of the group stage. Who thinks they'll make it further in 2018?'

Priestley unfolded his arms and raised his right hand, with the accompanying words in eager schoolboy style, 'Me, sir.'

Oxley offered a lengthier response. 'FIFA is in a position to engineer results without resorting to bribery – I expect there are refs who'd do anything for the chance to referee a really top match. But if it did just come down to bribery, it would certainly make more sense to target the officials than the players. Nowadays some players are paid a small fortune, so bribing them would be very expensive. There's also the pride that so many of them have in playing for their country; they might just refuse to go along with it – except if their families are threatened, or some other sort of pressure is put on them. Agreeing to throw a full international just for money could be out of the question for many players, though some of them might be willing to fix a friendly.'

Priestley asked, 'Refs don't get paid a fortune, do they? So, if it is just straightforward bribery, then they should be cheaper targets.'

Oxley recalled a case of financial inducement. 'There's no comparison between the wages a player gets nowadays and what a ref's paid. Back in 1984 the average pay of a top tier player was nearly twenty-five thousand pounds – that's per year, which is less than many get per week nowadays. Back then, it took a bribe of twenty-seven thousand pounds by Anderlecht to get a referee to cheat Nottingham Forest out of a place in the UEFA Cup final. If someone wanted to bribe a ref with the average pay of a Premier League player nowadays, it would cost them more than a million.

'As you go further down the scale, players are paid less, but so are referees. At any level it's always got to be cheaper to bribe a ref, as you might otherwise need to bribe nearly a whole team to guarantee a result. By the time it reaches my level, the bribes aren't much more than beer money.'

'So how much is a bribe at your level, Clive?'

'Fifty quid, apparently.'

Priestley found himself sobering up with this revelation. He nodded his head a little too vigorously as he encouraged Oxley to continue – not that he felt Oxley would need much encouragement.

'Not that I've ever taken a bribe, but I was offered one last Wednesday at the school. Mr Newhouse, the one who died, tried to give me a brown envelope with fifty quid in it. At first he made it sound like it was just a match fee, except I'd volunteered to do it for nothing, being for the school. Then he came on with how it would look bad for the teachers to lose, because they needed to be blokes that the kids could look up to, and how could they look up to them if they'd just beaten them in a football match. I told him straight, I went into refereeing because I wanted to see matches reffed fairly and that's what I was going to do. After that the other players came in, so I collected up my kit in my bag and went outside to inspect the pitch. That's why I didn't need to go back into the changing room at the end of the match – I'd taken my kit with me.'

Priestley turned to Berry. 'Did you get that, Sergeant.'

Berry frowned, unsure how to respond. He eventually answered, 'I'm a Detective Constable, sir, unless you're promoting me in the field.'

Priestley accepted the error. 'Slip of the tongue, Tony. Now get me another one of these, will you? Clive, what will you have?'

'It'll have to be my last. Let me get these Marcus.' He took out his wallet.

Priestley pushed away Oxley's hand and wallet. 'This is Tony's round; he was a naughty boy today.'

Oxley grinned at Priestley. 'What's he been up to?'

Priestley stumbled over his words. 'He's been telling tales out of school.'

Oxley tutted. 'There was a naughty girl at school last week, though I don't know if she'd been telling tales. She was running home before the bell had gone. I saw her when I was driving through the school gates after the match.'

Priestley nodded. 'Yes. I heard about it.' He turned to Berry. 'You'll be driving me home later, won't you my friend?'

Berry sighed theatrically. 'Driving or carrying, I'd guess.'

A man with a beer-belly came over to Oxley to say the darts match was about to start. Oxley explained with a broad smile, 'I'm helping the police with their enquiries. This policeman says he'll stand in for me.'

Priestley told Berry to get him another pint before he played in the darts match. While Berry was playing darts, Priestley took a comfort break and returned via the bar, where he bought another pint.

Priestley turned his head to look in the direction of the darts match; he could see the players but was unable to see the board. Oxley was giving Priestley a throw-by-throw account of past successes and failures by the pub team when Berry returned. 'I'm sorry, Clive, I've let the side down – in a way.'

'Don't worry about that – you could only do your best.'

'That's the trouble – I did my best, and we won. The other team accused me of being both sober and a ringer – I'm not sure which they thought was the greater offence.'

Priestley nodded. 'Sobriety is undoubtedly an offence in a pub, Tony, but not in the home – you should hear my wife on the subject.'

Berry noticed how Priestley looked to have headed past the glassy-eyed stage of drinking and was now heading for the comatose. As he himself was not permitted to have a beer, he decided on a course of action to rescue his mentor from enjoying any more. He went outside and telephoned Priestley's home phone number. 'Mrs Priestley?'

Professor Helen Priestley hesitated before allowing the incorrect form of address. 'Yes?'

The conversation tiptoed back and forth. 'This is Detective Constable Beresford. Tony. Yes, we have met. No, Helen, there's no problem. Everything's fine. I'm fine. Marcus is fine. His car's fine. He's not available to come to the phone right now. I think he's gone to the loo. We're in a pub. I'm doing the driving for him. My car's fine. I wanted to make sure there was someone at home in case he couldn't find his house keys. No, I don't know if he's lost his keys; it's just that he may not be able to find them. Well, yes, they probably are in his pocket, but it isn't somewhere I should be looking. Of course you're right, Helen, he should be looking in his own pockets, but he may not find them.'

Helen asked for clarification. 'May not find the keys in his pocket?'

'May not find his pockets. He's had a few drinks. Well, several. It's a bit awkward for me to ask him direct. Do you think you could phone him and tell him to come home? And if he doesn't answer his phone, call me back on mine and I'll pass it to him.'

Berry went back into the pub and sat near to Priestley. The call came through straight away. After locating the pocket with the phone, Priestley answered the call. 'Helen, my love, how nice of you to phone me at work.' ... 'Yes, it sounds like a pub. It also looks like a pub because it is a pub and I'm working here. I've had a very interesting conservation with my friend Clive.' He nodded and smiled at Oxley, who nodded only with his eyes as his head seemed unwilling to make the movement. 'No, I'm sure I said con-ver-sa-tion.' ... 'Well if you're sure I didn't then I'm sure you're right, that you heard the word con-ser-va-tion, even though the word I spoke was con-ver-sa-tion.' ... 'Very well Helen, if that's what you say then that must be true because you're always right.' ... 'No, I didn't mean it like that. I only meant that you're always ... not wrong.' ... 'I don't know where this ... talk is going.' ... 'Yes, we can talk some more at home. Tony is driving today, this evening.' ... 'He doesn't need to know the way; I'm here to navigate.' ... 'Yes, just a minute.' He passed the phone to Berry.

'Yes, I know the way.' Berry passed the phone back to Priestley.

'We are leaving now. Goodbye; I shall see you soon, my darling.'

Oxley declined Berry's offer of a lift. Priestley raised himself on unsteady legs. Berry walked slowly behind Priestly, opened a rear door for him and put the seat belt in place around him. They travelled in silence and arrived at Priestley's home, where Helen opened the outer, inner and living room doors, insisting Berry enter with her husband. She asked Berry, 'How many has he had?'

Berry felt more than a little awkward, talking about his boss as though he were not there. 'I couldn't say. I was playing darts for some of the time.'

Priestley admonished Berry. 'Never add unnecessary detail to your story, Tony. Keep it simple – do not offer additional information – that way there's less chance of you being caught out in a lie.'

Helen ignored Marcus and spoke again to Berry with a hint of a smile. 'I may have to start giving you instructions on how many he's allowed.'

Marcus tried again to be heard. 'You must follow her orders, Tony, to the letter and without questioning them; the orders of she who must be obeyed.'

Helen spoke very quietly to Berry. 'It isn't good for him to have too many.'

Marcus interrupted again. 'Put the sound on, will you? It's the weather forecast.'

Helen picked up the remote control; she pressed a button and the mute symbol disappeared from the corner of the screen. A woman explained what was to be expected the next day, using a continuous stream of words that Tony followed with only limited success, Marcus failing entirely. Helen pressed the mute button again. Marcus asked her, 'What did she say? What's happening tomorrow?'

Helen turned to Marcus with a hint of exasperation. 'She said there'll be some rain and no sun tomorrow.'

Marcus reacted as though this news was devastating. Initially aiming for monosyllabism so as to avoid words that might disintegrate into their constituent parts, he wailed, 'Do you mean the sun will cease to exist? But if there's no sun, then there'll be no warmth for the world.'

At this point in Marcus's little oration, Helen indicated to Tony with a tip of her head, a downturned mouth and the brief compression of her eyelids, that she had heard it all before. Marcus continued boldly, 'We're doomed to live on an increasingly cold and in-hos-pit-able planet, with an in-ev-i-ta-ble end to all life as the stored food and energy supplies diminish and are finally consumed.' His crescendo culminated with a triple-f: 'We're all going to die!'

At the end of the speech Helen snapped at Marcus, 'Keep it down – they're asleep.' Then she turned to Tony and asked in a honeyed voice, 'Would you like a coffee? I'll be making some anyway.'

Berry declined, wished them a goodnight, and headed out with haste that bordered on the unseemly. In the car he wondered whether he could justify phoning Susan, but decided he should not run the gauntlet of her questions in case he let slip something about what had just been happening.

CHAPTER 29

Lesson on Greek Mythology

Wednesday

Berry arrived early for the eight o'clock meeting and took his preferred seat at the right of the head of the narrow, boat-shaped, beech-veneered table in the small conference room he had previously reserved. Witty and Martello arrived slightly ahead of time. Priestley, someone who would regularly complain whenever anyone arrived late to a meeting, walked in at three minutes past. He began, 'Yes, I know what I've said before. Three minutes late, four people, that makes twelve minutes lost. I had to have two shaves this morning, so I took three minutes longer to get ready for work.'

Witty asked, 'Why two shaves?'

'I knew someone would ask. I always have an electric shave at night so I don't bristle the missis, and a wet shave in the morning to look smooth. I didn't do the electric one last night, so I did it this morning without thinking. Then I had to do the wet one because it's smoother; and anyway, the morning shave is when I have some of my best ideas.'

'If you don't mind my saying so sir, rather than looking smooth I'd say you look a bit rough, and I'm not just talking about your bristles.'

'Well, thank you for saying so, Neil; you're too kind.' Turning to Berry he added, 'I didn't come in the car this morning – my wife brought me in. You can be my driver again.'

Witty asked, 'Again?'

'Yes, again. Yesterday evening Tony acted as my driver as I undertook a difficult mission to extract information from the school football match referee. Tony, would you like to paraphrase that?'

Berry decided to play it for all it was worth. 'Acting DCI Priestley courageously undertook to drink the referee under the table so that he would spill the beans.'

Witty enquired, 'And did he?'

Priestley responded with a heavy sigh, 'I don't know if he spilled the beans, but I certainly did when I got home. Helen told me I'd have to clear it up myself next time.'

Smiles ricochet around the room amid expressions of sympathy.

Witty persisted, 'But did he talk?'

Priestley sighed heavily, 'Oh yes, he talked alright. The difficulty was getting him to shut up.' He straightened himself in his seat to suggest the start of the meeting proper. 'The referee, Clive Oxley, explained the mystery of the fifty pounds. It was, in essence, an unsuccessful attempt by John Newhouse to bribe him into helping the teachers to win the match. End of story. I see no reason to upset his family and friends by revealing this; would you agree, Tony?'

'Yes, definitely. Susan is upset enough without knowing about that.'

'All members of the family, Tony, are to be treated with the same consideration.'

'Yes, of course. I understand.'

Priestley picked up the next thread. 'Mr Oxley also mentioned having seen a girl running from the school prior to the normal end-of-day. You obtained testimony from a bird-watcher who saw a girl running along the public footpath that skirts the school grounds at the top of the sports field. As she didn't reappear further along the path, he assumed she'd entered the school through the gate that's set into the fence. We have an elderly woman who was sitting looking through her front window and saw a girl running along the road at the other side of the school grounds and in the vicinity of the school's main gate, again before the rest of the schoolchildren had been let out. If these sightings are of the same girl, then we can join them up and ask ourselves what she did between entering the school grounds at the top of the field and exiting at the other side of the school. That route would have taken her past the girls' changing room block where Mr Newhouse met his end.'

Witty highlighted a restriction on this route. 'The gate at the top is kept locked, and is only unlocked by members of staff to let in children who have been doing cross-country running. So there must be someone on the staff who can tell us who the girl is; that's if it was the same girl.'

Next, Witty placed on the table the photographs of the three girls who had been at the funeral. 'We also need to identify these girls, and to interview them if appropriate.'

Berry added, 'They all looked very young; I'd estimate fifteen to seventeen. They'd need a parent or guardian with them.'

'That's quite a precise estimate. Are you an expert – have you observed lots of girls in that age range very closely? Be careful how you answer.'

Berry tried unsuccessfully to stop himself from reddening. 'I could be wrong about the ages; I should have said "guestimate". They were wearing makeup as well, which can be misleading for … guessing ages.' Priestley nodded at Berry in acknowledgement.

Priestley asked 'AOB?' No one put forward any other business, so he stood up to indicate the meeting was over. He turned to Martello, 'You're very quiet today Lily; everything OK?'

She adopted her ready-for-anything look. 'Yes, everything's just great.'

Priestley indicated he was unconvinced, by responding, 'Well, tell me about it whenever you're ready. For now, I need you at the school if we're to be interviewing girls.' He turned first to Witty and then to Berry as he added, 'You two can get on with your other work, but be ready to join us if necessary.'

* * *

Priestley and Martello arrived at the school and went to Oaken's office. He asked if she could identify the girls in the photograph. In view of her helpfulness on the inquiry to date, he was initially taken aback by her response. 'I do know who they are. All three are my students, but I have no intention of revealing their identities to you. Mr Verbane recognised them at the funeral and reported them to me yesterday. I have spoken to them, so the matter has been dealt with.'

Priestley had not previously seen this feisty version of her. He responded, 'With respect, Miss Oaken, we need to interview whomever we believe we should interview, in the furtherance of the investigation.'

She remained unflinching. 'Ah yes, that "with respect" says it all. You say "with" but you mean "without". You're refusing to respect my judgement in the matter.'

Priestley decided to take a placatory line. 'Perhaps if you could explain to me in more detail how you reached your judgement, I could consider whether to accept your point of view.'

'Very well; this is how it is. I'd had strong suspicions for months about the inappropriate behaviour of Mr Newhouse with female students. Back in September I interviewed on a one-to-one basis several girls I strongly suspected of being victims of his, but they all refused to speak out, so I was powerless to do anything about it.

'When Mr Verbane came back from the funeral he told me there'd been three of our girls there. He'd previously supported my recommendation to ban all students from attending, so that made it a serious disciplinary offence – not just truancy but also going against the Headmaster's orders. As they're girls, he left it with me to deal with the matter. I thought it was very likely they were more of Mr Newhouse's victims, so I contacted their parents and told them their girls had been playing truant and I wished to see the girls about it straight away. I made it clear to the parents that they could also attend if they wished, but I didn't mention to them where the girls had been seen – only that they'd been missing.

'At five thirty all three girls presented themselves to me here. None of their parents came, which at first I thought was quite surprising, but my guess is the girls talked them out of coming to school with them.

'I had the three of them in my office together rather than separately. I told them what I believed had been happening. I explained about the police inquiry and how the best chance of not having their identities revealed to the press would be if they told me everything there and then, so that I could speak to the police on their behalf if necessary. I now know what happened to them, and I can't go back on my word to keep it to myself.'

Priestley felt a need to speak up in defence of the police force. 'I'm sure we have no intention of revealing their identities to the press.'

Oaken responded with a thickening of her voice that spoke of bitterness and anger. 'Just as you had no intention of revealing the identity of our lovely Hugh.'

Priestley felt guilt well up inside him – there was no denying the police's collective responsibility for that death. He offered a lame response. 'We never intended to reveal Hugh Cassidy's identity – it was the press who found out without us telling them anything.'

Priestley had not observed Cassidy's fallen body, so his mind's eye offered others that he had seen. Three comrades lay unmoving in the desert, leaving only him and one other alive to say what had happened; and seventeen dead insurgents, with no survivors left breathing to tell it differently. Camp Bastion was in that place Alexander the Great rightly called the Desert of Death; the blood from all twenty had looked just the same, as it seeped into the orange-red dust. He expelled the air from his lungs to expunge the remembrance, though unable to wipe clean the original slate.

Oaken would not be moved. 'The road to perdition is paved with good intentions. With respect, Mr Priestley, I do not believe the police as a whole can be trusted to protect the girls well enough for me to give them over to your tender mercies. This is not a criticism of you personally, but of the police force taken together in its entirety; it only needs one bent copper, to use the old expression, for any good work of the others to be undone. That's why I have no intention of revealing the girls' identities.'

Priestley recognised the validity of Oaken's argument and the sincerity of her belief. 'We could identify them without your help if we had to, but I'd rather work with you on this as you know facts that they might be unwilling to reveal to the police. Perhaps, if you wouldn't mind explaining in more detail, we could dispense with interviewing them ourselves.'

'I accept you need to know enough to make your assessment, but do I have your word of honour...' She turned to Martello and looked her full in the face. '... and yours also, Miss Martello, not to document what I say, only to listen? If you then believe you have to take it further, then and only then do you formally interview me. Do you accept this approach?'

Priestley turned to Martello, 'I'm happy to give my word for this specific meeting to be off-the-record. Are you happy to do so as well? You're under no duress from me. If you feel it goes too strongly against laid-down procedures then do feel free to refuse.'

Martello trusted Priestley's judgement on virtually anything, so had no hesitation in confirming her willingness to proceed as requested. 'I accept, for this specific meeting.'

Oaken began her explanation. 'I spoke to the girls as a group, in the hope that one of them would reveal what had happened to her, with the more reticent ones then doing likewise. The youngest girl was the first to reveal her experience. Rather than celebrating her sixteenth birthday last month with her friends as she had planned, instead she sacrificed her virginity on the altar of Mr Newhouse's ego.'

Priestley and Martello were both desperate to smile at the way Oaken was describing the event, but were fully aware that the seriousness of the occasion forbade them from showing it. Nevertheless, they were certain Oaken's terminology bore very little resemblance to that used in the original testimony. Priestley found himself wondering if the experience she was describing was one of which she herself had had no first-hand experience.

Oaken continued, 'She imagined it was love, whereas I knew it was just a man's base desire. The other two girls had similar stories to tell. One of them had also given herself for the first time on her sixteenth birthday, earlier this year. The other had had intercourse with Mr Newhouse shortly after her sixteenth birthday, though she had indulged in such behaviour beforehand with others – I shudder to think how many others.'

Priestley wondered what world Oaken lived in; clearly not that of the liberated woman. He waited a moment to accord dignity to her testimony, before asking the key question, 'Are you able to say exactly where the girls were at the time of Mr Newhouse's death?'

'Yes I am. The youngest one was definitely in class. The two older ones were on the sports field watching the School v. Staff football match, and I myself recall seeing them by the side of the pitch at the end of the match.'

Priestley decided for now to accept Oaken's testimony at face value, though keeping his options open. 'If the investigation into the death of Mr Newhouse fails to make progress, then we may have to revisit this matter of the three girls, but for now I'm prepared to accept your word about where the girls were at the time of death.'

'Thank you, Mr Priestley – I appreciate it.'

After a brief pause, Priestley began again. 'Could we now turn to another matter, and this is on the record. I'd like to identify a particular girl who was out on a cross-country run last Wednesday afternoon.'

SEND OFF SIR

'I believe there could have been any number of girls having a run. Normally, we provide our students with a wide choice of sports, but last Wednesday the girls only had the choice of watching the football match or going running. Could you describe the girl?'

Priestley gave a brief description and asked for a list of contenders; Oaken printed off the entire list of all Year Twelve and Year Thirteen girls. He then asked for another interview with Clifton. She gave directions to the small office that Clifton shared with another teacher. Before they reached the office, Priestley explained to Martello that he had no wish to plough through a long list of girls to find the relevant one, and as Clifton had been on the games field she may have noticed the girl they were looking for.

On finding the office occupied by Clifton and another teacher, Priestley asked if there was somewhere they could go for a private discussion. Clifton looked at her colleague and flicked her head in the direction of the door; he immediately stood up and walked out, looking down to avoid eye-contact.

Priestley began, 'I didn't mean to disrupt your colleague's work.'

Clifton replied, 'We're completely flexible about sharing the office. If I need a private conversation he goes somewhere else, and if he needs a private conversation he finds somewhere else. I find the system works very well.' She made a noise like a cross between a laugh and a snort at her own daring at having broken a PC rule.

Priestley explained they were looking for a girl who had been cross-country running and who had returned between about three ten and three thirty. Clifton immediately responded, 'Becky Worthington.' Priestley asked if she were sure about this. She elaborated, 'I had a key to the gate in the fence at the top of the field, and I let her in at about twenty past three. She was the last girl by a good twenty minutes. I know some of the students go for a walk and a smoke, but I've never caught them at it yet. Becky actually does go for a run; her mother is a personal fitness trainer, so Becky probably gets lots of encouragement to go running. Anyway, it's something she enjoys and is quite good at, so she runs with some of the boys. They leave her behind when they sprint at the end, the poor lamb, but she's always back the next time for another go.'

Priestley checked the list of all Year Twelve and Year Thirteen girls that Oaken had provided. 'I can't see her name on the list of girls who do games on Wednesday afternoons.'

Clifton peered at the printed sheets. 'That's a full list of the older girls all right. But Becky is one of our less academic, younger students. There are currently fifteen of them who're allowed to have extra games lessons, including Wednesday afternoons. After all, there's no point in putting such students through hours of lessons that they're never going to get to grips with; they might as well just be enjoying themselves by having a run out.' She raised a finger to her lips, and in a loud whisper added, 'The Ofsted inspectors would probably have a fit if they knew.'

Priestley decided to check if there could be other contenders who were not on the list Oaken had provided. 'Do you have the only key?'

'No; there are lots of copies. Often it's whoever's nearest that lets them back in, so any teacher going out there tends to take a key with them.'

'Is it possible someone else let in an entirely different girl while you weren't there?'

'It's possible, I suppose, but very unlikely.'

'When could we speak to Becky?'

'That's a bit awkward, to be honest. Becky has a form of autism called Asperger's syndrome; she answers direct questions with direct answers, but struggles to understand subtle questions. I assume you're thinking she might have seen something last Wednesday, but you can't really ask her about what you might describe as "anything suspicious" because that would mean she'd need to understand the concept of suspicion. You see the problem?'

Priestley thought he needed to have a better understanding of Becky before he could decide how best to proceed. 'May we sit in on one of her lessons, perhaps? She wouldn't need to know we were there to observe her. We could just sit quietly at the back.'

'I don't see why not.' Clifton checked on her laptop to identify where Becky would be that morning. 'You probably need something where there's a decent chance of seeing her interacting with the teacher or other students.'

'You're very perceptive; are you a psychologist by any chance?'

'We're all psychologists nowadays, aren't we? Teachers and police.'

'Some police are; others haven't a clue.' He thought of Dunn for a moment.

She echoed, 'Some teachers are; others haven't a clue. Your best shot is the last lesson before lunch. It's a bit of a wait, but it's probably the best one of the entire week for getting an insight into what Becky "gets" and what she doesn't. It's Classics in English; not to be confused with English Classics. It was Hugh Cassidy's idea, God bless him. He thought it would be good for some of the less able children – who obviously won't be studying Classics in their original Greek – to read English versions to the best of their limited abilities, or even have the teacher read out loud to them while they follow the words in their books. Sometimes they have actual translations; other times they're just stories loosely based on the originals. It's a small class and they all love it. Miss Cleese used to alternate with Hugh; sometimes they even did lessons together so they could read two interacting parts, even though the timetabling system only gave them credit for half the lessons. Sophie says she'll be doing all the lessons herself for the rest of this year, as a mark of respect for Hugh, even though she's now over-allocated on the timetable.'

Priestley and Martello agreed with Clifton they would return later to attend the lesson. They headed back to the station, knowing there would be general administrative items waiting for them that had a tendency to build up quickly unless e-mails and work queues were processed regularly.

* * *

Lily had discussed with Neil the ideas suggested by Anthony about a possible career change. Neil understood Lily's unhappiness with certain aspects of police work and so had offered his full support, despite his misgivings about Lily being exposed to pressures of a personal nature in those working environments. He could imagine wealthy and powerful men offering her inducements and the superficial attractions of a sophisticated lifestyle, and so he feared for the future of their relationship. Nevertheless, there was almost nothing he would not do for her happiness, so he had kept his worries to himself.

They agreed that making her intentions known to line management could remove any hopes she might have of advancement within the police force, but the more they discussed her future the more certain she was that it lay elsewhere. Consequently they had decided she should let Priestley know, but should ask him to keep it to himself for now in case it all came to nothing. She took the opportunity of the drive back to the station to apprise Priestley of her immediate intentions.

'That conversation I had with Anthony Ashbourne – he thought I should consider a change of career; maybe handling security at conferences, things like that. I'm seriously considering my options and thinking about leaving the force. I know you were instrumental in getting rid of one of the nastiest people who had it in for me, but there's other things I've hated about police work that I don't see changing. Could you keep it under your hat until I find something else?'

'You can rely on me to keep it to myself.'

'It might come to nothing, so I wouldn't want to burn my boats with the police force.'

'You say you don't wish to "burn your boats"; actually, it should be "scuttle your ships" – it's what Cortés did in Mexico.'

'What a fount of information you are.'

'When I was in the army I studied such things as strategy, tactics, motivation, all that kind of stuff. Cortés kept one ship for bringing back the treasure, so he didn't entirely cut himself off from Spain. If you do leave the police force, don't think it means you have to cut yourself off from the people you worked with. I want you to know I'll always be there for you, if there's anything I can ever do for you.'

'That's very kind of you, Marcus, though I don't know why you'd offer to help a deserter.'

'This isn't a conversation we can have properly while I'm driving. Just put it down to the fact that you're a lovely young woman and I like you a lot.'

'Before today, I could never have imagined you saying that.'

Priestley sighed. 'Yes, you're right. We're all so worried about saying the wrong things – the politically incorrect things – that we sometimes don't feel able to say the right things. But you know I meant what I said, and you know how I meant you to take it.'

'I get the impression you think I'm definitely going to be

leaving, so you're saying things while you can.'

'I think you should be leaving, because I don't think you're entirely suited to police work, and you may be a lot happier elsewhere.'

'It's not great for my ego to hear you say that – it sounds like you don't think I'm very good at my job.'

'Honestly, Lily, there are things where you're really good – that's why I wanted you with me this morning, in case something came up that you're the best at handling. But there are other aspects of the work that you don't like – and quite right too – no one in their right mind should like some of the things we have to do. The difference is, you can take your talents elsewhere and not have to do those horrible things, whereas plodders like me have to stick with it.'

Martello laughed. 'Plodders, Detective Chief Inspector? Just eight years on the force? You don't need to be modest with me.'

'Well, I did get a head start. But you don't need to be modest either – you can be great, so long as you use your talents and don't fret about any weaknesses.'

They continued in silence until they stopped at traffic lights. Martello began again. 'It would be a big step – leaving the force. I'm not sure it's ever going to happen.'

Priestley put the car into gear and set off, not responding until they were on a clear stretch of road. 'I'd say there are two ways of looking at it: you can stay on the force until you find the ideal job, but it might never come along; or you can leave the force, which will give you an incentive to find a suitable job. Practically, I expect any job application will look better if you're still on the force than if you're unemployed. In the end, maybe you'll need to take a risk and accept something less than perfect to get you started in your new career – something where you can prove yourself – and then apply for other work on the strength of what you'd just been doing.'

'I always appreciate your advice, Marcus, though I hadn't expected you to be encouraging me to leave.'

'I'm just thinking of your best interests. Don't let others know I encouraged you, though, because that would really drop me in it; there's a lot of people who'd miss you.'

'You really are ever so kind.'

Priestley briefly looked at her and smiled before turning back to watch the road ahead. As they approached the station, he timed a series of quick glances to see how she reacted to some key questions. 'What about Neil? I wouldn't want to lose him – he's a good bloke.'

'He's committed to the force – he's no intention of leaving.'

'How do you see your relationship with him in the future?'

'I'm determined to make it work, whether I'm struggling to make a living and depending on him for money, or whether I'm successful and making a load of money myself. Either way, he's the right man for me because he cares about me for what I am and not for what I achieve or don't achieve.'

'You may be looking for something new for work, but it sounds like you've already found what you've been looking for when it comes to a life partner.'

He parked the car and turned off the engine, then gripped the edges of the seat and raised himself slightly, easing himself around so he could face her more easily. 'I'm very happy for you.' After a pause he remembered he should mention the other party. 'And for Neil as well of course.'

She looked at him with the beginning of a smile. 'Go on; just say what you're thinking.'

Priestley stage-grimaced, 'The lucky blighter.'

Martello laughed in response. 'Yes, he is.'

* * *

When Priestley and Martello returned to the school, they were in good time for the Classics in English lesson, though they hurried from the car park to be out of the drizzle. In the staffroom they were introduced to the teacher.

'I'm Acting DCI Priestly. Call me Marcus. And this is DC Martello, Lily.'

'I'm Miss Cleese. My first name is Sophie; parents have such a lot to answer for when they name their children, don't they?'

Priestley gave a smile and a nod of recognition. Martello gave a general purpose smile, having failed to make the connection. Priestly began, 'Your surname is a familiar one in these parts.'

'Yes, my grandfather was a big cheese on the council. My father didn't follow him into politics though – he's a university professor – Classics, you might not be surprised to hear.'

'We were talking to Ms Clifton about sitting in on your next class.'

'Have you been DBS checked? You're not allowed to be with children without one.'

'Actually, we don't have DBS checks as such, but we are authorised to be with children. We've been subject to even stricter vetting procedures to get into the police force.'

'Does that mean you don't see DBS checking as strict enough?'

'What's checked is valid enough, though it only deals with a minority of problems.'

'Really? I thought it was meant to be the be-all-and-end-all.'

'Well, when you think about it, if three in five cases of paedophilia are committed by first-time offenders, then the DBS checks can only pick up two in five at best. If DBS checking is seen as the only vetting that's needed, any character deficiencies that don't register on the DBS checks are more likely to be ignored. Also, the DBS system itself looks like it was designed more for generating income for the government to pay for the system, than for stopping potential offenders.'

'I've not heard anyone say that before.'

'Well, I see it this way. Individuals are DBS checked when an organisation applies; employers pay a fee that depends on the type of check. DBS checks never officially expire, but an employer may have a policy of repeat checking, which means they pay again. Also, another employer might check on the same person, and they'd also have to pay a fee. Each fee is income for the government.

'The big problem is finding out about new entries. A repeat DBS check would reveal any offences that were committed since the last check, but they could have taken place much earlier. So, for that period of time, the organisation doesn't know.

'It would be better if organisations registered their continuing interest in someone, with fee payable depending on the type of registration, and then if something relevant is recorded against that person, the system automatically advises each organisation that has a registered interest. Repeat fees could be generated by invoicing registered employers, who would have the option of remaining registered and paying the fee, or de-registering.

'But a bigger problem is that many DBS checks relate to teachers who have just come through school and university, and who may not yet have committed an offence that an assessment of their character might have suggested was a distinct possibility.

There's a question of which way around the burden of proof should be, when it comes to looking after children. Should it be enough just to have not yet been convicted of a relevant criminal offence, or should it be necessary to have positive vetting based on personal assessment?'

Cleese looked genuinely concerned that there might be a flaw in the system. 'What can we do about it at school level?'

'I suppose you should report any concerns upwards, though to a large extent you may find it as frustrating as we do in the police force: until someone has actually committed an offence – and been found guilty – we're often powerless to take any action.'

'In some ways I wish you hadn't told me this.'

Priestley and Martello followed Cleese to her classroom. She unlocked the door and they walked in behind her, staying at the front of the class until she had introduced them to the children. 'Inspector Priestley and Constable Martello will be joining us today for our lesson.' She turned on her laptop, called up the class list and read from it the name of each child, who in turn put up a hand and waved or smiled or said "Hello, Miss," as they preferred. The detectives identified from the roll-call the child they wished to observe, having deliberately not revealed the subject of their interest to Cleese.

'Last week Mr Cassidy and I gave the lesson together, which was his last ever lesson with us all before he died suddenly at the weekend. We're all very sad about that.' She slowly looked around the room, so they could all see how sad she was and recognise it was appropriate for them also to look sad. 'I'll be giving the lessons on my own for the rest of this term. Now, who can remember last week's story about Actaeon and Artemis?'

Every hand went up. Cleese responded, 'Everyone put your hands down and we'll start again. Mr Priestley is not a School Inspector, so only put up your hand if you can answer the question.' Three hands went up, one of which was the right hand of Becky Worthington, which seemed to be stretching her so high that it raised her off her seat. 'Becky, you can remind us what happened.'

'A man was hunting in the forest. Then he went into a cave and saw Artemis with no clothes on, taking a shower. She didn't like that so she threw water at him and he ran away. Then he was turned into a stag and was chased and killed by his own dogs.'

'Brilliant, Becky. I couldn't have put it better myself. You must have really been paying attention to that story.'

Becky beamed in all directions, delighted to be the first to be praised in the lesson, though they all knew any answer could expect to be received with "brilliant, great, fantastic, marvellous, wonderful", and so on.

Cleese picked up a zapper and turned on a projector that was suspended from the ceiling. 'Now for this week's story. It's about two people whose names are Narcissus and Echo. First of all, does anyone know what a narcissus is?' No one offered an answer. Cleese pressed a few keys on her laptop, then went to the interactive whiteboard at the front of the room and used the touch-sensitive screen to reveal a picture of a host of white flowers with short orange trumpets. 'This is a picture of lots of them in a garden. We can see that the word "narcissus" is Greek, because the correct plural is "narcissi", not "narcissuses". So, one narcissus, two narcissi. Does anyone know any other words that change their ending in that way when there's more than one of them, and end up with an "i" on the end? Isaac, I thought you might know one from maths.' A boy shook his head very firmly from side to side. 'Can you think of a maths word to do with circles that has "i" as its last letter?'

He responded immediately, 'radii.'

'Well done, you just needed a little bit of a hint, didn't you?'

'No, miss; you changed the question. Radii ends with two "i"s, not just one.'

'You're quite right Isaac. It ends with an "i" and another "i".

'Now we'll look at the next name: Echo.' Cleese decided to use the negative form of a question to be confident she could press ahead with the lesson. 'Does anyone not know what an Echo is?' It achieved the desired result: no one raised their hand, indicating either they knew the answer or they did not wish to raise their hand. 'I'm now going to play an echo.' She went to the laptop and pressed a couple of keys, and a voice was heard shouting "Hello", which then continued with ever-quieter repetitions until it finally died away. 'Now we're all going to take it in turns to stand up and make our own echo sound. I'll start it off by saying the word "echo", and then I'm going to keep repeating it, quieter and quieter, until there's no sound left. Let's see how many times we can say the word before it's too quiet to hear.' She began with a fairly loud "echo" and repeated it a further five times before she stopped. Each child then took their turn, the first one saying the word seven times before stopping, others saying the word seven or eight times, though sometimes the repeated word was at least as loud, if not louder, than its predecessor. After the last child had finished, Cleese called over to the detectives who were sitting on a table at the back. 'Would you like to try?'

Priestley woke up from his daydreaming and stood up, beginning with a loud "echo" and reducing his volume over five iterations to stop on a quietly spoken one.

Martello then stood up and with a far-away look began with a fairly loud "echo", repeating with small reductions and finally stopping with a stage-whispered twelfth. The children applauded spontaneously because she was tall and beautiful and had the highest score. She smiled at the children so much she felt she could cry.

Priestley and Martello stayed for the entire lesson – to do any less would have felt insulting to the children and their teacher. As the last child left the room, Priestley asked Cleese, 'What happened at the start of the lesson, with all the children putting their hands up?'

Cleese looked abashed. 'It's a fair cop guv'nor – you've got me bang to rights.'

The two detectives smiled, uncertain what lay behind the confession.

'We had the Ofsted inspectors around recently. The game was, put up your right hand if you know the answer, put up your left hand if you don't. It looks better than just getting the same few hands every time.'

Priestley looked at her with clear admiration. Martello appeared a little shocked.

Over the lunch break Priestley and Martello were unable to locate Oaken, who was rumoured to be dealing with a disciplinary matter relating to a Year Eleven girl. They went to Verbane's office; Priestley knocked on the open door before delivering an especially polite request without stepping over the threshold. 'I'm sorry to trouble you, Headmaster, but there's something I need to arrange, and Miss Oaken is currently unavailable. May I ask you instead?'

'Of course, do come in.'

They stepped toward the desk behind which Verbane stayed seated; they remained standing. 'I'd like to interview one of your students, Becky Worthington. I understand she has some form of autism, and I know she's very young, so I'd like her mother to be present – I'll need her contact details. I'm intending the interview to take place at four o'clock sharp in the room that's next door to the staffroom; it's the one that's used by matron – I mean your Child Protection Officer. I'll interview Becky in there with her mum if that's alright; could you get a message to Becky not to leave school today, but to wait for her mum? DC Martello will also be present for the interview.'

'Yes, I can do that for you.'

'As soon as that interview is over, I should then like to speak to all the members of staff who may have been alone around the time that Mr Newhouse's body was discovered. Here's a list of the people.' He handed over a sheet of paper with the following names printed on it: Anthony Ashbourne, Victoria Clifton, Joanna Jackson, Jane Leveret, Christine Nunn, Glenda Oaken, David Pratt, Margaret Webster. 'It's important that all eight of them are in the staffroom ready to be interviewed as soon as I've finished talking with Becky and her mum. Other staff can use the staffroom up to three fifty; after that, I don't want any other staff in there, but I'll make an exception for you if you wish, otherwise I'd like you to be in your office.'

Verbane provided Mrs Sylvia Worthington's contact details and stated he would be in his office from ten to four onwards. Priestley added, 'Just so that there's no doubt about the importance of this arrangement, let me say there will be several police officers stationed at key exit routes from half three onwards who will arrest any of the eight that attempt to leave the school premises. I'm sure that won't be necessary though – if you give them all a sufficiently strongly-worded instruction.'

Once Verbane was alone in his office he found his legs shaking a little, which he put down to the after-effects of being spoken to by Priestley, and the sense that things were coming to a head. He immediately began scribbling a note for the eight people on Priestley's list, then decided to deliver the message to each of them personally.

CHAPTER 30

Priestley Sets a Trap

Priestley went back to the office with Martello. He phoned Sylvia Worthington, explaining some of the background and agreeing the time of four o'clock for the interview. He offered to arrange for her to be collected by car, but she assured him she would be there in good time. He noted down her car registration, marque and colour. He then contacted Witty, Berry, Plummer and Dunn, arranging for all of them to be at the school by three thirty, where they would meet up with Martello and himself.

At half past three the team met in the school car park. Priestley explained the first stage of the plan, using first names to engender a sense of team spirit. 'I've given each of you a copy of the guest list. They're all being instructed to assemble in the staffroom by four o'clock, so we need to be on the lookout for any of them trying to leave before then.

'Elias will stay in the car park.

'Linda will go to reception.

'Neil will go to the staffroom.

'Lily will go the side gate.

'I shall go to the main gate.

'Tony will stay with me until Mrs Worthington arrives. When she does, I shall leave Tony to man the gate while I accompany Mrs Worthington.

'Does anyone have any observations on this deployment of troops?'

Berry immediately responded, 'There's no one covering the top entrance gate from the playing field out onto the public pathway.'

'You're quite correct, Tony. If someone decides to do a runner, we'll know who they are because they'll be the one not in the staffroom at four o'clock. For them to scarper, they have to have an exit route, hence we need to leave one way open; we'd have to track them down later of course. If anyone tries to leave by any other route, turn 'em back; if necessary, 'cuff 'em.'

Witty suggested, 'Across the face? Or where it won't show?'

Priestley sighed, 'Not now Neil; please.'

Berry waited a moment before asking, 'So that's what this is all about, is it? Flush them out; see who breaks cover?'

'Not really, Tony. I'd be pleased enough with the result if it happens that way, but I'm not at all optimistic it will. Any other questions?'

'How will you recognise Mrs Worthington?'

'I have her car details. Any more questions from anyone?'

After a short silence, Priestley continued. 'Everyone is to remain at their post until ten to four, at which time you should all make your way to the staffroom. Lin, make sure you bring Mrs Webster with you.

'Finally, the meeting is scheduled for four o'clock, but if everyone is assembled before that time, then we can start early. Whatever time it is though, before or after four, we won't start the actual interview until we know all eight are in the staffroom. Any questions?'

As no one had anything else to say, Priestley gave some final instructions in a jokey manner to mask the serious intent. 'Those of you with common sense, use it; those of you without, phone me if something unexpected arises and you're unsure what to do.'

Plummer went to the Administration Office and explained to Webster, 'I'll stay on reception with you, so we can remind anyone on the list that they need to stay, otherwise someone might forget the appointment and set off home.'

Mrs Worthington arrived at three forty in her red Peugeot. Priestley flagged her down and introduced himself. He left Berry on duty at the main gate with Martello watching from nearby, accepting a lift to the car park where Dunn was patrolling. He and Sylvia walked to reception where Plummer was with Webster, and where Becky was sitting waiting. He walked mother and daughter to the interview room where he exchanged a few pleasantries with Sylvia. After a couple of minutes he looked in on Witty, quickly counting the eight members of staff who were sitting patiently. On second viewing, he realised Webster was absent and Pratt was talking to an interloper. Witty mouthed, very slowly, 'so-li-ci-tor'.

Priestley recognised Sol Schaeffer, a man of similar age to himself, though looking much older and more monk-like due to his tonsure. He beckoned Witty to come to the door. 'Get Mrs Webster and our team in here straight away. When Lily arrives, send her in next door; I'd like to have a chat with Mr Pratt and Mr Schaeffer before I interview the Worthingtons.'

Priestley returned to the small room where Sylvia and Becky Worthington were seated. Sylvia asked, 'When do I get to know what this is all about?'

Priestley responded, 'Please bear with me a little longer; maybe ten minutes, and then we can all have a chat. Would you like a drink? I'm sure I could rustle up a tea or coffee.'

'No, thank you. I always have my water bottle with me. I can share with Becks if she needs a drink.'

The officers arrived at intervals over the next five minutes, until all six of them were assembled. Priestley asked Lily to sit with the Worthingtons while he went for a chat with Pratt and Schaeffer. Berry sat near to his mentor to see if he could pick up some tips for dealing with solicitors – Susan excepted. Priestley greeted his old friend, or old adversary, depending on the occasion. 'Hello, Sol. What brings you here?'

'You do, Marcus.'

'Really? I never suggested anyone needed a solicitor.'

'Mr Pratt is concerned about his lack of an alibi.'

Pratt joined the conversation. 'You haven't given any explanation of why we have to be here.'

'I asked the Headmaster to issue an invitation.'

'It read more like a threat.'

'I'm sure that's just a misinterpretation. Take DC Beresford here; as honest as the day is long, and entirely unthreatening. He used to be in computing like yourself.'

Pratt turned to Berry, 'What did you do before you joined the police force?'

'After university I stayed in Sheffield and became a senior analyst on what I was told was the world's largest customer database, until I decided I needed to do something different to expand my outlook on life.'

Pratt turned to Schaeffer, 'The biggest in the world, in

Sheffield? I don't believe what I've just heard.'

Berry began to explain. 'It's a distributed database that holds data from dozens of countries across multiple continents in several physical locations. Sheffield is the place where the design ...'

Priestley interrupted Berry and spoke to Pratt. 'I just heard you call a police officer a liar. Would you like to put it in writing? Damages awarded by the courts for libel tend to be significantly higher than for slander.' Turning to Schaeffer he enquired, 'Would you expect to be representing your client in any civil suit, Mr Schaeffer? It could be problematic, as you may be called as a witness to what was said by Mr Pratt.'

Schaeffer waved a finger in the direction of a far corner of the room and invited Priestley to join him there. 'May I have a quiet word with you?'

They walked over in silence and pressed themselves into the ends of a well-worn settee, turning their heads to facilitate eye contact. Schaeffer began, 'Off the record, Marcus. Why are you trying to wind up my client? I don't see how it helps your investigation.'

Priestley answered indirectly. 'I have a case to solve, and Pratt lived up to his name when I interviewed him yesterday. One interpretation of his attitude is that he has something to hide. And now here he is with a solicitor; another possible indicator. Why did he ask you to attend this meeting?'

'We're still off the record, aren't we? I think he's paranoid. He seems to believe all police officers are out-and-out liars; perhaps Helen could trace it back to some traumatic event in his childhood. I haven't asked him about the Newhouse case because he might have disclosed something material and detrimental, and then I wouldn't have been able to represent him, but I really don't see him as responsible for your homicide – if that's what it is. What's your view?'

'Sorry, Sol, we're on opposite sides of the fence today. Just don't get in the way of justice, or we might cease to be best friends.'

'It's good to know I'm a B.F., but he's my client and I'll be doing everything I can to protect his interests.'

'Even if he's guilty?'

Schaeffer remained unmoved. 'You know how our legal system works. Guilt and innocence have nothing to do with it.'

'Alright, if that's how you see it, but if I think you're doing something unethical then I'll be after you with no holds barred.'

'Oh, come off it Marcus, let's be realistic; there's virtually nothing a solicitor does that the Law Society classes as unethical. Am I right or am I right? I can only think of one example in Shawton in all the years I've been here. Do you remember that firm of solicitors who billed two separate clients for the same work? One of them was the government. They made tens of millions out of something the rest of the country saw as not only immoral but illegal, and yet all the Law Society did was to suspend them for a while. Personally, I think the head of the firm should have been prosecuted and sent down for years. That's off the record, of course.'

'Well, let's forget legal ethics – it sounds like a contradiction in terms, anyway. I'm aiming for justice, and I trust you won't interfere with that.'

'Sorry, but I'm not here to support justice either; I'm only here for the rule of law.'

'In that case I hope the two are compatible this time.'

Priestley stood up and walked away, joining Martello in the adjacent room. 'It's time now to explain what this is all about. Becky, you were out running last Wednesday, and I think something may have happened that you need to tell me about. At the end of your run, the two boys you were with had a sprint and left you behind. Is that correct?'

'Yes.'

'When you reached the gate in the fence at the top of the school field, Ms Clifton let you in; is that correct?'

'Yes.'

'Could you tell me what happened after that?'

'Yes.'

'Go ahead then, tell me everything that happened.'

'I went into the changing room. I took off my clothes and went into the shower. I had my eyes closed because I had lots of shampoo on my hair. Then I opened them and Mr Newhouse was there at the edge of the shower, looking at me, so I splashed water at him and shouted at him to go away. He said I was in the wrong place, but I wasn't because it was the girls' changing room. He walked away and I ran out of the shower and put my clothes on but

I didn't get dried first. Then I ran home.'

'Did you see anyone else in the changing room?'

'No.'

'Did you see anyone else outside the changing room?'

'No.'

Priestley paused for a moment. 'When I was at school I was told that if someone did something they shouldn't, such as stopping their car and trying to grab me when I was walking on the pavement, I should scream and run away. Have you ever been told anything like that?'

'Yes, that's what I've been told as well.'

'Did you think about screaming when you saw Mr Newhouse, when you were in the shower?'

'Yes.'

'Why did you decide not to scream?'

'Because I threw water instead – like Artemis did.'

Mrs Worthington interrupted, 'Who the hell's Artemis?'

'A Greek goddess – she can explain it to you later.' Turning back to Becky, 'Have you ever practised screaming, as though you were being attacked, or something like that?'

'No.'

'Do you remember how we practised doing echoes in class, today? I remember my friend Lily was very good at echoes.'

Martello smiled at Becky, who smiled back.'

'Yes, she was the best.'

'I wonder if you would be the best at screaming.'

'I don't know.'

'If your mum doesn't mind, when I ask, would you do a really good scream here?'

Mrs Worthington objected. 'She's very sensitive to high-pitched sounds, so she wouldn't like it – it's part of her condition.'

'Well, I'm sure you're right to protect her from sounds she doesn't like, but someday a really loud scream could protect her from something even worse. Would you mind letting her do just one scream?'

Mrs Worthington gave a brief nod of approval to Priestley before turning to Becky. 'Alright Becks, you do one really loud scream when Mr Priestley says so.'

Priestley explained exactly what he wished her to do. 'You'll need to fill your lungs by taking a great big breath. Then let it come out in a really loud scream. Don't try to do it like you're trying to scream; do it like the air has to come out as fast as it can and you just can't stop it. Keep it going until it feels like there's no air left. You need to stand up to do it. Are you ready? Do it now.'

Becky took the biggest breath she could, then let it rip without restraint. The sound was the high, piercing note which comes when the vocal cords make no attempt at control; she felt it vibrating inside her skull and projecting from the centre of her forehead like a unicorn's horn, in the way tenors experience their highest notes. The shock of the first burst was painful to everyone in the room, becoming less so as it gradually died away with her reducing air pressure. Just as the scream finally petered out, Oaken thrust open the door and burst into the room, shouting at Priestley. 'What in God's name are you doing to that poor girl? I'm the one you need to be talking to – I did it. Now just let her go.'

Priestley quickly organised the release of everyone but Oaken, using the briefest possible instructions. Plummer and Berry were to go with Priestley and Oaken to her office; Martello was to expedite the departures of Sylvia and Becky Worthington, then join them in Oaken's office; Dunn was to send the seven other members of staff plus Schaeffer on their way; and Witty was to advise Verbane of the recent development.

Priestley invited Oaken to sit in her own chair behind her desk, knowing it could be for the last time. Desperately wishing not to be silent, but unable to think of anything relevant to say, she finally offered up, 'Is this where you put me in handcuffs and chains?'

Priestley responded in as kindly a tone as he could manage under the circumstances, choosing his words carefully to emphasise the positive aspects. 'Happily, this is not America, Miss Oaken. Admitting to the offence means there'll be no need for you to reveal the names of those three girls we talked about earlier, or for Becky to have to describe the ordeal she suffered when Mr Newhouse found her in the changing room, naked.'

Berry appeared about to speak, but Priestley silenced him with a raised finger. When Martello arrived at the office, he invited Oaken to leave with her and Plummer. 'Would you mind going with Lily and Linda to the police station, please, where you can make a full statement about everything that happened last Wednesday in the time between John Newhouse leaving the football field and the staff players entering the changing room. I'll be there myself to make sure all the relevant detail is recorded. We'll need to start off with a caution. You have the right to a solicitor, but you don't need to decide just yet – you can wait until you're at the station.'

Oaken took the office keys from her handbag and placed them on the desk, as she prepared for the last time to leave the daytime home of all the children she had loved like a mother, or at least a maiden aunt.

When they had the room to themselves, Priestley invited Berry to say what he had stopped him from saying before. 'What did you mean about the ordeal Becky had suffered in the changing room? You made it sound like Newhouse had interfered with her.'

'Before the interview, I didn't know for definite that it wasn't Becky who'd pushed Newhouse. When it became clear she hadn't, I had to narrow down the suspects from the eight people next door. Some of them may have had the opportunity, all of them had the means, but none had a known motive. Of the four women teachers, I thought three of them may have the character to own up if they thought a child was becoming distressed from being accused; I wasn't sure about Miss Leveret. Of the two men, I was thinking Ashbourne may own up but Pratt wouldn't. Of the admin staff, I thought Jackson wouldn't own up but Webster might. So, if no one owned up, then at least I'd have separated the list into the more likely and the less likely, and if someone did own up then the last remaining hurdle would be to establish that the confession was genuine.

'Now, as to your question, you need to recognise that until we have the confession signed sealed and delivered, she could retract it at any time. By suggesting she'll be protecting a vulnerable child, as well as the identities of those other three girls, I'm hoping she'll be motivated to stick with her confession. You have to bear in mind we're out of potential witnesses – no one saw her go in or come out of the girls' changing room. Forensics didn't turn up anything we could use, bearing in mind we know she had a valid explanation for any contact trace evidence from when she tried to resuscitate him.

'I thought the strategy of the scream might work because, whatever their other shortcomings, teachers on the whole – with notable exceptions – tend to be highly moral individuals when it comes to the protection of children. My belief was an essential factor in formulating the plan – I wouldn't have tried it with a group of lawyers, estate agents, journalists, politicians, and certainly not police officers.

'If you'd highlighted there was no interference with Becky, she may right now be considering whether to retract her confession. As it is, I expect her to see it through.

'It's like Clive Oxley was saying in the pub about refereeing football matches: do what's needed to obtain a fair result, rather than blindly applying the rules. I may have misled Miss Oaken, but if the result is a fair one then I would say the end justifies the means.'

Berry appeared to remain troubled, so Priestley invited him to speak freely. Berry explained his other concern. 'You didn't let me know what you planned to do. I was as shocked as anyone when I heard the scream. If we're all part of the same team, shouldn't we have been told what to expect?'

'I didn't know exactly what to expect myself, but I thought it was unlikely to have been Becky who pushed Newhouse, as she's only a slip of a girl. So yes, I was expecting to need to move to the next stage – getting her to scream. Now, I don't know how good your acting skills are, but I took the view that it would be better if you and the others reacted genuinely and spontaneously, which meant I had to keep you all in the dark. People can be surprisingly perceptive to the tiniest action that doesn't ring true, so I didn't want someone deciding not to reveal themselves because they'd spotted it was a trap. You shouldn't take it personally.'

Berry nodded and pushed forward his lips, confirming he was both appeased and impressed.

Back at the station, Priestley decided it would be safer to exclude Berry from the formal interview with Oaken. He arranged for both Martello and Plummer to be present, continuing in his belief that she would find the presence of the two women supportive. After the caution, Priestley asked Oaken if she required a solicitor, to which she gave what in his experience was an original response. 'Solicitors try to get people off, don't they', she asked rhetorically. 'So any guilty person is being immoral if they ask for a solicitor.'

Priestley knew of many people who had demanded to have a solicitor present, not because they were guilty of anything, but because they did not trust the police to deal with them fairly. Nevertheless, he had no intention of dissuading Oaken from declining the offer. 'Everything is being recorded, so we can rush through the whole saga as quickly and as painlessly as possible. DC Martello will be typing as we speak. Would you like to go ahead and explain everything that happened?'

Oaken settled deep into the comfortable chair that Priestley had himself fetched for her after she had initially been provided with a standard, hard seat. Priestley wondered if he was overdoing things, though Oaken appeared to accept his concern for her comfort as entirely genuine. Her body wobbled a little as she visibly inhaled deeply in preparation for giving her willing, if not cathartic, statement of events.

'I noticed Becky Worthington running along the footpath and heading back to school. I saw her from a long way away, through the fence, so I didn't need to hurry to unlock the gate for her. Ms Clifton had evidently also seen her, because, by the time I was half-way to the gate, she had come from the other side of the pitch and was letting her in. Ms Clifton headed back to the football field at a brisk walking pace, and Becky jogged toward the changing room.

'I had a look at the trees through the fence; they've lost nearly all their leaves, you know. Eventually I turned around and started to walk back, fairly slowly as I tend to do, and as I was getting close to the bottom corner of the pitch I saw Becky run out of the changing room; her long brown hair was all wet, and she was carrying her coat and bag and was trying to put on her jumper at the same time. So I rushed down to help her, and I kept calling her back while I went down the steps, but she didn't hear me. I went into the changing room, to find out who she was running away from. I thought she might have just been bullied by another student – statistically, almost half of all autistic children suffer from bullying in schools; my school has it well under control, but we have to remain vigilant.

'When I went into the changing room, John Newhouse was there by himself. He was standing near to the shower area with water dripping from him. He said to me, "Becky's been splashing me." He laughed when he said it. I shouted at him, "How could you, John." I wanted to give him a telling off, but I didn't feel I could because he was towering over me, so I rushed at him to push him and make him sit down on the bench.'

Priestley thought her testimony so far was highly credible. He had noticed over the years how some small and otherwise gentle women behaved aggressively toward tall men, as though the simple fact of the man's height had made them imagine they were somehow being threatened; perhaps if Newhouse had not been so tall, she may not have felt the need to push him down.

Oaken became more animated as she continued, 'I was so angry with him, I stepped toward him to give him a hard push, but the floor was slippery from the soapy water and I fell onto him. He stepped back from me, but he slipped as well. I tried to stop myself from falling by grabbing at him, but he was already falling, so I couldn't hold myself up on him. I fell on him with my whole weight. He hit the back of his head on a coat hook and fell on the floor. I ended up on top of him on the floor, and I didn't want anyone to see me like that, so I jumped up and ran out. I had no idea he was really badly injured.

'I went to see the Headmaster to tell him Becky had run away from Mr Newhouse, but Ms Clifton was also heading for him and she got there first and started talking – she was saying something about boys' bad behaviour. So I thought I'd tell him later, especially as there were a lot of students around and it would have been difficult to say anything without being overheard.

'Then Dr Hunter arrived with the shocking news. I rushed after the others, and when I saw Mr Newhouse on the floor I tried to revive him, but I couldn't. I knew it must have been from hitting his head on the coat hook, but for days I tried to convince myself it just couldn't have been. You don't expect someone to die from something like that, do you?'

Priestley took the question as rhetorical, so remained silent. Oaken also maintained silence, as she felt she had said everything that needed to be said. Priestley decided it would be better to have the statement signed without delay rather than risk getting bogged down in detail. He therefore formally terminated the interview, asked Martello to finish any typing outside the interview room, and to print off the statement for signing.

With the recording equipment visibly turned off, he enquired, 'How are you feeling, now, about Mr Newhouse's death?'

She settled back into the chair, as though discussing the weather with a friend. 'I know people say not to speak ill of the dead, but the more I've learned about his antics, the less I like him, or at least the memory of him.'

Priestley had the opposite thought: the best time to speak ill of someone is when they are dead – so they cannot sue.

Oaken continued. 'Until last Wednesday I had no more than strong suspicions; seeing little Becky running away from him like that just seemed to confirm everything I'd imagined. I think it was the fact that he laughed about whatever he'd been doing to her that made me angry enough to try to push him down. Do you know exactly what he did do to her?'

As the statement was not yet signed, Priestley decided to keep that aspect of the case obscured for now. 'We were trying not to upset her, so we didn't go into too much detail about that.'

Oaken assumed this confirmed her worst suspicions. 'He would have been sacked of course for what he did to Becky, and I assume you'd have prosecuted him too, but at least he would still have been alive. He could have mended his ways, but now he can't.'

Priestley was concerned Oaken may consider taking her own life, depending on the extent to which she blamed herself. He thought how an immoral person may be upset only at being caught, whereas a moral one may seek forgiveness through various ways and means, some by doing good works, others by the self-deception of allowing a religious leader to absolve them. He knew the hardest judge for the most moral was always themselves. He decided he should investigate the extent to which she held herself responsible for the second death. 'How do you feel about the other tragedy – Hugh Cassidy?'

'Hugh was what I believe the military call "collateral damage". There's a long chain of people who could claim a share of responsibility, starting with Mr Newhouse for his own behaviour and me for pushing him and accidentally killing him.'

Priestley looked closely at Oaken to see if this might have been intended as the start of her defence; her distant gaze suggested it was no more than she genuinely believed.

Oaken continued, 'The police for failing to keep his identity secret; the newspapers for publishing his personal details; society for discriminating against Gays; I'm sure there's more that could be added to the list if I knew all the facts.'

Priestley was relieved to hear her spread the responsibility. If she had heaped all the blame on herself for the death of an innocent, he could have expected her to be merciless in her self-condemnation, and consequently he would have needed to put her on suicide watch. He undertook to reinforce her current attitude so that she would be less tempted to increase her sense of guilt by discounting ameliorating factors. 'I agree there's more: the civil service and the government for encouraging the obscuring of same-gender relationships, first of civil partnerships and then of Gay marriages, by pressuring institutions into grouping them with marriages between men and women, and thereby reinforcing the idea that same-gender relationships are not something to be identified openly but are to be hidden away from the prying eyes of the prejudiced.' He had carefully chosen the term "same-gender" rather than "homosexual" in order not to utter the word "sexual" for fear of offending her sense of propriety. 'Then there's society at large, with some people who object to the term "Gay marriage" and others who object to the underlying principle. There's also Gay spokespeople' – Priestley had sought the politically correct word – 'who harm the perception of Gay people by pursuing activities apparently aimed at cultural dominance. I was recently reminded how the opening ceremony of the Glasgow Commonwealth Games included a kiss between men that was a reference to Gay marriage. Considering how many very young people will have been watching the ceremony on TV, this could be deemed to have undermined the drive toward reducing the early sexualisation of children – which is something, I am sure, you will have been concerned about at your school. As some of the Commonwealth countries deem homosexuality illegal, the message is that Gay Rights trump even national laws. I suppose the choice of a Gay man to play host was unsurprising, given what appears to be a high proportion of homosexuals and lesbians working in British media compared with the population at large. The media seems to have lost the principle of "fair share" – which is also a concept I'm sure you support.' These abstruse, overly-long sentences with their irrelevant references were designed to obfuscate by suggesting intellectual credibility to his supportive arguments in a manner that Oaken would be unlikely to remember in detail and consequently would be unable to unpick in the dark watches of the night.

Martello arrived with the printed statement for checking, signing and witnessing. Once the formalities were concluded, Priestley walked with her to the prisoner processing area and then to the cell where she would be spending the night. He offered her various facilities, including use of a telephone; it saddened him to discover there was no one she wished to contact.

She asked, 'Is it really necessary for me to spend tonight in a cell? I expect there'll be much more of this to come in the future, but for now there are things I'd like to sort out at home.'

Priestley asked quietly, 'Is there anything that can't wait until the morning?'

She looked down at her feet, 'I don't suppose there is, really.'

He checked there were no animals needing attention, 'Do you have any pets?'

She looked up again, 'No; I've never felt the need. Besides, I wouldn't have wished to neglect them, being out all day.'

'Well, if there's nothing urgent, I suggest you try to sleep and we can sort out everything in the morning.'

'Sleep? I doubt I'll be able to.'

'You could try saying "and" lots of times; just keep saying it over and over, but make the gaps different every time. I know it might not sound like it would work, but it can tire the mind, and sleep can come without you realising it.'

'Is that something you've tried yourself?'

'Yes, the technique worked for me. I didn't like the idea of taking sleeping-pills, as it's a sort of drug-dependence, which is something I was warned to avoid.' He realised he had disclosed too much information about himself, so tried to make the advice sound more general. 'Everyone should be warned against drug dependence.'

Oaken recognised the unsuccessful attempt to obscure the disclosure. She helped him to believe it may have passed unnoticed, by referring back to the earlier advice. 'Saying "and" sounds like it might work a lot better than counting sheep.'

Now that the statement had been signed, Priestley felt no further need to keep away lawyers who might interfere with the process of getting to the truth. He therefore added, 'You'll need to appear in court in the morning to get everything formalised. Maybe we could arrange for you to have a solicitor to help you through the system? You really could do with one to help you understand what's happening.'

'You're very kind, Chief Inspector.'

As he left her in the cell he remained concerned about the risk of suicide, despite having done everything he could think of; he therefore spoke to the duty sergeant about the need for vigilance, and had it put on record. As he went to gather his team for a de-briefing session, he reflected on a time when he himself had been the subject of a suicide watch.

* * *

Priestley began the team meeting by expressing his belief that Oaken's statement represented the truth, or at least a close approximation. Berry asked what the Crown Prosecution Service would be charging her with. Priestley offered his analysis. 'At one extreme it could be Voluntary Manslaughter with no extenuating circumstances, or maybe with a Partial Defence of Loss of Control. At the other end of the scale it could be treated as Accidental Death. In between, there are various flavours of assault. The CPS could argue there was an intention to cause some harm, though I don't believe any jury could be persuaded she intended to kill him. I'm second-guessing here, but I think they might go for Involuntary Manslaughter resulting from an Unlawful Act.'

Witty asked, 'What do you think she should be charged with?'

Priestley responded, 'I'd be tempted to save the taxpayer the cost of a court case and rule it an accident. If not, I'd hope any sentence didn't involve prison – she's more likely to prove a danger to society if she has to serve a spell inside, because she could come out mean and bitter and twisted. So I'd hope the worst she'd get is a suspended sentence.'

Witty responded immediately, 'As in hanging?'

Priestley sighed heavily, 'You really...'

Witty interrupted the reprimand, 'Sorry, sir; it just came out.'

Priestley shook his head slowly from side to side for a few seconds before continuing. 'It's up to the CPS to decide on the charge.' He looked directly at Berry. 'Tony, how do you think John Newhouse's sister would react if the CPS decided not to prosecute?'

Berry looked thoughtful. Eventually he replied, 'Being a

solicitor, I'm sure she believes in justice.'

Priestley reflected on how naïve that sounded.

Berry continued, 'Susan's really a much nicer person than you might think when you first meet her, so I'm certain she wouldn't be vindictive – wanting vengeance. It worries me she'll find out about her brother's background, and that could be really upsetting for her. Do we have to reveal everything we know about him?'

Priestley gave him a hard stare. 'There's a woman's incarceration at stake here; Oaken has every right to have all the facts placed before the judge, so that any sentencing recognises the reality of her understanding of the behaviour she expected from the deceased. If it goes to court I expect Susan would feel a need to be there, in which case she'll need to know the background so that she can accept the fairness of any sentence. Oaken's right to have the facts put before the judge far outweigh any wish you may have for Susan to maintain an idealised memory of her brother.'

Berry looked abashed. He changed tack to break the silence. 'It's a successful outcome to our involvement, anyway. Aren't we all supposed to go to the pub, or get some drinks in here to celebrate?'

Priestley continued to give Berry a hard stare. 'What do we have to celebrate, really? We've closed the case, certainly, but think about Glenda Oaken. She assumed John Newhouse was responsible for a sexual assault on Becky Worthington because she knew what kind of a person he was, but in fact the girl had simply gone into the wrong changing room, perhaps because her poor reading ability led to her failing to understand – or even to read – the notices that were posted on the doors. Oaken pushed Newhouse because of the reputation he had earned – not for what he had done that afternoon. She was evidently aiming for a very hard push, but I don't imagine for one moment she anticipated it would result in his death. Whatever the CPS decides, her life has been ruined by chance events conspiring against her. So it may be OK for TV cops to party, but I don't see anything here for us to celebrate.'

They all maintained silence, each of them feeling Priestley was right, but at the same time wishing their collective success could be reflected in a positive way with an upbeat ending. Priestley recognised the need for a little team-building, if only for the sake of the next case they might work together. He offered, 'What I would like to do is treat you all to a drink or two at the pub by way of a wake for both of the dead – John Newhouse and Hugh Cassidy. Are we all in favour?'

Berry's response suggested he had not entirely appreciated the subtlety of the argument against celebration. 'So we do still go for a booze-up at the pub.'

Priestley handed two twenty pound notes to Witty and sent him off to the local with Martello, Plummer and Dunn. He kept Berry back for a brief word on the subject of disclosing information. 'When should we be informing Susan Newhouse about progress?'

'She should be told straight away, and I'd like to be the one to do it – before it becomes public knowledge.'

'Everyone affected has a right to know. Should the mother be informed first?'

'I suppose so. Perhaps we could tell them at the same time. If you phoned the mother, I could phone Susan.'

'What about the other sister? Doesn't she have an equal right?'

'One of us could phone her after.'

'You sound like you're not thinking beyond how you can be the one to break the news to Susan. You need to avoid letting your personal feelings get in the way of your professional duty. I'm going to help you out, though. I'll phone Cynthia Newhouse to let her know that Glenda Oaken has admitted causing the death, but that it was to some extent unintentional and so it's for the CPS and the court to decide what's appropriate from hereon. Before I finish the call, you can phone Susan and let her know the same thing. I'll give Cynthia the option of telling her other daughter, Mrs Janet Henshaw, or of letting me inform her. After that, we'll join the others in the pub.'

Priestley explained the situation to Cynthia, who asked him to phone Janet in case she had any questions she wished to put to him. In parallel, Berry phoned Susan, and was still on the phone when Priestley had finished his second call. Priestley gave the throat-cutting signal to Berry, who guillotined his call with, 'I have to go now; my boss needs me for something. I'll talk to you soon.'

Priestley decided to meet the Crown Prosecution Service lawyer alone, just in case Berry disclosed something about the investigation that he would rather remained unsaid. 'I have to meet with our man from the CPS. I'll give him an investigation summary and then go through Oaken's statement. There's no need for you to be there – it's all fairly straightforward. You get off to the pub and I'll see you when I'm done here.'

'Will I be driving you home?'

'Not this time – I'll be on soft drinks.'

'Helen's orders?'

'Don't be cheeky.' He flicked his fingers as though to shoo away an annoying fly.

Priestley had a frustrating meeting with Edward Tomkins of the CPS, a young man who applied the perverted adage, "Why use five words when fifty will do."

Priestley explained his wish to keep his bargain with Oaken not to trace any of the girls who had had sex with Newhouse. Tomkins argued such evidence should not be adduced in the absence of identification of the girls.

Priestley suggested the girl in the shower should not be required to give evidence as she may be traumatised by the ordeal of being questioned in court. Tomkins argued her evidence could be deemed pivotal to a defence that soapy water had been a major contributory factor in causing the defendant to slip and fall on the deceased.

Priestley expressed concern that the girl, on being cross-examined in court, may imagine herself as being in some way responsible for Newhouse's death. Tomkins insisted a suitable explanation should suffice to overcome that concern.

Priestley referred to the girl's Asperger's syndrome as likely to make it difficult for lawyers to extract details from her without being accused of leading the witness. Tomkins countered that the girl could make an excellent witness as she may be incapable of lying.

Priestley suggested the school's management – the headmaster and the governors – should be prosecuted for gross negligence, having failed to replace several broken hooks including the one that spiked Newhouse's skull. Tomkins indicated he had no remit to expand his brief beyond Oaken.

Priestley suggested the government should be prosecuted for failing to provide sufficient funds to maintain the school premises in good order. Tomkins responded briefly, for once, 'Now you're just having me on.'

Priestley highlighted how Oaken had decided not to engage a lawyer and had voluntarily made a statement. Tomkins responded by gleefully rubbing his hands together, gloating, 'Another lamb to the slaughter.'

Priestley pointed out his reaction appeared to be immoral. Tomkins agreed it could be so construed, though his only concern was that it was not unethical.

Priestley suggested Oaken may not have thought her action dangerous, being simply a push. Tomkins elucidated how her thoughts were irrelevant, as it had been clearly defined in Regina and Ball that one must consider only how the action may be viewed by a sober and reasonable man.

Priestley suggested he no longer wished to be a sober man, though he hoped he would remain reasonable. Tomkins enquired as to why he seemed unhappy with their discussion.

Priestley highlighted how everything he suggested appeared to evoke a negative response, and that perhaps he himself would like to put forward some constructive proposals.

Tomkins proposed a charge of Voluntary Manslaughter. Priestley responded that such a charge would be bound to fail.

Tomkins proposed a charge of Voluntary Manslaughter with a partial defence of Loss of Control. Priestley responded that such a charge would be likely to fail.

Tomkins proposed a charge of Involuntary Manslaughter by an unlawful and dangerous act. Priestley explained that pushing is only slightly unlawful and not generally dangerous, and that such a charge would be unlikely to succeed. Tomkins reminded him of exactly such a case in London that resulted in a successful action against a member of the constabulary. Priestley glared at him and remained silent.

Tomkins proposed an alternative charge of Involuntary Manslaughter with subjective recklessness. Priestley suggested the defence might accept this if the sentence was an unconditional discharge, but if she engaged even a half-decent lawyer, then the prosecution would be very likely to fail. Tomkins agreed it was important they give themselves the best chance of success by not encouraging her to engage a capable lawyer.

Priestley suggested the death itself was accidental. Tomkins argued this would make his own rôle redundant.

Priestley expressed the opinion that Oaken did not represent a threat to the public, and that her incarceration would be a waste of money. Tomkins accepted a minimal sentence would benefit the public purse.

Having finally reached agreement on something, Priestley proposed that Tomkins should reflect on the case and decide in the morning what charges should be made. Tomkins agreed to postpone the decision pending deliberations and confabulations with his colleagues.

Immediately following the meeting, Priestley contacted Sol Schaeffer at home, giving him the background to the case and suggesting he should take on Oaken as a client. Priestley added, 'The police have a responsibility to ensure the law's upheld, but I can't see how locking her up is in anyone's interests.'

Sol's response was predictably upbeat. 'I can see no reason why my soon-to-be client should be incarcerated for her noble and protective action, which of itself could not reasonably have been expected to result in the unfortunate outcome. How's that for starters?'

'I didn't hear you – there was some crackle on the line. See you tomorrow.'

Priestley headed for the pub, optimistic that justice may gain the upper hand.

Witty saw Priestley enter the pub and dashed to the bar to pay for his drink out of the remainder of the fund.

'Orange juice and lemonade – make it a pint.'

'Are you on the wagon, then?'

'I'm not a condemned man.'

'What?'

'On the wagon – it's from when the condemned used to be allowed to stop off for a final pint before their execution.'

'Fascinating, I'm sure – but you still haven't answered the question.'

'My darling wife explained to me why I might prefer to remain an alcohol-free zone for a little while. She put forward a very persuasive argument.'

'Surely, not withdrawal of conjugal rights?'

'I don't think legislation supports the idea of any such rights anymore.'

'She'd be cutting your nose off to spite her face, anyway.'

'Detective Constable Whittington, how you any idea how far

you've just overstepped the mark with that comment? Just because we're in a pub, that doesn't mean you shouldn't show some respect for ... Is there any point in me spelling it out? I've obviously been too much of a nice guy, all these years. You're not the first DC who thinks they can say anything they like to me. I'm going to have to make some changes – no more Mr Nice Guy. Besides, I always thought your humour was to cover up your troubles – wearing the painted smile of a clown to hide the sadness, and all that. As far as I can see, you've struck lucky, so maybe you should be thinking about hanging up your clown costume in the wardrobe.'

Witty looked genuinely concerned that he had strayed into dangerous territory. 'Sorry, sir; I didn't realise your sex life was such an issue.'

Priestley leaned in closely and spoke through gritted teeth. 'It's nothing to do with my sex life.' He thought Witty looked unconvinced. 'It's actually to do with my fulfilling other obligations, such as making breakfast every alternate day.' Witty still appeared to be unsure whether to accept the testimony. 'There are times when I see you as ready to make sergeant, and other times – such as this – when I think you may be a liability. Do you wish to be promoted, ever?'

'Yes sir, especially if Lily takes a chance on trying something new and I'm left the only breadwinner.'

'Then you need to avoid ill-considered humour – sometimes what you say isn't appropriate, and other times what you say just isn't funny. You need to knock it off and grasp opportunities with both hands – like you have with Lily.'

Witty was almost certain Priestley was using sexual innuendo to be amusing – the very type of thing he had just been reprimanded for. He decided it may be a test and that he would be safer not to hint he had made a humorous interpretation. 'I'll mend my ways, sir.'

Priestley nodded. 'But don't forget you're obliged to laugh at jokes told by superiors – even if they're not funny.'

Witty gave a short laugh, hoping it was of regulation length.

They joined the other officers around a table. Berry immediately asked if Oaken had been charged. Priestley explained how everything would be decided and dealt with in the morning, adding, 'Let's not think about work for now – let's just relax a bit.

It's only a suggestion, but let's not forget who's making it.'
Everyone laughed except Witty; he felt he needed to be more
certain it was definitely humour and not simply an instruction.

* * *

Oaken lay quietly in her cell, listening to the hum of a distant
strip-light and the whistling of the wind. She had a feeling of fear
for what would follow, but also relief that her guilty secret was
now known. She compared and contrasted this with how Hugh
must have felt at the exposure of his own secret – except she knew
it never was a secret. The Head of Art had heard about the
marriage from a friend of a friend when he was holidaying in St
Ives, and at the start of term he told the headmaster who in turn
informed the senior staff, who spread the word with the proviso
that it should remain a secret as Hugh had not formally advised the
school. Consequently, virtually all the staff knew, but no one
publicly acknowledged it.

CHAPTER 31

Priestley Assesses his Team

Thursday

Priestley visited Oaken in her cell, recommending she eat the breakfast that lay untouched. She attempted to show her non-existent savvy. 'I suppose I'll be getting a dock brief?'

'No, Miss Oaken, that's something that was given by a court rather than received by someone such as yourself, and doesn't sit comfortably with Article Six of the European Convention on Human Rights, your right to a fair trial. I know you have concerns about the morality of instructing a clever lawyer, but really there's nothing wrong with getting a decent one to represent you.'

'An honest one?'

'You may be asking too much, there. But certainly I know a good one; I hope you don't think I've taken too much of a liberty, but I've already spoken to him and suggested you may wish to engage him.'

'Is that normal?'

'No, not really, but I'd like to make sure you don't suffer an injustice at the hands of the legal system. And if you wonder, there isn't any sort of kick-back mechanism in operation.'

'The idea of a "kick-back" hadn't occurred to me. Will I have to understand a lot of jargon?'

'Only if you attempt to represent yourself, but you really don't want to do that. As Abraham Lincoln said, "He who represents himself has a fool for a client." Even lawyers hire lawyers to represent them.'

'When may I see him?'

'He's waiting upstairs, but he won't speak to you on your own ahead of being charged, in case you divulge something that makes him ethically unable to represent you. I suggest we get the formalities over with – I'll charge you myself, with him present, once I know what the Crown Prosecution Service's intentions are. You'll then be brought before the court and given bail – the police have no reason to oppose it.'

'Let's get it over with then.'

* * *

The millstones of justice were still turning exceedingly slowly when Priestley returned to his new office – the one that had formerly belonged to DCI Castleton. On his desk he found a message to call on Chief Superintendent Barbara Watt. In her office the conversation was brief and to the point.

'Well done for clearing up the Newhouse case. You can expect the promotions board to confirm your elevation. Richie's looking at candidates for sergeant – he'll be asking for your views. That's all.'

'Ma'am.'

Priestley returned to his new office, wondering whether to fill it with pot plants. His phone rang almost immediately, a call from Superintendent Richard Yelland.

'Marcus.'

'Superintendent.'

'Congratulations on your promotion – I'm told it'll be going through 'ere long, subject to the usual formalities. I'm taking a look at who else may be due for a step up. I could do with an update on those who've been working for you on the Newhouse case. Well done, by the way; we all did our bit on that one.' Priestley wondered what Yelland had contributed that justified his saying "we"; perhaps sitting in a press conference and saying nothing, or maybe helping to dispose of Castleton. 'Come to my office for a chat when you're free; now would be good for me.'

Priestley correctly interpreted this as an order to attend at once. 'I'll be right there, sir.'

Priestley knocked and received an immediate 'Enter.'

'Sir.'

'Call me Richie. Babs told you what I'm after?'

'Yes, Richie. Babs said you're looking at filling the "sergeant" vacancy.'

'Whoa, hold on their, Marcus. One rank up only. I said you can call me Richie. I call her Babs. You call her The Chief Super.'

'Right you are; and what about ranks down?'

'She calls me Richie, I call you Marcus, and she calls you … anything she damn well pleases.' Priestley laughed good-naturedly.

Yelland picked up a buff file. 'It was good you got a quick result on the Newhouse case. You ran the investigation on a shoestring, Marcus; that's just what's needed nowadays, budgets being the way they are. Now, tell me how your people performed.'

Priestley had responses prepared without written notes, to suggest familiarity with the subjects and confidence in his opinions. 'I'll start with DC Whittington – Witty by name, witty by nature; but it can be Neil's biggest weakness – sometimes he uses his wit when it would be better to play the straight man. I've mentioned this to him, and if he keeps it in check I can see good reasons to support him being promoted. He's done some really good work on this case. He had an idea for processing witnesses efficiently that was original and really excellent. He's definitely "sergeant" material. Just one thing to bear in mind at the moment is that he's intending to get a divorce, so things are a bit "up in the air" for him as far as home life's concerned.'

'Always a tricky time, that. Maybe once he's got himself sorted out we can take a closer look. Next?'

'DC Martello. Lily has been ever so useful to me on this case. She has a presence in interviews that people respond to.'

'Yes. She's damn good looking as well, isn't she? Have you been tempted in that direction? It's better you tell me now than I find out later.'

'It's difficult not to be tempted – her beauty stands out a mile; but I'm determinedly uxorious.'

'And quite right too,' responded Yelland, having no idea of the meaning of the word "uxorious". 'Though I think "a mile" is a bit of an exaggeration – they're not that big, eh? Eh?'

Priestley laughed whole-heartedly, Yelland being his line-manager. 'Lily's beauty's a big asset.'

'Really? I haven't looked at her from behind.'

Priestley laughed again, trying not to let the edges of his mouth turn down. After a moment, he adopted a more serious expression. 'I've noticed that men, women and children all seem to respond to her looks. The downside is that she isn't consistently great at detection, and I think it's fair to say there have been times when she's shied away from some of the grislier aspects of our work. So I don't see her as taking on a more senior position in terms of straight detective work, but if there were something that enabled her to by-pass that weakness and be employed in a more PR-type rôle, then I'm sure she'd prefer it to what she does now.'

'And she's unmarried, so no divorce issues hanging over her.'

'I wouldn't quite say that, Richie. Neil's living with her and they're both claiming it's going to be permanent.'

'He's a lucky so-and-so. It sounds like Lily's another case where we need to let the fog clear before we consider awarding gongs. Who's next?'

'WPC Plummer. Linda. Excellent at working with people, and very good at other aspects of her job, too. She hasn't had much opportunity to display any leadership skills, and I wonder whether she's too nice a person to be particularly strong when it comes to giving orders. Though she's probably the best at what she does now, she may not be sergeant material.'

'Well, the only way to resolve that is for her to be given the chance to show her mettle. Look for an opportunity going forward.'

'There are aspects of detective work where I believe she could be a real asset. I'd like to invite her to join my team as a DC.'

'Then look for an opening for her. Next?'

'DC Beresford. Tony only joined in April, and he's on the fast track based on entrance assessment criteria. He has a quite exceptional mind when it comes to analysing technical matters like data and plans, but right now he can sometimes be a liability as far as people are concerned – he's too honest.'

'Well, you'd better knock that out of him straight away – honesty's the last thing we need.'

'I'm working on it. He's very keen and willing to learn, and has the right attitude to improve his understanding with every new experience, but the "people" side doesn't come naturally to him. To my mind the question is whether to put him in a position where he can use his current strengths, or to take our time developing him slowly so that he can end up holding the full bag of tricks.'

'That's a very insightful assessment, Marcus. I'll make sure it's put into the mix when he comes up for review.'

'That just leaves PC Dunn, who I understand is making his surname change official from Jobs-Dunn.'

'Good idea, get rid of that damn stupid name. And when do you think he might be a candidate for promotion?'

'When Hell freezes over, Richie. And even then I'd need some convincing.'

Priestley walked through the main office – he had heard it described as Management By Wandering Around, MBWA. He noticed Witty looking pleased with himself. 'You look like you've just thought of a good joke, Neil.'

'I've taken what you said very seriously, sir; I'll be keeping humour to a minimum, and there won't be any at all where it's the wrong type of situation.'

'Then what is it that's making you look so pleased with yourself? And don't tell me if it's anything to do with what you and Lily were up to last night.'

'Sexual innuendo is also a thing of the past, sir, where it might cause offence. If in doubt, I'll not speak out.'

'I'm starting to think you're serious, this time.'

'Yes sir, I'll be doing whatever I can to justify promotion; I hope I'll be able to earn your full confidence in my ability to perform as a sergeant, sir.'

Priestley wondered how long Witty would be able to keep up this behaviour. His last response also suggested to him the term "brown-nosing"; well, it was a common enough attitude when someone had recently experienced a life-changing event, such as becoming a parent, getting married, or moving in with a new partner.

'So, why the smiley face?'

'I've just received a call from a Mrs Ginny Bakewell, to tell me she's been diagnosed with diabetes.'

'And that's something to smile about?'

'I'm smiling because she was phoning to thank me for diagnosing her. She was quite upbeat about it – apparently there's some stem cell-based research coming out of Harvard that looks really promising for future treatment.'

'So, you're moonlighting as a doctor now, are you?'

'Well, credit where credit's due – it was actually a Chocolate Labrador that did the diagnosis.'

'This conversation is becoming increasingly bizarre by the minute, Neil. Are you talking about a real dog, or one made of chocolate?'

'It's a real dog called Brownie that's the pet of a girl called Rosie. The girl has diabetes and the dog warns her if her blood-sugar level needs correcting. When we were called out about Newhouse, Lily had the idea of getting a sniffer dog to pick up any trails from the changing room. There wasn't time to get a police dog, so Lily took a gamble and tried it with the medical dog. It drew a blank at the front door, so I suggested the back door, and we followed a trail that took us to a dead end street. We walked about a bit but didn't find anything, except the dog went up to a woman who'd just got off a bus. I guessed she might have diabetes, so I suggested she get herself checked out by her GP. It turns out Brownie was right.'

'Why wasn't this included in your report?'

'Because we drew a blank, and I didn't want us to look like idiots for trying something that didn't work.'

'You say Brownie led you to a cul-de-sac. Just check it against Becky Worthington's address, will you?' Priestley sat on the edge of the desk, doing his best to look casual and approachable.

Witty soon looked up from his computer screen, a desperately troubled expression having replaced his smile. 'Brownie led us right to the Worthington's house. If we'd followed that lead through, we could have got straight to the bottom of things. Christ Almighty!'

'Thou shalt not take the name of the Lord thy God in vain, Neil; add that to your list of personal objectives along with including everything in your reports in future.' Seeing how disheartened Witty appeared, he added, 'Don't beat yourself up too much about it, Neil; with Castleton as SIO, there's no guarantee he would have made anything of it and put the investigation on the right track. Even so, you'd best keep this between us and Lily, otherwise it could screw up your chances of making Sergeant.' Priestley sighed as he wandered back to his office, feeling as though a cloud had drifted along and darkened his personal sunny day.

* * *

Verbane called Hunter and Clifton to a crisis conference. 'Glenda's been charged with John's death, but I can't see her returning to this school even if she's found "not guilty". So, Vicky, if you feel you're up to it, I'd like you to become Acting

423

Headmistress with immediate effect.'

'Of course I'll step in, Headmaster, but I need to make sure my duties as Head of Sixth Form aren't neglected.'

'Well, run them in parallel and let me know what extra help you need. I've spoken with the governors and they've given me their support for filling vacancies internally in the short term, but with three staff gone we'll also have to advertise externally. It could be next term before we can bring in permanent replacements – the best candidates are likely to be already employed, so they won't be able to join us straight away. That means we'll be needing agency staff, which is something Glenda always used to deal with. So, Vicky, that's your first task as Headmistress.'

'I know what's involved – I'll get it sorted.'

'Good. Now, Brian, we need to consider how the school should mark Hugh's death.'

'Actually, Headmaster, it would be more normal nowadays to refer to "A Celebration of Hugh's Life". I had to arrange one at my previous school when a sixth-form girl died unexpectedly; it's difficult to get the balance right, when everyone's upset and no one really feels like celebrating anything.'

'You've convinced me you're the right person to deal with it.'

Hunter thought Verbane had not needed any convincing, and was simply trying to avoid becoming too involved himself. He wondered if Verbane had his own demons regarding death.

Verbane continued. 'Glenda was against the idea of asking John's family to allow a deputation of students to attend his funeral, and I now understand why. There's no such issue with Hugh, so I'd like the school to be fully represented tomorrow – staff and students. Make sure we give Hugh a good send-off.'

Hunter paused, choosing his words carefully. 'John's family didn't really want anyone from school at the service – except you, of course – so there wasn't any issue there, but we don't know what Hugh's family would like.'

'Well, I'm sure you could persuade them if necessary; we've lost a colleague, after all, and the students have lost a teacher.'

Clifton interjected vehemently. 'Though we may miss Hugh, the sense of grief for a lost colleague or teacher can never really be compared to the pain felt by family, especially parents who've lost their only child.'

Verbane and Hunter turned to Clifton, searching her face for an explanation behind her strength of feeling. Verbane responded, 'You're quite right, Vicky. We should start by finding out Hugh's parents' wishes.'

Hunter nodded, 'Not forgetting Hugh's partner, of course.'

Hunter phoned Cassidy's parents' home number and listened to a recorded message which included mention of Gareth's work number; he called it and spoke to someone who would have been willing to give him a mobile number – only neither Gareth nor Gwen possessed a mobile phone. He had not been expecting that response, so terminated the call without thinking to enquire further about where they may be located. Next, he tried Hugh and Michael's home number, but there was only an answering machine; he decided not to leave a message, as he had no way of knowing when it might be read.

Hunter decided to enlist the help of the police to track down Hugh's parents. He phoned DC Whittington's direct line that was noted on his card, believing he may be due a favour for not revealing the marijuana saga. 'Detective Constable Whittington? This is Brian Hunter from Midshaw School. You may remember we met last week.'

Witty steeled himself for a complaint. 'Yes, of course. What can I do for you?'

'Hugh Cassidy's funeral tomorrow is at Midshaw church, and the Headmaster has asked me to contact Hugh's parents, Gareth and Gwen, and his partner, Michael, to find out how they'd feel about having some members of staff there, and maybe some students too. I've tried Gareth's home and work numbers, and Michael's landline, but I haven't been able to make contact. Apparently Gareth doesn't have a mobile phone, and I don't have a number for Michael's. Could you help me to get in touch with them? It's quite urgent, as we'd need to start organising parental permissions today if any students are to go.'

Witty logged Hunter's mobile number and undertook to call him back. He went to see Priestley to relay the request, adding 'Should I ask them if they'd permit the police to be present as well? It could be good for appearances, in view of the bad press we might still get.'

'That's "Officer Thinking", as we used to say in the army. Do you have any other reasons why we should be there?'

Witty hesitated – he had a reason but felt it may not be a good one for someone who had "Sergeant" aspirations.

Priestley pressed him for an answer, 'Come on – spit it out, man.'

'It's my conscience – I mean my collective police conscience. I have a sense of shared guilt over Cassidy's suicide.'

Priestley looked directly into Witty's windows, attempting to see through them into his soul. 'Well said, Neil. Offer them as few or as many officers as they wish out of yourself, Lily, Linda, Tony, Elias and me.'

Witty went back to his desk and phoned Gough's mobile number.

'Michael Gough.'

'Hello, it's DC Whittington.' Knowing how people could fail to register names in times of stress, he added, 'Do you remember me? I'm the officer who started the search for Hugh when he was identified as a missing person. I'm ever so sorry about how things worked out for you.'

'Of course I remember you; didn't you say your name's Neil? I should have phoned you to thank you for doing your best for Hugh.'

Witty found himself shocked at being thanked by someone who had suffered loss as a consequence of behaviour by police officers. 'That's ever so kind of you to say so. I'm calling to pass on a message from Hugh's school. They'd like to be allowed to attend the funeral service if you and Hugh's parents wish them to; that would be teachers and students. I haven't yet been able to get in touch with Hugh's parents – would you be able to find out how they feel about it? I don't have a contact number or address for them up here.'

'Just a minute.'

Witty wondered if Gough would take long to decide how many he might like to attend.

Gough spoke again. 'Are you there, Neil? They said they'd be happy to have as many children and teachers as the school can spare.'

'How did you contact them?'

'I just asked them – they're with me – we're outside Hathersage church.'

'I thought the service would be at Midshaw church?'

'It is; I've been showing them local places of interest. I'm not sure they believed "Little John" was real until I showed them his grave. Do you want to speak to them yourself?'

'Maybe when I've finished talking to you – there's something else I need to ask you.'

'If you prefer to call them later, you have my landline number, don't you. They're staying with me at the cottage.'

'That's useful to know. Anyway, the other thing I need to ask you is if you'd like any police officers to be present at the funeral; I completely understand if you'd rather not, as it's really a time for family and friends, but I do want you to know that we share your sense of loss, even if it's only from getting to know about Hugh after he'd died. Everybody I spoke to said he was such a nice guy.'

'He was the nicest of guys. I'd be happy for you to be there, Neil, and anybody else who thinks like you do. Just give me a moment.' After a short delay Gough spoke again. 'Gwen and Gareth say they'd be ever so pleased to see as many officers as you wish; they really appreciate all the effort you put into trying to find him.'

'Well, thank you for being so … welcoming. Perhaps I could just have a quick word with one of them.'

'I'll pass you onto Gareth; if I put Gwen on she'll keep you chatting all day.'

Witty heard a woman's lilting voice in the background, 'Oh, you are a card, aren't you Michael?'

A Welsh baritone sang out, 'Hello, Gareth here.'

'Hello, it's Detective Constable Neil Whittington. Michael was saying you're alright with the school sending teachers and students to the funeral service, and police officers as well. Do you have any idea of the maximum you could make room for?'

'We'll make room for as many as wish to come; we won't turn any away.'

'Well, I'll pass that message to the school. Is there anything else I can do for you?'

'I don't think so. Does Michael have your number?'

'Yes, he has.'

'Then I'll let you go.'

'OK. Goodbye.'

Witty thought Gareth sounded the stalwart type. He found

himself wondering how Michael could have seemed so relaxed on the day before the funeral of his partner, considering how distraught he had been when Hugh had gone missing.

Hunter received the information from Witty and informed Verbane, who himself typed one letter for staff and another for students. The staff letter included a tear-off strip to request permission to attend the funeral service. The student letter had a similar tear-off strip, except the signature must be that of their parent or guardian. Verbane signed the upper sections of the two letters and took them to the administration office. 'Jo, here are two letters for copying; one for staff, the other for students. Get a copy to every member of staff and every student without delay.'

'You should have let me type them for you, Headmaster.'

Verbane thought, 'Yes, but the funeral's tomorrow, not next month.' He responded to her, 'This is a rush job – your top priority; could you get it all done within the hour? Distribute them at the start of the next period, so all the students are in one place and you don't have to go chasing them up.'

'I'll certainly try, Headmaster.'

'I don't want to hear "try" – I want to hear "I've done it." And when you've finished, come to my office and I'll see how long you took. It's ten past, so away you go.'

Verbane returned to his office, thinking, 'I should have taken that attitude with her years ago.'

* * *

Sol Schaeffer phoned Priestley and requested a private meeting, off the premises. They met in the park and walked around the empty boating lake, the boats themselves having been removed and stored for the following spring. Schaeffer explained the problem. 'I'm on the trail of some exculpatory evidence, Marcus. Glenda Oaken's determined to admit to Manslaughter by an Unlawful and Dangerous Act, when I say she shouldn't. I've finally got to the bottom of why she's being so stubborn. She believes a young teenager was sexually assaulted by John Newhouse, and she doesn't want this to be made known. I can't find anything in the evidence that says that's what happened, so have you any idea where she got that idea?'

Priestley recalled how he had been economical with the truth in order to encourage her to make a full and frank confession. 'I think she may have made an incorrect assumption. The girl in question was in the shower when Newhouse came in, but I don't believe there was any sort of sexual assault. If that's the only reason she says she should plead guilty, you ought to get her to change her mind.'

'She also mentioned she knows of three schoolgirls who had sex with Newhouse – she doesn't want their names to come out either, and she says there's probably plenty more who could be revealed if anyone started digging. How would you feel about Newhouse's behaviour with teenage girls being stipulated?'

'That's a question for the CPS, surely.'

'I've spoken to Mr Tomkins already; he's agin' it. Don't you have any leverage in that direction?'

Priestley noticed Schaeffer's pronunciation of leverage was in the American style. 'Have you been abroad recently, by any chance? To the US, perhaps?'

'Fairly recently. How did you know?'

'I am a detective, Sol.'

'And you've been keeping tabs on me?'

'It's just your use of language and your pronunciation.'

'Oh well, I'm guilty as charged – I've recently been working in Houston. Anyway, you haven't answered my question.'

'I don't have any leverage', Priestley emphasised his English pronunciation, 'with Mr Tomkins, but I think my boss's boss may have with his boss's boss. I'll see what I can do, but I really can't promise anything.'

'It's appreciated anyway.'

'Don't mention it.'

'I'll not forget your help.'

Priestley pretended to look deeply concerned. 'No, I meant it – don't mention it! Mr Tomkins might take it personally and hold it against me.'

Schaeffer's laugh rumbled around his belly for a good few seconds. 'And congratulations, by the way; it couldn't have happened to a more deserving … dude.'

Priestley nodded and smiled. 'I think we may have to start quarantining people when they came back from the States – make sure they haven't caught some linguistic disease.'

CHAPTER 32

A Second Funeral

Friday

Verbane went into the staffroom ahead of the regular morning meeting, breaking his habit of arriving exactly on time. He stood and looked out of the window at the trees that lay beyond the boundary fence, unseasonal sunshine playing on the last of the leaves. He checked his watch for the sixth time and found the appointed moment had arrived. He turned from the window to find the staff were already assembled and facing him in silence. He steeled himself for another difficult day. He rattled through the notices without a pause. 'There are no further exclusions to report. As well as our usual three staff absentees, you all know why Glenda is away.' There was a murmur around the room that Verbane silenced with a rapid horizontal chopping gesture of his right arm. 'Vicky is now Acting Headmistress, as well as remaining Head of Sixth Form. I expect she'll need to offload some of her duties, so everyone should be ready to assist in any way she asks.

'It would seem every member of staff wishes to attend Hugh's funeral service. Unfortunately, nearly all of you will have to remain in school for the benefit of the students, most of whom will not be wishing to be there. At the start of form time, I need you to collect together the slips from any students who wish to attend the funeral, and to send someone with them directly to my office. Nil returns are required.' Another murmur began. 'I mean, if there's no one from your form who has requested they attend the funeral then let me know there aren't any. When I know the number of student requests, I can calculate how many staff can be released. If any of you feel you have a particular justification for being at the service, please let me know directly after this meeting. In fact, just let me know now – other notices can wait until Monday.'

Cleese immediately squeezed her way past colleagues to reach Verbane. With a voice that seemed unsure whether to argue or to weep, she stood directly in front of him. 'Hugh and I were good friends as well as colleagues. We talked about Classics together, but it was more than that – we often understood each other without having to say everything we were thinking. I really have to be at the service, to say a proper goodbye.'

'I agree entirely, Sophie – I thought you should be top of the list. It'll be necessary to arrange cover for your lessons.'

As she turned to leave, Cullen pushed her with his shoulder to encourage her to move aside so that he could be second. 'I played football with Hugh, which made us more than just colleagues. I'd really like to be at the service, to show him all the respect he deserves.'

'I'll let you know.'

Collins had moved to one side of Cullen. 'Headmaster, would it help if I provided a few sheets of paper for people to write down their reasons, so that you can assess them later when you know how many staff can be spared?'

'Yes, Tom.' He raised his voice to the assembled staff. 'Change of plan: write down your reasons and I'll look at them as soon as I know how many students will be attending the service. Tom's putting out some sheets.' He hurried back to his office.

Hart unlocked the door to his biology lab and allowed his form to swarm past him; they climbed onto high stools around the four large, island desks that could each seat eight students. 'First order of the day is to let me have your slips if you're been given permission to attend Mr Cassidy's funeral.' Twenty-six slips were produced from the thirty students. He noticed a boy and three girls separately whispering to those around them with heads bowed; after a minute the remaining four slips appeared, with signatures he knew were unlikely to correspond to those on file as belonging to their parents or guardians. He decided this was one of those occasions when it was better not to check – otherwise four students would miss an experience that the others would share. He found an old envelope in a drawer and put the slips in it, sealing it with clear tape and writing on it, "HAR 30/30". He held out the envelope to one of the three girls whose requests had arrived in the second wave. 'Donna, take these slips to the headmaster and tell him that everyone in this form has asked to attend Mr Cassidy's funeral.'

Donna took the envelope, responding 'You mean "Celebration of Life", don't you?'

Hart gave a weak smile, 'Changing the name doesn't alter what it is.'

Verbane began to receive bundles of request slips, some in envelopes, some held by paperclips, some in rubber bands and some stapled together. Several form groups had one hundred per cent attendance requests, others slightly fewer. He quickly typed another note, which he took to the administration office and handed to Jackson. 'Quick as you can, Jo. Photocopy this and get one to every form teacher before the end of Form Time. Peggy, you and I will take some; I'll circle the rooms you're to do, and another set for Jo, and I'll do the rest.'

He took three school layout leaflets and drew circles around different areas. Jackson produced a large pile of photocopies which they divided up, and the three of them rushed around the school. Those teachers who were honoured by Verbane's presence invariably looked worried as he entered their classrooms – it was unprecedented for him to deliver anything personally.

The note explained briefly that, as there had been so many requests, it made more sense to ask if anyone did not wish to attend the service. He returned to his office and waited for responses. Within ten minutes every form had produced a nil return, as he had hoped – it made the administration easier. He wondered how much of this was down to personal feelings for Cassidy, how much to the day being bright and sunny, and how much to a feeling they might miss a new experience; he was certain many of the students had never been taught by Cassidy, and suspected some may not even have recognised him. Nevertheless, with so many initial requests to attend, he felt it was appropriate to close the school for the duration of the service.

He prepared another note for the staff, for them to relay the instruction that everyone except the currently disabled – one permanently so, another with a broken leg – would walk to the church; the two exceptions would be driven there. Only a limited number would be permitted to go inside the church, due to space limitations. The teachers were to remind students of the solemnity of the occasion; there should be silence when the mourners were entering and leaving the church. He despatched the note via Jackson, before returning to contemplate who should be on the list of church invitees.

He started with the two disabled – though he knew Robin Loxley found it hard enough to sit still for any length of time even before he broke his leg. He added those from what had been Cassidy's Form and was now Cleese's. He contemplated including the students from the Classics in English class, wondering if they would appreciate being asked to sit quietly for any length of time. He thought the seniors from the Classics class were a safe bet to be well-behaved. He wondered how many other groups or classes could be included. He decided to send Cleese and her students on ahead, and wait for feedback from her on available space, before selecting others. Using the school timetable to locate Hunter, he invited him to come to his office at the first break, to discuss arrangements.

* * *

Priestley assembled his troops for inspection.

Plummer and Dunn looked slim in uniform without the bulk of stab-proof vests that he trusted would not be needed on this occasion, though their black ties were clip-on to avoid the danger of strangulation – probably a good idea in Dunn's case. He nodded to them in turn, 'Very smart Lin, Elias.'

Witty and Berry wore plain, dark suits with black ties; though not principal mourners, Priestley thought it was always better to be overdressed than underdressed for funerals. He commented to Berry, 'It's the second time this week you've looked almost presentable.'

He had to admit Witty's full Windsor knot looked more *à propos* than Berry's half-Windsor, despite his Army prejudice against it from its association with the RAF, to say nothing of its historical connection with Edward VIII. Looking closely at the tie, he remarked, 'Nicely tied, Neil.'

Witty flashed a smile at Martello before responding, 'Lily did it for me.'

Priestley turned to Martello, 'I should have guessed.' She looked perfect, as always, her red and black dress expressing the correct degree of formality whilst avoiding upstaging the principal mourners. 'Impeccable, Lily. Now, how do I look? There aren't any gravy stains anywhere, are there?'

'You're fine, Marcus.'

'Honestly?'

'This isn't a time for honesty, is it, sir?'

Priestley winced stagily, 'Well, I don't wish to let the side down, so give me your expert opinion of my sartorial elegance.'

Martello looked him up and down. 'A dark grey suit is fine, and having a pinstripe in it is OK, but a purist might say that particular silver is a bit too bright for a funeral. Also, the police motif on your black tie may be a bit too prominent, but there's nothing that can be done about that. So, overall, ...'

Witty interjected, 'The only other thing is your fly's undone.'

Priestley's hand shot down to his trouser front, only to find it was zipped up. 'I fell for that one.' He relaxed his frown before adding, 'We'll all set off together in five minutes.'

They walked the short distance to the church, avoiding the difficulty of finding somewhere to park; though there was a ready supply of "POLICE" notices for putting in car windscreens, the glorious sunshine had been enough to dissuade even Dunn from complaining about having to use Shanks's pony. As they approached the church, Priestley recognised Cleese leading a crocodile of more than forty students of various ages, with Becky Worthington in the front pairing. Priestley walked toward them. 'Hello. Are you here for the service?'

Cleese changed course, the children following close behind, and Rendel bringing up the rear. As they converged, in a voice loud enough for the pupils to hear, she explained, 'We're the chosen ones – Mr Cassidy's Form Group and his Classics in English class.' She had felt it was only right, today, to refer to them as Cassidy's, though both groups were now entirely hers. 'The Headmaster has given us permission to go to the church for the Celebration of Mr Cassidy's life.' She looked briefly at the other officers, then back to Priestley, having observed how they were dressed. 'So, you're also here for the service, and these are your acolytes?'

Priestley tipped his head to one side in the direction of the five statuesque police officers. 'You know DC Martello – Lily. She and DC Whittington – Neil – will be going into church. The rest of us will keep an eye on things outside.' Turning to his subordinates, who had remained a little way away, he called out quietly, 'Lily,

Neil, why don't you go in with Sophie and her students.'

Martello and Witty ambled over to join Cleese; Priestley strode back to the remaining three officers.

The official start time of the service was just ten minutes away when Verbane arrived with a boy in a wheelchair, another on crutches, twelve adults and about a hundred children; they filed into the church through the carved stone portal that over earlier decades had been blackened in streaks with soot-laden rain. Priestley found himself wondering how many more could squeeze in, and hoping they had remembered to leave room for the principal mourners. He decided not to look inside to check, as he thought, contradictorily: 'One, as a non-believer I should not be entering the church; and two, if I step over the threshold, God may strike me down for my past sins.' He decided to delegate the task to Plummer and Berry. 'You two, just check everything's alright in there, then come back and let me know – Elias and I will be standing outside.'

Priestley walked with Dunn in silence. As they neared the entrance porch, he asked, 'How do you feel about being here, Elias?'

Dunn looked at Priestley with staring eyes, like a rabbit caught in car headlights. 'Is this why you wanted me here? To see what I'm responsible for? I can't wind back history, but I would if I could.'

Priestley shook his head. 'It isn't why you're here, though I'm glad you're thinking about the consequences of ...'

Berry and Plummer emerged from the church, so Priestley halted his conversation with Dunn. Berry gave an explanation of the set-up. 'The front pews on both sides have been left clear for the principal mourners; the rest of the church is crammed full. There's an area partitioned off just inside the door – they call it the narthex; it has sound-proofed glass doors that I'm told are very effective – anyone in the narthex wouldn't hear the service when they're closed. Right now there's more noise inside the church than out here – which seems a bit strange for a funeral – but no doubt everyone'll quieten down when they're supposed to.'

Two large black cars swept in and stopped directly outside the church entrance, where the ancient-looking vicar had appeared dressed in traditional vestments of black cassock and white surplice with black tippet. Priestley observed how the four men who extracted the casket were of quite contrasting dimensions, yet they appeared able to keep the coffin on an even keel. He remembered how the army had carefully selected three sets of four pairs of soldiers of successively slightly shorter stature to form wedges of pall-bearers for his three dead comrades.

A fifth man stepped around the car and adjusted the position of the drape on Cassidy's coffin; Priestley wondered if the pall of green field and white sky with its bejewelled embroidery and appliqué red dragon – now faded – was a family heirloom.

From the second car, the driver stepped out smartly and opened the rear door; there emerged just three mourners. Gwen was dressed entirely in black: pillbox hat with gauze veil; long-sleeved dress that reached a third of the way down her calves; four-buttoned, single-breasted woollen coat, three of them fastened – despite the warmth of the day; 80 denier stockings and low-heeled patent-leather shoes. Gareth wore a black suit with white shirt, black tie, black socks and black brogues. Michael looked less sombre in a dark blue suit and light blue shirt, with a black-and-silver criss-cross-patterned tie. They were ushered into the church by the vicar, now assisted by a verger – a stooping woman in her seventies, dressed in a black cassock. Priestley decided to risk the wrath of God; he led his three colleagues into the narthex. He realised he had no wish to witness the service in the way one might see a silent film, so he slid open one side of the sound-proofing doors and beckoned his colleagues to follow. As he closed the door behind him, he found the sound of traffic and people in the square outside was entirely silenced, giving the church an air of tranquillity amidst the town's daily noise. There were no spaces to sit in the nave, so they remained standing at the back.

Sophie noticed how the vicar genuflected at the altar, wondering if that was still standard procedure. She noticed how Michael had dressed in similar colours to the bereaved partner in Four Weddings and a Funeral. She watched the vicar as he turned to the congregation and began, 'Good morning and welcome to you all on this sunny day. In a few moments we shall begin the funeral service of dearly belovèd Hugh. Before then, Michael, Hugh's life-partner and husband, wishes to address you all.'

Michael stepped forward and up one step, before turning and scanning the front and second rows where he recognised some of his old friends; he knew he and Hugh had done little to add to their number in the past year. He began, 'When I set out to contact friends, I realised Hugh had his friends and I had mine. Though, given time, we may have joined the two groups, time was the one thing Hugh did not have – his life was cut terribly short, which left me feeling angry with the world. Then I spoke with Hugh's parents, and I realised my loss was less than theirs, yet my anger was far more. So I must thank them for helping me to see, with their all-forgiving outlook on life, that I must put aside my anger in order to begin the process of healing.

'Hugh had a passion for poetry. I should therefore like to read a poem that expresses how I feel about Hugh's passing.'

The four congregated police officers all heard the same words but each interpreted them differently. Priestley was relieved nothing was said that directly implicated the police force. Dunn felt uncomfortably visible, standing at the back of the nave in Michael's full view; he thought some of that anger was directed at him, even though his part in the tragedy remained untold outside the force. Plummer assessed Michael as rather self-focused, judging by the number of times he used "I" in his short speech. And Berry simply wondered if this was normal for a funeral service, having never been to one before.

Sophie had a feeling of déjà vu; she was fairly certain she knew what was coming next – Funeral Blues by W. H. Auden. She was taken by surprise when Michael began, 'Do not go gently...' She found she had released a loud, high sob, as she recalled the villanelle by Dylan Thomas, despite Michael's word-ending error. Gwen turned around from the pew in front to give her a sweet smile, as though in thanks for a beautiful gift. Sophie gave up trying to stop her tears from flowing.

The service followed the structure laid down by the Church of England. A student barely into her teens was despatched from the rear pew with two hymnbooks for the four standing officers to share; Plummer stepped toward Priestley in anticipation, but he indicated Dunn should share with him on the basis of closest match by height. Priestley tried to give Dunn the easier view of the words, believing he himself still remembered the once-familiar

"Dear Lord and Father of Mankind"; as he squinted to read the
first line of each verse as a reminder, he found he had sung
"hearts" instead of "heats", causing him to sing more quietly to the
end.

When the service was coming to a close, Priestley slid open
one of the two doors to the narthex and led the other three officers
outside, quickly closing the door behind them. He felt they would
have been in the way, standing at the back; and besides, he
thought, police on duty were largely exempt from following
correct C of E service procedure. As they emerged into the
sunlight, he found himself facing a thousand schoolchildren and
teachers. A corridor defined by two rows of boys had already been
formed from the porch to a clear area near the hearse. Priestley
acknowledged Alex Peveril with a nod. Alex explained, 'With so
many people here, Mr Collins thought it would be a good idea for
the school football team to form two rows to hold everybody back,
for the coffin and the family to come through.'
Priestley suggested, 'Something like the end of a football
match.'
Alex highlighted the dissimilarity. 'The Headmaster gave
instructions for everyone to remain silent, what with it being a
funeral – I mean a Celebration of Life.'
Billy Huntsman turned to Alex. 'We never got to applaud Mr
Cassidy after the match.'

Gwen and Gareth were first to follow the coffin. As they
looked at the masses standing silently in respect for their son,
Gwen turned to her husband as she choked back a newly-sprung
well of tears, unable to say anything beyond, 'Oh, Gareth.'
Verbane positioned himself behind Gough as they filed out
through the porch, looking at the assembled throng and pleased
that his instructions were being obeyed. As the coffin approached,
Billy decided he preferred the style of appreciation used at football
matches, and began to applaud. Verbane pointed at him and then
gave him the shushing gesture of a vertical index finger in front of
his mouth, but was too late to stop the eruption of sound; it was as
though an avalanche had been generated by a single snowball.
Gareth turned to Verbane, almost shouting to make himself
heard. 'Would it be allowed for a student and a teacher to come to

the crematorium with us?'

Verbane responded, 'Yes, of course.' He turned to look for Alex.

Gareth laid a hand on his arm and pointed to Billy, 'Would this boy here be allowed?'

Verbane realised why Billy had been chosen, and felt a little annoyed. The response to Billy's initial applause had been unanimous – including himself, following the philosophy "if you can't beat 'em, join 'em". Nevertheless, Billy was the student who had triggered the mass disobedience. He suggested, 'If you're sure – otherwise I could recommend someone else.'

Gareth responded, 'He's the right boy – you ask him if he'll come with us in the car.'

Gwen added, 'And the teacher – the young woman over there.' She indicated Sophie.

Verbane performed the introductions, staying to see them all safely into the funeral car and waving them goodbye.

In the car, Sophie used her ability – common to teachers – of non-stop talking so as to avoid uncomfortable silences. She described working with Hugh, and explained how much of himself he put into his teaching. Eventually she turned off the flow, being concerned she was stopping others from speaking.

Gwen started a conversation with Billy. 'It isn't so very long to Christmas – do you have plans?'

Billy offered an enigmatic response. 'It depends.'

'And what is it that it depends on, Billy?'

'L.A.'

Michael joined the conversation. 'Ah, Los Angeles, Hollywood.'

Billy responded, 'No; the Local Authority. They look after me.'

Gwen looked quite upset at the thought of Billy being in the care of the local authority, notwithstanding the fact that they were heading to her own belovèd son's cremation. 'Well now, I wonder if you couldn't come and stay with us this Christmas. Michael has his own plans, so there'd just be Gareth and me; what do you think, Sophie?'

'I'm sure that's ever so kind of you, Gwen, but I don't know if there are rules about that type of thing. It'll need some investigation, I think.'

The short journey was almost complete, so they fell silent in keeping with the occasion.

At the crematorium, Hugh's friends were transfixed as his coffined body floated away on electric rollers to be consumed by fire. Michael's friends, being one step removed, silently witnessed the departing coffin, but also cast glances of unspoken sympathy to the surviving husband. Gwen gave in to another flood of tears that quickly saturated her handkerchief. Gareth's eyes watered and trickled, as much for Gwen's loss as for his own; he felt that to show tears was unmanly, so tried to hide them by spreading them thinly to the sides of his face with a hooked index finger. Michael looked at the coffin with unbowed head so that his own stream could be witnessed by all. Sophie attempted to remain stoic in the Greek tradition, but failed again, the brook flowing down her unblemished cheeks and dripping onto her black skirt. Billy looked at the tears of those around him and found they had triggered some of his own, though he was unsure how much they were for Mr Cassidy and how much for his abandoned self.

CHAPTER 33

Epilogue

Glenda Oaken was found not guilty of manslaughter. Both the prosecution and the defence in the Crown Court accepted the coroner's finding as to how John Newhouse had died. The jury construed the circumstances that led to the impact as indicating death was accidental. The Shawton News quoted the judge's *obiter dicta* in which he referred to the second life that had been lost as a consequence of Oaken's failure to report to the police how the accident had happened.

In the court of public opinion, Oaken was castigated for her failure to set a good example to the children at her school. In her own assessment, she found herself guilty as charged – guilty but not culpable. She retired to Bourges in the Centre Région of France, where the distinction would be lost in the ambiguity of the French words *pas coupable*. There, she studied the French language and adopted the local dialect in the hope that she might merge with the scenery. When she was able to speak and to think like a native, she moved to Lyon in the Rhône-Alpes Région and started all over again. She found employment at a school as a language assistant, where those people who were unaware of her origins were impressed with her understanding of English, and those who did know were impressed with her comprehension of French. All of them appreciated her deeply caring attitude toward the children.

Michael Gough had his fifteen minutes of fame when the Shawton News proclaimed him the first local man to have a second same-sex marriage. He and his new husband opened a niche restaurant where they presented dining experiences to small numbers of discerning gourmets who appeared delighted to pay their exceptionally high prices for the privilege.

Billy Huntsman stayed with Gwen and Gareth at Christmas and again at Easter. In the summer he went to live with them and to work for Gareth. First, he learned how to operate the printing presses; then, he helped to expand the business and increase its profitability by becoming a successful salesman. He was the very opposite of slick, with his tendency to speak in short bursts; yet people responded to his genuine, warm smile, which came from his all-pervading feeling of happiness – now he belonged to a family.